MW01616034

Copyright ©2022 Rob J. Hayes
(http://www.robjhayes.co.uk)
All rights reserved

Titan Hoppers #1

By

Rob J. Hayes

Chapter One

An explosion shook the titan's hull. Fire vented into space, sucked away and snuffed out in a heartbeat. It all happened in moments. No sound, just fire and debris flying off into the black.

Iro watched out the little window of his room. He shuffled on the crate he had pushed up against the wall and pressed his face against the cool glass, waiting for the next sign of the titan's demise. The glass steamed with every breath and he wiped a ragged sleeve across the portal to clear it.

A series of detonations, more fire venting into the cold darkness. A small section of the titan came away, drifted apart from the larger mass. Small was a relative term, Iro admitted. The titan was massive, beyond any scale he could fathom. The Home Fleet consisted of thirty-eight ships, each one housing nearly ten thousand people. The section of titan that had just come away was larger than the entire fleet. The titan as a whole was a construct on a scale that defied reason. And it was dying.

And when the titan died, the Home Fleet would perish with it.

An alarm bleated out at uncomfortable volume, warning everyone on the Courage that the ship was changing course. With the titan ripping apart, the whole fleet would be moving. They had to pull away from the wreck before debris scuttled the fleet. No ship in the Home Fleet had used shields in centuries. Most had dismantled the systems long ago to shore up failing life support. That's why they had clung to the titan when they found it so many generations ago.

Food, electronics, technology, clothing, minerals. Everything the fleet needed to survive could be found on the titan. Whoever had built it, constructed it to be entirely self sufficient. A ship the size of a planetoid drifting through space. Of course, whoever had built it was long gone. Now it was filled with horrific monsters and deadly traps. Each section further in more dangerous than the last. The Home Fleet had been sending Hoppers to the titan for centuries, and they had barely got past the surface levels. And now they never would.

"Iro?" Neya shouted. "Slug, where are you?"

His older sister sounded excited, her voice full of an energy that put a grin on Iro's face without knowing why. He clambered down from his box and rushed to the door, pulling it open. The rooms he shared with Neya and their mother were small, but a boy of Iro's size could still hide in them if he wanted to.

Neya charged around the corner of the hallway from her own room. She was struggling to pull on an armored boot, and hopped into the metal wall. A laugh erupted from her and she grinned at Iro. She was tall and strong, made even bigger by her white, titan-forged armor. "They picked me, Iro!" Neya shouted. She finished pulling on her boot, lurched forward, and grabbed Iro up into a bear hug. She spun him about and then dropped him. He stumbled as he hit the floor.

"You're going?" Iro asked. He couldn't keep the tremor from his voice. The titan was dying. He knew the Home Fleet would send a final Hopper party or two across, but the thought of Neya going scared him.

Neya grinned through the nest of freckles across her nose and cheeks, and nodded energetically. Her short, dark hair flopped over her face, and she reached up and tied it into a tail, though a few strands immediately escaped and made a bid for her nose. "Old Brecka from the Vermillion is forming a party. He's got a Vanguard, a Corsair, a Berserker, and a Surveyor." She jumped and punched a hand against the wall in excitement. "You know what that means?"

Iro did. That was a mostly physical party of Hoppers, and that meant they needed a Paladin. That meant they needed a Hopper from the Courage. "And they picked you?"

Neya shrugged. "Brecka wanted Phusone, but he's still injured from his last Hop. Second choice is better than none, right?" She laughed again, still grinning. "We're going to the Dome, Iro. That's the furthest in I've ever been by... uh..."

"Three levels," Iro finished for her. He idolised his sister, envied her even. She was a Rank Three Paladin. She had just discovered her unique talent and that made her the best Hopper the Courage had after Phusone. Iro knew everything about every Hop she'd ever been on. Most of the time she only ever got to go on surface Hops, exploring the first few levels of the titan where the danger was lowest. After all, she was still young and inexperienced despite having recently opened her Third Gate of Power.

Iro dreamed of exploring the titan. Fighting the monsters and dodging traps, just like Neya. At eighteen, she was only six years older than him. But he was small and weak. And worse than that, he had no talent. Without a talent, he'd never be a Hopper. Normals like him were destined for nothing but ship repairs, food cultivation, general maintenance.

"Have you seen my sword?" Neya asked.

Iro nodded eagerly and darted back into his room. Neya's blade was leaning against the wall and he scooped it up in both hands, struggling to lift it, and carried it out to her. "I was cleaning it," he said. It was only partly a lie. He'd also been swinging it about, dreaming of slaying monsters.

"Course you were," Neya said. She grinned, ruffled his hair, snatched up the sword in one hand and gave it a practice swing. Not that there was room to really swing it in the hallway. She paused mid-swing and stared at the blade. "Scrap it, Slug. Did you chip the blade?"

Iro paled and stared at the floor. He'd accidentally hit the wall with it just yesterday and a tiny chip came loose. He was hoping she wouldn't notice.

"How the scrap did you chip a titan-forged blade?" She laughed. "Here," Neya handed him the sword back. He staggered as she dropped it into his hands. "I'll pick one up from the armory. You need to get that repaired."

Iro nodded and took the sword, nipped back into his room and leaned it against the wall. When he turned back around, he found Naya staring over his head out the window in his room. She drew in a deep, trembling breath. "Last Hop before it all falls apart," she said, her voice faltering with anxiety.

"Bring me back something nice," Iro said.

Neya snorted, already squeezing past him and heading for the door. "Brecka's taking us to the Dome, Iro. That means its a food run."

"Bring me an apple?" Iro suggested hopefully.

"We'll see, Slug," Neya said. She stopped and pressed the button on her earpiece. "I'm coming. Jeez, Brecka can wait another minute." She pulled open the door and strode out, letting it swing slowly closed behind her. "Then get the pod ready, I'll be there in three…" Her voice trailed off into the distance.

Iro shifted about uncomfortably. He felt strange, his stomach fluttering. He stumbled back into his room, climbed his wooden crate once more, and stared at the titan. Another explosion rocked the outer hull, silently shedding bits of the massive titan into space. It looked peaceful, but Iro knew it was anything but. If one of those shards of titan hull came towards the fleet, it could scuttle a ship easily.

After a few minutes, one of the Courage's pods launched, speeding away on thruster fire towards the titan. Neya would be on that pod and Iro watched it until it was too small to see against the hull of the titan. He quickly fetched his makeshift radio and carried it back to the window. He'd scrounged together parts, stolen wires from non-critical systems, and charged the battery by hooking it up to the lights in his own room. If the ship's wardens caught him with the radio, he'd be reprimanded, but it was worth it to listen to his sister's Hops. Iro might not have a talent, but he knew enough about electronics to build a radio.

Iro tuned it in and connected it to his own earpiece. He could listen in to his sister's comms, but the radio was only one way. He heard her pod make landing. Listened to her meet up with Brecka and the others. They opened the outer doors and breached the Dome. The comms went frantic then, but Iro pieced it together. There were khornids in the Dome. Vicious multi legged beasts with armored skin, venomous fangs, and claws that could shred even titan-forged armor. He listened to Brecka call for an enhancement. Neya would be boosting his strength and making his great sword vibrate to cut through the khornids' armor. She was amazing, throwing enhancements onto all four of the other members of her Hop. The fight was over quickly. Beter, the Vanguard, had taken a nasty bite, but Neya's enhancement had made his skin as hard as stone, and the fangs hadn't penetrated the skin. Neya's Hop proceeded to the next level of the Dome. They'd need to reach level three before they could gather enough food to make the Hop worthwhile.

Another explosion tore Iro's attention away from the radio. This one was larger than before. An entire section of the front end of the titan was blown away violently. Debris the size of ships scattered into space in every direction. A massive chunk of the hull detached, scraped along the titan's flank. The alarm bleated again and the Home Fleet made another course correction. They'd have to leave soon or risk being caught in the death throes.

"Take cover!" Iro heard Brecka shout over Neya's comms. He was an old man, built like a bull and stronger than a mechalift, but he sounded scared.

"Those are Vhar casters, Brek," shouted another man. "What are they doing here?"

Iro jumped off his box as the Hoppers argued. He pulled out his Titan Bestiary, the one he'd been compiling since he was six, and began flicking through the pages. Vhar were humanoid in shape but twice as big. They rippled with muscles they took from their kills then patched into their own skin. The casters were capable of casting themselves over short distances, disappearing and reappearing in a blast of cacophonic sound. Iro found the entry in his bestiary.

They shouldn't be at the Dome. Vhar casters were only ever found further in. Eighth level and higher according to his own hand-written notes. Iro ran back to the window and stared at the titan again, hands gripping the ledge around the glass, fingernails scraping across the bulkhead.

A blast of static ripped across the radio, drowning out the comms. A few moments later, Iro heard a woman's voice he didn't recognise. "Brecka? Brek? Scrap it, he's dead!"

They were fleeing the interior. Trying to escape. The thought occurred to Iro. *But the Vhar wouldn't be fleeing the interior of the titan unless…*

Another series of explosions ripped away part of the titan. It was close to the Dome this time. Too close.

No. No. Please be alright, Neya. Please.

"Scrap!" Neya cursed over the radio. "The titan is going down around us. They're fleeing the explosions."

"What do we do?" asked the other woman. "Those casters are between us and the pods? Brecka is dead. What do we do?"

Silence drowned out the radio for a few moments. Iro heard his heart thumping in his ears. His fingers hurt from digging into the window ledge. "Come home," he whispered. His vision blurred and he wiped tears on his Courage jumpsuit. "Please, sis."

"You there, Slug?" Neya asked over the radio. There was a lot of noise suddenly. Explosions ripping through the hull of the titan. Iro could see them from the outside. The entire megastructure was coming apart, bending, warping, breaking. He could hear the Vhar casters screaming. And over it all, Neya's voice. Calm. Far too calm for the chaos happening around her.

"I'm here," he said even though he knew she couldn't hear him.

"Course you are. Always listening, aren't you." Neya sniffed. "I don't think I'm making it back this time, Slug. Look after mom for me. She's gonna be sad, and you gotta be brave for her. You gotta be her courage." She chuckled. "Just like you've always been mine, yeah?"

Iro heard a human scream across the radio. It went dead for a few moments. He looked out the window again and saw a massive explosion rip through the titan, sawing it in half. Each half the size of a moon, tearing apart, venting fire and precious oxygen out into the cold dark. Another explosion rocked the titan's wing where the Dome sat.

"Scrap it!" Neya swore over the radio. She was

breathing hard like she was running. "You deserve to know. Iro, listen to me. Mom won't tell us. I think she blocked it out. Forgot it. But I found him. I know where our dad is. He's…"

The radio went dead as the Dome shattered.

Iro listened to the static of the radio, hoping Neya would come back. "Sis?" He shook the radio. Picked it up and slammed it against the window. *Neya.* He didn't care about their father, or the titan, or any of it. He just wanted to hear Neya's voice again. He just wanted his sister to come home.

Another series of explosions blew through the titan. The alarm bleating across the Courage sounded distant. They were moving away. The Home Fleet was putting distance between them and the dying titan. He clawed at the window as if he could crawl across the void. What if they were still alive? If Neya was still alive? He needed to rescue her.

It seemed to last for hours. Or maybe it was only minutes. The titan got smaller and smaller in the window until he could see most of it. He knew just how far away they had to be. Then, in one final act of violence, the titan's extensive engine core exploded in a light bright enough to rival the stars.

Chapter Two

Iro ducked into a roll and came up swinging his sister's old sword. His feet caught together, and he tripped with a panicked yell. The sword flew from his hands, bounced off the training dummy, and skittered to a halt on the fraying, padded floor of the training room.

I'm still as graceful as a bent screwdriver. He had no idea how Neya had always made it look so easy.

He stood slowly, rubbing a hand at his aching rear and wondering how big a bruise he'd have. Worse still, someone might notice in the showers. He missed the old days when the Courage had enough water that its crew could still use the showers in their own quarters. Now they had to use the communal ones that only turned on for twenty minutes once every three days.

"What's going on in there?" Master Tannow shouted.

"Nothing," Iro shouted back. He ran for his sister's sword, scooped it up, then made for his tool bag and threw the blade inside, clattering against the spanners and screwdrivers, just as Master Tannow ambled through the doorway. The old Hopper scratched at his bearded chin and scanned the room with a suspicious stare.

"I heard you cry out," the old master said. He had once been a renowned Titan Hopper with over a hundred successful missions. But something had happened, Iro wasn't sure what, and he had refused to ever board the titan again. Since then he'd taken over as martial master of the Courage. Not that he had anyone of note to train anymore, or any reason to train them. It had been five years since the titan had exploded.

Five years since we lost Neya. The wound still felt fresh.

"I, uh, tripped?" Iro said. He nodded and rubbed at his backside again, taking the opportunity to push his tool bag behind him a little further. If anyone knew he still had Neya's sword, they'd take it from him. "I was replacing the servos in the dummy and stood up too fast. Head rush made me dizzy."

"Scrap it, lad, be more careful," Master Tannow chuckled. "Your mother will have my hide if you brain yourself on a dummy. Especially a stationary one." He jabbed a lightning fast punch at the dummy's head. It rocked from the force but quickly settled back into mocking stillness. They were built to take a beating. Long ago, someone had painted a crude, leering face in pink and purple ink on this one's head. "Is that what's wrong with it then? The servos?"

Iro nodded and advanced on the dummy with his old screwdriver. "I think so. But we can't replace it. Don't have the parts. I've been trying to repair it, but I think it's just shot."

Master Tannow sighed. "Just like everything else, huh?" He wasn't wrong. The Courage was falling apart beneath them. And above them. And all around them really. A full quarter of the ship had fallen into such disrepair, they had simply sealed it off and let space have it. The rest of the Home Fleet wasn't much better. Of the thirty-eight ships that sailed away from the titan, they had lost three to failing systems, and one to catastrophic debris damage they simply didn't have the resources to repair. On top of that, food rations had dropped to half what they were five years ago. Iro wasn't privy to knowledge about fuel, but he guessed the situation was bordering on dire. The Home Fleet was dying. Without a titan to scavenge from, they wouldn't last much longer.

Iro poked at one of the exposed servos with his screwdriver. "I don't think it's jammed, just burned out." He retrieved the metal casing and started screwing it back into place.

"Probably for the best, lad," Master Tannow said with a smile. "The poor excuse for Hoppers I'm training these days aren't good enough to train with moving targets." Too many of their strongest Hoppers had been lost when the titan exploded. Too many didn't make it back. The Courage was particularly badly hit, with over ten rank three and higher Paladins never coming back. They were lucky Phusone was injured. He was the only rank four Paladin the Courage had left. Not that any of them had anywhere to Hop to.

"Want to try again, lad?" Master Tannow asked.

Iro grinned and nodded. He felt good about today. Like his current had been building inside of him for weeks and it was ready to be unleashed.

"What talent haven't we tried recently? Steel?" The old master asked. Steel skin was the easiest Paladin talent to learn. It involved projecting your current onto another, infusing them with it, then hardening that current into something as solid as metal.

"Number three still works," Iro said. Master Tannow approached training dummy number three. Someone, probably the same person who had painted a leering face on the other dummy, had painted a winking face on this one. Master Tannow pressed the button on the floor with his foot. The dummy's arms started spinning up faster and faster until they were a blur of whipping metal and padding.

"Ready, lad? First, activate your crest."

Iro breathed in, released it slow and steady. He felt inside for the current of power flowing within. Activating his crest was easy. Anyone and everyone could do it. From the mightiest Hopper, to the lowest drudge, they all had crests. But not all were created equal. Iro's crest formed behind him as a small, barely glowing circle of icy blue light. It was empty, blank. He knew from experience, having seen them, that most people's crests were filled with arcane letters and symbols detailing the most important experiences of their lives. Hoppers had the most extensive crests, brighter than others, and each Gate of Power they opened increased the size, complexity, and glow. Neya had shown him her crest enough times, and it had filled the space behind her, as tall as she was and just as wide. It had concentric circles around the edges, and a triangular shape in the centre for each of the three gates she had opened. It glowed with a fierce orange light, and was filled with arcane lettering and sharp lines. The complexity of it had awed Iro. Especially as his own crest had always been so utterly blank. Lifeless.

"It's fine, lad," Master Tannow said. "We all start somewhere. Now focus your current through the crest and into me. Give it the command of Steel."

Iro nodded and reached out a hand. He pointed at Master Tannow, focused on the current of power flowing through him like electricity through wires. "Steel," he said. He felt it move. The power shifted inside of him, flowing through his crest and into his hand. Master Tannow stepped in range of the training dummy. The dummy locked on its target, and struck, both arms flailing at the old master.

Master Tannow grunted once, then again, as both arms of the training dummy struck him about the chest. He staggered back, chuckling. "Ow! Should have used a lower setting, huh?"

Failed. Again. Iro sagged, a wave of tiredness making his arms heavy.

Iro sighed. His crest remained dim, dull azure and utterly blank. Nothing but failures. He couldn't even manifest the easiest talent. He was increasingly certain the current he felt inside was nothing but his imagination. The desire to prove himself as more than just a tech playing tricks on his mind.

Master Tannow pressed the button and number three slowed down and stopped spinning its arms. He turned to Iro with a wide, sorry smile. "Don't beat yourself up, lad. Not like we have a titan to Hop to. Besides, many people don't manifest a talent until they're older."

"You know any Hoppers who didn't have a single talent by seventeen?" Iro asked, feeling dejected.

Master Tannow opened his mouth to answer, but they both knew any denial would only be a lie.

Laughter sounded from the hall outside the training room. Iro ran to his tool bag and zipped it shut to hide his sister's sword. A moment later, the Courage's three trainee Hoppers sauntered into the training room.

Cali and Mia noticed him immediately. They were sisters, both strong enough Paladins that Master Tannow claimed they were close to opening their first gates, not that they ever would without a titan to Hop to. They were also ruthless.

"Oh look," Cali said, grinning at him. "It's Useless." She was the taller of the two twins and wore her hair shorter, shaving the left side down to stubble and leaving the right side to grow.

Mia skipped over to Iro, crouched down in front of him, and stared up at him. "Are you finished with the dummy? Did it win?" She snickered. Mia looked just like her sister only a little shorter and broader, with dark hair that hung down past her shoulders. She was strong enough to lift Iro off the floor, and had proved it more than once.

"Leave him alone, Mia," Cali said. "He and the dummy have a lot in common. I'm sure they have a lot of deep and meaningful conversations. Like what's it like to be completely useless?" They both laughed at that.

Iro knew from painful experience there was no point in fighting back. Both sisters knew a talent and had the power to use it. As far as everyone in the Home Fleet was concerned, that made them a higher class of citizen. It didn't matter that only one in a hundred people could use the current inside to fuel talents. Nor did it matter that without a titan to scavenge from, Hoppers were less useful than techs like him. All that mattered was they had the power, and that made them better than him. Nobody would stick up for him, not even Master Tannow. And every time he stuck up for himself it ended in bruises.

It was better just to leave. Not to give them a reason to focus on him. Iro hefted his tool bag onto his shoulder. It was heavy, especially with his sister's sword inside, but he was used to it. He had been carting it around for years now. He dodged around Mia and headed for the exit, keeping his head down. The trick to surviving on the Courage was to keep his head down and try not to get noticed.

Iro paused as he reached the training dummy. Cali was leaning against it. She saw him stop and winked at him.

Don't say it.

"We're allowed to be useless," Iro said, already regretting it. "Neither of us have talents. What's your excuse?"

Mia burst out laughing, but Cali's face went red with rage. "What did you say?" She pushed away from the dummy and started toward him, fists balled. It was a fight he couldn't win. Even without her talent, she'd turn him into paste without trying. Iro still struggled to swing his sister's sword without falling over, but Cali had been training to fight for years. On top of that, Mia could throw an enhancement on her sister.

Iro burst into a run, heading for the door. He bumped into Emil just before the door and almost fell back onto his arse. The bigger boy was the same age as Iro, but broader and stronger. He was also a Paladin, the best trainee Hopper the Courage had. Emil glanced at Iro, shook his head, then continued walking.

Cali paused, obviously waiting to see if Emil would give Iro a beating. When he didn't, she lurched after him again. Iro turned and fled, the sisters' threats chasing him down the metal corridors.

Iro found Roret working on the algae irrigation system. The other boy was a year younger than him, but knew his way around the Courage's mechanical systems like no other. Iro dumped his tool bag on a nearby bench and slumped down next to the vat his friend was working on, then explained the encounter with Cali and Mia.

"One day, they're going to catch you and beat your arse blue, Iro," the younger boy said.

Iro shifted and winced at the painful bruise he found. "The dummy already did that for them."

"Because you were trying to fix it, or because you were swinging at it?" Roret was one of the few people who knew Iro carried his sister's sword around with him.

"Let's just say I tripped and leave it at that."

Roret fished something out of the vat, stared at it for a moment, then shoved his arm back into the churning algae. They had run out of real food two years ago. Iro had all but forgotten what fruit or bread tasted like. Algae was the only thing they could grow in the meagre light that reached them from the stars. The windows above the vats showed those stars twinkling at them.

"You hear about the Sunset?" Roret asked as he fished in the algae for something else. The Sunset was the second smallest ship in the Home Fleet. It produced Mechanists for sending over to the titan. Hoppers who could create and control powerful automatons. "It's running out of fuel. None of the other ships are willing to send any over so…"

"So they're going to leave it behind?" Iro asked. Another ship abandoned to drift out in space. Iro didn't really know much about the other ships in the fleet. The different crews didn't mingle anymore. It was a waste of fuel sending people off ship. Each ship bred a specific class of Hoppers though. The Sunset bred Mechanists. The Courage bred Paladins. There were two other ships in the fleet who also bred Paladins, but Iro couldn't remember their names.

"Yep. Ahah!" Roret pulled something new out of the vat and held it up victorious. It was a clogged filter, the mesh black with mold. "This is for you." He dumped the filter in Iro's lap and held out his hand impatiently. Iro fished about in Roret's tool bag, found a mostly clean filter, and handed it to the other boy. He looked at the moldy filter with distaste and wrapped it in cloth before putting it back in Roret's bag along with a dozen others. This was what the Home Fleet had come to. Eating algae from vats, and re-using moldy filters.

And a thrilling job for us to do tomorrow. Scraping the mold off filters.

"Don't you wish it was different, Ror?" Iro asked. "If we still had a titan to Hop to, we'd have food, fuel, parts."

"Oh yes," Roret said enthusiastically. "And you'd take your sister's sword, Hop across to the titan, slay a few monsters, and save the fleet." He chuckled and shook his head at Iro. "No point in wishing things were something else, Iro. Accept them how they are and deal with it. So we eat algae now. It's not so bad. Sure, it tastes like my foot and smells like your foot, but it keeps us alive."

Roret was far too positive, but Iro knew there was one thing that would change that. "My mom said they're cutting back water rations again."

"What? No, no, no. Don't say it."

"Showers every fourth day from tomorrow."

"I hate you, Iro."

"Wasn't my choice."

Roret grunted as he fitted the *new* filter into place. "The bearer of bad news always always tells it to the boot." He chuckled, then sat down next to Iro, sighed, and wiped a sheen of sweat from his forehead on his arm. "We're dying, aren't we, Iro?"

That seemed far too pessimistic a question from his young friend. Iro decided to cheer him up. "Nah. Not if I can help it, Ror. You remember what Neya always used to say?"

"Who's your little friend with the big nose?"

Iro laughed. "That too." Iro coughed and put on his very best big sister impression. "Courage will get us through the darkest times. You just have to be brave." It was a terrible impression, he had to admit, but he was starting to struggle to remember what his sister sounded like.

"You know that's a metaphor, right, Iro?" Roret said and shook his head.

Iro had never really thought about it before. He'd always just taken Neya's words at face value.

"Fool," Roret said and stood. "Come on. I've got the filters in two more vats to check before I can call it a day."

Iro arrived back home before his mother. He expected that. She was a senior officer on the Courage, third in command. She almost never got back before him, no matter how long his days. He dropped his toolbag in his room, next to his old handmade radio, and a box of spare parts he somehow never found time to sort.

He made his way to the kitchen where the family had once cooked meals, sat and ate together. Nobody cooked anymore. Iro glanced down the hall to where Neya's rooms sat untouched. His mother kept it just as it was the day she left. There was a public shrine close to the docking pods, dedicated to all the Hoppers who lost their lives the day the titan died. But his mother kept Neya's room as a personal shrine. He sometimes found her standing at the door, staring in, a sad smile on her face as if she was having a conversation with her daughter.

Iro crept along the hall, ignoring the rusting metal bulkheads. He paused at his sister's door, staring at the handle. Neya had always been the brave one. The genius Paladin. The fearless Hopper protecting her team.

And I'm just a talentless coward, hiding in her shadow.

His hand fell away from the door handle. In five years, he'd never managed to work up the courage to open it. Too scared he'd find the ghost of his sister waiting for him.

The front door opened, his mother sighing as she stepped inside and pulled the door closed behind her. Iro hurried away from Neya's old room and quickly set about wiping down the breakfast bowls they'd left this morning. The fleet couldn't spare water for washing dishes anymore. Now they all wiped bowls down with disinfectant cloths. It left an aftertaste that transferred to the algae, but at least it made the stuff taste of something.

"Hi, you," his mother said as she squeezed past him. "How went the repairs?"

"Brilliantly," Iro said, putting as much cheer as he could into his voice. "I fixed the whole ship. Runs like new."

She chuckled. "You know, I did hear it purring while at the controls earlier."

Iro finished wiping the bowls, then placed his own

underneath the dispenser. "It was easy," he said. "I even invented some new fuel to use."

His mother paused at Neya's door, brushing it with her hand without looking at it, then turned and opened her own door. She looked tired. Her skin, once pale, was now waxen. She had cut her hair down to her shoulders a few years back, then more recently cut it again above her ears. It was easier to clean that way. There were bags under her wood brown eyes, and her smiles never quite reached past her lips. Still, she stood straight-backed despite her exhaustion, and never once did she complain.

The food dispenser chimed and Iro took his bowl and pushed his mother's into place. Green algae slopped into it through the tubes. It smelled like sweat and tasted like nothing. He hated it and missed real food. The dispenser chimed again and he took his mother's bowl and placed it next to his own. They looked more empty than usual. *Rations decreasing again, and mom already looks thin.* Iro grabbed their spoons and quickly ladled a couple of spoonfuls from his bowl to his mother's, then pushed it to the other end of the table and sat down to wait.

When his mother reappeared, she was dressed in a fresh uniform. It was mostly clean, which was to say it was one she hadn't worn for a few days. Iro should have thought of that. He looked down at his own clothes, still sweaty from the day's work and spotted with dried algae from the vats.

"You're growing out of that fast," his mother said as she sat down. "Seventeen is too old to still be growing, Iro. We'll have to put in you Neya's old clothes soon." The name dropped like a stone between them. Iro couldn't think of anything to say.

"Well, this looks wonderful," his mother said, pulling her bowl in front of her. "You must have spent hours preparing it."

He smiled at the old joke. “Only the best tasteless green slop for my mother.” He’d lost count of the number of times they’d shared the same exchange. It was comfortable and brought a smile to both their faces.

They ate in silence. Iro swallowed each spoonful quickly. *How can it taste of nothing, and yet still taste horrible?*

“How goes the training?” his mother asked once they had finished.

“I think I’m improving. I only fell over once today.”

“Definitely an improvement. And it looks like you didn’t fall on your face this time. I’m impressed. Are you still struggling to hold the sword steady?”

Iro shook his head. “The weight’s fine these days, I’m used to carrying it. I just can’t seem to find the proper balance.” He sighed. “It would help if Master Tannow would train me.”

His mother crossed her arms. “You’re not a Hopper, Iro.”

“I know that.”

“There’s no shame in it. Techs are just as important as Hoppers. More so these days. Without you…”

“Without me the engines don’t work, the doors don’t open, the algae doesn’t grow.” He sounded more petulant than he meant to. “I know all that. The Hoppers still get treated differently. Special. They get more food, fewer duties. They get to train.” None of that really mattered to him. “And she was a Hopper.”

His mother glanced at Neya’s door once more. Another awkward silence settled between them. Iro sulked. He knew he was sulking, felt the familiar weight pressing down on his shoulders. He could never quite think of the right words. He wanted to be a Hopper, even without a titan to Hop to. He wanted to face down monsters, to train to fight. He wanted to be someone who would make Neya proud of him.

But it was also more than that. He needed to atone. Because maybe if she'd had her own sword with her, instead of some dull-edged armory blade not weighted right for her, she might have fought her way free and made it home. *Maybe she'd still be alive, if not for me*. It was a foolish thought, he knew, but no matter how many times he told himself that, the thought never went away.

His mother leaned forward, moving her head about until he couldn't help but look at her. She pulled a face, squinting with one eye and sticking out her tongue, still green from the algae. Despite himself, Iro laughed.

"There he is," she said. "Maybe I can help. Teach you the basics at least." She stood and rolled a shoulder. "I think I can just about remember how to hold a sword." She'd been a Hopper in her youth, a Paladin who made two forays onto the titan. But she'd failed to open her first gate, and that ended her career. You only got one chance to open the Gates of Power.

Iro jumped up, knocking his chair over. "Really?"

His mother nodded. "Sure. You know the training room schedule? We'll find an hour every couple of days to get down there. I'll try to remember how to swing a sword, and you can try to learn from an old woman too used to a comfy chair."

Iro skirted the table in a moment, bent down, and wrapped his arms around his mother. "Thank you!" He knew it wouldn't make him a Hopper, that without a talent he'd never be a Hopper. But at least it would be some progress. At least it would be a change to the normal ship routine.

An alarm sounded across the ship. The general alarm that bleated through every room and loud enough to penetrate the cold of space. Both Iro and his mother stopped, frowning and staring up at nothing for a few moments. Nobody had heard the general alarm since the day the titan died.

As suddenly as it started up, the alarm stopped. His mother frowned at Iro for a few more moments, then rushed to her feet and ran to the comm panel.

Chapter Three

Iro's mother pressed the button on the comm panel for the bridge. "Captain?"

"Serah, is that you?" Captain Galen's voice came across the comm panel with a hiss of static accompanying it. It had been a while since they'd used it, and it was possible some of the wires were degrading.

I'll fix it tomorrow. He could try to find some replacement wiring, though it was one more thing they were starting to run low on.

"Yes, captain. What's going on?" Iro's mother glanced at him, frowning. He couldn't decide what that meant, but he felt nerves tingle through his stomach. When she turned away, Iro set about cleaning the bowls just for something to do.

The radio was silent for a few seconds. Then it hissed again and Captain Galen's voice came through. "We've got a contact, Serah. It's big, metallic. Not close." He fell quiet, but the radio still hissed with static so he was still transmitting. Iro heard a few rushed voices in the background. The bridge of the Courage sounded busy. "It's a titan, Serah. We've found a new titan."

Iro dropped the bowl he was cleaning and turned to find his mother staring at him, her eyes wide. A new titan meant hope. Hope for the fleet, for survival. His gut churned. On one hand, it was everything they needed. On the other, nothing would change for him. Only the Hoppers would get to go aboard the titan.

His mother was trembling as she pushed the button on the comm panel once again. "How far away, captain?"

She sighed, her breath catching in her throat.

"We'll get to eat real food again, mom," he said. It wasn't the most important thing about finding a new titan, but it was the first to come to his mind. He'd work a hundred double shifts for a bite of an apple again.

Serah let go of the button and grinned at Iro. He grinned back.

"Is that your son, Serah?" The captain's voice had gone cold.

"Yes, captain." Iro's mother frowned at him again.

"Send him away. I have an urgent communication coming from Admiral Nmayer for command staff only. And tell him he can expect punishment for attacking a Hopper."

His mother rounded on him. "You attacked a Hopper? Iro, who? Why?"

"I didn't," Iro said urgently. "I don't know who…" Then it dawned on him. Cali and Mia were Captain Galen's daughters. He'd insulted them by sticking up for himself in the training hall. He hadn't expected them to run to their father for retribution, but it didn't surprise him. "It's not my fault, I…"

"Go!" His mother said sharply, pointing down the hall to his room. "I have to hear what the admiral has to say, but we'll talk about this later."

Iro thought of arguing, but he knew it would be pointless. Even if his mother did believe him, no one else would. They'd take the word of a Hopper over his any day. Besides, he couldn't keep his mother from her work, and he really wanted to hear what the admiral had to say. Iro lowered his head as if in a sulk, and trudged down to the hall to his room. He forced himself to pull open the door slowly and ducked inside. But as soon as the door was closed, he grabbed his old handmade radio from the floor and rushed to the window. Of course, he didn't have the clearance or the frequency to listen in to the admiral's broadcast, but he also didn't need it. He'd long ago tuned his little radio into the apartment's comm signal. He spent a few agonising moments finding the right channel, then turned the volume low and leaned in close to the speaker to hear what was being said.

Ship to ship transmissions had never been particularly good. The truth was, no one really knew how the technology aboard the fleet worked. They simply knew that it did. Sometimes parts burned out and needed replacing. The controls flew the ships and operated the various systems like engine control or communications. But that was as far as anyone understood it. Some of the Mechanists seemed to think the ships were alive, a rudimentary sort of intelligence like they gifted to the automatons they created.

"Have all ships checked in?" The voice was tinny with static, but Iro recognised it. He'd heard it only once before, when the titan died. Admiral Nmayer had made a fleet-wide announcement, praising the heroics of all those lost Hoppers, and delivered a rousing speech about flying into the dark unknown with passion and bravery and hope. Five years later and all three of those seemed in short supply.

"Yessir," said another voice, this one Iro didn't recognise.

"This is Admiral Nmayer aboard the Vermillion." His voice sounded like a grinding servo, all its teeth filed off, but unwilling to stop spinning. "As your captains have probably all informed you by now, we've detected a large metallic mass. Analysis indicates by size and shape, it's a titan." The radio went dead for a moment. Iro could almost imagine bridges across the fleet echoing with the cheers of their command staff.

"We have a number of problems," the admiral continued. A hiss of static might have been a sigh. "This new titan is not close. With a course change, and at our current speed, we would reach it in one-hundred-and-seventy-five days. Ten of our ships won't make it. They'll run out of fuel half way there."

The radio went silent again. When it clicked on once more, a new voice came across. A woman Iro had never heard before. "Admiral, this is acting captain Troy of the Serendipity."

"Acting captain?" the admiral asked. "What happened to Osidus?" Iro guessed that was the previous captain of the Serendipity."

"He's missing, admiral."

"Missing? How…" the admiral paused. "Continue, Captain Troy." Iro understood immediately. No one went missing aboard a ship. There was nowhere to go missing except not on the ship. Captain Osidus was not the first person to give in to despair and step out into the darkness.

"We're one of the ships who won't make it, Admiral," Captain Troy said.

"Do you have a question, Captain?"

Captain Troy coughed. "No sir." *She just wants to put a voice to those we might be leaving behind.*

Admiral Nmayer continued as if the interruption had never happened. "I've had the math run and triple checked. If we increased speed, we can cut the arrival time down to twenty-eight days. The fuel we'll save on essential system usage will allow all thirty-three ships to arrive. It will be at the very limit of our reserves though."

"Assuming the ships don't shake themselves apart, Admiral." Said another new voice, a man even more tinny than the others. "This is Captain Ecktov of the Lament. The Lament is falling apart, Admiral. We don't have the parts to repair it, and we can't be sure it will survive the acceleration." From the notebooks Iro had read, and his discussions with Roret, it was the deceleration that would be the real problem. That's when the most stress was subjected upon the ship.

Captain Galen's voice came across clearer than the others. "Captain Galen of the Courage, sir. What if we take the people and fuel from the ships that won't make it, scrap them for parts, and carry on at this speed?"

"We don't have the food production facilities," said a woman with a high voice. "Uh, sorry. This is officer Tanny of the Burning Ember. The fleet's food supplies and algae growth are balanced on a fine edge, sirs. If, um, if we inject new members into the crews, it will upset the balance. We won't have the food production capabilities to feed everyone." She went quiet for a moment and Iro heard her arguing in the background with another woman. Then she came across clearer once again. "A quarter of the fleet will starve before we reach the new titan."

The argument continued for what seemed like hours. Iro leaned on the window ledge and stared out at the black beyond, daydreaming. Five years ago, he'd needed a box on the floor to stand like this. Now he could reach it comfortably. It gave him hope that he might still have some growing left to do and he wouldn't end up the shortest member of the adult crew.

"So we are agreed," the admiral's voice sounded firm. Iro realised he hadn't really been listening for some time. "Any trainees are to be given dispensation. Extra rations and freedom from duties. Any youths with even a single talent manifested are to be pressed into training immediately. Get your Hoppers trained. We'll have only one chance when we arrive. If we fail, we lose the fleet." He was greeted by silence.

"Prepare your ships, captains. Inform your crews. We make for this new titan at full speed."

Twenty eight days passed as a blur of exhausting work for Iro. The ships of the Home Fleet might once have been designed for hard accelleration through the void, but after half a hundred generations of people living and dying aboard them, they certainly weren't anymore. Not a day zipped by at nauseating speed where some critical system didn't fail. Water supply, fuel management, food delivery, thruster control, door motors. Everything failed, and the tech core simply didn't have the parts or the people to fix it all.

By the thirteenth day, most of the apartment doors had to be cannibalised so the locks no longer worked. However, this allowed them to change the motors in the algae vats. Roret assured Iro that stirring the algae was of great importance. Not that the tech core got to eat much of it. With Hoppers and trainees receiving double portions, the techs were down to one quarter rations. Every day he felt his stomach clawing at itself.

On the twenty third day, just five days from contact with the new titan, the water purification systems crashed. Literally crashed. The bulkhead wall fractured from the strain and vented the entire purification system out into the black, along with half the Courage's remaining water supply. That was the end of showering. Roret's complaints only got louder.

Worst of all was not the exhaustion from the constant repairs, nor the feeling of fighting a battle that couldn't be won. Worst was that he found no time to train. He carried Neya's sword everywhere in his tool bag, but the few times the training halls weren't in use, he was either too busy or too tired to take advantage.

As they burned through the black ever closer to the

new titan, Iro had to admit to himself the truth he had been hiding from for five years. He wasn't ever going to be a Hopper. There were a dozen talents Paladins could manifest to allow them to open up their crests and use the current of power all people carried inside. He had tried them all. And he had failed. And now the new titan was so close, he was out of time. He could no longer pretend it would happen eventually.

On the morning the Home Fleet flew into the space around the new titan, Iro finally admitted the truth to himself. He was going to be a tech for the rest of his life. He'd never see anything beyond the rusting metal walls of the Courage.

Chapter Four

Iro and Roret hurried through the halls as quickly as they could, both carrying heavy tool bags. Iro's even more heavy for the sword hidden within. They scooted past another couple of techs working on a bulkhead that had ripped itself apart. The two women had a welding torch, but it was sputtering, too low on fuel to maintain a good flame.

Roret had been right, the deceleration was worse. The Courage was tearing itself apart from the stress, and it wasn't the first ship. They'd already lost the Broken Mirror, its people scattering throughout the remaining ships.

"Stop running," shouted the older of the two women working on the bulkhead.

"Can't," Roret shouted.

"They need us at the Hopper pods," Iro added.

Two of the Hopper pods were malfunctioning. That was on top of bays three and five, which had already been shut down and cannibalised for parts. They barely had enough Hoppers to fill two squads, but that didn't matter if they didn't have the pods to launch them onto the titan when they arrived.

The halls were filled with people. Mostly techs and ship officers all going about their jobs. There was an air of excitement in the atmosphere. Five years floating about in the dark, twenty-eight days of full speed travel, and now they were finally here. Iro passed a window on the outer bulkhead wall and slowed to a stop. He took a few steps back and pressed his face to the glass, staring at the titan.

Scrap! It's even bigger than the last titan. It seemed longer and thinner than the old titan, though Iro had to admit that might be another trick of scale. It had four wings, each one jutting out from the titan, two on each side, around the central body. Its tail branched out into six thinner lengths, each one longer than the main body. Then, each of the six tails spread out into a luminescent solar sail. Iro knew enough to assume that was how it collected the energy it needed to keep going, swimming through space as it did. But the old titan didn't have a solar sail, and they had no idea how it generated its power, nor produced its fuel.

Everything they *knew* about titans was nothing but conjecture. Where they came from? Why they existed? Who built them? All the people of the Home Fleet knew, was that titans existed, and without them they would all be dead.

"Come on." Roret grabbed Iro's arm, tried to pull him away.

"Look!" Iro said, stabbing a finger at the glass window.

Roret pressed in close, his cheek cool and sticky when pressed against Iro's own. They both stared out the window. "Is it bigger than the old titan?"

"I think so." They were still hours away and already it dominated the view.

"Scrap." They both fell silent for a few seconds. "Now come on. If we don't get the pods working before the fleet gets there, they'll make us get out and push the damned things." Roret tugged him away from the window.

The pods were scrapped. Iro and Roret spent half an hour diagnosing all five of them, and only two were fully functioning. The other three were in various states of being canabalised, all of which stopped them from doing what they needed to. That left them with only two functioning pod bays, and eight functioning pods between them. It also left the Courage in the rare situation of having too many Hoppers for the working pods. Though Iro had to admit that was only because they were sending the trainees. He shuddered at the thought of having to tell Cali or Mia they were grounded due to lack of parts. He couldn't imagine getting out of that conversation without at least a broken arm.

"Whoever did the last diagnostic was an idiot," Roret said. "Two malfunctioning pods is scrap. It's clearly three."

Iro stalked over to the bay entrance and looked at the paper pinned beside the wall. It had been scribbled over and re-used so many times, it was hard to tell which entry was the last. "Last diagnostic was run ten days ago by Chief Petros. I'm not saying you're wrong, Ror. I just wouldn't go insulting him to his face."

"Good job he isn't here then, because he's a scrapping tool!"

Iro looked over the list of problems again. Pods two, three, and five weren't working. Pod two's life support was down. Given that the trip over to the titan would take a few minutes at least, that meant whoever tried to use it would both freeze to death and suffocate long before they arrived. Pod three's thruster line was scrapped, so it couldn't manoeuvre. Pod five's hydraulics were down so the doors wouldn't open or shut, and its navigation controls looked like someone had breathed flame on them.

"How many pods do we need?" Iro asked.

"Four," Roret said.

Four, or one of them had to explain to a trainee they weren't allowed to go on the first Hop to the new titan. Literally the one thing they had all been training for their entire lives.

Getting out and pushing would be preferable to delivering that news.

"Let's shut down number two, use the parts to get three and five working. We'll have to hope they find the new parts to fix them while on the titan." With a plan in place, they set about working. It took a couple of hours to strip down two, and get three working. They were still working on five when the trainees and Master Tannow marched into the pod bay.

"Stay close and stay together," the old master was saying. "Remember, there's nothing stronger than a group of Paladins who trust each other."

Iro poked his head out of pod five's door to see Master Tannow in full titan-forged armor. It was an old suit, painted bone white, the Courage's color. Much of the paint had faded or was chipping and scarred, barely clinging to the metal. The chest piece was dented, the left pauldron was cracked and taped back together, and the weave beneath the armor plates strained around his ample mid-section, but at least it was a full suit. He also had an ax with a head the size of Iro's torso strapped to his back. "I thought you didn't Hop anymore, Master," Iro said.

Cali and Mia skipped around the old master, one either side of him, and advanced on Iro. "Oh look, sis. It's Talentless." Cali said. Her suit of armor was not titan-forged, but ship-printed. That meant it was flimsy at best. It also meant it was old, likely a hand-me-down as the printers hadn't worked for longer than Iro had been alive. That also explained why it was missing the left vambrace and the left greave. She had a couple of thin knives strapped to her hip, her weapons of choice.

Mia stalked up to Iro and punched him hard in the arm before he could back away. He staggered back, crying out, then the aching numbness turned the pain into agony. "I'm not getting in that pod, if he's been working on it. It'll blow up half way to the titan." Her suit of armor was bone white just like all the Hoppers from the Courage. It was cracked down the chest plate, held together by fraying strips of tape. She had no pauldrons, her muscly arms bare and on display, and only one vambrace on her right wrist. A hefty two handed hammer sat strapped to her back, but despite the weight it didn't seem to encumber her at all..

"At least being blown up would improve your looks," Iro said quietly.

Not quietly enough, apparently. Mia turned on him, raising a fist, a snarl on her face.

"Enough, Mia," Master Tannow said. "If you kill our tech, who will fix the pod?"

"I'm not going in that one," she snapped.

"You are."

Mia turned back to Iro and pushed him hard enough in the chest, he stumbled back against the pod door. "Fix it right or I'll feed you to the void."

Iro heard a *thunk* from inside the pod, and Roret's head popped up out of the open hatch in the floor. "Is the door closed yet."

"Nope," Iro said, backing away from Mia, keeping his eyes on her in case she lunged at him.

Roret disappeared back into the hatch. "What about…" Iro heard a *clunk*. Nothing happened. "No, that's not it. Hand me the hydrospanner."

Iro inched out of the pod door. Mia was still glaring at him, close enough to lash out and punch him again. He hefted his toolbag from the floor and dropped it inside, close enough for Roret to reach.

He noticed Emil leaning against the door of pod two. "Not that one," Iro said, pointing. Mia made a lunge for his hand and he pulled it back quickly. "Pod two is down."

Emil didn't even look at Iro as he pushed away from the door and sauntered forward to lean against pod three's door, staring into the cockpit. His armor was dented, scratched, clearly cobbled together from different sets, all of it slightly different shades and none of it seemed to fit right. A pair of oversized gauntlets with spikes on the knuckles dangled from his belt hooks.

"What are those lights off the front wing?" Emil asked, nodding into the pod.

Master Tannow's face twisted like he'd found a rat in his algae. "It's another fleet."

"What?" Iro said, unable to keep the surprise from his voice. Mia spun about to stare at the old master, and Cali's mouth hung open. Only Emil didn't seem to care.

"Another fleet has already staked a claim on the titan," Master Tannow said as if it didn't matter. As if finding another fleet of ships wasn't an unprecedented event. "That's as much as we know, and it doesn't matter. We're here now and we can't turn around."

Iro nodded. "Nowhere to go and not enough fuel to get there."

Master Tannow sat on the bench and buried his head in his hands. "Not enough fuel to get here. We're running on fumes already. It's amazing the lights are still on."

"Haven't we contacted them to make sure they're friendly?" Cali asked. Iro thought he detected a quiver in her voice and saw her patting the knives strapped to her belt.

"We can't," Iro said. "Our comms barely make it past the fleet."

Master Tannow nodded, head still in hands. "We don't even know if they're human. For all we know, they could be Vhar. We don't know what sort of tech they use, nor what comm channels they have. Without flying in close and waving out the window at them, we have no way of communicating. And again, it doesn't matter. We have nowhere else to go." He looked tired, or maybe scared. "They're on the front starboard wing, so we're heading to the rear larboard wing. As far away from them as possible.

That's a whole lot of space between us."

"What if they've already scavenged that wing?" Cali asked. She scratched at the shaved side of her head.

Emil snorted but said nothing.

Master Tannow sighed. "The Home Fleet was attached to titan 01 for twenty-two generations. We never even made it past the ninth level. That means we barely even searched the outer skin of the one wing, let alone ventured into the main body of the titan. And we never needed to. Everything we needed, we took from the outer levels of that one wing.

"That other fleet is roughly the same size as ours, maybe a little bigger. This titan is big enough for both fleets and then a dozen more. We'll be fine."

Iro considered the possibility of a dozen other fleets. So many people. All he'd known, his entire life, was the Home Fleet. He thought they were all humanity had.

But what if there are more of us out there?

The general alarm bleated throughout the ship. A moment after it fell quiet, Captain Galen's voice sounded across the main comm speakers. "The fleet is beginning its approach. Hoppers, prepare to launch. We only have one shot at this."

The speakers fell silent. Iro held his breath, waiting for something else to happen. After a few seconds, Master Tannow took his head out of his hands and hauled himself to his feet.

"OK, trainees, assemble." Emil, Mia, and Cali all jumped to attention, standing before Master Tannow. Iro stared at them. Even in patchwork armor, they looked a formidable bunch.

"This is a large scale joint Hop," Master Tannow said. "That means Hoppers from all over the fleet are assembling at the landing zone. No official squads have been organised, which means *we* are a squad. You watch each other's backs. Protect each other. We are Paladins. It's our job to enhance others. Leave the fighting to the Corsairs and Vanguards wherever possible, but keep your weapons at hand."

He paced, and Iro saw sweat trickling down his brow. "Landing zone is the thruster control. I'll do the flying, your pods will be set to follow the leader." He stopped pacing and stared down at Emil. The other boy wasn't much shorter than Master Tannow. "Fuel is the mission critical resource here."

"Not food?" Iro clamped his mouth shut too late. The words were already out. All eyes turned his way. They ranged from condescending to outright hostile. Iro lowered his head and backed up a step into pod five.

"Not food," Master Tannow growled, moving to stand in front of Cali. "We have all the algae we want and the means to grow it. But without fuel, the fleet is dead. We expended everything to get here. So much…" He sighed. "This Hop is a one way trip."

"What?" Mia said. She looked at her sister, and then back to the master. "What do you mean one way?"

That explained the diagnostics reporting there wasn't enough fuel in the pods. The pods could manage a short trip at best, and once they were on the titan, they weren't coming back. He had assumed they would be fuelled up before they left. The fuel pellets were handled by ships officers, not trusted to tech grunts like them.

Master Tannow stepped in front of Mia. "Scared, trainee?"

Iro saw Mia gulp. "No. I just… How do we get back?"

"Why do you think we think we're going to thruster control, trainee?" He shook his head slowly. "Fuel is the mission critical resource," he repeated. "Every Hopper down there is going to be looking for fuel pellets. We find some, fill the pod cargo holds, fill the engine, and get back to the Courage before she goes dark. Which gives us about…"

"Three hours, sixteen minutes," Roret said without even lifting his head from the guts of the pod.

"It's going to be chaos down there," Master Tannow continued. He straightened up and walked back to the head of the line. "There will be Hoppers from other ships everywhere. We don't know what sort of monsters or traps we're likely to encounter. This is a whole new titan. But if the wing hasn't been scavenged, then you can expect it to be crawling."

He paused and looked over his trainees one last time. "Stay close. Watch each others' backs. Courage!"

"Courage," Emil, Mia, and Cali said together with little enthusiasm.

Master Tannow nodded and stared at pod one. His eyes took on a glazed look for a few moments, then he shook his head. "Emil in three. Cali in four. Mia in five."

"What?" Mia all but shouted. "I'm not getting in that one. If Useless here has been touching it, it'll probably blow up half way to the titan."

"Wouldn't worry about that," Roret said, climbing out of the hatch, spanner in hand. "If I can't get the door working, you won't even leave the bay." He squeezed past Iro, still loitering at the pod door. The cockpits were barely big enough for one person, and Iro's tool bag took up a bit of space itself. Roret pulled open the panel underneath the pod controls and frowned at whatever he saw.

"See," Mia said. "I…"

"Get in the pod, trainee," Master Tannow shouted. "We launch in thirty seconds."

Iro glanced out the pod window. All he could see now was the titan. It was beyond massive.

Mia stepped into the pod, tripped on Iro's tool bag, then caught herself on the seat, and gave Iro a solid push. He stumbled back, hip bouncing off the controls, head hitting the outer bulkhead.

"Get out of my pod, Useless," Mia snarled at him.

"I'm trying," Iro snapped back, already trying to squeeze around Mia as she tried to manoeuvre herself into the seat. "But you take up so much room."

"What the scrap did you just say?"

"Only that you clearly love algae a bit too much."

Mia grabbed Iro by his collar and slammed him against the pod wall, lifting him off his feet. He instantly reevaluated his position. She was all muscle and scarier than he gave her credit for. A few strands of dark hair wafted in front of her face and she blew them away, still glaring at Iro.

"Ten seconds," Master Tannow's voice was tinny over the pod comms.

"Is the door closed yet?" Roret asked. He sounded like his head was inside the wall.

"Not yet," Iro's voice trembled. He held up his hands as non-threateningly as he could and smiled down at the girl pinning him to the wall.

"Get out of my pod," Mia hissed each word carefully.

"I can't. You're holding me here," Iro said slowly as if speaking to a child.

With her free hand, Mia punched Iro in the stomach. He doubled over, the air driven from his lungs.

"How about now?" Roret shouted.

"Nope," Iro wheezed.

"Launch," Master Tannow said. The pod bay rumbled as pods one, three, and four detached from the Courage and rocketed toward the titan.

Mia dropped Iro to sprawl on the cluttered floor of the pod. She turned to the window and pressed her face against it, watching the other pods go. "No!" she cried. "You can't go without me, Cali." She turned to Iro, face like a sparking wire. "My sister is down there alone because of you."

"I think the hydraulics tube has come loose again," Roret shouted. "Can you secure it?"

Iro crawled on elbows and knees to the service hatch and peered into it. It was a tiny space, he had no idea how Roret had fit inside with space to work. Sure enough, the hydraulics tube was dangling, unconnected. He plugged it in, twisted it to lock it. It flopped free again. The locking screw had been stripped.

"Mia, can you hand me the silver tape?" Iro asked, flailing a hand back at her. "Top of my bag."

Mia grumbled something, nudged him again a couple of times, and then he heard her rifling through his bag. A moment later, the roll of tape was shoved into his hand, and Iro plugged the hydraulics tube back in and started wrapping tape around it.

"Why do you have a sword in here?" Mia asked.

Iro froze. "Get out of my bag!" He flipped around onto his back. Mia stepped on his chest, pinning him to the floor, and picked Neya's sword out of his tool bag.

"What does a tech need with a sword?" Mia asked. Iro tried to sit up, but she pressed down on his chest, slamming him back to the floor. "A chipped old piece of scrap.Don't tell me you still want to be a Hopper, Useless. You got no talent."

"Put it back," Iro wheezed.

"Or what?"

Roret cheered. "I got it!" The pod door slammed shut.

Mia's eyes went wide, a grin splitting her face. She dropped Neya's sword back in Iro's bag and scrambled for the chair. There wasn't enough room in the pod with both of them cluttering it up, and she shoved Iro hard with her feet. "Get out."

Iro scrambled to the pod door and pulled himself up. He hit the controls to open it. Nothing happened. He pressed the button again. Still nothing. Roret shouted something, but with the pod door closed, Iro couldn't hear what.

Suddenly the pod shook violently. Iro was thrown back to land in Mia's lap and they both squeaked in alarm. Out of the window, Iro saw the black void. Then the titan swung into view as the pod rocketed towards the wing.

Chapter Five

There wasn't room in the pod for two. Mia strapped herself into the chair. Iro collapsed to the metal panelling on the floor, curled into a ball, clutched at Mia's leg to stop himself from being thrown around. The pod shook hard enough to make Iro's teeth rattle. They flew through space on the same course Master Tannow had taken to the titan.

After minutes that stretched on for an eternity, the pod docked with the titan. It was not a clean landing. It clipped a wall, sending it into a violent spin that made everything go black.

Iro woke to the sound of retching. Mia was on her hands and knees next to him, vomiting up her breakfast of algae. He turned away from the sight. The pod was a painful blur, hazy around the edges. Iro lifted a hand to his head and winced in pain. He was bleeding.

Neya's sword!

In a daze, he looked around for his toolbag, found it had fallen into the open hatch. Most of the tools and parts and fallen out, were clattering around the guts of the pod, but Neya's sword was still in the bag. Iro wrenched it out of the hatch and clutched it tight, hugging it to his chest. He couldn't bear the thought of losing his sister's sword.

A loud thumping sounded from somewhere. Outside, Iro realised through the dizziness. Someone was hammering on the pod door. He flipped over, stretched out and and reached up for the release button.

"Stop!" Mia snarled. She grabbed at his leg, tried to pull him back from the door. "What if it's a monster?"

Iro stared at her for a moment, trying to understand.

Why would a monster knock? He shook his head, gripped Neya's sword tight, and pressed the release button on the door. It unlocked with a hiss of escaping air, and then was wrenched open.

"It's about time, sis. I thought you weren't..." Cali stopped as she pulled the door all the way open and found Iro's sword point swaying in her general direction. "Scrap! What are you doing here?" She frowned at him, then looked past Iro to where Mia was still throwing up in the corner of the pod.

Iro staggered forward out of the pod door, bumping into Cali. His legs felt like loose wires, but he needed to get away from the smell of Mia's vomit. A large hand landed on his shoulder.

"What are you doing here, Iro?" Master Tannow asked. "And why do you have a sword."

Iro shook his head, still trying to clear the cobwebs away. It was so noisy wherever they were. He heard people shouting, cries of anger, of pain, an explosion.

"It was my sister's sword," he said before he could think better of it. He blinked away the last of the confusion, and looked up to find himself standing at the edge of a battlefield.

They'd landed in a large open dock that led to the thruster section. There were pods everywhere, each with the ship name painted on the side. There were Hoppers from the Courage, from the Vermillion, the Swift, the Grey Haven, the Stormhold, and many more. Further in, past the docking area, the titan opened out into a cavernous space that stretched on into the darkness. The ceiling was so high up Iro could barely see it. The walls were all near seamless bulkheads, and he smelled the warm, acrid tang of engines in use. And then, of course, there were the monsters and Hoppers fighting each other.

Iro stared as a Vanguard ripped a length of metal from the floor and held it up before her as a shield. As he watched, her crest, a huge glowing glyph of purple symbols, lit up behind her. The length of metal she clutched sizzled, the air around it wavering from heat. A giant insect-like creature with a segmented body ten feet long, reared up before her. Half a dozen bladed legs flashed out at the Vanguard. She blocked them all with her shield. A section of the metal sheared away, but she held the monster back. Iro desperately tried to remember what the monster was called. He wished he had his bestiary with him, where he had written about all the monsters Neya encountered on her Hops.

A kharapid, he suddenly remembered. *But it's so much smaller than the ones Neya fought*.

Over the other side of the engine room, he saw a Mechanist raise his arms. His crest appeared behind him, drawn in sharp, golden lines. Dozens of little automatons scrabbled out from his robes and took flight. Only Mechanists could give life to the automatons. The little things swarmed a four legged monster with shaggy fur, stomping hooves, and a horned nose. Each of the automatons slashed gouges from the monster's hide until it collapsed, blood pooling beneath it.

A huge brute of a monster roared from within the engine room. A moment later it charged forward out of the gloom. It almost looked human, but it stood twice as tall as Master Tannow. It twirled a massive hammer in each hand, swinging them at Hoppers as it charged. Iro saw a Paladin from the Courage point at the Vanguard in the monster's way. One of the giant hammers slammed into the Vanguard and crushed his shield, sending him tumbling away. He rolled to a stop, unharmed thanks to the enhancement, and brought his hands together with a resounding boom that shook the entire chamber. Every monster in the engine room turned its eyes on the Vanguard. Iro unwittingly took a step towards it and had to shake himself to get control. Taunt was a talent only the strongest of Vanguards could use. That meant the man was ridiculously powerful.

Monsters swarmed over each other to get to the Vanguard. A trio of Corsairs, bolstered by Paladins, picked at the rear lines of the monsters, their swords slashing. They moved so fast Iro could barely see them. One sent a wave of crackling yellow energy slashing out from her sword's arc. It cut down half a dozen little rustlings, severing limbs and spraying blood.

The giant monster with the two hammers reached the Vanguard, screaming in fury, its hammers raised to strike. The Vanguard crossed his arms, screamed his own challenge back. His crest appeared before him, bulky green lines and circles glowing in the air. The hammers struck the crest and sparks erupted from the impact, engulfing both the Vanguard and the monster.

Master Tannow stepped in front of Iro, blocking his view. "I said what are you doing here, Iro?"

Iro shook his head, still in shock from the sight of the battle. *Is this what Neya experienced every time she set foot on the old titan?* He'd always known she was strong, she made it through her third Gate of Power, after all, but to face off against monsters like he was seeing now. She was so brave.

"The door shut," Iro said dumbly. "The pod launched before I could open it again."

"Scrap!" Master Tannow grabbed his chin, ran his fingers through his beard. All his trainees were here now, they assembled around him. Mia finished throwing up and stared at the battle with wide eyes. Iro hoped he hadn't looked so stupid when he was gawking. Cali was next to her sister, twirling her knives in her hands, eyes wide and darting. Emil stood slightly apart from the rest, hands clenching and unclenching. He watched the battle unfolding with a calmness Iro couldn't understand.

"I'll take the pod back," Iro said. "I shouldn't be here."

This was what he had always wanted. To be a Hopper just like Neya. *But I'm not like her. I've never been like Neya. I don't have a talent. I don't know how to use her sword. Even my crest is dull and blank.*

He couldn't fight anything more dangerous than a rusted gear. And now he was here, on the titan, it was terrifying. To see monsters up close. To hear them, smell them. It was all too much.

To his right, a burly Hopper dragged a slight woman out of the battle, towards the pods. Blood trailed behind her, and Iro realised her left leg was missing past the knee. She was unconscious, green froth bubbling at the corners of her mouth.

"Can't go back," Master Tannow growled. "One way trip, remember. Until we find some fuel to fill the engines, none of us are going anywhere." He sighed and shook his head. "Can't leave you here either. Stay close." He grabbed Iro's shoulder and shoved him towards the others. Mia glared at him, and Iro dropped his gaze to the ground.

Iro saw Mia reach for her sister's hand, a moment later they were clinging to each other, fingers intertwined. Iro understood. He gripped Neya's sword so tight his knuckles were white, and the sword danced in his grip.

"Stay at the back of the battle," Master Tannow said, his voice quiet as though he were talking to himself. "We're Paladins. No need to get in the thick of it." He started forwards, already raising a hand and bestowing an enhancement on another Hopper. Bolstered by a burst of speed, the Corsair darted around a plume of spat flame, and rushed the toad-like monster, gutting its bulging red belly with a single slash. A flash of flame roared out of the monster's open gut and engulfed it. That was a fuel spitter, Iro remembered. They were a particularly odd type of monster only found near the engine sections of titans. Neya had described their squat frames and gaping maws in great detail, and that they consumed fuel pellets and exhaled fire.

Mia, Cali, and Emil followed their master. As trainees, they hadn't even opened their first gates yet. That meant they only knew one talent, the easiest for any Paladin to learn, the ability to harden another person's skin like steel. They bestowed their enhancements liberally, often only on Vanguards, taking it in turns when the effort of holding the enhancement in place became too great. Each of their crests were small things, only just larger than his own, but brighter and with symbols and lettering he didn't understand. Despite that, their crests dimmed in seconds whenever they used their talents. Iro had heard Paladins who opened their Fourth Gate could hold enhancements for hours, but for trainees it was tough to hold it for a few moments.

The front lines of the battle moved further into the engine section as the Hoppers pushed out from the landing zone. Iro gawked at the sheer size of it. He'd done some study of the old titan maps, and had stared at the new titan out of the window for hours as the Home Fleet approached. The engine section here was a single feeding line into a single thruster. According to the maps from the old titan, each thruster would have two dozen feeding lines to ensure enough fuel pellets were funnelled to the engines. The wing they were standing in now had thirty-two thrusters. That meant three-hundred-and-eighty-four feeding engine sections like this for each wing. And the engines were only a small part of the overall wing. And he was fairly certain they could fit the entire Courage in this one section. The sheer size of the titan being revealed to him made him feel small in a way he never had before. He'd spent his entire life aboard the Courage. The cramped apartments, close halls, and crowded workstations were all he had ever known. But their entire civilisation could live inside a single wing of the titan without even venturing down to the lower levels.

That wasn't quite true. Monsters were drawn to humans for some inexplicable reason, so if they ever tried to live on a titan, they would come under constant attack.

A young woman with a split lip, still bleeding, and a jaw like a bulkhead, limped toward them. Her armor stopped at her pauldrons, leaving her heavily muscled arms bare. Her chest plate was flaking yellow and spattered with green blood, but Iro saw an emblem on her breast of a clenched fist. She was a Berserker, specialising in martial combat. Iro knew little about the Berserkers other than that they were the most powerful of the physical Hopper classes.

"Tannow, we need a Paladin in there," she pointed into the gloom. The noise coming from from the engine section was intense. An explosion lit up the struggle for a moment, and Iro glimpsed a huge monster standing almost to the ceiling. It appeared to be made from metal, its scaly skin shining. It stood on two legs, with a long, bladed tail, and a giant maw already dripping with gore. Iro had never even heard of such a monster before. A Vanguard stood beneath it, struggling to hold a shield above her head as the monster tried to crush her with one of its clawed feet. A Corsair leapt thirty feet into the air, glowing sword slicing down on the monster's nose. Sparks flew from the impact. The monster lurched to the side, slamming the Corsair from the air. Iro never saw what happened then, the gloom reclaiming the distant battle other than the blurred glow of crests as Hoppers charged about.

Master Tannow clenched his fists, trembling. Then

turned to the trainees. "Stay back here. Protect each other." He turned and ran off into the gloom with the Berserker. Iro stood behind the others, clutching his sister's sword. He was out of his depth. Way out of it. He'd dreamed of this for years. To board a titan and fight alongside his sister for the good of the fleet. To join her in her adventures. To take her place after she was gone. But Neya had only ever told him of how exciting her Hops were, the thrill of battling monsters and dodging traps. She never told Iro about the fear of facing monsters who were trying to kill you. The horror of watching comrades hurt, killed. Iro saw it all now and he was terrified. Part of him wanted to go home.

They weren't the only Hoppers hanging back away from the front lines of the fight. The injured were dragged back to the pods, Surveyors tending to their wounds. Surveyors were both trap hunters, and the best battlefield medics in the fleet. Their talents were so variable, Neya once told him a Surveyor who had opened their fourth gate could slow down time around a wound. There were trainees from other ships, those also experiencing their first Hop. Not all were Paladins, and many couldn't help from the backlines, but at least they were getting the experience.

Mia and Cali stood close to each other, talking in whispers. Emil paced ahead of them, squinting into the gloom as though he could see the battle taking place further in.

A scream of rage startled Iro and he spun about to see two rustlings bounce over a metal crate, heading straight for them. The rustlings were only three feet tall, their bodies almost perfectly spherical, their skin a pitted, rusty red. They had beady eyes, huge mouths full of razor sharp teeth, and each one ran on overly muscled legs, with spindly arms topped with a crude claw that gripped shards of metal like knives. One screamed like it was on fire, and the other garbled a string of unintelligible words.

"Cali," Mia shouted, already slipping her hammer from her back. She stepped in towards the rustlings and swung her hammer, grunting at the effort. The first of the rustlings dropped to the ground and rolled under the swing, but the hammer connected with the second. It crunched into the monster, sent it sprawling, half its grotesque body pulped by Mia's strike. The rustling garbled some more nonsense, and began crawling towards them with its one good arm. The first rustling recovered and leapt on Mia, knives stabbing.

"Steel!" Cali shouted, her silver crest flaring into a glowing complex of lines and circles behind her, just as the rustling hit Mia. Both girl and monster staggered, fell, the rustling on top of Mia, stabbing at her again and again. It's knives bounced off her scraps of armor, scraped against her enhanced skin, and Mia screamed. A steel enhancement might stop the knives cutting her, but they didn't stop the impacts or the pain.

"Get it off. Get if off!" Mia squealed, desperately trying to cover her face from the monster's strikes.

Cali collapsed to one knee, sweating and panting from holding the enhancement on her sister for so long. Her silver crest dimmed to dark flickering lines as her current ran out.

Iro stared. Unable to move. He wanted to. To run to Mia's side and stab Neya's sword into the rustling, but his feet wouldn't move. He just stared, hearing Mia's screams as if from far away, drowned out by the deafening rasp of his own breathing. Neya's sword trembled in his grasp and he didn't move.

Emil ran to Mia's side. Metal gauntlets on his hands. He thumped two solid blows into the rustling's bulbous body, grabbed one of its arms, dragged it off the screaming girl. It roared at him, spun about in Emil's grip, flailed with its unhindered arm. The knife found a gap between Emil's armor, sliced along his arm. He shouted in pain, dropped the monster, staggered away, clutching at his wounded arm. The rustling took only a moment to right itself, then leapt at Emil, both knives flashing. Mia rose from the ground, screaming, her hammer rose with her, then she brought it down with enough force to crack metal. The rustling's body crumpled from the blow, orange ichor spraying from its eyes and mouth.

Mia let go of the hammer now lodged in the monster's body and collapsed to her hands and knees. She was shaking, breathing hard. Cali staggered upright, wiped sweat from her head, ran to her sister's side. Emil just stared down at the dead rustling at his feet. His eyes were wide, and he was frowning at it. The monster's body twitched, and Emil stumbled back, holding up his fists, ready to defend. Then he winced and clutched at his wounded arm.

Iro couldn't quite understand. Rustlings were one of the lowest grade monsters. Neya told him stories of facing down hordes of the things. Dozens of rustlings rolling over each other to get to her and the other Hoppers. Five Hoppers against fifty, and that was the easy Hops. Mia, Cali, and Emil had fought just two of them, and nearly lost. *That's the difference between a trainee and a Hopper whose opened one of their Gates of Power.*

Cali screamed in agony. Iro looked to see the wounded rustling wasn't quite dead. It had crawled towards her as she saw to her sister, and stabbed a knife into her thigh. The wounded monster wrenched on the knife, dragging its grotesque body closer, opening a mouth full of dagger-like teeth to bite her.

Emil rushed to the rescue again, dragging the rustling away. "Mia, get her to the pods." He wrestled with the wounded monster for a few moments, then knocked its remaining knife away and knelt atop it, punching it again and again.

Mia hauled Cali up, supporting her sister, and dragged her away towards the pods where the Surveyors could see to the wound. Meanwhile, Emil kept thumping away at the rustling. Shouting wordlessly at it with each strike. After a dozen punches, the monster stopped twitching. It was dead. Emil got up, staggered away, turned and collapsed. He was clearly exhausted, sweat pouring down his face, chest heaving.

Iro cursed himself for the coward he was. The other three had fought for their lives against the two monsters, and he just stood there and watched, unable to even move. Neya's sword trembled in his grip, and he felt tears blur his eyes and run down his cheeks. He stared at the sword. A solid three feet of bulky titan-steel, chipped where he had been carelessly swinging it about. It had a slim cross guard without ornament. The hilt was wrapped in some leather taken from a monster from the old titan. The pommel was weighty, to balance the heft of the sword. How many monsters had the sword slain in his sister's hands?

Useless in my hands. Just like me. Useless and talentless.

Emil cried out in alarm. Iro wiped tears on his sleeve and stared to see the other boy backing away, fists held up before him defensively. A kharapid scuttled towards Emil and lurched up before him, bladed limbs slashing. Emil deflected two of the limbs, but another caught him on the arm, the same one the rustling had injured. Emil fell back, clutching at his wound. The kharapid scuttled forward, the front half of its body reared up, limbs slashing.

Kharapids were not the sort of monsters a trainee could fight. Even Hoppers who had opened their first gates were ill-advised to face such powerful foes. Emil, injured and alone, and still a trainee stood no chance.

Iro had to help. He thrust his hand forward, focused on the idle current of power nestled within, summoned his icy crest, and projected it out to Emil. "Steel!" he shouted. Nothing happened. Just as it had every time before.

The kharapid slashed at Emil again. He tried to block with his one uninjured fist, but the monster was too strong. It crushed through his defence and buried a bladed limb in the boy's shoulder. Emil screamed in pain, and the kharapid flung him away to sprawl on the floor.

"Move," Iro said through gritted teeth, ordering his legs forward. The kharapid scuttled on. Emil pushed himself to his knees. He couldn't even raise his arms.

"Move!" The kharapid closed on Emil and reared up for a finishing strike.

"MOVE!" Iro screamed at himself. He raised his sister's sword to strike and the world lurched beneath him.

Chapter Six

Iro's vision tunnelled to a fine point. He felt like gravity shifted, dragged him forward. The world went fuzzy and he blinked. When he opened his eyes he found himself stood between the kharapid and Emil. Neya's sword was in his hands and he was swinging it. The kharapid lurched back, arms flailing, and the sword bit home. The blade severed one of the monster's limbs, and clanged to a halt against another, the carapace stopping it from cutting any further. The kharapid leaned into Iro and he growled, staggering back a step from the monster's massive strength. Another bladed limb slashed out over the top of the sword and Iro squeaked in alarm.

"Steel!" Emil breathed.

Iro felt his skin tighten just as the limb smacked him in the face hard enough to throw him down beside Emil. The other boy collapsed, exhausted, his fiery crest flickering once then fading completely.

The kharapid thrashed about. One limb was severed, another broken where it had connected with Iro's steel-enhanced face. But it had plenty more limbs to use, and any one of them could kill them both. Iro staggered back to his feet and held Neya's sword up, ready to defend. "I won't let you," he snarled at the monster.

The kharapid scuttled forward, limbs reaching back to strike.

"Look out below," a distant voice shouted. Iro glanced up to see a man soaring through the air above him. The man spun once in mid-air, then started falling towards them. He had a massive slab of metal as a big as a door over each of his arms, and his crest was a neon pink light shining behind him. "CRUNCH!" The Vanguard shouted as he landed on top of the kharapid, bringing both slabs of metal down on the monster so hard he crushed the carapace and squashed the monster like a bug. Blood and ichor sprayed out everywhere, hitting Iro in the chest.

"Oh yeah!" the Vanguard shouted. He was tall and lithe, dressed in a full, heavy suit of titan-forged armor that was painted a brilliant white and more pristine than any Iro had ever seen. His hair was dark and tied into a bun at the back of his head, and he grinned at Iro despite the green blood splattering his face. "That's one for me already. You're falling behind, Lara."

The air shimmered beside Iro and a woman appeared. She was short and plump, her hair just as dark as the Vanguard's, but tied into a tight braid. She wore a light suit of dark green armor. She did not smile. "Your vainglory almost got these trainees killed, Ben."

The Vanguard chuckled. "They had it under control. I just got in the way really. Right, kid?"

"Uh…" Iro mumbled.

"Thank you," Emil grumbled from behind. The other boy was still kneeling, cradling his right arm with his left, though both were bleeding.

The Vanguard waved a metal-clad hand in the air. If the giant slab of titan steel that extended up his arm weighed him down at all, he didn't show it. "Not needed. Really, I'm sure you had it under control." He stared straight at Iro. "You got some good instincts there, little Corsair. Always protect your Paladin."

"Corsair?" Iro asked.

"Sure," the Vanguard said. He stepped forward and swung the metal door at Iro, but pulled back before he hit. "Whoops, sorry about that." He dropped the metal slab and clapped Iro on the shoulder. "What is it you Corsairs say? *Your life is your sword.*"

The woman sighed. "Your sword is your life."

"Same thing, no?"

"No."

The Vanguard shrugged, picked up the metal slab again with such ease it might have weighed less than a sock, then turned away to face the gloom of the engine room. His crest flared into neon life behind him, all the lines bulky. It had symbols Iro almost recognised, but he had no time to study it. "Time to get into the mix. You ready for this, Lara. SPEED!" And he sprinted away, disappearing into the gloom in seconds. A moment later, Iro heard him shout *SMASH*. He had a feeling the monster hit had probably not survived.

"Take your Paladin back to the pods," the woman snapped. "And if I see you in the fight again." She leaned forward and stared Iro hard in the face. Her eyes were dark and looked lifeless. "I will kill you myself." Her crest appeared, flaring white in front of her for a moment, a blinding brilliance, and suddenly she was gone.

Iro stared into the engine room for a few seconds. He could still hear the sounds of fighting further in, but it had moved far beyond them now. The beachhead had been established, and the Hoppers would now have to hold it long enough to fill the pods with enough fuel to cart back to their respective ships.

He looked down at the sword in his hands. Shining silver blade, a splash of green blood where he had chopped off the kharapid's limb. He still had no idea what had happened. He couldn't be a Corsair. Classes ran in the family, passed down through blood. His mother was a Paladin, so he should be too, like Neya was. Like all the Hoppers on the Courage were. But what about his father?

Iro had never known his father, didn't even know who the man was.

"I'm a Corsair," Iro said quietly.

Emil grimaced at Iro and struggled to get a foot beneath him. Iro rushed forward to help, but Emil shoved him away with his less injured arm. "Get off me. I don't need your help." He staggered back to his feet, then turned and started limping towards the pods.

Iro twisted his hands around the grip of Neya's sword and stared at the blade again. He was a Corsair. A Hopper. Or he could be at least. He could be a trainee, just like he'd always wanted. He looked about at the spilled blood, the slaughtered monsters, the Hoppers having their injuries treated at the pods. The fear came back hard. Did he still want to be a Hopper after seeing what it was like? He didn't know the answer to that.

Iro trailed after Emil. He didn't know what to do now, but the Vanguard had told him to protect his Paladin, and the woman had threatened to kill him if he went near the battle again. Iro figured the pods were probably the only safe place for him.

Cali and Mia were slumped by one of the pods. A Surveyor loomed over them, tutting at Cali's arm. A tablet floated nearby, a pen floating next to it. Whenever the Surveyor spoke, the pen scribbled on the tablet. A titan-looted artifact. Powerful items that could only be found on the lower levels or in spires. They were almost always guarded by the most vicious monsters.

"Superficial cut, three inches down the left forearm, close to the ulna," the Surveyor said. He was an older man, hair grey and cut short, and with dark bags beneath his eyes. "Recommend fifteen stitches, no further surgery required. Chance of significant scarring: forty percent."

"Significant scarring?" Cali asked, panic clear in her

voice.

"Yes," the surveyor said in a gruff voice. "You want to Hop, get used to scars."

"What if I don't want to anymore?" Cali asked in a quiet voice.

The Surveyor didn't answer. He moved on to Mia and started cataloguing her injuries, the floating pen and tablet recording every word.

Emil stood nearby, cradling his arm. Iro formed up in front of the others, holding Neya's sword out before him in what he thought was a ready stance, just in case any other monsters slipped past the lines.

"What happened?" Mia asked as the Surveyor poked at her leg.

Emil ground his teeth and said nothing. Iro couldn't keep quiet. "I saved him. I'm a Corsair."

Emil glared fury at him, and Iro took a step away from the other boy, but kept his sword up and held in both hands.

"What?" Cali asked. "How?"

"I… uh… don't know." Iro said. It still didn't make any sense to him, but he had felt his current of power move. It flowed into Neya's sword. He had disappeared and reappeared between the kharapid and Emil.

Iro activated his crest, brought it up shimmering before him. It was still dim, barely more than a flickering LED on the verge of dying. The lines were icy blue and thin as a sword cut. But it wasn't blank anymore. At the very centre of his crest, inside the circle, was a symbol he didn't recognise. It had three slashing lines, all straight and intersecting, forming a triangle. He stared at it in wonder. His crest. No longer blank. He finally had a talent.

A roar sounded from further within the engine room. Everything shook. Iro felt the vibrations through his feet.

Another explosion rocked the cavernous room, so far back Iro could make out nothing but the flames. Screams drifted out of the gloom.

A few moments later, Hoppers started running back towards the pods. First there were just a few, then a lot. Master Tannow was with them, carrying a metal crate in his arms, and clearly straining from the effort. More Hoppers ran from the gloom, most of them carrying similar crates, or bags straining from the contents.

"Time to go," Master Tannow said as he dropped the crate to the ground before them. He wiped a sheen of sweat from his head, and staggered, putting a hand on Iro's shoulder and leaning against him. Iro struggled to stay upright. "Put that sword down before you hurt someone."

"Did you know Useless is a Corsair, master?" Cali asked.

Master Tannow stood straight again and stared down at Iro. Under the weight of that scrutiny, Iro wanted to crawl into the dark and hide. "What?" Master Tannow asked.

"He's a Corsair," Emil said. "He teleported in front of me or something. There was a Vanguard, Ben. He saw it all and said it was a Corsair talent."

Master Tannow nodded slowly. "We'll sort that out later." He ripped the lid off the metal crate to reveal hundreds of fist sized black pellets. "Put that sword down, Iro, and help me fill the cargo holds quick."

They spent the next few minutes filling their own four pods' cargo holds. All the while, more Hoppers, many of them injured, staggered back to the landing area. The noise from the engine room was growing closer, the roaring more frequent, the stomps shaking the metal flooring more violently.

Master Tannow sent Mia and Cali off first. With their pods refuelled, it was easy enough to set them to return home. Then he shoved Emil into his pod and ordered Iro in as well. Emil secured himself to the chair, and Iro knelt at his feet, clutching the metal frame. As Master Tannow wrestled with the pod door, trying to get it to close, Iro saw the monster charging out of the engine room. Vanguards fled before it, all hope at holding the thing at bay discarded. The monster roared, a sound like tearing bulkheads, and molten metal sprayed from its maw. It caught one of the fuel crates and the explosion ripped through the engine room.

Chapter Seven

Serah paced aboard the bridge of the Courage. She knew it was driving Captain Galen to distraction, but she didn't care. Until she got word of Iro, she couldn't be still. She had to at least feel like she was doing something. That little tech friend of Iro's, Roret, had come to her just after the pod launch, told her what had happened. Serah had wanted to demand the pods recalled immediately, but that was not within her power, and they didn't have a choice anyway. They needed the fuel.

"Pods are starting to return, Captain," called out Lena from the observation panel.

Unfortunately, they had very little they could actually observe. Half the systems on the Courage no longer functioned, and half of those never would again because they didn't understand how they had functioned in the first place. Serah turned on her heel, started pacing back the other way. She didn't have a lot of room to move on the bridge. The captain had his own chair, but everyone else had no choice but to stand. There were ten consoles arrayed around the cramped space, each with their own function and their own officer assigned to monitor the readouts. Serah was officially off-duty, given her shift had ended two hours ago, but she couldn't be anywhere else. The bridge was where the news would arrive first, and so on the bridge she would remain until she knew Iro was safe.

"How many?" Captain Galen asked.

"Three so far, Captain," Lena said.

Galen motioned to Rafial who was manning the viewing console. The tall youth pressed a couple of buttons and the view screen flickered to life. It dominated the wall before them, was fuzzy around the edges, and had thousands of dead pixels that no one knew how to fix. Every time they switched it on, more dead pixels appeared, so they rarely risked it. Most of the time they just hung a ragged, fading banner with the ship's symbol— some ancient bird-like animal no one even remembered the name of— and name written on it. But of course Galen would risk it for this; his own daughters were down on the titan as well.

The view screen fuzzed a little, and then an image of the titan brightened into view. The sheer scale of it took Serah's breath away. And she had lived all her life around the old titan. She had been aboard it, trained as a Hopper, though she failed to open her first gate, and that put a premature end to her career of adventure and combat. This new titan though, it was truly massive. An artificial wonder making its way through the universe, two fleets all but attached to it, feeding off it.

A host of tiny lights flared near the engine section. Pods rocketing out of the landing zone and returning to their respective ships. She hoped Iro was aboard one of them. Her poor, talentless boy had no business being aboard a titan. And she couldn't even begin to consider the possibility of losing another child to the monsters and traps. Not after losing Neya.

More and more of the pods detached from the titan, pin pricks of light zipping away against the backdrop of the giant ship.

Then the unthinkable happened. An explosion ripped out of the titan's wing, venting flames into the void to be quickly swallowed by suffocating space.

"What happened?" Serah asked, hearing the hysteria in her own voice. She stopped pacing and clutched at the railing, leaning over the back of the captain's chair.

Captain Galen frowned up at Serah and shook his head, his hands clawing at the arms of his chair. "Lena, report."

Lena leaned close over the observation panel. "It looks like an explosion in one of the engine feeders, sir."

"Was it the same one our Hoppers were aboard?"

Lena nodded and Serah almost collapsed. She had to lock her knees and lean on the railing. She watched through the view screen as the flames stopped venting into space. The engine linked to that section flickered and then went dark. It looked so small and peaceful from distance, but she knew that single engine was large enough to destroy the entire fleet if they ever drifted too close.

"Any word on our pods?" Serah asked.

Theodora, the big woman on the comm panel, pressed the button on her earpiece. She spent a few seconds staring into nothing, the tinny voice barely audible to Serah. Then Theodora nodded. "All eight of our pods have returned with full cargo holds, Captain," she said, ignoring Serah. "Some injuries, but nothing fatal."

Serah laughed, tears coming unbidden to her eyes. She was still leaning on the railing and had to pry one of her hands free to wipe her eyes on a sleeve. She felt a hand on her shoulder, opened her eyes to see Captain Galen standing there, squeezing her shoulder gently. He was clearly as relieved as she was.

Theodora pressed the button on her ear piece again. "Captain. It's Master Tannow, he wants to see you and Serah immediately."

All eyes on the bridge turned to Serah, and she felt her legs go weak all over again. "No," she whispered. "Please no."

Theodora took pity on her. "Iro is alive, but… Master Tannow doesn't say. Just needs to speak with you and the captain urgently."

"Nikolaos, you have the bridge," Captain Galen said. He turned to Theodora. "Tell Master Tannow we'll meet him in the pod bay."

"They're on their way to Serah's quarters, sir," Theodora said.

Serah and Galen left the bridge at a brisk pace. It was too slow for Serah. She wanted to run through the halls, and she didn't care who stared at her and thought it strange. She flung open the door to her quarters and rushed in to find it empty, they had beaten Tannow and Iro there. Galen walked in behind her, closing the door, and made his way to the table in the kitchen area. He stared at her with obvious concern, but she couldn't find it in herself to care.

The moment the door opened and Iro stepped through, Serah launched herself down the hall and wrapped her son in a crushing hug. Iro startled and laughed, but hugged her back. For a few wonderful moments, nothing else mattered. She had her son back. She ignored Tannow as he squeezed past them in the hall, and into the kitchen.

Suddenly, Serah realised Iro was saying something. She couldn't hear him. She was hugging him so tightly his face was pressed into her shoulder. She let him go reluctantly, and found him grinning at her. "I'm fine, mom. Really. You hurt me more with that hug than the kharapid did."

Serah felt all colour drain from her face. "You fought a kharapid? What were you thinking?"

"Emil was in trouble."

"That boy is a Hopper," Serah snapped. "He can look after himself. You are not. I know you want to be, to follow in Neya's footsteps, but you're not a Hopper, Iro." Her voice grew higher, tighter, but she couldn't stop it. She shook him once by the shoulders. "You're just not."

Iro grinned at her and Serah felt an irrational anger inside. How could he laugh at a time like this? He fought a kharapid. He was lucky to be alive.

Galen coughed from the kitchen before Serah could tell Iro off. "Can we get on with this. I have a ship to oversee, and…" He trailed off.

"Cali took a bad cut, but she'll be alright," Tannow said.

Galen sighed, deflated, slouched into one of the kitchen chairs. "Are you hurt, Tannow?" he asked.

The old Hopper trainer grunted. "It's nothing. Not considering the things we encountered over there. There was… It's not important right now. We're here to talk about Iro."

Serah pushed her son on ahead of her. As soon as they were all seated around the little kitchen table, knees knocking beneath the thin metal, she reached out and grabbed his hand, squeezing it in her own. He smiled back at her, and Serah still couldn't fathom why he seemed so happy.

"You should have sent him right back," she said, frowning at Tannow.

The old master nodded. "I should have. Under normal circumstances, I would have. But I couldn't, and it turns out that's a good thing. He saved Emil's life over there." Tannow leaned forward, his belly nudging the edge of the table. He stared hard at Serah. "Iro is a Corsair, Serah."

She shook her head. "That's not possible."

"I know," Tannow said. "But enough people saw it. He channeled through that old sword he carries about. Performed a Blink Strike on the kharapid and saved Emil's life."

"It was amazing, mom," Iro said, the grin still fixed

on his face. "One moment I was standing too far back. Then the world just… lurched, and I was between Emil and the monster. Ow! Mom, you're squeezing too tight."

Serah let go of Iro's hand. She glanced at Galen to find the captain frowning at her. "Who is his father?" he asked.

"It doesn't matter," Serah said. "He's not a Hopper. Had no talents."

"Spontaneous manifestation," Galen said, his voice almost dreamy.

Serah sent a panicked look at Tannow, he caught her meaning and nodded. "What's important," the old master said. "Is that I can't train Iro here. I don't know the first thing about Corsair talents. But I've already spoke to Alfvin over on the Eclipse, and he…"

"No," Serah said before Tannow could finish. She shook her head, feeling tears stinging her eyes. "I've already lost one child to the titans, Tannow. Not another."

"That's not your choice, Serah," Galen snapped. "Right now the fleet needs every Hopper it can…"

"Scrap you, Galen," Serah hissed at him. "He's my son."

"Compose yourself, officer," Galen said. "He's a potential Hopper at a time when some ships can't field a full squad. And I am well aware of the risk."

"One boy won't make a difference."

"What if he does?" Galen pressed. "What if one Hopper makes all the difference? And having a Corsair with ties to the Courage can only be a good thing."

Of course Galen would look at it from a greed-based perspective. He saw Iro as a potential for influence and scavengable goods from the titan.

"I'll do it," Iro said, his voice quiet but full of hope. "I want to." Serah felt his hand in her own again. "Mom, I want to train to be a Hopper. I always thought that would be as a Paladin like you and Neya, but if it's as a Corsair, then I'm happy with that too."

There was no arguing after that. Nothing Serah could say that would stop it. They were all arrayed against her.

Emil waited before his family apartment, one hand hovering before the door handle, his other in a sling. It was throbbing despite the pain medication the doctor had given him. His wounds hadn't been serious, not compared to some of the Hoppers, but the doctor had taken a while getting to him. It had been hours since Emil returned to the Courage. That was more than long enough for the story to make the rounds.

He drew in a deep breath, held it, pulled the door open. It squealed like blades against each other, and Emil cursed. They'd been asking the techs to get their door fixed for months now, but every time it was always a few days away on the list of tasks. He knew it was more likely they just didn't have the oil to spare. The techs had already been around to remove the rotors from all the doors, so they no longer opened automatically. His da' had a fit over that, declaring they were now one stop from living like beasts. Emil stepped over the threshold and pulled the door shut behind him to another rusty squeal. It was too much to hope that hadn't woken the old man, and he knew it.

The hallway was littered with old boxes. Metal crates filled with scrap his father deemed too useful to get rid of, too valuable to give to the rest of the ship. He was wrong, of course. It was all just junk. A box full of cables no one knew what they were for. Most of the wiring was stripped beyond use anyway. Another crate filled with ceramic shards from broken cups and plates, from before the fleet had switched over to printed plastic. That stuff was hundreds of years old and useless for everything but taking up space. Another box was bursting filled with broken tablets and ear pieces that his father had stolen from the reclamation bay. He claimed one day he'd sit down and fix them all, but the truth was the old man had no idea how to fix anything. Chances were most of it was scrap beyond salvage anyway.

Emil struggled to raise the strap of his armor bag over his head with one arm and placed it down next to the door as quietly as possible, nestled between a box of empty oil canisters and another with a single pillow inside, crusty with years old blood. The last remnants of his mother.

Emil considered his armor for a moment. It needed cleaning, but it could wait until tomorrow. He was exhausted. The high from the Hop, his first Hop, quickly gave way to the fear of actually experiencing it. He'd never admit it to the others, but he'd been terrified. Then there was the fight, enhancing that talentless tech. That had taken it out of Emil. The injury too. Then hours waiting for the doctor to see him. All he wanted was to crawl into bed and sleep.

"About time you came home," his father's voice echoed down the hall.

Emil sighed. All pretence at stealth was gone now. He pulled his arm out of the sling, grimacing at the pain, and shoved the thing into his pocket. Then he walked down the hall, picking his way between the piles of boxes, into the kitchen.

"Da'" Emil said as he reached up to the cupboards to look for a clean bowl. There wasn't one. All their bowls were dirty and in the sink, despite not having running water to clean them. Emil fished one out and rummaged around for a sterilising wipe. They were out of those too. Eventually he gave up. He was hungry enough to eat the bowls, but he was also sick to death of algae paste.

"That all?" his father said once Emil flopped into the

seat opposite him. "You come home in disgrace, and the only thing you have to say for yourself is *da'*."

Emil raised his eyes to meet his father's hostile stare for a few seconds. He was a tall man, thin as a stripped wire and tough as old bhur beast leather. His hair had long since fallen out on top, but the old man refused to give it up and grew out his horseshoe of hair to dangle around his shoulders. He stared back at Emil with dark, spiteful eyes set within a face like a uniform dumped and forgotten, all lines and creases. Emil quickly dropped his own gaze before his father could take it as some sort of challenge. It didn't take much of an excuse. "Sorry, da'."

"Well, an apology is a start," the old man snarled. "Doesn't make up for the disgrace you just heaped upon this family though, does it?"

Emil kept his gaze on the table top. The paint was long gone and the table was spotted with rust. That was his fault, he'd peeled off the paint in flakes when he was younger. A habit he'd taken too whenever his parents set to shouting at one another.

His father was obsessed with some sort of social standing he was certain existed aboard the Courage. He claimed that was why he'd never risen above the ranks of drudge. That was the impolite name of a sanitation expert, or unlucky scrap who has to clean the toilets and sift through the septic tanks. It was the worst job aboard any ship, and aboard the Courage, Emil's father was the chief drudge. Despite that, he was always talking about the social elite who danced about on the bridge and made the decisions that the rest of them had to suffer. He claimed he was smart enough to be an officer, to be captain even, but those jobs were passed down through families these days. The only way to climb the ranks was through playing what he called *the social game*. That was his own name for being friendly and polite with people.

"You knocked us down today, Emil," his father continued. "Thanks to you, I'll have to spend weeks kissing the wrinkly arse of that fool, Torken. He loves to lord stuff like that over me." Torken was the general worker foreman, the man who handed out most of the worst jobs aboard the Courage. And Torken's daughter was one of only two remaining Paladins aboard who had opened their third Gate of Power. That made her strong and strength meant she was special.

"You don't look hurt," his father said. Emil was doing his best to keep his left arm steady on the table, because any movement sent sharp agony tearing through it. His father wouldn't be concerned knowing he was hurt, only more disappointed. "So what? You started a fight with something bigger than you and some talentless kid had to save your arse?"

Emil scratched at one of the last bits of paint clinging to the table's surface. "He wasn't talentless. He just pretended he was." Emil couldn't understand it. Why had Iro pretended he was weak for so many years? At least it explained why he was always hanging around in the training rooms, and why he hid that sword in his bag, believing no one noticed.

"Is that supposed to excuse it?" his father snapped. The old man slammed a fist down on the table. "Only a coward needs someone else to protect them, Emil."

Emil stared at his father for a second and almost said *Like you*. His father had a talent too, had even passed through his first gate. As a Paladin, he could Steel people to protect them. He'd been trained to fight, but on his very first Hop he got scared and hid while the rest of his squad died because they didn't have a Paladin to back them up. That was the truth about their social standing and why his father was a drudge. It was because he was a coward who let others die to protect him while he hid. Emil forced his mouth shut, and went back to glaring at the table.

"Don't you dare be weak, Emil," his father snarled. "If I ever hear about someone having to protect you again, I'll…" He let the threat dangle. He always let the threat dangle, daring Emil to ask what he'd do. "Now go on. Get out of my sight before I get angry."

Emil stood, walking slowly so it didn't look like he was fleeing. He stepped past the piled boxes, plucked his armor bag from the floor and passed the strap over his head. His arm was throbbing again.

"Where are you going, Emil?" the old man called.

Emil didn't answer. He pulled open the door, drowning out his father's words with the rusty squeal, then stepped out into the waiting corridor and ran. He didn't stop running until he reached his squad's training room. It was empty, thankfully, and Emil dumped his bag down against the wall. He took a few moments to collect himself, gritting his teeth against the throbbing in his arm, then ran towards the nearest training dummy, stepping on the button to make it start swinging.

Emil ducked the dummy's first swing, and rose into an uppercut that thumped against its padded chest. The dummy lurched the other way, swinging at him again and he leapt back too slowly. The blow caught his injured arm and he cried out, clamping his teeth down to crush the rising scream. The dummy kept spinning, lurching one way then the other, attacking thin air to mock him. Emil leapt up with another cry and attacked again.

Chapter Eight

With all the ships in the fleet refuelled, there was no longer an issue with ships manoeuvres. Food, water, and spare parts were all another matter, but already there were plans being drawn up for future Hops. The assault on the engine room had gone poorly, or at least not as well as the fleet captains had hoped, but there was always a chance they would find less resistance in the garden, or perhaps even find the real treasure of a manufactory. Those were very rare unless the Hoppers ventured further into the titan's wing, but that was where they would find most of the parts they needed to fix their failing ships.

Iro knew all of that. It didn't matter for now though. It would be a long time before he was ready to Hop again. Weeks of training, he supposed. Maybe even months. Nobody had told him how long his training would take, but Mia and Cali and Emil had been training for all their lives. Training for all their lives and still they weren't prepared for that first Hop. Iro almost despaired when he thought of how far behind he was.

He waited at the docking hatch of the Courage, and stared out the window as the Eclipse drifted closer. All the ships had docking hatches and tubes, a much more efficient way to transport supplies and people than the docking pods. Though people rarely moved ships. He'd never thought about it before, but it was true. As long as he'd been alive, the only people who lived on the Courage were those born there.

Affinity for talents, and therefor Hopper classes, were passed down from parent to child, so it only made sense that people rarely moved ship. If Iro was a Paladin, there would be no better place for him than the Courage. But people were encouraged to breed across ships. Back when the fleet had orbited the old titan, people regularly moved across ships for what the adults had called social visits. But not Hoppers. Too much chance of an affinity being bred out of existence, Iro supposed. Again, he'd never really thought about it.

His mother fussed about him, straightening his jacket, tutting over the holes in his shoes. There was nothing to be done. He was wearing his best clothes, but after five years drifting through the dark, no one had clothes that weren't fraying at the edges and full of holes or covered in stains. Another thing they hoped to fix now they had a titan to scavenge from again. His mother had a large bag with her, though she hadn't told him why yet. Iro himself carried two bags, one full of ratty clothes, and the other full of personal effects. Neya's sword was strapped to his back, now he was allowed to carry it in full view. That was a point of pride for him. He openly carried his sister's sword and no one questioned his right.

"Don't think this gives you a licence not to come back," his mother said. She licked her thumb and tried to smooth down a petulant bit of hair on Iro's head. She needn't have bothered. His hair always had a habit of sticking up where it would. "The captain says the ships will be docking every few months, no reason you can't visit."

"I will, I promise," Iro said.

His mother stared at him for a moment, then lurched forward and wrapped her arms around him. Iro hugged her back.

A red light above the docking hatch flicked on. The ships had detected each other and the docking tubes were extending. No one knew how the ships knew to do it.

His mother pulled back and heaved the bag she had brought from the floor. She stared down at it for a moment, then thrust it at Iro. "This was mine," she said. "It was always too small for Neya, but she was…" She shook her head. "Bits of it will fit you and it's better to have some protection than none."

Iro took the bag, struggling under the weight of it, and looked down into it. A jumble of old pieces of ship-printed armor clinked together inside. It was painted bone white, Courage colors, though that paint had faded and was peeling off in chunks. It was also made for a woman, rather than a man.

"Mom…" Iro started.

"I know," his mother said as the light above the door switched to green and the docking hatch opened. "You'll get your own suit eventually. Once we find a manufactory, but for now at least you'll have some armor." She sniffled. "It's the best I can do, Iro." She hugged him again.

Master Tannow cleared his throat. Iro's mother sent him a glare, but released Iro and stepped back. "Do the Courage proud, lad."

Iro shouldered his bags, struggling under the weight of his new armor, and nodded. He was ready. Ready to leave the Courage and start his training to be a Hopper. He stepped forward and found his feet failing him at the door. The docking tube swayed a little before him as the ships matched speed and course. The tubes had to be flexible to account for fluctuations. But it wasn't the fear of passing through the tubes that caused him to hesitate. It was leaving. He'd been looking forward to it for days, ever since discovering he was a Corsair, but now he was there and the Eclipse was waiting for him. He didn't want to leave his mother behind, nor his friends. Roret wasn't happy about it all. He'd sulked when Iro told him, and refused to come and see his friend off.

Iro glanced over his shoulder to find his mom watching him, tears in her eyes. He found his own stinging too and had to wipe them on the back of his sleeve. "I'm gonna miss you, mom."

That broke her and his mother collapsed into Tannow's arms, bawling like a child. Iro turned and fled down the tube, barely noticing it as it swayed. The door closed behind him, cutting off the Courage and his old life.

When Iro reached the far end of the docking tube, the door slid open on silent motors. The smell that hit him was a shock. It smelled like the Courage hadn't for years. It smelled clean. He stepped across the threshold into a gleaming white docking chamber that looked freshly painted. A couple of passing techs stared at him, whispered something to each other, then hurried away. The door closed behind Iro, and he turned suddenly. The light above the door flicked from green to red, and the docking tube detached and began receding back into the ship. Through the window, he saw the Courage start to drift away, as both ships moved back into their normal fleet positions. He fancied he saw a face at the window on the Courage, his mother staring back at him across the void.

"Iro, is it?" said a man.

Iro spun about and snapped to attention. The man waiting for him was tall and rangy. He wore an impeccable uniform the likes of which Iro had never seen before, with deep blue cloth and black trim. Despite the uniform, he slouched, hands buried deep in his pockets. He had a bored look on his face that said he'd rather be anywhere else, and his blond hair fell around his face in messy waves.

"Yes sir," Iro said, still standing to attention.

"That looks painful," the man said. He cocked his head to the side. "How long can you keep it up?"

"Sir?" Iro said, relaxing a little.

"Not long, I guess," the man said, shrugging without taking his hands out of his pockets. "Come with me, I'll show you to your quarters." With that, he turned and sauntered down the corridor away from the docking hatch, leaving Iro to hurry to catch up.

"Uh, who are you, sir?" Iro asked as he struggled to keep his three bags from toppling him. The pace the man set was lethargic at best.

"Rollo. Master Rollo, to you, I guess." He sighed as if the conversation was more effort than he cared for. "Welcome to the Eclipse, Iro." He sniffed. "Is that you? Don't you people bathe?"

Iro dropped his gaze to the floor, suddenly self conscious. He sniffed at himself, but could smell nothing over the scent of disinfectant in the air. "Every four days, Master Rollo."

"Four days? Urgh. No wonder you left." He said nothing else about the matter and Iro wondered how often the people aboard the Eclipse got to wash. And how often the walls were cleaned. And how everyone appeared to be wearing clothes without stains or patched over holes. As he followed Master Rollo along corridors and past rooms that had doors that still opened on automatic motors, he wondered how the people here kept their ship working as they did, and so spotlessly clean.

Iro almost bumped into Master Rollo when he stopped. The man didn't pull his hands from his pockets, but kicked at the door they stood outside. He stared at Iro under half lidded eyes like he was falling asleep.

Iro glanced at the door, then back to the master. "Should I…"

The door slid open to reveal a massive young man with arms thick with muscle, and a face still pudgy with youth. The boy sniffed and grimaced.

"It's the new kid," Master Rollo said. He turned and started striding away. "Show him how to wash. Apparently they don't do that over there."

Iro watched the master go for a moment, then turned to find the other boy staring down at him. He wasn't sure if he should be following Master Rollo or not.

"Got a name, new kid?" the huge boy asked. He took a step forward, filling the doorway and looming over Iro. He crossed his arms and his shirt looked fit to burst from the pressure.

"Iro. Uh, Courage Iro."

"Hah!" the other boy said loudly, immediately brightening up with a grin. He stepped back and aside to let Iro in. "I'm Bjorn. Eclipse Bjorn, if you must, but I hope you won't. Come on in. I'll introduce you to the others."

Iro stepped over the threshold and the other boy immediately clapped him on the back and sent him stumbling. "I'll take those, new kid," Bjorn said, grabbing Iro's bags and pulling them from his shoulder. Iro immediately clutched at his sword strap. "It's alright. No one's gonna touch your sword. This way."

Bjorn hefted Iro's bags onto his shoulders as if they weighed nothing, squeezed past Iro, and strode down a hallway that was almost spotless save for a single bulkhead that had three names scribbled on it and a tally beneath each one. The other boy stopped at a doorway and waved inside, dumping Iro's bags just inside the door.

"You're with me," Bjorn said. "Only spare bunk."

Iro approached cautiously and peered around the doorway. The room inside was small as his own back on the Courage, but with a bunkbed pushed up against one wall. The rest of the space was dominated by a rickety metal chair, some weights of various sizes, and a host of clothes dumped half on the chair, and half on the floor. There was barely enough room for his bags. He couldn't imagine unpacking them anywhere.

"I'm on the top bunk," Bjorn said.

Iro nodded. He had never shared a room with anyone before. Their apartment on the Courage had enough space for him and Neya and their mother to have a room each. The idea of having no privacy was a daunting one.

"Who's this?"

Iro spun about. Opposite the room he was to be sharing, was another of the exact same layout, only without the weights and dumped clothing. One rakish boy leaned against the door. He had dirty blond hair that looked wet and slicked back on his head, and he had a gap in front teeth that made him whistle a little with his S's. Behind him, another boy lounged on the bottom bunk. He had dark hair, though still lighter than Iro's, and was as big as Bjorn but was pudgy with it rather than muscled.

"This is Courage Iro," Bjorn said with a wide grin.

The rakish boy laughed. "That explains the smell."

Iro fought the urge to sniff at himself again. He'd only been on the Eclipse for a few minutes and he was already getting sick of people telling him he smelled.

"A sword without a Hopper to wield it, shouldn't start a fight," said the pudgy boy from his bunk. He had his eyes closed and his arms behind his head.

"What does that mean?" the rakish one whistled through the gap in his teeth.

The pudgy boy cracked a wide grin. "It means I sleep below you, and the last thing you should be doing is accusing others of smelling bad."

"Scrap you, Torben!" said the rakish boy, but he laughed.

Bjorn reached out and tussled the rakish boy's hair.

He leapt back and tried desperately to push his hair back into place, telling Bjorn to leave off.

"This is Arne," Bjorn said, pointing at the rakish one. "And the lazy one over there is Torben."

"I'm not lazy," Torben said without so much as cracking an eyelid. "I'm just conserving energy."

"Like a marsh mite," said Arne, laughing.

Iro remembered the monsters from Neya's stories. Marsh mites lived in the gardens. They were horrible beasts with armoured backs, and a host of tentacles around a snapping beak of a mouth. They waited beneath the waters in the garden, only surfacing to ambush the unwary. They were also ugly as a hull breach.

Torben opened his eyes, pulled a face as though considering the statement, then nodded. "Yeah. Exactly like a marsh mite."

"Lazy, ugly, and stupid," Arne said.

Torben shrugged. "If the uniform fits."

"Come on," Bjorn said, starting towards the door out of the apartment again. "I'll show you the showers, then the mess hall. Then training tomorrow. You're gonna want to sleep before that."

"Mess hall?" Iro asked. "You don't have a kitchen here."

Arne laughed. "You see a kitchen, Courage?"

Bjorn shook his head. "This is it, Iro. Home. Our room on one side, those two fools on the other."

"What about back there?" Iro asked, pointing down the hall. A door sat at the end of the hall.

Arne laughed again. "Definitely from a lower ship. He wants to eat in the storage cupboard."

"Nothing in there but our armor," Bjorn said. "Come on."

The shower turned out to be remarkably clean

compared to the Courage. Not a spot of rust or mold to be seen anywhere. On top of that, there were individual stalls rather than a communal shower, and Bjorn claimed each crew member was afforded enough water rations for a single shower a day. He also said the rationing would probably disappear once the fleet was making regular hops to the garden. It would take a few weeks before all the ships' water tanks were full again, but apparently the Eclipse was likely to be one of the first in line. Iro spent longer in the shower than he ever had, and it was warm, and it was private. He'd never known such luxury. It was a real shame to put his dirty, patchy, sweat and grease stained clothes on again afterwards.

The mess hall was where everyone but the ship's officers ate. A large, open hall with banks of benches in neat, orderly rows. Hoppers and techs and drudges all ate together, often at the same tables. Iro and Bjorn each had a large bowl of algae, far larger than his rations aboard the Courage in recent months. Bjorn didn't know the names of everyone, but he pointed out all the Hoppers they saw. There were dozens of Corsairs aboard the Eclipse and easily as many trainees. Some of the Hoppers had even opened their fourth gates. Iro had to stop himself from gawking. Aboard the Courage, they had only six fully trained Hoppers left. On top of that, they had only one Hopper who had opened their fourth gate. Everywhere Iro looked, the Eclipse was an entirely different class of ship than the Courage.

Iro struggled to get to sleep that night, listening to Bjorn's bed rattling snores. He missed his own room. He missed the constant rattle and hum of the ship around him, the Eclipse was in such better condition it was almost silent. He missed Roret and even the smell of the Courage, even if everyone on the Eclipse seemed to think it terrible. But most of all, he missed his mom, and hoped she wasn't missing him too much.

Chapter Nine

Bjorn woke Iro early by rolling out of the top bunk and hitting the ground heavily enough the whole bed jumped. The big lad pulled Iro out of bed, and cajoled him into a morning run around the ship. The lanky Arne and chubby Torben joined them, and before Iro's stomach could grumble about the lack of breakfast, all four boys were swiftly jogging through the clinically white corridors, dodging around techs, drudges, and officers.

Iro fell behind the others. Bjorn set a quick pace, his longer legs eating up the distance. Arne kept up with ease. Torben occasionally had to stop to squeeze past others in the tight hallways, but caught back up easily enough despite his bulk. Iro was not used to running, or any sustained exercise really. The most he'd done aboard the Courage was swinging Neya's sword about on his own until he felt tired enough that he gave in.

By the time Bjorn stopped and Iro caught the others up, they had run around the ship five times. The bigger lad stopped them outside the showers, the others had already gone in. Bjorn grinned when Iro finally caught up. Iro collapsed, his breath burning in his lungs, sweat pouring down his face. Bjorn gave him only a minute before hauling him to his feet and pushing him into the shower block.

After the shower, they sat down to breakfast at the mess hall, where they hastily scoffed down a large bowl of algae. Iro was still hurting from the run and just keeping the paste down was a heroic effort. Then it was back to their quarters to get ready for training.

It was at that point that Iro realised something. He

had always secretly begrudged Hoppers a little for having easier lives when techs like him were busy fixing things all hours of the day. He resented the trainees most of all. But their lives weren't easy either. They had to train all the time or they might die on a Hop, or worse yet, others might die because they weren't fit enough or strong enough. He had resented the trainees, but there was a reason that Mia and Cali and Emil could beat him up so easily. Because they spent all their days training to be stronger. Well, Iro was a trainee now, and he was clearly not strong enough, not compared to the others. If he wanted to catch up, he would have to work just as hard as them. Harder even.

Bjorn told him to get into his armor and strap on his sword and Iro hurried to do it. It was tough. He'd never worn armor before. There was an underlayer of mesh like fabric that snugged so tightly to his body he felt uncomfortable and self-conscious. Most of the armor plates just about fit him, and they clipped together and slotted into each other. It was awkward and bulky and he was sure he'd be walking into things without meaning to. The right pauldron was too badly cracked to clip into the breastplate, so he left it behind.

The others were waiting for him by the time he finished.

"That's your armor?" Bjorn asked, an eyebrow raised into his hairline.

Iro felt his cheeks go red and nodded. He knew it wasn't a good fit. It was too slim, barely covering his arms and legs. And the chest plate was shaped wrong.

"You sure?" Bjorn asked.

Arne burst out laughing and even Torben was chuckling. "It's a hand me down," Iro said. "From my mom."

Arne and Torben laughed so hard they collapsed

against each other. Even Bjorn was grinning and clearly trying very hard not to chuckle.

"Go ahead," Iro said.

Bjorn snorted, roaring with laughter and slapping the wall with his hand. His own armor was dark blue, far bulkier than Iro's, and looked like it had been printed yesterday.

They set off jogging again, and Iro's legs weren't happy about that to say the least. In the two minute jog to the training hall, he stumbled twice, his feet almost giving up beneath him. He'd never in his whole life felt so tired, so achey, wretched. The extra weight from the armor and carrying his sword was a feat he hadn't even considered.

The training hall was larger than the ones he was used to repairing on the Courage. The floor was covered in a tough yellow mat that was somehow hard and also soft enough to cushion should a trainee fall. Two of the walls had racks of dull-edged training swords of various types and sizes, some with single edges and some with two. Some long and thin, others short and wide. The third wall had some training apparatus with metal sides full of holes, and a cushioned top pushed up against it. There were no training dummies.

Four girls stood about the hall already when Iro and the others arrived. They were moving through a series of stretches that looked painful to reach and even more painful to hold. They were all armored in the same deep blue as Bjorn, Arne, and Torben. Iro considered his own bone white armor.

Looks like I'm going to be the odd one out. Again.

"Is this everyone?" Iro asked Bjorn as Arne and Torben waved to the girls and moved to join in the stretching routine.

Bjorn frowned at him. "In our training squad? Sure.

We were seven, and you make eight. A complete squad."

"There are other squads?"

Bjorn nodded. "Two others full of trainees. They use a different hall, so you'll not see them much."

"Oh. The Courage only had six trainees."

"In a squad?"

Iro shook his head. "In total."

Bjorn shrugged. "The Courage is a little ship. Come on, I'll introduce you."

A large part of introductions consisted of everyone having a laugh at Iro wearing a woman's armor all over again, Arne leading the charge. After everyone had given up laughing, they handed out their names.

There was Eir, a tall girl with a head shaved to stubble. She had a wide grin and blue eyes that seemed full of mischief.

Ashvild was almost as short as Iro, but she stood so rigid it looked like it had to hurt. She wore her blond hair tied into a tight braid. She didn't smile, even when she was laughing. There was something dangerously severe about her. The type of person Roret would have said had a wrench up their butt.

Ylfa was the most beautiful girl Iro had ever seen, even more so than Mia. She had a kind smile that didn't seem to meet her dark eyes, and her dirty blond hair was short, but not as short as Eir's. Iro felt a stupid grin stretching his face when their eyes met, and Bjorn thumped him on the arm hard enough he couldn't feel his fingers afterwards.

The final girl was Ingrid. She was almost of a height with Torben and wasn't far off his bulk either. In fact, they had the same hair too, and the same goofy grin. The more Iro looked, the more certain he was that Ingrid and Torben were siblings. When they stood next to each other, they could have been twins.

They were just about finished with introductions when Master Rollo sauntered into the room, his hands buried firmly in his pockets, his uniform rumpled. Unlike the trainees, he was not wearing any armor.. All chatter quickly ceased and the others leapt into line and stood to attention. Iro hurried to the end of the line and stood as straight as he could, but his back was already aching like his bones were on fire. Master Rollo ignored them all as he walked over to the wall with apparatus stacked against it and hopped onto a high bench where he sat with his legs dangling, heels tapping against the metal structure.

After a few seconds that felt like hours, Master Rollo yawned. "OK, new kid. What was your name again?"

"Courage Iro, master."

"Urgh," Master Rollo said, somehow slumping even further. "Someone tell him his mistake."

Bjorn nudged him slightly. "It's Eclipse Iro now."

"You're not here on some little day trip, kid," Master Rollo said. "You live here until I either fail to make a Hopper out of you, or you die. My bets on the latter, but only because you'll die before I fail. So, what do you know, Eclipse Iro?"

"Uh…"

"About Corsairs," Bjorn whispered.

"Oh," Iro nodded. "Nothing, master. Not really. They… uh… We focus the current through swords to use talents." And Iro had to admit that was about the full extent of his knowledge. Master Rollo was silent, his legs kicking back and forth slightly as he stared at Iro.

"Um…" Iro looked down the line at the rest of the trainees but he found no help there, not even from Bjorn. "I used a talent that Master Tannow called a Blink Strike?"

Master Rollo rolled his half lidded eyes. "Ashvild.

Blink Strikes."

The painfully severe girl took a single step forward out of line. "One of the rarest first manifestation talents among trainee Corsairs. It involves focusing one's current through their sword and using it to slip through the world at extreme speed to deliver a single, powerful strike." Master Rollo nodded lazily and Ashvild took a step back, a self-satisfied smile creeping across her face.

Iro stepped forward, ignoring Bjorn's hissed intake of breath. "So it's a powerful talent?" Iro asked. "It seemed strong when I used it. I just teleported in front of the kharapid."

"You fought a kharapid?" this was from the tall girl with the shaved head. It took a moment for Iro to remember her name was Eir. She leaned forward, stared at him, eyes wide and an earnest grin that Iro felt the need to return. "I hear they're dangerous, but not as…"

Master Rollo cleared his throat loudly. Eir quickly fell silent, rubbed a hand over her bristly scalp, and leaned back into the line.

Master Rollo removed a hand from his pocket, and scratched at the back of his neck. "Blink Strike has its uses," he said slowly. "But…" He thrust his hand back into his pocket and rolled his head to stare at Arne. "Torben. Weakness of Blink Strikes."

The big, chubby boy hesitated a moment, then stepped forward. "It's not true teleportation. That's, uh, a Mage talent?" He paused, wincing as though he expected Master Rollo to contradict him. When the master said nothing, Torben continued. "It's more like really fast movement. And it's hard to control. Once you've started a Blink Strike, you're locked in to it."

"Locked into it?" Iro asked.

Torben stared at him with wide eyes for a moment,

then looked slowly to Master Rollo. Iro had a feeling he was speaking out of turn, but no one had explained the rules to him.

"You can't change the strike once you've started it," Master Rollo said. He pulled a hand out of his pocket and flicked a couple of fingers at Torben. The chubby boy stepped back into line with a grateful sigh. "You choose how you want to strike, where you want to be. Until you reach that position, you can't change it."

"But..." Iro was trying to understand. "It's instant. Isn't it?"

"Is it?" Master Rollo asked, his half-lidded eyes oddly intense. "I dunno. Maybe the new kid is right. Must have all of five minutes of experience, and here's me with just a couple of decades." One of the girls laughed, and Iro didn't dare turn to see who. "Try it, kid. Draw your sword." Master Rollo waited until Iro had Neya's sword in his hands. Now try to hit me with a Blink Strike."

Iro stood dumbfounded. "I don't want to hurt you, master."

"How chivalrous of you," Master Rollo said. He still hadn't moved from his perch, both hands were once more buried in his pockets, his legs dangling over the bench, kicking back and forth slowly. "Now use your Blink Strike on me. Try to hit me. Or, pack up your scrap, and go back to your hovel on the Courage. We might not dock for a while so you'll have to swim through the black to get there."

Iro twisted his hands on the grip of Neya's sword. He was being mocked, he knew that. He was used to it from the other trainees, but not from adults. Master Tannow had never mocked him. He ground his teeth. *I just have to bear with it. Learn everything they can teach me.*

"I don't know how," he said quietly.

"What?" Master Rollo asked.

"I don't know how I did it," Iro said again, more loudly, his eyes on the floor. "When I did it before, I just did it. But no one has told me how."

Another laugh from behind, but more than one person this time.

"Wonderful. We have a scrapping toddler on the team." He recognised that voice. It was the pretty girl with dark eyes; Ylfa. Iro felt heat flush his cheeks.

"No," Master Rollo said sharply. The laughter stopped. "You kids are here to learn. Ignorance isn't funny." His half-lidded gaze locked on Iro once again. "And neither is the desire to learn. You want to learn how you did it, kid?"

Iro nodded.

"First things first. Activate your crest."

Iro drew in a deep breath and let it out slowly. He activated his crest and it flickered to a dim glow behind him. He glanced over his shoulder at it. The luminescent lines seemed to stutter, so close to blinking out. But it held, floating behind him. A icy blue circle with the same strange triangular symbol in the centre, like three sword slashes. There was something else as well, something that hadn't been there before. Spreading out from the circle were dim, jagged lines. They had yet to take on any recognisable shape, but it was proof that Iro had awakened a talent. His crest was already growing.

"Interesting," Master Rollo said quietly. Iro looked up to find his eyes narrowed. The man scratched at the stubble on his chin. "You see something new every day."

"Is something wrong with my crest?" Iro asked.

Master Rollo shrugged and tucked his hand back in his pocket. "Now imagine the strike you want to make. Picture it. Standing in front of me, swinging the sword at me. How your feet are placed on the ground, the way your arms are positioned, the grip on your sword. The arc of the swing.

The way the edge of the blade splits the air. Hold it in your head, then focus the current through your sword. And swing."

Iro pictured himself standing before Master Rollo, his sword held above his head chopping down. He raised Neya's sword, reached inside for the current that flowed through him. Always before, he had tried to push it out of his fingers with a Paladin's command, but this time he forced it to flow into Neya's sword. He chopped downwards. Nothing happened.

Master Rollo stared at him a moment, then yawned loudly. "A common problem. Some trainees, and even some Hoppers need to use a crutch to use their talents. Activate your crest in front of you and let the strike you want to make pass through it."

Iro activated his crest again, this time floating before him, the lines and symbols a pale azure. It was mesmerising and he wished his crest was bigger so he could study it in detail. He pictured the strike he wanted to make again and raised Neya's sword, then chopped downwards through his crest. The world fuzzed around Iro for a moment, and he had the strangest feeling of being dragged. Then he was standing before Master Rollo, Neya's sword raised above him and falling, just like he had pictured.

Master Rollo kicked out with one foot, hitting the cross hilt of the sword and arresting Iro's strike. He lashed out with his other foot and kicked Iro in the chest hard enough to send him flying backwards across the room. The world spun, and Iro landed on the floor, the wind blasted from his lungs, Neya's sword spinning from his grip. He rolled onto his hands and knees and choked, desperately trying to remember how to breathe. How had Master Rollo hit him so hard while barely moving? How how he reacted fast enough to see the strike coming?

Bjorn grabbed Iro underneath the arms and hauled him back to his feet as Iro took deep, wheezing breaths.

"See what I mean?" Master Rollo said. "I'm faster than you, so I saw that strike coming and had a counter ready. Because it was not instantaneous. Now pick up your sword and try again."

Iro had to search around for his sword, it had spun away into the corner of the training hall. He picked it up and returned to the line of trainees. His limbs felt heavy and he was struggling to keep his legs from shaking.

"I said try again, kid," Master Rollo said.

Iro shook his head. "I understand, master."

"Not yet you don't. Try again."

Iro staggered forward and held Neya's sword up before him. He was trembling, exhausted, barely able to keep the sword point from swaying side to side. He activated his crest again and it flickered into dim light for a moment before fizzling out and disappearing. He pictured the strike he wanted to make again, this time standing side on and thrusting his sword straight at Master Rollo. Then he reached inside for the current, and found none. He was drained, exhausted. Iro just shook his head and slumped onto one knee. Sweat dripped from his head to splash upon the floor.

"Well, that makes my point for me," Master Rollo said. "Blink Strikes take a lot of current to perform. They're tiring, especially for trainees who haven't opened their first gates yet. Still, only having one in you is pathetic."

I've only been a trainee for a couple of days!

"Of course, once you're trained and have opened a gate or two…" Iro looked up just in time to see Master Rollo vanish. He felt the knife pass over his head. A finger flicked his ear. Then Master Rollo was in front of him, the knife in his hand slashing just a breath from Iro's nose. Then he was back in his perch on the apparatus, his knife slashing upwards into the air. Master Rollo tucked the knife back into his boot, and pushed his hands back into his pockets. It had all happened in the space of three heartbeats.

Iro collapsed to his knees.

"Get him back in line," Master Rollo said.

Iro felt Bjorn haul him to his feet once more and push him into position.

"Seeing as the new kid is new and clearly has no idea how to swing a sword, we're going to run through some basics today," Master Rollo said with a savage grin. The rest of the squad groaned.

Chapter Ten

The next ten days were the most gruelling, exhausting, and painful of Iro's life. He forced himself to wake early, even earlier than Bjorn, and spent the morning borrowing the bigger boy's weights. It was a struggle. At times, Iro found himself using both arms and still struggling to lift a weight that Bjorn exercised with while holding a conversation. His muscles quivered from the effort, and for hours afterward they burned so uncomfortably he couldn't stand it. Even lifting a cup made him shake.

On the third day, Iro startled when Bjorn let out a good natured chuckle. "You're going to do yourself an injury like that, Iro. Here." Bjorn fished some smaller weights from underneath the bed, and set them up. "You gotta start off small. Build up those wire-thin arms of yours." He wasn't wrong. Iro found it a lot easier to lift them after that, but the effort still burned and left him feeling wobbly.

After his own personal training, came the morning run around the ship. They did this every day without fail. Iro wanted to die afterwards every day without fail. But death did not come because after the run everyday came training with Master Rollo, and that was worse than the run. Possibly worse than death too.

Master Rollo continued to be a brutal taskmaster of a trainer who seemed to enjoy pointing out that Iro was holding the entire squad back while he caught up on what he called *the basics*. As though it was somehow Iro's fault that he had never actually been trained how to swing a sword. Every day was a series of cuts, thrusts, blocks, and parries. And the entire squad ran through the same motions every day, endlessly, until they were all sweating and on the verge of collapse. If one of them got a movement wrong, or let their sword drop from tiredness, Master Rollo singled them out. He would have them stand there in front of the rest of the squad and practice the motion while the others got to rest for a minute. Iro often got it wrong.

He could see the other members of his new squad wanted to progress. Even Bjorn occasionally sighed at the delay to his own training. That hurt. He was thrust into a new situation aboard the Eclipse, and the only people he had a chance of making friends with resented him for his lack of skill. But Iro refused to quit.

On the eighth day of training, Master Rollo took pity on Iro. Either that or he just had enough of Iro failing to learn.

Iro stabbed his sword into thin air. It was the same thrust he'd practiced fifty times in the last five minutes. The same thrust the whole squad had been practicing for almost an hour now. Iro's arms were already trembling, but he just couldn't hold Neya's sword up any longer and his elbow dipped. The other trainees groaned, all except Torben who sighed gratefully and placed his sword point on the floor, leaning on the cross hilt. Torben's sword was huge, the blade easily five feet long and half a foot wide. Despite its size and weight, Torben wielded it with apparent ease. Even after hours of training, his thrusts never wavered.

"You still haven't figured it out yet, huh, new kid?" Master Rollo said. He slipped from his perch and stalked toward Iro, his hands in his pockets.

Iro sighed. He let the point of Neya's sword drop and hit the floor. After eight days he already knew better than to drop the sword completely. Part of him dreaded what was about to happen, Master Rollo rarely left his perch to berate anyone, and when he did it usually resulted in being kicked across the room. On the other hand, at least Iro was getting in a few seconds of rest. "Apparently not, master."

Master Rollo stopped right in front of him and stared down at Iro. "So slow. Look." He pulled a hand out of his pocket and pointed. Iro followed his finger to see Eir shifting from foot to foot and looking nervous. He'd come to know the other trainees a little better over the past week, and one thing he'd noticed about Eir was that she never stood completely still. She had a sort of restless energy that was strangely infectious to be around.

"Eir, thrust," Master Rollo said.

"Can do." Eir whipped her slender needle-like sword into position and thrust in a perfect example of the motion. She pulled back her arm after completing the thrust, and grinned wide.

"Don't get cocky," Master Rollo said. "Torben, hand Eir your sword."

Both trainees hesitated for a moment. Master Rollo dug his hand back into his pocket in a fashion that from him seemed to be a threat. Torben lurched into motion and held his sword out to Eir. She dragged it from his grasp, and handed over her much smaller blade.

"Good," Master Rollo said. "Now thrust."

Eir rubbed a hand over her bristly scalp and pouted. "Do I have to? I'm sure he gets it. You get it right, Iro? The swords not right for you. See, he understands."

Master Rollo stared at her under his lidded eyes. "Thrust."

Eir groaned and settled in position. She struggled to lift Torben's sword even with both hands on the hilt, and right away Iro could see the sword point wavering in the air. Eir thrust it out with both hands, overbalanced, lost her grip, sent Torben's sword clattering to the floor. She stamped her foot on the floor and glared at the sword. "Too scrapping big to use."

"I use it just fine," Torben said.

"Well, you're also too big."

"Quiet, both of you," Master Rollo said. "Retrieve your swords and practice your thrusts. Five hundred each for failing."

"What?" Eir said, her voice high. "I only failed because you made me. Uh, master."

"I didn't fail at all," Torben said.

Master Rollo glared at them, opening his eyes wide enough they boggled. Both trainees quickly fetched their swords and settled in to practice their basic thrusts. Master Rollo turned back to Iro.

"I get it," Iro said.

"Do you?" Master Rollo asked. He reached out and plucked Neya's sword from Iro's hands. It was a struggle for Iro to let go of the blade. It felt like a betrayal to let anyone else hold it. Master Rollo held it up before his face and twisted it about, staring at it.

"How old is this sword?" Master Rollo asked.

"I don't know." Iro rubbed at the back of his neck, feeling awkward that someone else was holding it. "It was my sister's."

Arne snickered. "His sister's sword and his mom's armor. He's probably wearing his grandma's knickers too."

"Arne," Master Rollo said quietly.

"Yes, master?"

"A thousand thrusts."

Arne groaned. Master Rollo silenced him with a half lidded stare and the other boy quickly dropped into position beside Eir and Torben.

Master Rollo stepped back, still holding Neya's sword. He thrust the blade out, dropped into a crouch, turned and brought the blade arcing upwards. It split the air with a *whoosh* and the apparatus at the far end of the hall rattled. Then Master Rollo leapt to the side, spinning the blade about his body. The air seemed to thrum around him, his body going fuzzy around the edges. Master Rollo stopped spinning the blade and drew up into a straight stance, Neya's sword held before him. He ran a hand along its length, tested the edge with a finger, then flipped the sword up into the air and caught it on its point on a single finger. He balanced it there with apparent ease for a few seconds, then flipped it again and caught it by the hilt.

"It's a good sword," Master Rollo said as he approached. "Well balanced, and titan-forged so it focuses current well." He tapped a finger against the blade, right where Iro had damaged it as a child. "The chip will weaken it over time there. That will need fixing. Not easy to do. Impossible unless we find a new manufactory. Better off replacing it. Besides," he handed the sword back to Iro who took it a little too eagerly, "it's all wrong for you, new kid. You're too short for a blade this long, and too weak for a blade this heavy."

Iro stared at Neya's sword in his hands. He knew Master Rollo was right. He felt it every time he held the blade. It was a struggle to perform every cut and thrust. He was constantly fighting against the weight, against overbalancing.

Master Rollo walked to the wall where the practice swords sat on racks. He stopped and stared at Torben for half a minute. The chubby boy was sweating and performing the same lunging strike over and over. "Your arm is dipping on the return," Master Rollo said eventually. "Another hundred thrusts." Then he continued to the weapon rack. He spent another minute examining them, then selected one and turned around.

Master Rollo tossed the training sword to Iro. He

barely caught it. "Try that one," Master Rollo said as he pulled Neya's sword away from Iro.

Iro lifted the training blade. It was blunted metal, but forged to be the same weight as a real sword. It was also a lot lighter than Neya's sword. This one had a single edge, and a slightly curved blade. It was long, but not so long it was unwieldy, and had a square cross guard, and a hilt long enough Iro could have fit three hands on it if he'd had an extra one. He dipped into the correct stance, holding the sword up and ready, then stepped into the thrust. It was so much easier than with Neya's sword. The blade felt like an extension of his own arms instead of a weight dragging him down.

Iro stepped back and held the sword up before him, marvelling at how different it felt. Master Rollo stepped in and shoved Iro's back leg out a bit, then cajoled him back into the thrust stance, and made Iro raise his elbow a little higher. Iro thrust again, stepped back, thrust again, stepped back, thrust again. It was all so easy.

"See," Master Rollo said. "The right sword is the difference between a swing and a slice, between a block and a parry, between death and life. Your sword is your life, Iro. It's easier to find one that suits you, than force yourself to suit one that's wrong for you." He turned and started walking back towards his usual perch on the apparatus. He took Neya's sword with him.

"Master?" Iro said before he could think better of it. Master Rollo stopped, glanced over his stooped shoulders at Iro, half lidded eyes curious. "Is it a choice? Is it my choice which sword I use?"

"Yes."

Iro looked down at the training sword in his hands, then back up at Master Rollo. He could hear the others whispering to each other. Could hear Eir, Arne, and Torben continuing their practice thrusts. "I want to keep using my sister's blade then."

Master Rollo walked back toward Iro, Neya's sword held tight in one hand. "You sure, new kid? You know what this means? You'll have to work harder. You might never be tall enough to use it properly, and you sure as scrap aren't strong enough yet. You'll not be going anywhere near a Hop until I'm satisfied you won't be a danger to others. You use a sword like that," he pointed at the training sword, "you'll be there soon enough. You use this one," he lifted Neya's sword again, "who knows when you'll be ready."

Iro met Master Rollo's half lidded gaze. "I understand, master." He held out the training sword.

Master Rollo considered Iro for a few moments longer, then shrugged. He retrieved the training sword, and handed back Neya's blade. Straight away, Iro felt the extra weight of it dragging on his arms and back, a strain across his shoulders. He would work harder, longer if that's what it took. He couldn't even properly explain why, but it was Neya's sword, and he would learn to wield it properly no matter how long it took.

Rollo pushed open the door to the Hopper's private lounge, walked the three paces required to reach the nearest couch, and collapsed into it face first. Scrap, but teaching was hard work. There was the constant paying attention to everything the kids did, watching them make the same mistakes over and over again. Not to mention daily assessments. He had no idea why Alfvin had chosen him to be a master. Well, that wasn't entirely true. He knew why. Because Rollo was one of the only rank four Corsairs left aboard the Eclipse, and because the kids found him young enough to be relatable, and scary enough to jump to his every command. And, of course, because Alfvin was bitter as stewed coffee and loved to torture Rollo. But scrap, did he hate teaching.

"How's it going, Rollo?" Frigg asked. She was sitting on the couch across from him, a steaming cup of coffee in one hand. Only it wasn't coffee because the fleet had run out of it years ago. It was algae treated to smell like coffee. Everything was algae. He hated algae.

Rollo extricated a hand from his pocket, extended a thumb either up or down — it was hard to tell which while he was face first on the couch — then let his hand fall to the floor.

"That good?" Frigg said with a smile. He could tell she was smiling without looking. It was in her voice. When you knew someone as well as he knew Frigg, you could hear a smile in their voice.

"I hate this scrap," Rollo said into the couch. He was fairly certain it muffled his words beyond comprehension, but Frigg laughed all the same.

The door to the Hopper lounge opened again and Alfvin walked in. Rollo could tell it was Alfvin by the way he walked, every footstep rang with purpose and conviction. A born leader. Rollo grumbled something obscene into the couch.

"Frigg, Rollo," Alfvin said as he walked through the lounge. He pressed the button on the not-coffee making machine and waited while it spurted hot algae into a cup. There were no other Hoppers around. The lounge was for all of them, and there were well over two dozen aboard the Eclipse, more than enough to make the lounge uncomfortably cramped. Luckily, most of the Hoppers preferred the mess hall where they could mingle with the rest of the crew. Rollo preferred the lounge because it had couches to sleep on. Frigg preferred the lounge for the peace and quiet. Alfvin just like to disturb them both. But he was the lead Hopper aboard the Eclipse, so that was his privilege. Still, he didn't have to enjoy it quite so much.

"How are the kids?" Alfvin asked once his not-coffee was steaming in his hands.

Rollo rolled over on the couch until he was staring up at the metal roof, the oppressively white and bright neon light glaring down at him. "They're idiots," he said around a yawn.

Frigg chuckled. "How are the officers?"

"They're idiots."

"What about us?"

"You're scrapping idiots," Rollo said.

Alfvin sighed. "Is there anyone you don't think is an idiot?"

Rollo considered the question. "Me."

"That must be a terrible burden for you," Frigg said. Rollo checked, but of course she was grinning.

Alfvin paced. He never sat down, never stopped moving. Rollo hated that about him. "I mean it, Rollo. How's the boy from the Courage? What was his name?"

"Iro," Rollo said. It was just like Alfvin not to have bothered learning the kid's name. People weren't worth remembering until they were useful as far as Alfvin was concerned.

Alfvin grunted. "How's he progressing?"

"Slowly."

Alfvin didn't seem to like the answer. He grumbled into his not-coffee cup. "Do I need to remind you how important he is, Rollo?"

"Nope."

"That boy might be the key to unlocking new Hoppers in the fleet," Alfvin said, ignoring Rollo. "If he can open the first Gate of Power, it's proof that Hopper classes aren't limited to the ships they're born on and who their parents are."

"You told me all this," Rollo said. It was, in fact, the fourth time he had the speech from Alfvin.

"Spontaneous manifestation of a talent is unheard of," Alfvin said.

"It isn't," Frigg countered. "Records are spotty, but it's how we discovered talents in the first place, Alfvin. It wasn't until the fleet encountered the old titan, that people started manifesting talents. It's not unheard of, just forgotten."

"Lost," Alfvin said. "Until now." Definitely a natural leader. Bold, confident, full of purpose, and scrapping bursting with exhausting zeal.

It was all too much effort. Rollo rolled over to face the back of the couch.

"You have to push the kid, Rollo," Alfvin said. No doubt he had already forgotten the kid in question had a name.

"I am," Rollo said into the couch.

"Hard."

"I am."

"Push him harder, Rollo," Alfvin said. "Take him on a Hop."

Rollo spun about and sat up, staring Alfvin down. "No. He's not ready. Some of the others maybe, but Iro isn't ready for a Hop."

Alfvin waved the complaint away. "We're scheduled to make second landing in the garden in three days. We've already secured a breach zone, it's safe to land. Water supplies are running low on many of the ships. Did you know some people are only washing once every two days?" It was worse than that, but of course Alfvin didn't really care. "Take the boy. Take the squad. A Hop will do them good."

"He's not ready," Rollo repeated as clearly as he could.

Alfvin shook his head. "Then make him ready, Rollo." He stood. "Three days. Take the entire squad and make them ready. The Courage boy needs to open the first gate."

Alfin paused as he reached the door to the lounge. "Break him if you have to." He pulled open the door and stepped out into the hallway beyond.

Chapter Eleven

Iro slipped the belt over his head and tightened the strap against his chest, securing his sword to his back. Then he tiptoed toward the door. It was late, but he couldn't sleep. He pulled the door to his dormitory open as quietly as he could so as not to disturb the others, and then made for the training hall.

Iro stepped into the empty room and frowned. It seemed so different like this, empty and lifeless. He was used to it being filled with people, his squad, and noise, and pain. He rolled his shoulders and winced at the knot bunching up in his neck. He definitely felt stronger than he had been when he first arrived, but that didn't mean he felt strong. He still tired easily, long before any of the others, and while Torben or Arne or Ylfa could cut and thrust with speed like an electrical spark, Iro felt slow and clumsy by comparison.

He drew Neya's sword from over his back and held it in both hands. Already he could feel the weight of it was uncomfortable. He glanced at the banks of training swords. It would be so much easier to do as Master Rollo suggested. But no. He would use Neya's sword or die trying. And that was the truth of it. It was why he was having such trouble sleeping. Why he was here despite the exhaustion of a full day's training behind him, and the prospect of another in front. He was scared.

Master Rollo had told them all they were going on a Hop in just two day's time. Iro didn't feel ready. He felt weak and ill prepared and terrified. Last time had been different. It had all been a big accident. He'd been scared, but excited. And besides, there were other Hoppers everywhere. Even so, when the rustlings attacked, when the kharapid reared up before him… Iro shivered and tried to put it from his mind. He was going on another Hop. Iro still didn't feel prepared.

He moved through the slow warm up forms he'd been taught, trying to unwind his muscles and get the blood pumping. A slow horizontal slice to the left, circle the sword up and down in a vertical chop, step forwards bringing the sword back and level with his chest, thrust forward. So slow it was achingly painful and the sword danced in his hands as his arms and legs protested the strain.

Iro pulled up into a straight stance, sword held vertical and close to his chest. He imagined the strike he wanted to make, a sweeping upwards arc. He even imagined an enemy too. His blade would connect with the kharapid's lower torso, cleaving it in two. He activated his crest and it blossomed to electric blue light before him. Bigger than before, the sharp lines extending out from the inner circle were growing, reaching for… something. It was still so unclear. He let his current flow down his arms and into the blade. Then he struck. The world lurched. For a brief moment he felt himself being dragged by the force, the world became a dizzying blur around him, his arms and legs seemed to move without command. Then he was standing before the imaginary kharapid, his sword slicing upwards in a shimmering arc.

He overbalanced, stumbled forward. Neya's sword clanged against the wall of the training hall. Iro stepped back, breathing heavily, sweat beading on his forehead. His crest dimmed and flickered out of existence. He could still only use the Blink Strike once before he exhausted his meagre current, but at least he could control it now.

"That poor wall."

Iro spun about, fumbling Neya's sword and almost dropping it. Eir stood at the entrance to the training hall, leaning against the doorframe, grinning.

"You were watching?" Iro asked.

Eir nodded. "I was. And I'm on the wall's side. It was a totally unprovoked attack." She pushed away from the doorframe and sauntered closer. She had such an easy way of walking, almost skipping with each step, like she was bursting with energy. She bent down to look at the wall where Iro had hit it. "Oh dear. You dented the bulkhead."

"I did?" Iro leaned closer to look. She was right. There was a tiny dent in the wall where his sword had struck. "Scrap! Rollo is going to kill me, isn't he?"

Eir straightened up, rolled her eyes, bobbed her head a bit as if thinking hard, then nodded. "Yep. You're dead alright." She shrugged and patted him once on the shoulder. "It was nice knowing you." She sauntered away into the centre of the hall.

Iro stared after her, then back to the wall, panic rising in his chest. "What do I do?"

"Get your affairs in order," Eir said as she stopped in the centre of the training hall and lunged into a stretch. "Notify your loved ones. Make sure you're wearing clean underwear."

"What?"

Eir glanced over her shoulder and winked at him, her blue eyes sparkling. "Relax, Iro. I'm joking. No one will notice. Least of all Rollo. I swear, I think he sleeps through half our classes. Just wakes up occasionally to tell us we're doing it wrong. Even if we're not."

Iro clutched at his chest. His heart was racing. He swung Neya's sword up to rest against his shoulder and moved to join Eir in the centre of the hall. "That wasn't funny."

"I disagree," Eir said. She sank down into another stretch, one leg out to the side and the other bent beneath her. She was so low to the ground. Iro wasn't flexible enough to get anywhere near that low.

"Stop staring," Eir said, narrowing her eyes at him. "Either join in or turn around. You're making me self conscious." She ran a hand over her freshly shaved scalp.

Iro sank into the same stretch, though he made a poor imitation of it.

"Could you not sleep either?" he asked as Eir stood and started stretching out her arms and shoulders. He copied her.

"I never sleep much," she said. "So I come here." Like Iro, she hadn't bothered with her armor, but was wearing her training uniform. A light pair of grey trousers and a white, sleeveless shirt. Her slender sword was strapped to her belt. "I don't usually find anyone waiting for me."

"Oh, I wasn't waiting for you. I didn't know."

Eir rolled her eyes at him and shook her head. She lifted a single foot off the floor and extended her leg out to the side, holding the pose, watching Iro out of the corner of her eye. Iro stared at her for a few seconds, then lifted his leg and tried to extend it. He barely managed to get his foot above knee height and had to wave his hands about in the air to stop from pitching over, but he stayed upright and considered it a victory.

"So why are you here, Iro?" Eir asked as she lowered her leg. Iro gratefully copied her and sighed from the relief in his muscles. He was about to rub the ache out of his thigh, but Eir raised her other leg into the mirror pose. He groaned and tried his best to copy her again.

"I couldn't sleep."

"You said that already. Why not?"

Iro felt his leg wobbling, locked his knee, almost over balanced and had to fling both his arms out wide to steady himself. "I'm scared," he admitted. *Why is she so easy to talk to?* There was something open and friendly about Eir. "I think Master Rollo is wrong. I don't think I'm ready."

"Well, of course you're not," Eir said.

"Huh?"

She smiled at him and cocked her head to the side a little. "If you don't think you're ready, then you're not ready."

"But Master Rollo…"

"Isn't you." Eir pulled her leg back in and Iro copied her, already dreading what insane stretch she'd lead him through next. "How would he know better than you if you're ready?"

Iro thought about it for a moment, but the logic didn't quite make sense to him. "But he's our trainer, and an experienced Hopper. Surely he knows when we're ready to Hop?"

"Does he?" Eir asked. "Like he knew you were ready to try the cut-thrust earlier?"

The reminder of the day's training was like a gut punch. They were still working through what Master Rollo called *the basics,* but at least they weren't just repeating the same single movements over and over again. Today they started on a few easy combos, learning to move fluidly from one attack to another. A cut followed by a quick thrust. Of course everyone else had managed it easily, but Iro kept faltering. His arm would lock in the wrong position, or his shoulder would dip, or his muscles would tremble and the sword point would waver, or any number of other failures that all led to Master Rollo berating him for getting it wrong.

"Exactly," Iro said. "He was wrong. I failed at the cut-thrust every time."

Eir shrugged. "Not every time."

"Most of them."

"You got one right towards the end."

"It took all day though."

Another shrug, this time followed by a grin. "Well, you're definitely not ready for this." She turned away from Iro and pitched forward, springing onto her hands and raising her legs into the air until she was balancing there in the middle of the training room in a free standing handstand. "Feel free to quit," she said, her voice tightening only a little around the strain of holding the handstand. "I won't hold it against you. Though I will ask you to leave the training hall." Her face was flushing red, but her eyes sparkled.

Iro laughed as he stared at her. He understood. "You're telling me I might not be ready to do it, but I have to try a thing to get better at it. That I might fail a few times, but I have to keep trying to get better so I don't fail every time. And that's what the training is about, that Master Rollo is the safety net if I fall."

Eir snorted, her face growing a little redder. "I'm telling you to try the scrapping handstand or get out of the training room and leave me in peace."

Iro took a deep breath, placed Neya's sword on the floor, then rolled forward onto his hands. He overbalanced in an instant and sprawled on the floor. Eir was watching him, sweat beading on her forehead. She stuck out her tongue and started moving her legs as though she were walking upside down. Iro laughed, picked himself up, and tried again.

An officer sauntered into the training hall and cleared her throat to get Master Tannow's attention. He called a brief halt to the training session and went to confer.

They were training their talents, and though it was a good thing to strengthen, Emil ached to move. His arm still hurt where the monsters had slashed him, but it only slowed him down, not stopped him. He wanted to throw himself back into the physical combat, to hit something. But Cali was still limping from the thigh wound, so they were practicing their talents instead. Besides, as Master Tannow liked to point out, they were Paladins and therefore far more useful strengthening others than joining the fight themselves.

Emil knew the old master was right, but it annoyed the scrap out of him anyway. He wished he had been born on a different ship, born a different class. He wished he had been born a Vanguard or a Berserker, someone who could get into the thick of things. He wanted to fight, not stand at the back and enhance others while they protected him. He shouldn't need protecting. He clenched his fist and punched the air. The action felt good but he needed something to hit or it just wasn't satisfying enough.

Mia let out a dramatic sigh and sat down, then rolled onto her back to stare up at the roof. "Oh, I can't wait to shower again."

Cali nudged her sister with her foot. "Get up before Master Tannow sees you, or he might take away the privilege."

The fleet was making regular trips to the gardens now, collecting water mostly. The algae would keep them all fed for a while yet, but water was important and every ship was running out. It also took a lot of trips to collect enough to fill a ship's tanks. The pods could only carry so much. Luckily, they had collected enough already that both Hoppers and trainees were rationed enough to shower every day again. It was a luxury for them. It would have been a luxury for Emil too if his father hadn't demanded his shower rations. After all, he worked sanitation so he spent all day in other people's waste, it was only fair he get to shower more regularly. Emil didn't bother arguing. He didn't need to feel clean to train anyway.

Master Tannow finished talking to the officer and turned back to his trainees. "I have to go sit in on a meeting with Grand Ahmad."

Emil looked up at that. Grand Ahmad was a Vanguard and the leader of the Hoppers throughout the whole fleet and had as much say in governing the fleet as the admiral. He was also one of only four Hoppers who had opened the fifth and final Gate of Power. He was the pinnacle of strength and what could be achieved as a Hopper. Rumour had it, after the landing at the thruster control, so many Hoppers beaten back and injured by a single powerful monster, Grand Ahmad had gone alone to face the creature. Where two dozen Hoppers of the fourth gate level had failed, the Grand defeated the monster with a single strike. That was real power. Someone who needed no help or protection from anyone.

"Keep practicing your Steel training," Master Tannow said. "Not one of you can hold it for five seconds yet. That's not good enough." He sighed and rubbed a scarred hand over his face. "I'll see you tomorrow morning." And with that, he followed the officer out of the training hall.

Mia waited all of ten seconds before she flipped from her back to her feet and let out a whoop. "Early finish for the day!" She ran over to the wall and scooped up her great hammer, grunting as she hefted it onto her shoulder. "I'm going for a shower."

"That's not what Master Tannow ordered us to do," Cali said as both girls started towards the door.

"Feel free to stay behind and spend some quality time with Emil." Mia waved at Emil, then stepped out of the door and was gone. Cali followed, not even bothering to wave.

Emil relished the peace and quiet. He didn't mind the sisters really, but they were so noisy, always seeming to prefer to talk than train. Well, they were gone now and with them any chance of following Master Tannow's instructions. Emil had no one there to enhance, so he no longer had any choice but to work on his combat.

He approached training dummy one and pressed the button on the floor to start it moving. A whirring noise issued from the thing, followed by a clunk, a hiss, and an acrid smell like burning hair. Another one dead. And the tech core hadn't assigned them a new talentless repairman yet since Iro was gone. Emil growled, thumped the dead dummy, and stalked over to five.

Training dummy five had a laughing face painted on it in pink and purple. That was Mia's terrible attempt at artwork. A more recent addition was a little name written in purple on the chest. It read *Emil*. He wasn't sure whether he should be complimented or insulted. He didn't care.

Emil stamped on the button to get the thing moving and it whirred to life, spinning its arms in frantic, random patterns. The head rocked back and forth a little with the motion, but the leering face didn't change. Emil grinned back at the dummy and took a step back, settling into a ready crouch with his hands up before him. He watched the smiling dummy for a few seconds more, then sprang towards it.

It swung its left arm at his face and Emil ducked beneath the attack, blocked a follow up from the right arm, launched a one-two combo at the dummy's face. Both hits were solid and the dummy rocked back then forward, renewing its assault. Emil weathered another brief battering, dodging back, spinning around and inside the dummy's guard, thumping it with a thunderous uppercut that would have sent most opponents sprawling on the ground. The dummy simply accepted the beating in stoic silence, then swung at him again. Emil backed away a couple of steps. It was too weak, too slow. He needed to up the difficulty.

He pressed the button on the floor to speed the dummy up once, twice, then three more times until it was at its strongest setting. The arms moved so fast they were a blur, the noise of the grinding servos filling the training hall. It was perfect.

Emil rushed in and the dummy locked onto him as a target, spinning to face him and swinging for him with both arms. He blocked the left swing on his forearm, the pain of the strike sharp as a knife. He brought his knee up to block the other strike. Too slow. The dummy's right arm thumped into his side hard enough he cried out. The left arm struck his leg with such force it crumpled beneath him and Emil collapsed.

He crawled away from the dummy and struggled back to his feet, limping in a tight circle a few times until he could feel his leg again. All the while the dummy continued spinning its arms, waiting for him, grinning. Wearing his name. Mocking him.

"Just try that again, you piece of scrap!"

The dummy smiled at him.

Emil stepped forwards more slowly this time, watching the spinning arms, trying to find their pattern of attack. He got within range and the dummy lunged for him. He ducked underneath a wild cross swing, blocked a follow up, lurched forward to strike at the dummy's head. A flailing arm smacked into his chest so hard it drove the air from his lungs and left him gasping. Another arm cracked him across the face and Emil found himself launched away, spinning through the air before hitting the ground hard, still gasping.

The dummy spun and grinned.

It took a few moments before he could breathe again, then Emil was back on his feet. He tasted blood in his mouth, wiped a smear from his lips. Then he darted in again.

Chapter Twelve

Iro had his own pod aboard the Eclipse. He wasn't accidentally squeezed in with Mia or Emil. He wasn't just thrown into any old working pod. He had his own specific pod just for him. Number 3 in Bay 12. The Eclipse had so many Hopper pods. So many working ones. A far cry from the Courage where they were constantly cannibalising one to fix another. He guessed he was probably imagining it, but the trip over to the titan seemed smoother too.

Master Rollo flew them all to one of the garden domes on their wing. The fleet had designated this particular dome as Babylon. Iro had no idea what the word meant, and neither had any of the other trainees. Torben, who always seemed to have his head buried in a book, suggested it was an old word, by which he meant one from before the time humanity had boarded the fleets and found the titans. Iro struggled to comprehend such a thing. If there hadn't been fleets in that before time, then what was there?

The pod sailed quickly over to the titan, first stars, then the metal skin of the titan filling the window. The landing shook Iro up a bit, but at least it wasn't the spinning crash landing of his last trip. The pod aligned perfectly and Master Rollo's voice came over the short range squad comms, telling them all to disembark. Iro opened the pod door and stepped out into the freshest air he had ever tasted.

Trees stretched up before him, each one a massive pillar exploding from the ground up towards the domed roof and the stars beyond. A riot of emerald leafs hung from every branch, and here and there fat drops of crystal clear water fell tens of feet to detonate on the spongy ground below. Iro stood transfixed by the sight. He'd heard of trees. Neya had explained them to him in detail. But he'd never seen one before.

So many of them. And so big. Are they really all alive?

The noise was beyond anything he could have imagined. He was used to the electric hum of ships systems, the ever-present ringing of feet marching down hallways, of doors whooshing or squealing open. On the Courage, he had been comforted by the constant rattle the ship made as it flew through the dark void. Some people found it terrifying to hear the ship struggling not to come apart, but Iro had always found it bolstering to hear the ship laboring so determinedly to stay together. When it stopped rattling was when he worried. But the garden dome of Babylon was an orchestra of sounds he couldn't name. Whistles and howls and hoots and screams and clicks and the occasional roar.

"Trainees, fall in," Master Rollo said. Iro continued staring at the trees, watching the leafs rustle and shudder. It almost looked like there were creatures moving about inside the safety of the overlapping branches. A part of Iro wanted to climb back in his pod and fly back to the Eclipse where everything made sense. Another part wanted to run wildly into the dense forest and explore.

"I said fall in," Master Rollo repeated.

Iro ripped his gaze from the trees to find he wasn't the only one standing around staring. Bjorn was in line in front of the master, but his eyes were wide and his mouth hung open. Torben's sister, Ingrid had one foot still in her pod and looked scared enough she was considering getting back in and closing the door. Arne was staring up past the hanging leafs to the glimpses of the dome above, one hand on his head, absently gripping his slick hair between his fingers. Of all the trainees, only Ashvild didn't seem fazed. But then, Ashvild was so coldly clinical Iro doubted anything jolted her. She pushed a gawking Eir into line, then dragged Ylfa over as well. Iro stumbled forward to join them. Within a few moments, all the trainees stood in a line in front of Master Rollo.

"This is Babylon," Master Rollo said slowly. He was wearing a light suit of titan-forged armor, painted the same Eclipse dark blue as his trainees. There was a symbol painted on the right breast, a pale eye with a red iris. Master Rollo had somehow still managed to find his pockets underneath the metal plates and had buried his hands in them. Despite being a Corsair, he didn't seem to carry any sword with him, even on a Hop.

"What are they?" Bjorn asked, his voice slow and dreamlike.

"Trees," Master Rollo said. "You'll get used to them."

"They're so big." Eir ran a hand over her scalp and shuffled from foot to foot. Her armor was even lighter than Master Rollo's, with many of the plates just stitched or clipped into the underweave.

"Eh?" Master Rollo shrugged. "These ones are babies. They get bigger further in. Hopefully we won't get that far."

"How big is Babylon?" Iro asked. He seen it from the pod window on the way over, but it was so hard to judge scale when titans were concerned.

Master Rollo glanced over his shoulder toward the trees. "We haven't mapped it all yet. Too much space. The Surveyors have been working at it for almost ten days though. Rough guess, you could fit the entire fleet inside the dome two or three times over." He looked up at the dome high above. "Conservative guess, really."

"But what are they?" Bjorn asked again.

"Read a book, Bjorn," Torben said with a laugh. The big, chubby boy was always ready with a smile. "They're trees. Plants. Think of them as big, solid algae."

"Huh? You can eat them?"

"Bits of them."

Master Rollo sighed, looked around the ground for something, then shrugged and sank down to sit cross legged on the soil. "Babylon is almost entirely forested apart from a couple of decent sized lakes. Its perfect for us for now. We're going to the first lake which is about an hour's walk in. Mission resource is water. We've tried to lay pipes to collect it, but there are still monsters lurking about in the trees and they tend to tear up the pipes. Besides, the longer we stay here, the bigger and nastier the monsters that come calling. For now, that means it's easier to cart the water back by hand."

It was an oddity no one in the fleet had ever been able to explain. Monsters were drawn to humans. Almost as if they sensed the presence of people. They would leave the lower levels and swarm towards Hoppers if they stayed too long. It was why no one had ever tried to live on a titan. Any settlement would come under constant assault and the longer it stayed, the stronger the monsters that would find them.

"Why is the ground so scrapping soft?" Ylfa asked. Iro had noticed she punctuated almost everything she said with at least one curse. Her armor was the same Eclipse blue, but it was bulky. It was so encompassing it looked more like Vanguard armor than Corsair, but she wore it easily enough and it didn't seem to restrict her movement much. She knelt down and grabbed a handful of soil, rubbing it in her gauntlet until it fell between her fingers. "Ahh!" She dropped a small, wriggling creature to the ground. It was pale and as long as a finger. It struggled a few moments, then started burrowing back into the ground. "A little monster."

All eyes turned to Master Rollo. He groaned and

leaned back until he was lying flat on the ground, staring up at the branches and leafs above.

"It's soil," Torben said, ambling over. He looked uncomfortably in his own bulky suit of armor and was constantly tugging at the plates to rearrange them around his belly. "It's what allows the trees and other plants to grow. A substrate."

"What about the scrapping monster?" Ylfa asked, her voice shrill.

Torben scratched at his chin for a moment, then nodded. "A young form of a tarun. When they reach adulthood they can be dozens of feet long and can burrow through metal as well as soil. Have mouths full of rasping teeth and spit sticky webbing from glands at the side of their heads. Uh, well, they don't have heads really, just mouths. And no eyes."

Arne plucked the little creature from the soil and held it up to his face. "How do they see?"

Torben glanced at Master Rollo, but the lethargic Hopper didn't appear to be taking any notice. "They see with sound? I think." Torben said.

Master Rollo chuckled but said nothing.

The little creature wriggled and writhed, curling around one of Arne's fingers. He grinned and waved the finger at Ylfa. Her pretty face twisted into a snarl and she backed away from him, spitting insults.

"Why are we just waiting here, master?" Iro asked.

Master Rollo pulled a hand from his pocket and waved vaguely towards the pods. "For company."

Eir shuffled out of line and approached the nearest of the trees, cautiously extending a hand out towards it. Iro watched her, felt a smile stretching his cheeks, a not-unpleasant ache in his stomach. Eir brushed a finger against the tree's brown flesh then quickly pulled it back. "It's not dangerous is it, master?"

Master Rollo yawned dramatically. "Nope. Feel free to hug it."

Eir grinned, eyes sparkling, and turned back to the tree. She pressed her palm against it. "It's rough. I thought it would be smooth." She stepped forward, laid a cheek against the tree.

A heavy arm landed on Iro's shoulders, staggering him. He smelled Bjorn's sweaty presence. After weeks of living with the other boy, he had become intimately acquainted with the smell.

"Wha…" Before Iro could finish a single word, Bjorn gave him a meaty push, sending him stumbling towards the trees and towards Eir. He staggered to a stop, turned and glared at Bjorn. The bigger boy just laughed.

"I think there's something up in the branches," Eir said. She was staring straight up. Iro stepped closer and joined her. Despite the light streaming into the dome from the transparent roof, the canopy of branches were dark enough he had to squint to make anything out. He saw dark shapes that could have been more branches. Eir pointed and he followed her finger, saw two spots of light like eyes glaring out of the darkness. Then they were gone.

"A monster?" Iro asked.

"Not everything in the domes are monsters," Master Rollo said, still lying on the ground, his eyes closed. "Be glad of that. Once we start hunting some of the little critters we'll have more than just algae to eat."

Ingrid moaned. "We haven't had real food in so long."

"Never seems to stop you," Torben said. "You eat your weight in algae every day."

Ingrid thumped her brother on the arm. "You're one to talk." They were both as chubby as each other, though wore it well. It made them seem imposing and powerful, especially in armor.

Eir poked Iro with a finger. He found her staring at him, smiling. "How's the handstand coming along?"

Iro ran a hand down the rough skin of the tree. "Good. I've just about mastered the art of falling on my ass instead of my head."

The roar of thrusters cut off Eir's reply and all eyes turned to see three new Hopper pods alighting on the landing zone just outside the reach of the trees. Compared to the Eclipse pods, these new ones were old and battered and rusty in places. Iro recognised them all too well and felt his heart race in chest.

The first of the pod doors opened and Master Tannow pushed free of the close confines and into the light. He blinked a few times, squinting, then spotted Iro and grinned. The second pod opened up and Emil stepped out. Despite the injury he had taken during the last Hop, he moved easily, walking onto the soil and staring up at the trees with a open mouth. The third pod door didn't open and Iro heard pounding from within. Master Tannow stalked over to the pod and pushed the emergency release. Still nothing happened. The pounding grew more frantic.

"Urgh, Iro, can you get Mia's door open?" the old Paladin master said.

Iro leapt into motion and ran for the pod, sliding to a stop and pulling open the panel that accessed the door hydraulics. It was always more Roret's skillset to tinker with the pods, but he'd picked up enough to know what he was doing.

"What are you doing here?" Iro asked as he tightened a loose bolt with his fingers, then pumped a large button a few times to charge the hydraulics.

Master Rollo rolled onto his feet and thrust his hands

into his pockets. "Master Tannow doesn't have enough trainees for a full squad so he's tagging along."

Bjorn approached Emil and held out a hand. "That means you're from the Courage. Nice to meet you. I'm Eclipse Bjorn."

Emil glanced down at the offered hand, then went back to staring at the trees.

"Talkative, aren't you?"

Iro finished pumping the hydraulics, then replaced the panel and pressed the emergency release again. The door popped open far faster than he expected and Mia tumbled out, gasping and wild eyed. They collided and both hit the ground, Mia thumping him twice in the side as she scrambled in panic. Luckily his mother's hand-me-down armor caught both the blows.

Mia scrambled back to her feet, turned, kicked the pod. "I hate this thing! Why do I always get the scrapping broken pod?"

"Probably because you always tell Roret he has a big nose," Iro said as he got to his hands and knees and then stood.

"Who?" Mia turned on him. "Wait. Useless? Is that you? Why are you wearing your mom's armor?" She pushed him aside, her greater strength almost throwing him back to the ground, and walked towards the trees, gawking. "What the scrap?"

"She's charming," Eir said. Iro startled to find the girl standing next to him, staring at Mia. "Friend of yours?"

Iro only groaned in reply.

"Trainees, line up," Master Rollo said. He didn't shout, Iro had not yet heard him shout, but every member of his group quickly jumped to the command. Emil and Mia were slower to react and Master Tannow had to grab them both and push them into line. Master Rollo watched, then sighed. "We have company. They might act like untrained idiots, but I'm promised they're not. Right, Courage Tannow?"

"That's it?" Master Tannow asked. "That's your introduction?"

Master Rollo shrugged.

They spent a minute swapping names, then Master Tannow explained the mission. There was a small lake about an hour's walk into the forest. They were to head there, gather a few barrels of water, then return to the pods. All in all, a quick, low risk Hop. A far cry from the landing in the thruster control.

As Master Tannow finished explaining the mission, Master Rollo spoke up. "We don't expect to encounter any monsters. At least, not any truly dangerous ones. If you see anything, tell me or Courage Tannow. Do not engage unless I give you explicit orders. You're here to learn, not to die."

"We might scrapping die here?" Ylfa asked, her voice trembling a little.

Master Rollo shrugged again. "Probably not you. Arne and the new kid might though."

Iro felt the fear settle in his stomach again, like a ball of scrap weighing him down. He glanced across. Rather than finding a mocking sneer, Arne met Iro's gaze with a tremulous smile. Without another word, the two masters stepped past the tree-line, and all their trainees hurried to follow them.

Chapter Thirteen

Iro stared around in wonder. Everything was so strange. The ground was soft, almost springy underfoot, riddled with hard wires of wood that criss-crossed through the dirt like a badly fixed rotator servo. He could only guess they were part of the trees that surrounded them on all sides, crowding out the light from above. Unseen creatures called out constantly, hooted or whistled, rustled some nearby bush of green leafs then vanished before anyone got a good look at them. Neither of the masters seemed concerned about the creatures so Iro assumed they weren't monsters. But he didn't think anything that wasn't a monster lived on the titans. Was he wrong about that? Or did it mean that animals were monsters, or that monsters were just animals? He couldn't figure it out.

They walked in small, strung-out groups. Master Tannow and Rollo were up ahead. Master Tannow seemed to be doing all the talking. Mia and Emil were just behind, and neither of them seemed to be talking at all. Both wore armor painted bone white. The color of the Courage. He supposed he'd have to get his armor painted Eclipse blue at some point. Though the idea sat oddly with him for some reason. Emil kept his eyes fixed forward, while Mia gazed all around her, grinning at everything.

After them walked Eir, Ashvild, and Arne. Their conversation seemed lively enough and every time Iro saw Eir laugh he had the mad urge to run forward and inject himself into the conversation.

His group was the largest and consisted of himself, Bjorn, Torben, Ingrid, and Ylfa. Well, Torben lagged behind a bit, kicking his feet through the dirt.

"What the scrap is up with your friends?" Ylfa asked. She had her sword drawn and was waving it about dramatically as if fighting imaginary monsters. He'd seen her practice with it and the way she could spin it around her body was dizzying.

Iro rubbed at an itch at the back of his neck. "Bjorn's a bit dim, and Torben is actually asleep."

"Hey!" Bjorn said, punching Iro on the arm. Iro stumbled into a tree, laughing. His arm was already hurting. Bjorn didn't know his own strength.

"It's not sleep," Torben said sleepily. "I'm just…"

"Conserving energy?" Iro asked.

Torben stared at him a moment, then yawned. "I was going to say I'm lulling my enemies into a false sense of security. Only a fool grabs a sword by the sharp end."

"Huh?" Bjorn asked.

"He's mixing his analogies again," Ingrid said, shaking her head at her brother. "It actually means you shouldn't take a weapon you don't know how to use."

Torben kicked at a wooden wire running through the ground, stumbled a step. "It can also mean you shouldn't attack a foe you don't know anything about."

Ingrid rolled her eyes at her brother. "No. It can't." She turned back to the rest of them. "He's always been like this. Likes to pretend he's smart because he reads books, but he only understands every other word."

"No one ever learned to walk by sitting still," Torben said as if that somehow ended the conversation in his favour.

"Right," Ylfa said with a shake of her head, sending curls bouncing. She fixed Iro with a dark stare. "What I meant was, what's up with your scrapping friends from your old junker of a ship?"

"I wouldn't call them friends. The only time Emil ever noticed me was when something needed fixing. He's the one with the scowl and the over-sized gauntlets. And I think I was more like target practice for Mia. I'm pretty sure she hates me. She's the one with the hammer."

"You really were a tech until first landing?" Ingrid asked. She loomed over Iro, taller and broader than him. He felt like a child walking next to her. "No talents?"

Iro moved around a tree that was in the centre of the path. "Yeah. My mother and sister were both Paladins, but I could never get even the simplest of talents to work. So I was put to work in the tech core. I was really starting to think that was going to be my life."

"I've heard it's hard work," Bjorn said. "Especially over the last five years. My uncle is a tech. He lived with us. I used to come home from Hopper training all sweaty and tired, but he'd come back covered in grease and muck, and stinking like a low shipper."

"Low shipper?" Iro asked.

Bjorn shut his mouth, his eyes went wide and he stared straight ahead. Iro glanced at Ingrid and Ylfa to find them looking elsewhere too. He suddenly had the sinking feeling he didn't belong. A gnawing worry eating at his stomach like he'd just stepped into a nest of monsters and was waiting for one of them to wake up and pounce. He desperately needed to move on before the silence became too awkward.

"It is tough, being a tech. Dangerous too. Not like being a Hopper is dangerous, but definitely not without risks. I've seen people get electrocuted before. Chief Wasome lost a hand to a ventilation fan that started up too quickly. And then there's the systems we don't understand."

"Huh?" Torben grunted, sounding suddenly interested.

Iro scratched at the itch on the back of his neck again. "We don't really understand how the ships work. At least half of the systems are a complete mystery to us. We can repair a lot of things that break; corroded wires and blown resistors, but there's so much that is completely beyond us. Some of those systems have defences and don't like being tampered with."

A little furry creature the size of a child dashed out in front of them, stopping on the leafy path. It walked on four legs, had a bulbous body, an elongated face, and dark beady eyes. It reared up onto its back legs, sniffed at them all, then dropped back onto all fours and raced off into the depths of the forest. All of the trainees glanced at each other, but the other groups hadn't even noticed.

"What was that thing?" Bjorn asked.

Ingrid leaned forward to peer into the brush where it had ran to. "And more importantly, if we catch it can we eat it?"

Torben strode forward. "Can't taste worse than algae."

They shared a laugh at that and all continued on, speeding up to catch up with the others. Iro kept a wary eye on the surrounding forest though. He couldn't shake the feeling that if there were small critters about, there might also be large monsters roaming the forest.

Emil noticed Mia walking close to him again and edged away for the eighth time. Considering how hard she hit, even in the training hall, he was surprised how stealthy she could be. Every time he looked away for a moment, he turned back to find her so close they were almost brushing shoulders. He didn't like it. If anything attacked them, he'd need space to move. And Mia's great hammer was next to useless in close confines or surrounded by allies. The fact that she kept closing on him could only mean she didn't understand that.

Another noise from above, a hooting followed by a rustle, a fat green leaf twirled slowly down towards them. Emil flexed his hands inside his gauntlets and squinted at the branches above. If there was anything up there, he didn't see it. When he lowered his gaze, he found Mia close again, walking alongside him. Her hammer was still strapped to her back, her muscular arms crossed against her chest, and she walked with a slight skip to each step. Far too careless. Didn't she remember the last time they had been on the titan? How could she have forgotten so quickly?

"You should have your hammer ready," Emil said quietly.

"Really?" Mia grinned and looked around eagerly. "Have you seen something? A monster?"

"Not yet."

She pouted. "Oh. Well, let me know when you do." She inched closer again, nudging Emil with her pauldron. "Hey, I don't think they like us much."

"Who?"

"The Eclipse trainees, of course," Mia shook her head. "Do you think Useless has been telling them stories about us? Spreading lies probably."

"Who?"

"Useless." Mia sighed loudly enough Emil was sure it would bring a monster to them. "Iro. The boy who used to fix the training dummies. Hung around like he really wanted to be a Hopper. Saved your life a while back. Ringing any bells?"

"I know who Iro is. Just call him by his name." A flash of movement to the left and Emil stared after it. He saw nothing past the looming trees and small, thorny-looking bushes. "Why does it matter if he tells them stories about you?"

Mia hunched her shoulders, glared at him. "Because they might not like us if he does."

"Why does that matter?"

"Urgh! Why are you so dense?" Mia stamped at something wriggling through the dirt. "This is gonna keep happening, you know. Teaming up like this. We don't have enough of us on the Courage to form full squads, so they're gonna keep sending us out with others. Probably with this lot."

"So?"

"So don't you want us all to be friends?"

Emil shrugged and wished he'd never engaged in the conversation to start with. But now he was hip deep in it and couldn't think of a way out. "I'm not looking for friends. I just want to get stronger and open my first gate so I can be a full Hopper."

"What'll that change?" Mia said. "You'll still have to team up with other Hoppers. Maybe even find a regular group to squad with. It'll make things easier if you're all friends, right?"

Emil almost growled in frustration. He was sure he could smell something strange on the air. It was almost dusty, but thicker than that and more unpleasant. He cracked his knuckles within his gauntlets. "I don't care about making things easier and I don't care about being friends. These other trainees are no different than the officers you pass in the hallways. They're just blurs. Any other Hoppers I team up with will just be comrades, there to help me achieve the mission. That's it. Nothing more." It had to be that way. He couldn't get close to people who might die before the end of the mission. Couldn't rely on people who were weak enough to need helping. It'd be so much easier if he could just do everything himself.

Mia edged away from him. She was staring at him, brows pulled together. "So what? You don't do friends at all?"

"Nope."

"So what are we? Cali and me?"

Emil shrugged. "Currently an annoyance."

"Scrap you, Emil!" Mia braced herself and pushed him, putting all her weight and power into it. She was stronger than him and they both knew it, but she held nothing back and the push threw Emil to the ground. He slid in the loose packed dirt, stumbled back to his feet, used a nearby tree for support. Then he turned on Mia, fists balled inside his gauntlets.

Emil paused, cocked his head to the side as he heard something. He realised he wasn't hearing it, but feeling it. He glanced down to see the ground trembling beneath his feet, bits of dirt jumping as if alive.

"Well," the lazy Corsair master said, smiling. "It's about time something showed up."

Emil followed the Corsair's gaze just in time to see a huge four-legged, tusked monster come thundering out of the darkness towards them.

Chapter Fourteen

Rollo fished in one of his pockets and pulled out a flick-knife, pressed the button to reveal the little blade. It was no longer than his middle finger. He slashed it through the air and used a Blink Strike. The world blurred around him as he was dragged like gravity had shifted, speeding into his chosen position. He slowed just in front of the charging monster, still swinging his little knife. The blade connected with the beast's snout, spraying thick red blood across the forest floor. The monster staggered off course from the strength of the blow, howled in pain, crashed into a tree, it's eight tusks tearing up the soil and ripping chunks from the bark. The monster staggered, disorientated. Rollo turned away.

"Trainees, line up," he said it loudly enough they'd all hear him over the whining and snorting behind him.

"But master," Arne said, peering out from behind a tree. "There's a monster."

"Sure is. A bhur beast. I'd say…" He looked over his shoulder at the monster still trying to dislodge one of its tusks from the tree it had collided with. It stood about fifteen feet tall at the shoulder, powerful muscle underneath shaggy fur. "It's a smallish one, I think." He glanced over at Tannow.

Tannow crossed his arms over his white breastplate and nodded. "That one's a baby. Mature adults are at least twice that size."

Rollo shrugged, pressed the switch on his knife to retract the blade, and shoved it back into its pocket. "Come on. Line up, trainees."

They moved slowly, slinking out from behind trees and taking places before him. It was frustrating. Any longer and the beast would recover. He hadn't hit it hard enough to keep it down for long.

The Paladin boy was first in front of him, hands curling and uncurling inside his huge gauntlets. Eager was good, but the lad was two clenches shy of over eager, and that was potentially bad. Then came Bjorn and Iro, Eir and Ashvild. The others soon realised it wasn't a joke and slunk into line in front of Rollo.

"Good." He stepped aside to give them all a full view of the bhur beast as it snorted and stamped at the ground, wrenched its powerful neck side to side. It would be free soon. "This is a bhur beast," Rollo said. "Low grade monsters we usually find up here and abouts. Stay out of the way of the tusks and when it charges you, get out of the way." He glanced at Tannow, but the Paladin said nothing.

The bhur beast finally wrenched its tusk free of the tree in an explosion of bark, then roared. Rollo waited until the noise of the tantrum had died down. "Good. Work together, trainees. Kill it." With that, he turned and walked away, moving to stand next to Tannow.

"You sure this is a good idea?" the old Paladin asked quietly.

"It's a baby, and there's ten of them," Rollo said. Besides, Alfvin had ordered him to push the kids and this was about as weak a push as he could manage. He didn't want to think of what Alfvin might do if he got it in his dumb head that Rollo was coddling the kids. Alfvin could be very unpleasant when he wanted.

All the trainees were milling, sending each other worried looks, gripping their weapons too tight, exchanging panicked whispers. One of them needed to take charge before the monster did. The bhur beast faced them, swinging its head from side to side, snorting huge breaths. Then it chose its target and charged straight into the centre of the trainees. All the kids scattered, running from the charge, disappearing behind trees. All but one. Iro didn't move and the bhur beast stampeded right at him.

Tannow raised his hand, his crest flaring to light behind him, but Rollo pushed his hand back down. He hoped he was doing the right thing. Had to believe the kid had something planned, that he wasn't just frozen in fear and about to be trampled to death.

At the last moment, Iro activated his crest, swung his sword, used a Blink Strike to drag himself out of the way of the charge, his sword swishing through thin air. The bhur beast continued its charge between two huge trees, already starting to turn and hunt down new targets amongst the fleeing trainees.

"Huh…" Rollo grunted.

Tannow sighed in relief and sagged a bit. "What?"

"The new kid used a Blink Strike to dodge instead of attack."

"Yeah?"

Rollo unclenched his hand from around the knife in his pocket. "Pretty rare for a trainee to figure that out without being told." Iro was leaning against a tree, sword dangling from his loose grip, panting hard, sweat dripping from his forehead. His crest had dimmed to a stuttering glow, barely even visible. "He's weak. But he has a head for talents."

"He's not weak," Tannow said, a note of pride in his voice.

"Yeah, he is," Rollo argued. "But he might not stay weak. You know… assuming he survives."

Iro told himself to stand up. He didn't have time to

be out of breath or leaning against a tree or fearing for his life. The bhur beast was still around, he could feel the vibrations through the earth as it charged, hear the shouts of his fellow trainees from the nearby forest as they tracked it, fought it, maybe even fell to it.

"Scrap it!" He pushed away from the tree, locked his trembling knees to stop from collapsing, drew in a deep breath, and tried to settle his racing heart. His crest was so dim, the lines barely visible. *It'll be a while before I can use another Blink Strike. I have to find some other way to attack the monster.*

Iro staggered after the shouts of his friends, weaving between trees until he saw the battle. The bhur beast had stopped its charge and was bucking, slamming into nearby trees, frantic. Ylfa was standing on its back, one hand intwined in its thick fur, the other stabbing down with her curved blade over and over again. She wasn't even penetrating its thick hide and her blade remained clean of blood. She slipped, her sword spilling from her grasp, her footing dislodged. She pulled her hand free, kicked off from the side of the bhur beast just in time to stop it crushing her against the tree it slammed into. Ylfa hit the ground hard, rolling to a stop and scooting away behind the tree as the bhur beast slammed into it again and again. Leafs and branches rained from above at the violence of the impacts.

"Torben," Bjorn shouted from nearby. "Boost me."

Iro turned to see Bjorn running at Torben. The bigger boy knelt, braced his sword against the ground. Bjorn ran onto the sword and Torben stood, shouting as he pivoted the sword on his shoulder and flung Bjorn into the air. Bjorn sailed towards the bhur beast, a battle cry on his lips, his big two-handed sword swinging. The bhur beast staggered away from the tree, swung its head towards Bjorn. Tusks connected with sword, sent the weapon spinning away out of Bjorn's grasp. Another twist of its head and a tusk slammed into Bjorn's chest, cracking his cobalt armor and sending him flying away. He crashed into a tree, splintered the bark. The bhur beast lowered its head, sighted at Bjorn, and charged.

⚙⚙⚙

Emil darted around the tree, grabbed the bigger boy under the arms, and hauled him up and around the massive trunk just as the bhur beast slammed against it. Its tusks raked the bark, sending wood splinters flying. It roared loud enough to make Emil's ears ring. He dropped the big Corsair on the ground.

"Are you trying to get yourself killed?"

The other boy coughed, blood spraying from his mouth onto his cracked chest plate. He raised a shaky hand, clenched it into a fist, extended his thumb upwards. "Thanks." His voice was a wheezing croak.

Emil shook his head. "Can you stand? Can you move?" He helped the other boy up.

The bhur beast was still savaging the tree. Far too close for comfort. The Corsair staggered a step, used another nearby tree for support. "I can walk."

"Then get out of here," Emil said, turning away from the boy. "You're no good anymore."

He didn't bother to wait for the other boy to reply. Emil dashed around the tree and leapt at the bhur beast, slammed a gauntlet into the meat of its front leg, then ducked underneath its heaving chest even as it turned for him. He drew his fist back, punched as hard as he could straight into the beast's exposed neck. The monster staggered from the blow and Emil leapt back. Too slow. He got his gauntlets up just as a tusk smashed into him, sending him flying. The trees passed by in a dizzying blur. He hit the ground, tucked into a ball, rolled. A stick poked hard into his side and he cried out, finally came to a stop face down in a pile of rotting leafs. He groaned, struggling back to his hands and knees. Aching pain racing through him.

"What are you doing?" A girl stopped beside him, grabbed his arm and hauled him up. She was one of the Corsairs, short and stocky with braided hair, and a severe look. He hadn't bothered to learn their names. "You're our Paladin. Get behind us and stay out of the way."

"I can fight," Emil growled, squinting past the pain. He felt blood running down the side of his face. The bhur beast was already swinging its head about, looking for a new target.

"Shut up!" the severe girl snapped and pushed him behind her. "Your job is to enhance, not flail at things you can't hurt. What talent do you know?"

Emil ground his teeth in frustration. What the scrap did this girl know? He was strong enough to fight, no matter his class. "Steel," he growled.

The girl glanced over her shoulder at him, bright blue eyes shining with something like hunger. "I can use that."

Iro skirted the bhur beast, thinking better of attacking it alone. No matter what any of them tried, they weren't even piercing the monster's hairy hide. Master Rollo had almost killed it in a single blow, but none of the rest of them stood a chance.

The monster charged at Ylfa, but the wiry girl ran up a tree trunk, leapt, grabbed hold of a hanging branch, pulled herself up and out of reach. The bhur beast savaged the trunk, grunting and growling. Ylfa clung to the branch and shouted insults at the monster.

"Good work getting Bjorn to safety," Iro said as he arrived at Emil's side.

Emil glared at him for a moment then went back to

staring at the monster. Ashvild was just a couple of paces away, waving at others to join them. Eir, Arne, Torben, and Ingrid trotted closer.

"Master Rollo said this was an easy one," Ingrid said, rubbing at a graze on her cheek. "None of us can even hurt it."

"I hurt it," Emil said. Iro wasn't sure anyone else heard him, but none of the others paid him any attention.

Mia jogged closer, her great hammer clutched in both hands, a worried look on her face.

"My mother once killed a bhur matriarch," Eir said quietly. "On her own." She sounded sad rather than excited by it though.

"If only she were here instead of you," Arne said.

Eir shook her head, looking far more serious than Iro had ever seen her. "Oh, you don't want her here, she…" She trailed off.

"I have a plan," Ashvild said. She pointed at Mia. "You, Mia, was it?"

Mia nodded, none of her usual confidence showing.

"You know how to swing that chunk of metal?"

"You can bet your scrapping arse I do."

Ashvild nodded, smiling. Iro had never seen her smile before. She was always deadly serious no matter what was happening.

The bhur beast gave up trying to get to Ylfa and turned, looking for other prey. It spotted the group of the trainees and lowered its head to charge.

"Arne, Eir, distract it. Buy us some time," Ashvild said.

"Yes sir!" Eir said as she skipped into a run straight at the monster.

"Sure," Arne grumbled as he stalked after Eir. "Give me the dangerous job."

As the bhur beast pawed at the ground and started into a charge, Eir and Arne split up, flanking it. The monster slowed, unsure who to target, and swung its head back and forth. Eir darted in to score to a slicing attack down its flank with her thin sword. The bhur beast stamped, turned, whipped a tusk at the slight girl. Eir leapt into the air, brought her sword up to block, her purple crest bursting into light behind her. The tusk crashed into her, but rather than be crushed by it, Eir seemed to stick to the tusk like she was an extension of it. The bhur beast flung her away and she glided lightly down to the ground, completely unharmed. Iro gawked, wondering what talent Eir was using.

Arne took the opportunity of the monster's distraction and picked up a stone, threw it at the bhur beast's backside. The monster growled, trampled the ground as it spun about and sighted the tall boy. It leapt at him and Arne turned and ran, darting behind a nearby tree.

"OK," Ashvild said. Iro turned his attention back to the group. Mia, Torben, and Ingrid clustered around. "The bhur beast is big and powerful, but it's clearly stupid too. It goes after whichever target it can see and ignores everything else. That gives us an advantage. Ingrid, I need it to charge you."

"I can do that," Ingrid said, shifting from foot to foot. "As long as you can stop it getting me."

Ashvild nodded. "I'm going to knock it down. That should buy Torben and Mia a few seconds to get into place."

Mia glanced at Torben standing beside her. "What are me and tubby supposed to do?"

Ashvild gave her a pale stare. "Torben will position that oversized sword of his at the monster's skull. You," she pointed at Mia, "are going to swing that hammer as hard as you can and drive his sword like a nail into the bhur beast's head."

"Oooh, I like this plan," Mia said, grinning, gauntlets twisting around the haft of her hammer.

"Emil, that was your name, yes?" Ashvild said, then continued before he could answer. "As Mia starts to swing, enhance her with steel. It will increase her weight as well as strengthen her skin. That will mean she can hit even harder."

Emil narrowed his eyes. "It will. But how do you know about that?"

Ashvild pulled a face. "Because I'm not stupid and I actually pay attention in class. Are we all ready?"

Iro felt his spirits sink. "What about me? What do I do?"

Ashvild glanced at him as if she had forgotten he was even there. "Protect the Paladin in case something goes wrong."

Iro opened his mouth to argue, to point out that he could be useful, but Ashvild didn't give him a chance. "Are we all clear on our parts? Good. Let's bring this monster down."

As the others moved off to get into position, Iro felt forgotten and useless like he hadn't since back on the Courage, before he'd manifested his talent and become a Corsair. He hated the feeling. It twisted his insides and made him feel tired and angry. But he wouldn't let it get him down. Master Tannow had always said that protecting the Paladin was one of the most important jobs on any Hop, so that's what he'd do. Even if it was just a job Ashvild had given him to keep him busy.

He clutched Neya's sword in both hands and stepped in front of Emil. "Stick behind me. I'll protect you."

"Scrap you!" Emil snarled, shoving him aside. "Just stay out of my way."

Iro shook his head and turned away. Some things never changed. He stayed in front of Emil though, ready to protect him in case something went wrong.

Arne was frustrating the monster, popping around one side of a tree, then darting back to the other side. The bhur beast slammed against the trunk hard enough a crack raced up the length.

"Now please," Arne screamed. "Now. Do it now!"

Ingrid strode into a small clearing between half a dozen trees. She looked formidable in her bulky blue armor, more like a Vanguard than a Corsair, an immovable wall of muscle and metal. "Hey monster," she bellowed. "Let's play."

The bhur beast swung its head around to stare at Ingrid with dark, beady eyes set deep within the bony plates of its head. The Corsair grinned, held her long sword up above her head. Her crest, a soft orange fuzz of circular lines and swirling lettering, lit up before her. It was small, only a little larger than Iro's own crest. Ingrid's blade started to glow. Softly at first, but quickly growing to a bright golden shine that had Iro shielding his eyes. The bhur beast swung its head from side to side, pawed at the earth, throwing soil all over Arne as he peered around the tree. Then the monster lowered its tusks and charged.

"I got its attention, Ash," Ingrid said, her voice quavering. "Ashvild? Ash, where the scrap are you?"

The bhur beast tore along the earth toward Ingrid. Her crest flickered out, her blade lost its glow. She lowered her sword and backed up a step but had nowhere to go. No trees near enough for cover or to climb.

Iro started towards her, but his feet froze. What could he do? Nothing but get in the way. He turned to Emil. "Enhance her."

"Shut up!" Emil said.

Iro spun back around to see Ashvild step out from behind a tree to Ingrid's left. Ashvild drew back her arm and launched her short sword across the little clearing. It looked like a pod racing across the black, a golden zipping light. Then it sank into a tree across the other side of the clearing. Ashvild darted back behind the tree, ran around it once, knelt down and braced. Iro saw a thin golden line still hanging in the air across the clearing like a wire pulled taught. Ashvild's crest, a tiny fiery blur hovering behind her, flared bright.

The bhur beast roared as it closed on Ingrid, then hit the golden wire. Ashvild screamed, was yanked off her feet, slammed against the tree. The bhur beast stumbled then fell, hitting the ground head first, its tusks tearing up huge chunks of dirt and sending them flying like splashing waves from a thrown stone. The monster slid to a stop just two paces from Ingrid. The big Corsair staggered back a step, turned, and scrambled away.

Ashvild was down on the ground, wincing in pain. Blood dripped from her trembling hands, but she raised a finger and pointed, drew in a breath. "Now. Do it!"

Mia and Torben raced into the clearing. The bhur beast was still down, lying on its side, moaning and barely moving. Its cloven feet pawed at the air and its eyes rolled. Torben ran up to its head, his giant sword unslung and thrust it against the monster's bony skull, between its eyes. He ducked underneath the blade and moved out of the way of the hilt, supporting the sword by its cross guard. Mia's run turned into a sprint and she whooped. She slid to a stop just a few feet from the pommel of Torben's sword and drew back the hammer for a mighty swing.

"Steel," Emil said from behind Iro. Mia's feet sank an inch into the dirt as Emil's enhancement tightened her skin and increased her weight. Then she swung her hammer at Torben's sword.

The blade shattered against the monster's skull.

Torben staggered back amidst falling shards of metal. "What the scrap?"

Mia stepped back, clutching her great hammer against her chest and shaking her head. "Don't look at me. Your sword was scrap."

A ripple passed along the bhur beast's flank as it snorted and shifted, slowly moving to get its legs beneath it.

Ashvild leaned against a tree, her hands still trembling and dripping blood. She shook her head and sagged. Arne and Eir watched from a distance, waiting in case they were needed again. Ingrid jogged up to join Iro and Emil even as Mia and Torben turned away from the waking monster.

"If only it was titan-forged steel," Ingrid said. "So much stronger than the metal we can print on the ship."

Iro looked down at Neya's sword in his hands, his knuckles white around the hilt. They did have one titan-forged blade with them.

"Scrap scrap scrap scrap scrap," Iro said. He activated his icy crest and swung Neya's sword through it. The Blink Strike dragged him through the air so quickly his stomach lurched. He flew past the fleeing Mia and Torben, right up to the bhur beast. His sword hit its hardened skull, bounced off the bone.

The bhur beast grumbled and shifted.

"Do it again!" Iro shouted as he clambered into position with Neya's sword pointed between the bhur beast's eyes. The sword was shorter than Torben's, but it might work.

Mia slid to a stop. "Huh?"

"Titan-forged steel. Just hit it again!"

Mia turned, sprinted back toward him, leapt into the air, arched her back, hammer held behind her. The bhur beast's eyes flicked open and Iro stared down into the dark depths. The monster roared. Mia let out a triumphant cry and swung her hammer up and down towards Iro. Iro closed his eyes, certain she was going to hit him instead of the sword. He felt his skin tighten, his limbs grow heavy.

Mia's hammer struck with such force Iro felt his arms vibrate. He screamed from the pain. The bhur beast gave a violent lurch, flung him away.

Iro landed in the dirt a few paces away heavily enough he sank into the soil. Then his skin loosened and he felt light again. He quickly sat up and shuffled back, terrified of seeing the bhur beast lurching back to its feet. Or worse, of seeing his sister's sword shattered just like Torben's. Instead he saw Neya's sword sunk up to the hilt in the bhur beast's bony skull right between its eyes. Mia held her hammer over her head, carrying the massive weight as if it was nothing, jumping up and down on the spot and whooping.

Slowly, Iro got back to his feet and stumbled towards the monster. His arms hurt, though not enough he couldn't move them. But his legs felt wobbly and unresponsive, turning every step into a staggering lurch. He couldn't quite believe what had just happened.

Mia's gaze settled on him, her grin so wide it was infectious. He had the sneaking suspicion she was going to hit him. She dropped her hammer and pounced on Iro, grabbing him around the waist and hoisting him into the air in a crushing hug. He squeaked in alarm, but Mia just threw him into the air, caught him, then dropped him back to the ground. "We did it!" she said, still bouncing on the spot.

"Not so useless after all, huh?" Iro said, grinning back, caught up in her joy.

"Huh?" Mia grabbed him by the arms, spun him about, then let go and jumped again. "I guess not. We just killed a scrapping monster, Useless!"

Iro nodded. He couldn't match her energy, but he

laughed all the same. "Well, I did most of the work, but I guess you helped."

Mia laughed and thumped him on the arm. It hurt, but he didn't care. In the face of her energy and enthusiasm, it was hard to feel the pain.

Ashvild was the first to join them, then Torben and Ingrid. Arne kept his distance, but Eir danced closer, a curious look on her face as she stared from the bhur beast to Iro and back again. Emil was the last one to approach. He kept his distance from all the others, refusing to join in the celebration.

"You did it," Ashvild said, cradling her bloody left hand against her chest.

"Scrapping right, we did," Mia said. "Right between the eyes."

"We all did it," Iro said. "Your plan. All of our work."

"Sure," Mia said. "But *we* struck the killing blow, Useless." She wrapped an arm around his shoulders and pulled him so close she all but crushed him against her armor.

Iro basked in the brief celebration. He saw Master Rollo and Tannow approaching at a leisurely pace, Bjorn limping behind them. Rollo looked bored, but Master Tannow was smiling. Iro turned away from them, found Emil brooding at the edge of the celebration. He considered ignoring the other boy, letting him sulk. Then he drew in a deep breath and approached.

Emil glared when Iro came close. "What do you want?"

"To say thank you. You enhanced me. Probably stopped Mia's strike from killing me as well as the monster."

Emil snorted, crossed his arms and turned away. "Now we're even." With that, he walked away to stand alone again.

Chapter Fifteen

The day after the Hop, Iro grinned as he remembered the battle with the bhur beast. It had been terrifying at the time, but they had all come through it alive, and they had slain the monster. He was buzzing with the thrill of victory.

They didn't go on the usual morning run, partly because Bjorn couldn't. The bigger boy was limping, and had his left arm in a sling, but he, too, was in high spirits. They took their time, sauntering through the halls of the Eclipse, and Iro felt different for the first time since he'd arrived on the ship. He finally felt like he belonged, like he was accepted. Not just some little kid from another ship, but part of the Eclipse. Part of a new family.

The girls had, of course, arrived in the training hall early. They always beat the boys to the room, mostly because Bjorn usually pushed the limits of time on their morning runs. Iro felt his grin stretching even further at the sight of Eir moving through her morning stretches.

Bjorn nudged Iro with his good arm. "Make it more obvious."

Iro felt his neck and cheeks grow warm and locked his eyes on the floor. They all shuffled into the room.

"Besides," Bjorn continued too loudly for Iro's liking. "I thought you and that Courage girl were hitting it off."

"Mia?" Iro asked, incredulous. "She hates me."

"Steel is tested through battle, not idleness," Torben said sagely.

Iro laughed nervously. "What?"

Bjorn stopped next to Eir. "He means, Iro, that love is built on conflict, and you two were definitely very conflicting."

Iro glanced at Eir, she was staring back at him, a smile tugging at one corner of her mouth.

"Shut up, Bjorn."

"I mean," Bjorn continued. "You and Mia did slay a monster together."

"It was epic," Eir said. "Very inspiring. You two definitely had chemistry."

Iro felt like his cheeks were on fire they were so hot. He wanted to run away, to hide, to crawl into a service duct or eject himself out into the black. Anything to escape the conversation. Not that running would do him any good. Hoppers didn't run. Hoppers fought.

"It wasn't just us," Iro said quickly, trying to regain some control. "We all fought together to kill the bhur beast. Well, everyone except you, Bjorn. You had to get rescued by Emil. Then you spent the entire fight having a nice rest."

"Oh yes, very easy for some," Torben said grumpily.

Bjorn looked around to find the other trainees staring at him, nodding. "Hey! I tried to kill the thing. It's not like I just ran off for a nap while you lot fought it."

"I'm sure I saw you resting your eyes at one point," Eir said. "Lazy Bjorn, we'll call you."

Ingrid joined in, standing next to Torben and looking every bit his twin. "When the fighting gets tough, there's Lazy Bjorn, sitting on the sidelines with his feet up."

"He's not even injured," Arne said quickly, never missing a chance to poke fun at someone. "Just putting it on for sympathy. He asked me for a shoulder rub earlier."

"I did not!" Bjorn shouted.

"Line up, trainees," Master Rollo said as he sauntered into the training hall, crossed over to his usual perch, dumped a satchel on the floor, then thrust his hands into his pockets. He looked slightly more unkempt than usual, his hair a messy tousle, his shirt untucked on the left side, and the right pocket on his jacket was inside out. He stared at them all under lidded eyes as they shuffled into line and stood to attention.

"First real Hop," Master Rollo said eventually. "Exciting."

"Scrap yeah it was," Ylfa said.

Bjorn rubbed his arm in its sling. "Painful, really."

Iro thought about the others, Emil and Mia. The way Emil had claimed they were even had a strange finality to it, as though the other boy hoped they'd never meet again. "Will we be working with the trainees from the Courage again?" he asked.

"Told you," Bjorn said, pouting at Iro. "He just wants to see the girl with the hammer again."

"So you think it went well then?" Master Rollo said.

"Scrap yes, master," Ylfa said. "We killed a monster!"

Iro sensed a trap. It was something in Master Rollo's stillness, like a marsh mite about to erupt from the water and snare its prey.

"Wrong," Master Rollo said, the word cutting all of them in two. "You think you did well killing a baby bhur beast? If I was grading you, and be glad I am not, you would have all failed."

Awkward silence flooded into the room. Iro heard boots ringing on the hallway floors outside, snatched voices as people passed, the hum of electricity thrumming through the lights.

"But we succeeded," Bjorn said. "You told us to kill the bhur beast and we did."

"We?" Master Rollo asked. "Let's go through it, shall we."

Iro had to stifle a groan. *He's going to eviscerate us all.*

"Bjorn, you were an idiot," Master Rollo continued.

"You were specifically told to work together, but instead you flung yourself at the monster head on in a scrapping stupid attack and almost got yourself killed. You forced your Paladin to put himself in harm's way to protect you. And you were so beat up you spent the rest of the battle out of the fight. You didn't just fail, your actions were dangerous and put others in danger. Heroics aren't taking on the whole titan on your own. Protecting your squad is heroic. Working together to bring down a monster without injury or loss of life is heroic.

"You didn't just fail. If I had my way, I'd kick you out of the squad and stick you on drudge duty for the rest of your life."

Bjorn deflated as Master Rollo talked. He was the second largest of all the trainees after Torben, but in that moment and during that dressing down, Bjorn looked smaller than Iro. He sagged, arm cradled against his chest, and Iro thought he saw tears filling the boy's eyes. He had the urge to rush to Bjorn's defence, but he knew the bigger boy wouldn't thank him for it.

"Ylfa," Master Rollo said, swinging his half-lidded stare towards the girl. She paled before his icy blue gaze. "Your first attack was wild and stupid. The bhur beast's back is all wiry hair and thick skin, and no attack you could have made would have harmed it. You put yourself in danger. And you dropped your sword." He said that last with a weight that settled like a bulkhead collapsed on the girl. "You are a Corsair. Your sword is your life. Never lose it."

Ylfa locked her dark eyes on the floor and muttered, "I didn't know its back was so armored."

"Excuses now?" Master Rollo asked. "Ashvild, where is the bhur beast weakest?"

Ashvild stepped forward. Her bandaged hands hung

by her side. "It's belly, just below the armor plates on its chest."

"And how did you know that, trainee?"

Ashvild swallowed hard, glanced across at Ylfa, mouthed *sorry*.

"How?" Master Rollo repeated.

"Because I studied, master."

"Well, there's a novel idea," Master Rollo said. "Turns out expecting you all to study in your own time to keep yourselves and your squad mates safe was believing too much of you. So from now on, we'll be spending every fourth day buried in books, learning all about the dangers of the titans." He sighed. "It will *not* be fun.

"While you're front and centre. Ashvild, you came up with a plan. You rallied the others to you and put them to work. You showed forward thinking and leadership. Shame your plan was such scrap."

Iro saw Ashvild's jaw clench. She glared at Master Rollo for a moment and Iro thought she was about to argue with him. Then she lowered her gaze. "Master?"

"Despite knowing where the bhur beast was weakest, you made a plan to attack it where it was strongest."

"I thought a decisive blow would be best, to ensure it died quickly rather than…"

"I don't care about your reasoning, trainee," Master Rollo said, his voice flat. "Your plan put your squad mates in danger by attempting a risky finishing move. Victory lies in surviving the fight, not some flashy kill. Safety always comes first."

Ashvild clenched her jaw again, then nodded. "Yes master."

"And on top of that, your talent almost cost you both your hands," Master Rollo continued, relentless. "Thread Edge is a powerful talent, and that was an inventive use, but your skill in using it needs a lot of practice."

Ashvild nodded and stepped back into line.

"While we're talking about the plan," Master Rollo said, sweeping his gaze across the trainees. "Eir and Arne, you actually did quite well."

Eir grinned. "We did?"

Arne cracked his knuckles. "Of course we did."

"Can either of you tell me what you did well?"

"Umm." Eir frowned, thinking. "I was very graceful, and Arne did a fantastic job of running away."

"I was taunting it," Arne said.

"By showing it your arse?" Eir grinned at him.

Master Rollo removed a hand from his pocket, rubbed at his temple. "Correct. You were given the job of distracting the monster. You followed your orders and you kept yourselves safe while doing it. In a normal Hop scenario, that job would be fulfilled by a Vanguard or Berserker, but we didn't have either of those classes, so it fell to you. Well done."

Iro got the distinct feeling that was the last of the praise Master Rollo intended to dish out, though he had no idea what he had done wrong. He had followed Ashvild's orders, and even stepped in to help strike the killing blow when the original plan failed. Surely he had done everything right?

"Ingrid…" Master Rollo said.

"I followed the plan Ashvild came up with," Ingrid said, cutting him off. "I got the monster's attention just like I was told to."

Master Rollo nodded slowly. "You did. Well done on that. You also had no exit strategy. You froze. If Ashvild was off in her timing, or if her Thread Edge hadn't held, you would have been crushed by a stampeding bhur beast. At your current stage, that would likely mean death. Always have a backup plan, a way out of danger if things don't go as expected. And no, cowering in fear is not a sufficient backup plan."

Ingrid didn't argue with him after that.

"Torben." Master Rollo lowered his head and sighed. "Torben."

"I know what you're going to say, master," Torben said, holding his hands up placatingly. "My sword broke. I'm a Corsair. My sword is my life. But…"

"First I was going to point out that you launched Bjorn into his suicidal attack."

Torben looked at Bjorn for a moment, clearly trying to decide if it was worth defending himself. Apparently he decided it was not and shut his mouth.

Master Rollo grunted and looked up at the huge boy. "Glad we agree that was stupid. And yes, your sword broke."

"That's not my fault," Torben said quickly. Iro thought he was foolish to defend himself. Best just to weather Master Rollo's brief ire. "If I had a titan-forged blade, it wouldn't have broke."

"You don't get a titan-forged weapon or armor until you become a full Hopper," Master Rollo said. He left out the part that none of them would be getting any titan-forged gear until they found and secured a manufactory. The fleet simply didn't have the means to forge the stronger metal that could only be made on the titan. Their printed material was weak and flimsy by comparison.

"But that's not fair," Torben said. "In order to progress, we're expected to kill monsters that need titan-forged weapons to do so, but we don't get titan-forged weapons until we progress, and we need to kill the monsters to progress. It's a loop with no way to win."

Master Rollo sighed. "You don't need a titan-forged

weapon to kill a bhur beast. You just have to aim for somewhere that isn't armored scrapping bone."

Ashvild stepped forward again. "Master Rollo." Iro had to admire her courage to pull his attention back onto herself. Torben slumped and quickly stepped back into line, looking eternally grateful to Ashvild for saving him.

"Yes, Ashvild?"

"Why does Iro have a titan-forged sword?"

All eyes turned to Iro and he felt his stomach lurch. That earlier relief at finally starting to fit in was snuffed out like a flame in a vacuum, and he once more felt the need to run and hide.

"It was my sister's sword," Iro said quietly, hating how weak his voice sounded.

"That doesn't make sense," Ashvild said. "I thought a Corsair had to forge their own blade at a manufactory or they couldn't focus their current through it?"

Again all eyes focused on Iro and he felt like he was being accused of something though he didn't know what.

"That's true," Master Rollo said. "I assume it's because the sword originally belonged to Iro's sister and she was a Paladin so never focused her current through the sword, leaving it unattuned."

"Huh?" Iro looked about, but all the other trainees seemed to know what Master Rollo was talking about. Again he found himself far behind in his training and lacking knowledge that the others thought commonplace. "What do you mean unattuned, master?"

Master Rollo rolled his eyes. "Eir."

Eir bounced forward a step. "I know this one. Um, when a Corsair focuses their current through a titan-forged blade it becomes attuned to them. Right? That's right. Uh..." She ran a hand over her bristly scalp. "If another Corsair tries to focus their current through a weapon already attuned to a Corsair, it doesn't work. You're really lucky to have a titan-forged sword already, Iro."

Iro drew Neya's sword from over his shoulder and stared at the blade. It was long and wide, with an edge on both sides. The blade itself was silver, but the edges were strangely dark. The chip was half way up the blade, and the more he thought about it, the less he understood how it had happened. He had chipped his sister's titan-forged sword by swinging it around in his room and hitting a wall. The same sword had survived being driven like a nail into the hardened skull of a bhur beast. How had he managed to chip it at all? He peered closely at the little defect, and saw a tiny snaking crack spreading out from the chip. *I need to get it reforged before it breaks. But I can't do that unless the fleet finds a manufactory. And even then, there's no chance they'd give a trainee like me access.*

"Now we're on the subject," Master Rollo said. "Iro."

Iro looked up from staring at his sword and found the master watching him, a bored look on his face. Iro quickly sheathed his sister's sword.

"You did well getting out of the way of the initial charge. Quick thinking using a Blink Strike to dodge rather than attack."

"Thank you, master," Iro said. *Here's comes the but.*

"But it went downhill from there, didn't it. You were ordered to protect your Paladin. Instead, you left him vulnerable, charged in for the glory kill, and forced your Paladin to protect you."

"But Emil was safe," Iro argued. "And he..."

"Was he?" Master Rollo asked. "Safe? Did you know that? Did you know for a fact there wasn't another monster hiding nearby, waiting for a chance to strike a separated target? Not all monsters attack head on like the bhur beast. Many wait in shadows and strike without warning. You left your Paladin alone. Always protect your Paladin.

"All of you need to do better next time," Master Rollo said. "Learn. Improve. Being a Hopper is dangerous, and one stupid mistake means death. It's my job to train you, but also to prepare you for what is to come. To give you the knowledge, the experience, the strength, and the will to survive monsters, traps, and whatever else this new titan throws at you. So stop making my job harder by being scrapping idiots!"

He leapt down from his perch and grabbed the satchel he had brought in with him. He reached inside and pulled out a small tablet, then threw it to Iro. Iro almost fumbled the catch, but managed to keep hold. Master Rollo threw a tablet to each of the trainees, then dumped the satchel on the floor again.

"This is a bestiary," the Corsair said. "It contains everything we as a fleet know about every monster and trap we have encountered so far. Most of it comes from titan 01, but we have already encountered a few new monsters here on 02. Read it. Learn it. Read it again. It *will* save your life.

"Now, find the document on bhur beasts and lets go over what you idiots *should* have done yesterday."

Chapter Sixteen

Master Tannow had given them all the day off. Emil didn't like it. Time off was time wasted. Just because the old man was too tired to keep up, didn't mean the rest of them should be punished.

Emil made his way to the training hall alone, lost in his thoughts, trusting his feet to guide him. He was reliving the fight against the bhur beast again. Every day since the Hop, he had been over it all in his head. Ten times a day, twenty. What did he do right and wrong? What could he have done better? Master Tannow was no help. The old Hopper sat Mia and Emil down the day after the Hop and told them they did well. He offered no criticism and no advice. He just said he was proud of the accomplishment. Mia was obviously proud of herself too, endlessly chatting to Cali about how awesome it had been, and how she and Iro had worked together to strike the killing blow. It was all so useless. Emil needed to know what he should have done. He needed to be stronger so next time he'd kill the monster instead of just giving it a nasty bruise.

There were noises coming from the training room and Emil had a gut-wrenching moment of believing the others had gone ahead training without him. That they somehow thought him weak enough that he was slowing them down. He rushed to the door and peered inside to see the other trainee group, under Master Kelving, running through training drills. Heras, the oldest trainee on the Courage and the son of one of Emil's father's friends, spotted Emil and waved. Emil nodded back once, turned, and strode away.

He had no idea where to go. The training hall was busy. His father was off shift so their quarters would be as hostile an environment as the endless black. He briefly entertained the mad thought of stealing a pod and Hopping down to the titan, but he was too weak. His encounter with the bhur beast had proven that.

Emil found his feet quickening, anger and shame and guilt a burning churn in his gut. He needed to get rid of it all. He needed to move, to expend the tight energy making his arms and legs feel like coiled springs. He lurched into a run, dodging around a tech who was making repairs to a bulkhead, shouting at an officer to get out of the way. The Courage was a cramped ship, barely enough space for two people to walk abreast in the corridors, but Emil would make it work. He'd run until he couldn't. Until his legs gave out and his lungs burned. He'd run until he was too exhausted to think.

There was only one circuit he could currently run around the Courage. Too much of the ship was sealed off, the atmosphere vented out into the void. His path took him past the waste management and Emil sped his pace even faster. The place reminded him too much of his father. He ran past the food storage and their row upon row of algae vats, past the stairwell leading up to the bridge. His route led him through the observation lounge. It was one of the largest open spaces on the entire ship, and despite the fact that it could have been put to better use, it had been preserved as a place the crew could go to relax. It was filled with tables and chairs, most of which were in use. Some with crew talking quietly to each other, sharing jokes or griping about their day, others with people sitting in silence. Emil had never understood that. Silence was fine on his own but felt awkward around others.

He had to slow down at the entrance to the

observation lounge. There were people in the way, standing in the door arch chatting. They didn't move fast enough and he had to stop, lost all his momentum. He growled at the two officers, squeezed past, then started jogging again. Sweat trickled down his back and he hated the feeling of it.

"Emil! Hey, Emil, over here." Mia and Cali were over by the aft window. They were sitting at a table and Mia waved at him, grinning. He considered ignoring her, but she might view it as a snub. Word would get back to his father, and there would be hell to pay for his perceived slip down the social ladder.

Emil jogged over to their table. Both sisters were in casual uniforms, patched and sewed here and there but clean of stains. Both had tablets. Mia had a pen with hers and Emil could see she was sketching something onto it.

"What?" he asked, still trying to catch his breath.

"You're in a pleasant mood," Mia said, her pen stroking the screen of the tablet.

"Sit down," Cali pushed out a third chair with her foot.

"Why?"

Mia shook her head, smiling. "To relax a bit?"

Emil glanced between the two sisters. "Why?"

Mia sighed and rubbed her thumb across the tablet screen. "Because we're friends, and friends relax together."

Emil glanced between them again, trying to figure out a way he could decline without causing an issue that his father would hear about.

Cali pushed the chair out a little further. "Please."

Emil gave up. There was no way out of it. He slipped into the seat and sat, staring straight ahead at the window. He could see the titan through the glass. He could see nothing but the titan. It dominated the view. Smooth metal in places, jagged in others, tiny lights blinking on and off along the hull just like stars. He could just about make out the dome with the garden. Or at least he thought he could. There were a dozen domes on the wing they clung to. He really wasn't sure which one they had been to.

"Phew, you smell, Emil," Mia said. "You know we can shower now, right?" She grinned and sketched a few more lines onto the tablet.

"My father…" Emil caught himself. It was against the rules for him to give his daily shower privileges to his father, but the old man demanded it. He shrugged. "I've been running."

"Clearly," Cali said. "What else do you do on your time off?"

Emil fidgeted a little. The chair was uncomfortable. Mia was slouched in hers and seemed content enough, but he couldn't seem to find a way to sit in it properly that didn't press into his back awkwardly. "Usually I train, but the hall is busy."

Mia glanced at him, then back to her tablet. "You train on your days off?"

"Yes."

"What else?" Cali asked. "When you're not training."

Emil felt like he was being interrogated, and he didn't like it. "Sometimes I help my father. He…" He liked to get together with a bunch of other drudges where they could complain about the officers and Hoppers and their special privileges. The old man made Emil play lookout in case anyone too high on the social ladder came by and might overhear them.

"Don't you do anything for yourself?" Cali asked. "A hobby maybe?"

Emil stared at her, trying to decide if she was joking. He had no time for a hobby. If he did, it would just be wasting time.

"Mia likes to draw," Cali continued.

Mia turned her tablet around to show Emil. "I'm still working on it." It was a rather skilful drawing of a bhur beast in a forest with a young girl swinging an oversized hammer at the monster. Emil noticed she had missed out all of the other trainees. "I've got some others which are far better." She opened up another drawing, a portrait of Cali in grey lines, her eyes somehow distant and thoughtful. Another drawing was of Emil, mid strike against a training dummy. He looked at Mia when she showed him that one. She shrugged back at him.

"It was a good composition," Mia said. "Much better than a moment later where you were on the ground nursing a split lip."

"What do you do?" Emil asked, turning to Cali.

"I read mostly," she said. "The Courage has a good library of books. I think some describe a time before we found the titans, but it's hard to tell. So many different places and people. And missing sections. My dad says a lot of it is just made up. People wrote down their dreams. I don't know. I just like to read. Do you?"

Emil knew how to read, of course. It was required learning early on for everyone in the fleet regardless of familial rank or whether they manifested a talent. He even remembered his mother had a few paper books. They were rare and old, so old the paper was crisp and brown and brittle. He had vague memories of her sitting at the kitchen table, gently turning a page and smiling at whatever she found there. He had been too young to read them himself. When she died, his father burned the books, said they were a useless waste of space.

"I don't have a tablet," Emil admitted. He'd had one once, but his father had taken it apart to see how it worked in the hope that he could fix some of the broken ones he kept lying around. It hadn't worked once he put it back together and now sat with the rest of the broken scrap.

"Oh," Cali tapped her tablet a few times, then placed it on the table and slid it over to Emil. "Take this one. It's loaded with a ton of books already."

Emil stared at the tablet, frowned. "Don't you need it?"

Cali shook her head. "I have a spare back in our quarters."

It was so easy for her. The captain's daughter. Bigger quarters, probably more food, no need to give up her showers to her father. Emil and countless others aboard the ship didn't have a single working tablet to their family, and yet the captain's family had a tablet each and spare enough that she could just give one away like it was nothing.

Emil glared at the tablet lest he turn the fury on either of the sisters instead. "Thanks," he ground the word out between his teeth. They didn't even realise it. How easy they had it. How humiliating it was to be given something as if it was nothing.

"You really just train on your own even on your days off?" Mia asked.

Emil nodded, still not looking at either of the sisters.

"Why?"

"To get stronger."

"No, I get that." Mia whisked her pen across the tablet, sketching a few more strokes, the beginning of a tusk. "Why do you want to be a Hopper?"

"I have a talent."

"Right, I know. But why do you *want* to be a Hopper?"

Emil considered the question. He'd not really thought about it before. He had a talent so of course he was in training to be a Hopper. If he failed, never even opening his first gate, he'd probably end up a drudge just like his old man. That was just how things were. He'd never had a choice to do or be anything else.

"To protect the fleet," he said, hoping it would mollify the sisters. He wished he'd never sat down. This interrogation was uncomfortable.

He glanced up to find Mia frowning. "That's fine, I guess. But don't you have a reason *you* want to be a Hopper? More food, better quarters, the thrill of the fight. Better food!"

Cali laughed. "You can guess why Mia wants to be a Hopper."

"Hey! We killed the bhur beast. Least they could do would be let us eat some of it. Instead it gets chopped up and sent into cold storage, and we get— you guessed it— more algae." Mia dropped her tablet on the table and groaned, leaning back in her chair and staring at the ceiling. The metal panels above were rusting and one had fallen away completely, revealing a host of wires within the darkness. "One day, we Hoppers are going to eat nothing but bhur beast steak. I remember it from the last titan. It melts on the tongue and ahhhh." She dragged her gaze from the ceiling and grinned at Emil. He quickly looked away.

"What about you, Cali?" he asked before either of them could prod him with more questions.

Cali's mouth twisted as if she was chewing on something inedible. She was silent for a few moments. "Do you remember what it was like back at titan 01? Before it exploded. Do you remember the children?"

"We *were* children," Mia said, rolling her eyes.

"We were, but there were younger children. They used to run around the ship and play, get under foot. How many children do you see now?"

Emil turned in his seat, looked around the

observation lounge. The youngest children he saw had to be closing in on ten years old and there were only three of them. Now he thought about it, he rarely saw true youngsters these days.

Cali sighed. "Birthrate was declining even before titan 01 exploded, but it plummeted to almost nothing afterwards. We were low on food, supplies, space. So having children was discouraged. People didn't want to bring children into a dying fleet. Movement between ships was prohibited. It's like…" She frowned. "It's like a generation has just been lost. Gone. Only it's not because it's a generation that never existed.

"It's not right and it feels like we, the fleet, I mean, lost something. I want to be a Hopper to get that back. To bring the fleet back to the point where there are children running about again."

They were all silent for a few moments. Emil felt awkward to have heard Cali's earnest reason, but he couldn't say why.

Mia broke the silence with a sigh. "Well then, you best recover quickly so you stop missing the Hops. Not to mention my thrilling heroics."

The question rattled around in Emil's head. Why did he want to be a Hopper? Protecting the fleet, keeping it supplied felt too simple. It was true enough, but it didn't feel like the whole truth. Mia's reasoning was selfish, but at least it was honest, and he doubted it was quite as self-centered as she claimed. If bhur beast was readily available, it meant the whole fleet was being fed and not just on algae. She wanted to feed the fleet. Cali's reason was about the future, of seeing the fleet continue past their lives and onto the next generation and those beyond. They were both good reasons, but neither of them were Emil's reasons.

It came to him like a light switching on in a darkened

room. Inspiration lighting up all the corners no matter how dim. He wanted to be a Hopper to climb out of his position aboard the ship. To be more than a drudge or the son of a drudge. To have more. But his desire ran deeper than that too. He wanted to remove the barriers.

Cali and Mia, their entire family, had everything they needed. Tablets, clothes, shower privileges, space aboard the ship to live. Not everyone had that. Drudges were the lowest class on the ship. They didn't get new clothes. They still didn't get to shower every day. They didn't get extra food rations. With half the ship in disrepair and vented out into the black, they lived in cramped quarters. Emil knew of some drudges who lived three families deep in a single home. He doubted the sisters even knew about that, secure in their privilege.

That was Emil's reason to fight, to get stronger, to be a Hopper. He wanted the fleet to prosper. He wanted the Courage to be fixed to the point where they could open it up again and give people back the space they deserved. He wanted everyone to have the new clothing they needed, to be able to shower whenever they pleased. The class divide had always been there, but hardship had made it worse. He wanted to obliterate the divide entirely. If the fleet had enough supplies. Enough parts, enough food, enough clothes, enough everything. If the fleet had all of that there would be no need for the class divide to be there at all. Drudges, officers, Hoppers, techs could all live equally.

That was his reason. His purpose. And though he wouldn't tell the sisters, already knowing they wouldn't understand, he would hold his reason close. He would nurture it, fuel it and let it burn hotter and brighter. And now he knew his goal, he would train even harder to accomplish it.

Chapter Seventeen

A day off. Iro had almost forgotten such a thing existed. He hadn't had a day off since… He tried to recollect. Certainly not since starting work in the tech core back on the Courage. Back then, titan 01 had just exploded. He had just lost Neya and it felt as though all the joy had been sucked out into the cold void with her. He remembered feeling tired all the time, sick to his stomach whenever he tried to eat anything. He remembered the guilt, the damning certainty that it was his fault because Neya didn't have her titan-forged sword with her.

He'd started taking shifts in the tech core to distract himself at first. The Courage was in a bad state even then and the techs needed all the help they could get. After that, he just kind of fell into the job. And it did become a job. A full-time job with no days off. At least he got to work alongside Roret.

Iro missed the younger boy. He had made new friends on the Eclipse, but none like Roret. None where the friendship just felt easy. Where nobody had to try to be friends. Iro missed his mother, too. The comfort of her always being there. The smell of her, the sound of her voice.

He wiped a sleeve across his eyes. This day off was making him homesick. He had no idea what to do with himself. Master Rollo had told them all to take the day off and relax.

All the others had family they could visit aboard the ship. Iro's family was back on the Courage and the fleet had yet to reinstate ship to ship social visits.

So Iro had a day off and nothing to do. He could

have stayed in his quarters and caught up on the bestiary reading, but that felt too much like work and he didn't want to disobey Master Rollo. Besides, their quarters smelled too much like Bjorn, Torben, Arne, and Iro himself. Regardless of how many times they all showered, there was a smell to the quarters that even Iro found undeniable. He needed some fresh air.

He realised he'd never actually explored the Eclipse. Ever since arriving, his days had been structured and organised. Weight training, running, eating, showering, training, it was all laid out before him. He'd been to the Hopper pods once, run around the ship with Bjorn and the others, but he'd never looked at his surroundings. Iro let his feet guide him now, strolling through the ship without destination or purpose.

It really was so much cleaner than the Courage. The bulkheads weren't rusting, the walls were freshly painted and cleaned. The smell was less stale air with a hint of unwashed bodies and burning air filters, and more acrid disinfectant on the verge of stinging his nose it was so strong. He smiled at those he passed and most of the people smiled back. Techs going about their day, officers running to and fro, drudges laughing with each other. It all seemed so much more relaxed than it had on the Courage.

The Eclipse was a much larger ship, too. Almost twice the size and none of its sections were closed off to the cold black outside. He walked through a housing section where people sat in their quarters with their doors open. People inside, busy about whatever they were doing, shouted to others across the hall, laughed and joked. On the Courage, you never left your door open. It wasn't for fear of people stealing things. That happened occasionally, but the culprit was always found and punished. It wasn't like they had anywhere to run. It was just not done on the Courage.

People's quarters were private and even glancing in an open door was rude. Here, he glanced in on his way past and a woman mending a jacket with needle and thread smiled at him. A young boy of maybe eight years old grinned and ran out to greet him then proceeded to barrage him with questions about the Hops he'd been on. Iro had to admit he'd only been on two, and the boy soon lost interest.

He soon realised there was a guardedness aboard the Courage that simply wasn't present on the Eclipse. He thought it came from a ship full of people living on the edge. Maybe that wasn't entirely fair, the whole fleet was living on the edge of annihilation, finally saved after making it to titan 02. But, the people on the Courage were living more on the edge, dangling over it and staring into the abyss while the people on the Eclipse could see the edge, were caught in its gravity, but had yet to stare into the nothing.

Iro was so lost in his maudlin thoughts, he wasn't paying attention to where he was going until his found himself in the main tech bay. Engineering on the Courage was an oily place where the air smelled thick and fiery. The air filters rattled loudly enough to make everyone need to shout and were in constant need of replacing due to the fumes coming off the engine. Tetricos, the head tech, said something had cracked in the engine housing a generation or two back and they didn't have the time to power down the engine to fix it, so the fumes it gave off were both viscous and noxious. People who worked too long near the engine passed out and took days to wake.

Engineering on the Eclipse was as clean and pristine as the rest of the ship. The engine itself hummed rather than roared. The air was clear and didn't feel like wading through water, it didn't stick to your clothes and make you smell of fuel. The air filters whined softly above, so quiet Iro could hear that one of them was loose and needed the housing tightened a touch. Even the floor was clean rather than covered in dusty footprints.

"Can I help you, Hopper…" a young tech asked, stopping in front of Iro. She wore a dark blue overall spotted with a few oil stains but nothing worse. Rather than carrying a toolbag, she had a belt festooned with pouches. Iro could see spanner heads, a wrench, a handheld welding torch, loops of spare wire. He'd have killed for supplies like that back on the Courage.

Iro snapped into a salute, straight-backed and with a hand flat against his chest. "Eclipse Iro."

The young tech tried to suppress a laugh, failed and burst into a cackle. Her chestnut hair flopped in front of her face and she pushed it back with a grease-spotted hand. She was perhaps the palest person Iro had ever seen and had a rash of freckles on her left cheek but nowhere else.

"Well, Eclipse Iro," the woman said, putting on a deep, formal voice. "I'm Eclipse Frea. It's quite rare we get Hoppers down in the Burn, so what can I do for you?"

Iro glanced down at his clothes. Of course she had known he was a Hopper, he was wearing his cleanest training uniform, one of the four they had given him when he arrived on the Eclipse. Freshly printed just for him. All the other trainees had more casual clothing as well, but he didn't. All his clothes from the Courage were rags when compared to the Eclipse, so he stuffed them all in a bag and hid them under his bed to forget about.

"Frea," said a burly tech with a bushy black beard. "The secondary thrust feed is sputtering." Iro smiled at that. He knew well enough that half of a tech's job was listening to the ship and hearing what was going wrong before it became too big a problem. He'd spent countless hours listening to the whirring of servos; he could tell the moment they started to grind.

"Shut it down, expunge the feed, flush it with solvent. Then run a level five diagnostic and lets hope the ship doesn't throw any errors at us." Problems with the mechanisms, the tech core could fix. Errors within the systems were something else. Iro had often wondered why and how such important knowledge had been lost, but no one understood how the systems worked, and the tech core just hoped they wouldn't break down.

"You're in charge?" Iro asked.

Frea raised an eyebrow at him. "That surprises you, Eclipse Iro?"

"No!" Iro raised his hands in surrender. "I mean, yes. But it shouldn't. Sorry. I come from the Courage and our… their head tech is older than the titans."

"Huh. It's you. I heard they found a Corsair from one of the low ships." Iro frowned at the term. That was the second time he'd heard it. "So what do you want, Eclipse Iro? Light in the training hall flickering?"

"You can just call me Iro."

"Oh, can I? Well, thank you, Hopper. I'll be sure to do that with your permission."

Iro winced. He hadn't intended to annoy the head tech of the entire ship. "Sorry."

"What do you want, Hopper?" Frea asked.

An idea struck Iro. "Do you have anything that needs fixing?"

Frea's eyes boggled and she shook her head. "Really? A low shipper steps on to my barge and thinks she needs fixing?"

"I was a tech aboard the Courage."

"Good for you, Hopper. You should probably know then that we're sailing through space in a bucket we barely understand. Everything needs fixing all the time." She leaned forward a bit, stared at him until he looked away.

"But my crew can handle it. We don't need a low shipper messing with systems he doesn't understand."

Iro thought that was a little harsh considering Frea had just pointed out none of them understood the ship. But he could see her point. He turned away. "Sorry." Then he stopped. He had to tell someone even if it was someone who hated him. "I just… I used to be a tech and I'm feeling homesick, so I thought maybe you had something I could fix. I'll go."

He made it two steps toward the exit. "Wait," Frea said. Iro turned to find her frowning at him. "What did you work on back on the Courage?"

"Servos mostly," Iro said. "Fixing doors and dummies and feeds."

"You know how to strip a rusty gear?"

Iro nodded.

"Come on then."

Frea marched him into a dimly lit corridor off the main engineering, then pulled open a door into a storage cupboard. The door grated like gravel as she wrenched it open.

"I could look at the door if you like," Iro said, aiming for helpful. Frea shot him such an incredulous look he actually stepped back from her. "Or not."

She fished out a large box filled with old gears. Some were coated in rust, others were chipped or stripped down to nubs. "Here." She hefted the box into Iro's arms. "I've been meaning to get someone to sort this forever. I've got no space for you here, so you'll have to take them elsewhere to sort. And if they're not back by tomorrow, I'll come looking for them." She leaned closer again. "Do not make me come looking for them." With that, she turned and strode away leaving Iro alone with a box of useless scrap he had foolishly committed to fixing.

Iro considered where to do the work as his feet carried him from engineering. He still didn't want to return to his quarters yet, Master Rollo had banned them all from the training hall, and he didn't think cleaning rusty gears in the mess hall would go down well. They ran past an observation lounge each day, and there were usually some tables free, so he made his way there instead. Most ships had at least one observation lounge, a place where the crew could relax and look out upon the stars or the titan. The Eclipse had three. Iro made his way to the port lounge where the windows looked out upon the rest of the Home Fleet. He liked that. He found himself a table, unfortunately away from the windows, dumped his box on the table and sat down to go about cleaning them.

He glanced out the window from time to time as he worked and wondered which of the tiny blocks of metal and light was the Courage. It was impossible to tell from such a distance, but he liked looking. He wondered what his mother was doing, whether she was on the bridge or maybe back at their… her quarters, all alone. He imagined Roret elbow deep in the algae vats again, trying to change the filters.

Iro laid out a few of the worst gears and went to work. Wiping off the loose rust, then oiling, sanding down the gear, oiling again. It was all mechanical to him, something he knew how to do without thinking. It was comfortable, an action he could fall into and not think about anything for a while.

He was lost in the work, probably looking like a bored tech, when he heard voices he recognised a few tables away.

"I'm still not sure it was fair Rollo raked us over the jagged blade for it." Iro recognised Torben's deep voice. The big trainee was trying to keep his voice down, but it carried even over the general hubbub of the lounge filled with chatter. Iro almost turned in his chair and waved to Torben, but that would probably lead to questions about why he was doing tech work, and that would lead to being mocked for being homesick.

"Nah, he was right, Tor." That was Ingrid's voice. It made sense, they were siblings after all. Iro remembered sitting in the observation lounge on the Courage with Neya once. She had pointed out the window to titan 01 and all the places she had visited along its vast hull, sharing a story about each one. Iro had sat there rapt the entire time, wishing he would one day have the chance to go on a Hop with Neya.

"Bah!" Torben said. "It was our first Hop, sis. I think we did alright, everything considered. Even a tree starts off as a seed."

"Shut up!" Ingrid said. "You're not half the philosopher you think you are, Tor. I just hope the low shippers are catching as much of a beating as we did."

There was that term again. Iro had a sinking feeling he knew what it meant. He had seen the differences between the Eclipse and the Courage first hand.

"Their master looked a bit soft," Torben said.

Ingrid made a sound like a hissing hydraulics line. "Did you see the way that girl with the hammer pranced about like she'd done all the work? And that boy just stood at the back. Lazy…"

Iro heard footsteps right behind him, drowning out the sound of the two siblings for a moment. He strained his ears to hear past the noise.

"They're not all bad, sis. Iro is alright."

Ingrid mumbled something. "Tell me, Tor. Does he smell? They all smell."

Torben was quiet for a few seconds. "Yeah, a little bit.

It's not their fault. Their ship is a wreck."

Iro felt like he'd been punched in the gut. He shrank down in his chair, pulled his arms close to his chest. It suddenly felt like people were avoiding him. The table next to his was empty. Was it because everyone knew he was from the Courage? Did they all label him a smelly low shipper and keep their distance? He almost sniffed at himself, fought the urge and won through a sheer act of will.

"Their ship is a wreck because they don't maintain it. They smell because they don't clean it and don't wash. It's laziness, Tor. And look, they send two Paladins out to our eight Corsairs. Two! But they expect the exact same share of the supplies we bring back. Does that seem fair? Does it seem proportionate?"

Iro wanted to flee. To grab up his box of gears and run from the lounge, find a hole to hide in. But if he got up now, they'd notice him. They'd realise he'd heard them and that would be so much worse.

Later, after Iro had finished on the gears and taken the box back to Frea, he slunk into his quarters and climbed into his bunk. His fingers ached from the work of cleaning the gears, and his mind was raw from the thoughts spinning around his head. Bjorn was already in bed, the bottom of his bunk sagging from his weight. He shifted and sighed.

"Good day, Iro?"

Iro considered answering. He could tell the truth about it all, but Bjorn would want to talk about it and Iro just didn't have the energy. He just wanted to sleep. To let that little slice of oblivion claim him even for only a few hours. He turned in his bunk, faced the wall, pulled the pillow over his head.

"Hey, Iro," Bjorn said. "I asked you if you had a good day off?" Bjorn's weight shifted in his bunk again and Iro knew he was leaning out, staring down at him.

Eventually Bjorn sighed and shifted again, the bunk groaning from the strain. "Fine. Suit yourself. Hope you're in a better mood tomorrow. Master Rollo hates sulkers."

Chapter Eighteen

Master Rollo's training settled into a gruelling routine. Each six day consisted of two days of combat training; one spent on the basics running endlessly through chops, stabs, blocks, slashes, and the other day spent on more advanced techniques like parrying, positioning, footwork, and turning a defending move into an attacking one. No member of the trainee group was spared the hard work, or the punishment if they got it wrong. They were all sweaty and exhausted and aching by the time they moved on.

The third day out of six was a relative rest compared to the previous two, but that was a lie. That third day was spent studying, memorising, and being tested on the various monsters and traps documented in the bestiary. They focused mainly on those they would find on the higher levels of the titan where trainees and first gate Hoppers spent most of their time. Master Rollo claimed there was no point learning about Vhar and fingoids until they had a chance of meeting them. Iro occasionally tapped forwards on the tablet to read about the more powerful monsters. He wished he hadn't. There was one monster that attached itself to a person's head, threaded needle-like tendrils through their ear and into their brain, then controlled them like some sort of puppet while also sucking their life out of them to feed itself. Iro had nightmares about that one.

The fourth day was the most fun, and the most painful, of the routine. Sparring. Iro wasn't entirely sure how fighting against other people with swords was supposed to help him prepare for monsters. It was true some of them wielded weapons, most notably the various classes of Vhar they encountered. Vhar behemoths had multiple arms — as many as they could graft onto their bodies from people they had killed — and loved to wield sharp objects in them. Mostly it was crude axes or swords they fashioned from shards of metal, but occasionally one had been known to wield titan-forged blades they had taken from slain Hoppers. Regardless, the majority of monsters would not be wielding weapons, so it seemed odd to Iro that they would spend an entire day learning to fight other people with swords. It was fun though.

Iro was still behind the others in terms of strength, skill, speed, knowledge, and just about every other measurable metric, but that didn't mean they went easy on him. He threw his all into every bout and every opponent he was pitted against. And they all battered him about the training hall like he was a child.

He had expected Torben and Bjorn to be the most fearsome of his opponents, their strength was irresistible. Iro quickly learned that blocking their attacks was pointless and painful. They crushed through his defence with greater power and knocked him flat easily. After a few times of taking that sort of beating, Iro started trying to dodge and parry instead. That led to another discovery. Just because the boys were big and strong, did not mean they were slow. It seemed unrelentingly unfair that both boys were bigger, stronger, and somehow faster than him. Both of them helped him up every time they put him down though.

Unfortunately, Torben and Bjorn were not the worst opponents he was pitted against. They put him down hard and fast with powerful blows that ached for hours, but at least they were friendly about it. Ashvild was another matter entirely. She was cold, calculating, and brutal. Despite the fact they were using training swords, her blade was a blur of motion Iro couldn't track. He flailed left and right, and somehow the tip of her sword still bent around his defence, punched into his flesh, and left him howling in pain. Every time she hit an arm or leg, it went dead for a minute or so, and hurt even worse when it was waking up. And she was never content with a single strike. Each bout she would tag him a half dozen times until he was mewling on the floor unable to stand. That was far more embarrassing than being smacked around by the bigger boys.

Despite all the pain and embarrassment, Iro enjoyed the sparring days. They felt like progress. He promised himself he'd score a hit on one of the others eventually. That would be his starting point. First he'd score a hit, then he'd take a whole match.

The fifth day out of the six should have been the most exciting for Iro. It would have been once. It was a day to train their talents and it was always a strange one. All trainees manifested a single talent, but they didn't all manifest the same talent. Iro was the only one in his squad who could Blink Strike, not including Master Rollo, of course.

Eir and Arne used a talent called Riposte. When their blades connected with an enemy's weapon, they seemed to both attach to it and become weightless for a brief time, allowing them to flow with the enemy attack and be completely unharmed by it. It was fascinating watching Eir catch a swing of Arne's sword and simply float away like a flake of rust on the breeze. Arne wasn't so skilful at the talent and often found himself falling on his ass instead of floating.

Iro practiced his Blink Strike alone. He imagined the attack he wished to make, focused his power through his sword, let it pull him across the hall into his strike. But his crest was still dim, lit like the dying glow of a torch whose battery was too low.

He activated his crest and stared at it, studied it. It had grown, still spreading outwards from the inner circle. A straight line cut through it diagonally, bisecting it, and two flowing lines were snaking out from the centre either side of that bisection. Symbols were starting to appear along the flowing lines. On one side, he was certain a cog was forming, lit in the same ethereal blue glow as the rest of the crest. Opposite it was something else, something that looked a lot like the crossed tusks of a bhur beast. Master Rollo explained that a crest was formed by the experiences of the Hopper. In its complexity, you could find every talent the Hopper had learned, along with symbols referring to many of the most important events in the Hopper's life. It made sense to Iro, that the bhur beast would be there, his first real fight against a monster. Despite the crest growing in size and complexity, it had yet to get any brighter, and that meant he had yet to get any stronger.

He could still only Blink Strike once before the light flickered out, and his crest vanished. After about ten minutes, he could summon it again, perform another Blink Strike. Master Rollo told him he just had to train it. The more he used it, the stronger his current would become, and the brighter his crest would shine. Still, after three of those days training his talent, Iro did not feel like his crest was any more luminescent.

The sixth day, Master Rollo gave them to rest, recuperate ready to start the routine all over again. In truth, those sixth days were Iro's least favourite. Before they found titan 02, he'd have traded a week's algae for a single day off. Now he'd rather be training. He didn't like not having anything to do. Didn't like the reminder that everyone else belonged on the Eclipse, had family to see and spend time with, while he had no-one and nothing. He spent most of those days helping Frea down in the tech core. She still wasn't exactly friendly to him, but neither did she turn him away.

Four weeks into the routine, Master Rollo changed things. Iro and the other trainees turned up ready for basic combat training, armor and swords equipped. Iro still hadn't found time to paint his armor Eclipse blue so the bone white made him stand out, one more thing marking him as different. They found the master waiting for them in the training hall. That was already strange enough, he was always late, but he'd also brought a portable screen with him and had set it up next to his usual perch.

"Come on," Master Rollo said around a yawn. "Sit down. Drop your weapons. You won't be needing them today."

"What about our armor?" Arne asked, already detaching his sword and leaning it against the wall.

Master Rollo rolled his lazy gaze toward Arne. "Lad, if you start undressing in front of me, I'll have you assigned to drudge duty for a week."

Iro sunk down into his usual spot at the edge of the group, closest to the door. He wasn't really sure why he'd chosen that spot, it just kind of happened, though Bjorn still occasionally pulled him into the centre.

"We'll be Hopping over to the titan again soon," Master Rollo said once all the trainees were seated. "And the more you Hop, the more likely you will be to encounter your first gate. So it's important we discuss the gates. You need to know what they are, what you might encounter, and what it means."

Master Rollo fell silent for a few seconds, looking around them all. "I'm going to start with the basics, assuming none of you have a clue what I'm talking about because you're all idiots.

"For a start, gates are linked to your crest." Master Rollo thumbed over his shoulder and activated his crest. It flared to light behind him, a brilliantly burning emerald green. It was huge, easily nine feet tall and wide, dominating the training hall behind the master and so bright Iro had to squint against the glare. It was complex too, hundreds of symbols all swirling around each other, arcane lettering spaced between, intersecting and flowing lines creating a mesmerising pattern Iro could have studied for hours and still have found new sections.

"I have opened four of the Gates of Power, and, as you can see, there are four open locks on my crest." He was right. Threaded throughout the shining sigil were four smaller circles forming a square with lines shooting between them. In each of those smaller circles was an emblem. One of those emblems was the same eye Master Rollo wore on the breast of his armor. The others looked like an ax blade, a length of rope, and a trio of curved lines Iro didn't recognise. There was also a fifth circle near the very top of Master Rollo's crest, but it was empty and detached from the others.

"That the fifth lock has appeared means I am almost ready to open the Fifth Gate of Power. That it is empty, means I have not opened it yet. Understand?"

Arne raised a hesitant hand. "Why haven't you opened it yet?"

Master Rollo's crest faded away, the burning green lines fizzling out. "Because I haven't encountered the fifth gate yet."

"Why not?"

Master Rollo coughed a noise that sounded almost like a growl. Then he pulled a tablet out of the duffle bag and a pen and started scribbling on the little screen. His drawing took shape on the larger, portable screen standing beside him. He drew an archway.

"This is a Gate of Power," Master Rollo said. "Or sometimes this is a gate." He wiped out the archway and drew a door. "Or sometimes this." He wiped out the door and sketched a rough circle. "What's important is a gate can look like many things." He wiped the screen again and went back to the archway. "You'll know it when you encounter yours.

"The gates are locks keeping you from your potential. There are five of them and they exist inside all of you. Not physically inside of you, Ylfa, so don't go cutting yourself open to find them."

"What the scrap?" Ylfa asked. "Why are you picking on me?"

Master Rollo shrugged. "Thought I'd give Bjorn a rest."

"Much obliged, master." Bjorn sent a grin at Ylfa. She glared back at him.

"Think of it like this," Master Rollo continued. "Your body is a ship. There is an engine inside of you and the closer you get to it, the more of its thrust you can use and the faster you can go. But there are doorways between you and the engine. So to get to the engine, you need to find those doorways, open them, walk through.

"Right now, you're about as far from the engine as can be. You can hear the power of it, but nothing more. Trainees like you who haven't opened their first gate can manifest a single talent from their class. You might be able to learn the theory of the other talents, but you can't use them because neither your body nor current can handle the strain of multiple manifestations. Put simply, you're not strong enough and no amount of training will ever make you strong enough."

"So what's the point of all the training?" Torben asked.

Master Rollo sighed and dragged a hand down his face. "Don't be an idiot, Torben. The point of training is to get stronger, to survive Hops over to the titan in the hope that you might have the chance to open your first gate while you're over there."

"But..."

"Because nobody has ever encountered one of their Gates of Power anywhere but on a titan," Master Rollo said. "The gates and the titans are linked in a way we don't yet understand. What we do know is that you will never encounter your gates here on the Eclipse. Only by Hopping."

Iro frowned. He'd never heard any of this. Neya and his mother had always been vague about the gates, despite both having opened at least one. He wondered if they had been so secretive on purpose, if there was some sort of rule about talking to non-Hoppers about it. He held up his hand.

"What are you doing?" Master Rollo said. "Don't put your hand up, Iro. If you have a question, just scrapping ask it."

Iro dropped his hand. "So the first gate will make us stronger?"

"Among other things," Master Rollo said. "Each gate will make you stronger, faster. It will swell the current inside of you and bolster your crest, making it larger and brighter. But they're also more specific than that.

"The first gate will allow you to learn two new Corsair talents. One will manifest on its own, you'll have no choice about it. Some people say that manifestation is linked to your growth as a Hopper. If you're a sneaky scrapper and like to stab your opponents in the back, you might manifest Shadow Blade as your talent. That sort of thing."

Arne opened his mouth to speak, but Master Rollo shook his head at the boy and continued.

"The second new talent you will get to choose."

Master Rollo paused and swept a stern gaze over them all. "This is important. Maybe your most important choice as a Hopper. The talent you choose will help determine how you fight, how you progress. It's important to choose a talent that will work well with those you've already manifested, and that will allow you to fight in a way that suits you and your style. You'll also need to find a Corsair who knows the talent and is willing to teach it to you."

Master Rollo picked up his tablet again and drew a little stick figure with a sword in front of the gate, then drew a little flame around the stick figure. "Along with the two new talents, your crest will grow larger, and will start to fill out with representations of all the talents you learn. That's a lot. It will allow you to be versatile. But strength-wise you will still be too weak to take on any of the more powerful monsters."

He drew a bigger flame around the stick figure. "The second gate gives you a significant boost to the current inside of you. Your crest will vastly increase in luminescence. Most of you currently struggle to use your basic talents once every ten minutes. If you manage to open your second gates, you'll be able to use those same talents ten times every minute with ease. It will also give you a big boost to your physical abilities. Torben, come here."

Torben stood slowly, nervously. Master Rollo stood to meet him. "And by physical abilities, I mean things like speed and strength. It is a big boost." He grabbed the collar of Torben's armor and lifted the boy off the floor, holding him up at arms length with no effort. Torben flailed in panic, but even that didn't cause Master Rollo any problems with holding him up. "If you've ever seen a Hopper leap twenty feet into the air, or match strength with a charging blur beast, this is how. The second gate."

He dropped Torben and patted the boy on the

shoulder. "Go on. Sit back down."

Torben nodded and stumbled away on shaky legs, falling back to sitting as soon as he reached Ingrid. Master Rollo went back to the screen and sat down next to it again.

"The third gate…"

"That's the one that manifests a Hopper's unique talent, right?" Arne asked.

Master Rollo nodded as he drew an even larger flame around the stick figure. "Yes. Hoppers who open their third gates all manifest a talent unique to them." He drew a little sword flying through the air.

"My sister opened her third gate," Iro said. "She was a Paladin and manifested the ability to enhance a Hopper's weapon so it vibrated. Blades that could slice through metal."

"Huh?" Ingrid said. "That's not a Paladin talent. Paladins only buff people not weapons."

"Correct," Master Rollo said. "However, unique talents manifested by opening the third gate are not constrained by class. A Paladin might learn to throw lightning, or a Vanguard might learn to teleport. There's no limits apparently and no way to know what a Hopper's unique talent will be unless they open their third gate." He paused then and winced as if he was debating whether to continue. "But the truth is only about a fifth of all Hoppers manage to open the third gate. Some never even encounter it, and others fail to open it and stall."

Stalling was what they called it when someone failed to open a gate. It had happened to Iro's mother. She had opened her first gate well enough, but had failed to open her second gate, and that had been the end of her Hopper career. Knowing she would never progress any further, she had quit and become an officer instead.

"Know this," Master Rollo said. "You only get one

chance to open each gate. If you fail, that's it. You'll never get any stronger. We don't know why."

"What's your unique talent, master?" Eir asked. "I've always wanted to know. I bet it's powerful."

Master Rollo gave her a half-lidded stare for a few seconds, then sighed. He drew a much larger flame around the stick figure, and drew a beam of something extending from the sword as if the blade was shooting a laser. "Opening the fourth gate manifests what we call a passive talent. These are talents that are always on. They are unique to the Hopper and often completely change the way the Hopper fights. For instance, if a Corsair manifests a passive regeneration talent, they can focus more on offence and ignore wounds that might have been fatal before. Or if they manifest some form of ultimate perception they could see every attack coming before it happened. Or if a Vanguard manifested armoured plates on their skin as a passive talent, it would make showering really scrapping difficult."

"What's your passive talent, master?" Eir asked, needling Master Rollo again.

"Putting up with idiots like you." He drew a flame surrounding the little stick figure that was almost as big as the archway. "The fifth gate, the final one, gives an immense increase to both strength and available current, and allows the Hopper to learn hidden talents." He drew little question marks all over the screen.

"What are the hidden talents?" Iro asked quickly. He wasn't the only one. Almost all the trainees leapt on the question.

Master Rollo shook his head and stabbed the pen all around the question marks. "How would I know? They're hidden. Hunt down one of the Grand Hoppers and see if they'll tell you. Idiot children.

"Look, don't waste your time pondering the higher

gates for now. You need to be concentrating on one thing." He paused, wiped the screen, and looked expectantly at them all.

No one said anything for a few seconds. "The, uh, our first gates?" Iro said, entirely unsure of himself.

"Finally!" Master Rollo exclaimed. "Why is it I've been training you idiots for years and it's the new kid who figures that out?" He sketched a new archway on to the screen, giving it some flourishes that looked like wires crawling around it, then drew a new sword-wielding stick figure standing before it.

"There's only so much I can prepare you for the gates. Each one is different for every person. When you encounter your first gate, it might be as simple as breaking the lock and pushing it open." He drew some chains around the archway, then scratched them out. "Some have a puzzle to solve." He wrote *12+314/9x3 =??* on the screen. "Some require a sacrifice to open." He scribbled out one of the stick figure's arms. "They are personal to each Hopper so there's little I can do to prepare you for that."

He wiped out the chains and numbers, and drew another stick figure flying through the air, sword raised above them. "I can tell you this. The world will freeze in place and go gray. It's a timer." He drew an hourglass on the screen. "You only have so long to figure out how to open your gate. Colour will start to bleed back into the world starting from above you, and if you haven't opened the gate by the time all the colour has returned, the world will lurch back into motion, your gate will vanish, and you'll have failed. Failed and stalled." Master Rollo drew the flying stick figure landing and cutting the other stick figure in half. He scribbled red all over the dead stick figure. "So don't stand around gawking at everything being frozen. If your gate appears before you while on a Hop, push your surprise aside and get on with opening it before you run out of time."

"That's not a lot to go on, master," Ashvild said.

"I know. And I'm sorry about that. Some Hoppers like to pretend we know everything about the gates, but it's a lie. We know they exist. We know they are linked to the titans and to our crests. We know that opening them gives us Hoppers access to greater current and new techniques. That's about all we know. Still, knowing even that little might help you when the time comes."

Master Rollo started drawing on the tablet again. "There's a couple of other things you need to know as well." He wiped out the stick figures and drew a new one with huge muscly arms and something that looked like sparks flying off them. "If you do manage to open the gate, you'll feel strong. Powerful like you could take on the entire titan on your own." He looked up at them all. "Don't trust that feeling. You'll be stronger alright, but that feeling of ultimate power and invulnerability has led more than one Hopper into a fight they couldn't handle."

He went back to the tablet again and started drawing monsters. A little bhur beast that looked far too cute to be the real thing, with great big, round eyes. A fat ball with arms, legs, googly eyes, and pointy teeth that Iro assumed was meant to be a rustling.

"And monsters are always drawn to humans on the titan, but if a Hopper opens a gate nearby, every monster in the vicinity will claw through the walls to get to them if they can." He finished by drawing a seven-armed, musclebound, sword wielding humanoid thing flying out of nowhere to attack the little stick Hopper. Again he scribbled out the stick Hopper with a red smear and looked far too pleased with himself while doing it.

"Any questions?"

"Um, I have one," Eir said glancing around at them

all. "Why did most of the scenarios you drew end up with the little stick Hopper dying?"

Chapter Nineteen

Rollo paced through the corridors of the Eclipse wearing as grim a face as he could manage. It wasn't that he was feeling particularly grumpy, but that he had realised people were less likely to talk to him if he looked like an angry tripcarn. Though he could never really match the monster's ferocity what with having three heads and all. People still waved or nodded or said hello to Rollo as he passed, but none of them tried to stop and entangle him in useless, idle conversation.

He preferred being alone, always had. There was a simplicity in only having his own thoughts to contend with. Besides, other people had opinions and they were usually wrong. Which only reinforced his certainty that most people were idiots. Most people. There were a few Rollo counted as worth putting up with. Frigg was one of them. He hoped to push open the door to the Hopper lounge and find her waiting, a cup of steaming not-coffee in her hand, and a smile on her face. Rollo preferred being alone, but for some reason it was just easier to be alone with Frigg.

Unfortunately, Frigg was not in the lounge. Bolder, however, was. The fat Hopper grinned and waved at Rollo. Rollo scowled back and deposited himself on the couch, spreading out so there would be no room for the other man. He leaned back and stared up at the pristine, uniform ceiling. He spotted a single drop of water beading between two of the panels. That would need reporting to the tech core. Water leaks were a serious problem for everyone.

"We're pushing further into the wing today," Bolder said.

Rollo grunted as noncommittally as he could.

"Level five, if you can believe it, and we've still not found a manufactory." He paused as if waiting for a response. Rollo heard him groan as he settled into the chair opposite the sofa. "Last Surveyor I hopped with was flummoxed. Said they'd not even found a hint of a manufactory. Though he also said we'd barely explored one percent of the wing so far." Another pause. "Or maybe it was point one of a percent?"

"Doesn't sound so strange to me," Rollo said and instantly regretted it. The first rule of being antisocial enough that people left you alone was to never engage.

"But that's it," Bolder said, leaning forward and clearly warming to the topic now he had a participating audience. "It is strange. The Grand Hoppers have us pushing deeper into the titan rather than fully exploring the upper levels. We're running into traps I've never seen before. Finding monsters that are too strong for the level."

The drop of water detached itself from the ceiling and plummeted to burst apart on the sofa next to Rollo. "How strong?"

Bolder grinned, a manic light in his eyes. "Vhar on level four. Not just drones, but casters and brutes. Alexandros from the Stormhold lost an arm three days ago. He's only a second gate Vanguard, not prepared to face a Vhar brute."

"The squad killed it?"

Bolder shook his head. "They couldn't. Alexandros lost an arm, the squad lost its Surveyor. Torn in half when the Brute got hold of her. They dragged Alexandros away and ran."

Rollo pinched his nose. The only time a squad had ever encountered Vhar below level six was when titan 01 exploded and the monsters were fleeing the depths of the dying beast. But titan 02 wasn't exploding. Then again, they still knew almost nothing about the new titan. Rollo admitted it was entirely possible the whole place was more dangerous than 01.

"And still the Grand Hoppers have us pushing deeper," Bolder continued. "Level five already." He shook his head. "I'm scared what we'll run into."

The door opened and Frigg sauntered in. Her uniform was pressed, spotless, and straighter than a sword blade, and her pale hair was artfully tousled. Rollo smiled at her and she shook her head at him.

"Someone's in trouble," Frigg said as she sauntered over to the not-coffee maker.

"Is it me?" Rollo asked. "I have a feeling it's me."

Frigg nodded as she pulled a cup from the overhead cupboard and poured herself some algae. "Oh, it's you, alright. Morning, Bolder."

"Frigg. Have you heard…"

The door opened again and Alfvin stood framed by the bright light of the corridor. Suddenly Rollo remembered he had a meeting with the Lead Hopper, and it was supposed to take place a half hour ago.

"Scrap."

"I knew I'd find you here," Alfvin said coldly.

"In my defence, I only just got here. Ask Bolder."

Bolder's eyes went wide and he stood quickly, the chair cushion sighing with relief, and inched towards the door. "I was just leaving." He paused before the threshold and grinned at Rollo. "Good luck."

Alfvin strode over to the algae-not-coffee maker and shooed Frigg away. She took her cup and retreated to the chair Bolder had vacated, sat with an amused half smile. Rollo had the certain feeling she was going to enjoy this a whole lot more than he was.

Alfvin stood at the counter, brooding over his mug of algae. He seemed tense. Or more tense than normal at least. Just his presence made the lounge feel cramped and hostile. Rollo wondered how it could be so quiet yet seem so noisy.

"How is the boy from the Courage progressing?" Alfvin said eventually, still not turning around to look at Rollo.

"All my trainees are progressing quite well," Rollo said.

Alfvin waved an impatient hand over his shoulder. "I don't care about the others."

Rollo fought the urge to get up and punch the Lead Hopper. It wouldn't serve any purpose but to make Alfvin more hostile, and he already seemed out of sorts.

"Well, I do care about them," Rollo said. "And they're progressing..." He paused, searched for the right word. "Sufficiently." It seemed about right. Certainly none of them were blazing a trail, but none of them were lagging behind either.

"That's because you don't understand the situation." Alfvin finally turned and glared at Rollo. His eyes were red, puffy as though he hadn't slept in days. "None of the others matter because they're never going to be anything but trainees."

The smile fell from Frigg's face. "What?"

Alfvin glanced at her, then back to Rollo. He looked hesitant for a moment, then slumped and shook his head. It was the first time Rollo had ever seen the man look anything other than precisely composed. Even when they were kids, getting their butts whipped by monsters, Alfvin would be the height of formality, probably explaining to the monsters how they were killing him wrong.

"We've been attached to titan 02 for thirty-three days now," Alfvin said. "In that time, Hoppers from all over the fleet have made over one hundred Hops. Trainees from some of the upper ships have made close to five Hops already."

That made sense. The Legacy families lived aboard the upper ships. Those Hopper families who had been producing powerful Hoppers for generations. Three of the four Grand Hoppers came from Legacy families. It made sense they would want their youngest members making as many Hops as possible. It had been five years since any trainee had opened their first gate, the Legacy families would count it as a point of pride to have one of their youngsters be the first since arriving at the new titan. It would be one more piece of evidence that the Legacy families and the upper ships were better than the rest of the fleet. Still, Rollo didn't care. Let them have their political games and their useless pride.

"Do you know how many trainees have encountered their first gate since we arrived?" Alfvin asked.

"You know I don't," Rollo said. "So stop being an ass and tell me."

"None."

"None?" Frigg asked.

Alfvin turned his puffy gaze her way. "Not a single one. Neither have any Hoppers encountered their next gates. Since arriving at titan 02, it appears every trainee and every Hopper in the fleet has stalled."

The entire fleet. Every Hopper. It was terrible to imagine. It meant that even though they had found salvation at the new titan, the fleet was still dying, just more slowly. As Hoppers died of age or illness or injury, there would be no replacements. If progression was stalled, then delving deeper into the titan was suicide.

"Why are we only just hearing about this?" Frigg asked, her voice high with tension. Of course, she was only a third gate Hopper. She might have been keeping it from all the others, but Rollo knew how eager she was to open her fourth. And now she'd just been told she never would. "This is… It's important. It's… Why doesn't everyone know?"

Alfvin sighed. "Because of how you're reacting right now. It would cause a panic. So many of us are so focused on progressing that it would destroy morale across the fleet. The upper ships have decreed silence on the matter until the Grand Hoppers come up with a solution."

He was right. Hoppers would lose the will to board the titan and fight. They were still resupplying half the fleet with water and fuel, still setting up regular Hops to bring back food that wasn't grown in a vat. They still hadn't found anything resembling coffee. It would also mean the trainees, all of the trainees, had no hope at all. They would never even open their first gates. That meant they would all have to retrain as officers or tech or drudges. Rollo really hated to agree with Alfvin, and hated to agree with the upper ships even more, but they were right; a fleet-wide stalling of progression *had* to be kept secret.

"That's why you're asking about Iro," Rollo said as he realised the truth. "The Grand Hoppers think he's the solution."

Alfvin sipped at his algae and winced. "*I* think he's the solution. The Legacy families think he's a problem. The Grand Hoppers have yet to weigh in."

"He's the first spontaneous manifestation of a talent in generations," Frigg said. She was hugging her own cup of algae as if it was providing some comfort. "His mother was a Paladin. His father…" She paused and looked to Alfvin.

"Was talentless."

"And yet he manifested as a Corsair," Frigg finished. "If he can open the first gate…"

Rollo nodded. "Proof that there's hope for the fleet."

"That's one way of looking at it," Alfvin said. "But it's not the way the Legacy families view it."

"Because he's from a lower ship?" Rollo asked.

Alfvin grunted an affirmative. "The Legacy families' status and political power aboard the upper ships is based solely upon their ability to produce powerful Hoppers with each generation. If they can no longer do that, but talentless techs from the lower ships can, then it throws the whole system out of balance."

"But that's politics," Frigg said. "Surely the survival of the fleet is more important."

"Don't be naive," Alfvin snapped. "If the Legacy families wanted the Courage boy…"

"Iro," Rollo said. "His name is Eclipse Iro."

Alfvin shot Rollo a venomous look. "If they wanted him to succeed, they would have taken him aboard one of the upper ships. Probably the Sphinx. There, the Darwish family could have taken control of his training and, should he succeed in opening the first gate, they would likely have welcomed him into the family as a foster child. Any talk about him ever having come from the lower ships would be quashed."

"But they didn't know about the stalling at the time," Rollo said. "So they let him come here and hoped he'd vanish into obscurity."

"Exactly," Alfvin said. "Mid ships like the Eclipse are unimportant to the Legacy families. Right now we remain unimportant because the Courage boy has not opened the first gate. But when he does, he will become both a problem to them, and also a lifeline to the survival of the fleet."

"OK," Rollo said, holding up his hands in defeat. "I get it."

"I don't think you do. Push him."

"I've been pushing him, Alfvin." Rollo shook his

head and mourned the quiet of the lounge. "I've been pushing all of them."

"Not hard enough."

"They fought a bhur beast. Ten trainees killed a monster without any help from a Hopper."

"Bah!" Alfvin pushed away from the counter and started pacing. "You should have had the Courage boy take it on alone."

"You're scrapping mad." Rollo couldn't quite believe what he was hearing. It would be suicide for a single trainee to take on a monster like a bhur beast alone.

"It's well-known that hardship and peril are key factors in encountering the gates, along with training. If the Courage boy is to open his first gate, his life must be put at risk."

"That's only one theory," Frigg said quickly, a concerned frown creasing her brow.

"It's the preeminent theory. Have you ever known anyone to encounter a gate when sat idly at the back of a fight?"

"He's only been on two Hops," Rollo argued. "Give Iro time."

Alfvin waved a dismissive hand in the air. "You make my point for me. How many Hops did it take you to open your first gate, Rollo?"

"It's hardly fair to compare."

"How many?"

Alfvin knew exactly how many. He'd been beside Rollo every step of the way as trainees. "One. But considering it was to save you from a marsh mite, I'm starting to wish I hadn't."

Alfvin snorted and thrust his hand behind him, pushing his mostly empty mug onto the counter. He only half managed it and as soon as he took his hand away the cup pitched over the side and clattered to the floor, spreading warm algae all over the white tiles. Alfvin stared down at the mess for a few moments. It was unlike him, being so uncoordinated.

"Regular Hops," Alfvin said eventually, still staring down at the seeping algae. "Every fifth day." He finally turned from the mess and strode towards the door. "I'll be organising all your Hops from now on, I think."

Rollo waited until Alfvin was gone. He knew the man well enough to know there was no point arguing with him further. If Rollo wanted the decision overturned, he'd have to go over Alfvin's head to the Grand Hoppers. But if Alfvin was right, then bringing Iro's case before them and the Legacy families might just put Iro in even more danger.

"Scrap it!" Rollo hissed. "He's a mad man. Iro has only been a trainee for a few months."

"What if it works?" Frigg said. She was frowning at the mess of algae on the floor. "What if Iro is the start of a new generation of Hoppers, and pushing him opens up the door? If progression really is stalled, then kids like Iro might be the only hope we have left."

"What if pushing him into Hops before he's ready gets a young boy killed?" Rollo asked. It was all too soon for the boy, he could barely hold his sword firm without trembling.

"I'm not saying it's right, Rollo. I'm asking what if Alfvin is right?"

Iro couldn't sleep. It wasn't just Bjorn's bed rattling snores, or the way his right shoulder ached whenever he rolled onto it. There was a mixture of excitement and nerves and fear all souring up his stomach. They were going on another Hop tomorrow, not to the dome, but delving deeper.

Master Rollo had seemed hesitant to tell them, almost

like he was trying to stop it by sheer force of will. They weren't just Hopping to an explored area this time. They would have a Surveyor with them, and would be venturing out into parts unknown. The thought of it sent a thrill running through Iro and he wondered if it was the same nervous energy his sister used to talk about. The fear that followed curdled the energy though. He wasn't ready. *None of us are ready. What if we encounter traps? Or monsters more dangerous than a bhur beast?*

He gave up trying to sleep and grabbed Neya's sword before slipping out. He wandered through the sleepy halls of the Eclipse and tried to trick himself that he didn't have a destination. It was a lie. He was closing in on the training hall and felt a flutter pass through his chest. Iro hoped to find Eir in the hall. They'd met three times now at night, when most of the ship was asleep. Twice they'd gone through extra training, Eir teaching him some gruelling stretches, instructing him to hold poses which he was certain she made up on the spot to make him look stupid. Though she went through the same sets of stretches and there was no denying she was stronger, faster, and more flexible than him. Without her armor slowing her down, Eir was like a loose hydraulic tube under pressure, twisting and slipping around every strike anyone levelled at her, impossible to pin down.

Iro found his pace quickening as he drew close to the hall and had to force himself to walk more slowly. He stopped outside the entrance, hiding just around the corner, pressed himself to the wall and listened. Silence. He let out a breath and felt himself deflate a little with it, some of the energy leaking out of him. Then he heard a sigh, someone shifting position, the rustle of fabric.

Iro fixed a smile on his face, prepared a line in his head about how she must have been waiting for him, and tried his very best not to rush around the corner into the training hall. He laughed, looked up, the words forming on his lips. And found the training hall empty. He slumped and couldn't help the disappointment welling up inside.

At least no one is here to see how stupid you look.

Dropping Neya's sword by the wall, Iro walked into the centre of the room and lowered into the first stretch designed to loosen up his limbs.

"So eager, you couldn't even wait for me?"

Iro spun about out of his stretch, tripped on his own feet, and crashed to the ground in a tangle. He look up at Eir standing in the doorway, an amused eyebrow quirking upwards. He grinned at her and reached for something to say.

"I thought you practiced me more." He frowned even as the words left his mouth.

Eir laughed at him. "Was that supposed to be a complete sentence?"

Iro struggled back to his feet and tried to remember what he had meant to say. "I thought, uh, you needed more practice than me?" It still didn't make any sense.

"OK," Eir slipped into the room and patted him on the shoulder. "You keep telling yourself that. Lunging Shark, go." She stepped forward, slowly lowering onto one knee, raised her arms above her head, dipped forward, touched the ground, then straightened her back and brought her arms down in a wide circle. Iro attempted to follow her through the same stretch and almost managed it. His legs wobbled a little and he lurched onto one knee, couldn't quite lower himself enough to touch the ground with his hands without cheating. Flexibility was apparently a process. Thankfully, Eir never mocked him for failing.

"What is a shark?" Iro asked. All of the stretches she led him through had strange names and he understood so little of them.

"I don't know," Eir admitted as she led him through the Reclining Camel stretch. "My mother taught me all the movements and I don't think she knows either. And she learned them from her mother who probably didn't know. Just stupid names, I guess."

"It sounds made up," Iro said. "Or perhaps it's a type of mold."

They flowed through a few more stretches, ending in the hated handstand. Or as Eir called it, the Exploding Star. She rolled onto her hands, slowly raising her legs to point at the ceiling, then lowered her legs sideways until she was doing the splits. Iro, on the other hand, flailed onto his hands, tried to get his feet off the ground, toppled sideways and sprawled ungainly on the floor. Eir giggled at him. She might never mock him about failing the rest of the stretches, but she was merciless when it came to the Exploding Star. Luckily, the giggling unbalanced her and she had to quickly roll out of the stretch before she ended up sprawled next to him.

"How about some sparring?" Eir suggested. She extended a hand to him.

"Sparring with you?" Iro asked. He took her hand, felt a tingle of energy race through him and up his spine. She pulled him to his feet. "You mean you want to knock me around the hall a bit?"

"Hey, you almost dodged one of my attacks earlier today."

"That would be the feint you wanted me to dodge, so you could land the real attack."

"Yes. And you were very close to dodging the feint."

"But not the follow up stab?"

"Oh no." She grinned at him. "You were never dodging that."

They picked their training swords from the wall and

settled into stances opposite each other. Eir smiled. She always wore a slight half grin whenever she was getting ready to fight. Iro watched her, stared at her smooth, pale skin. Her blue eyes. Her bristly scalp. Her lips. Then her smile vanished and he readied himself as she darted in for the attack.

Eir thrust her slender sword at him and Iro flung himself to the side, bringing his own blade up to parry. Eir flowed into her next strike, whipped her sword up, then back down. Iro tried to twist out of the way, but her sword smacked against his forearm with a stinging pain that quickly faded to a bruised ache.

"That's one for me," Eir said as she took a few steps back to start all over again.

"We'll add it to your towering pile of wins," Iro said sulkily.

"Oh, don't pout. You'll wi.."

Iro rushed her, grinning as he delivered a cross slash with enough power to break through the guard of her wispy sword. Eir leapt into the air over his strike, her back foot touched the flat of his blade and she seemed to spring off it, twisted in mid-air, kicked him between the shoulder blades. Iro stumbled forward, turned, sword brought up… It was too late. Eir was standing just a couple of feet away, the tip of her blade hovering before Iro's face. She grinned at him.

"One day that pile of wins is going to topple over and crush you," Iro said as he backed away a few paces.

They clashed another dozen times. Each trading of blows ended the same way and Iro was sore all over again by the time they quit. A couple of times he almost came close to landing a hit, but Eir always seemed to twist or caper away. Even without using her talent she was slippery as wet soap. The only victory he could claim was that she was sweating by the end of their session. It was a poor victory, but Iro clutched at it all the same. They placed their training blades back on the wall and sank down to sit beneath them, side by side, catching their breath.

Iro found himself unreasonably aware of how close they were, their shoulders touching as they slumped against the wall. It sent that same tingle of energy through him as when she took his hand to pull him up. Exciting and terrifying all at once, just like the upcoming Hop.

Say something funny. He tried to think of something, anything to say. His mind drew a blank.

"You're really putting in the effort, Iro," Eir said after a while. "It shows."

Iro scoffed. "Doesn't feel like it." If anything, he thought he was getting worse. He felt slower not faster. He could clearly see how clumsy most of his attacks were.

"Really!" Eir said. "Wasn't too long ago you couldn't even hold a sword still, let alone swing it. And honestly, you almost got me once or twice there."

She was humoring him, he knew, but it felt good all the same. Yes it also felt awkward, like praise he hadn't earned.

"No one else is putting in the effort you are, Iro," Eir continued. "Well, except me." She turned her head and grinned at him. "But I'm special."

"You are," he said and somehow it felt like the most awkward two words to ever leave his mouth. He felt hot all of a sudden and had to turn and look away. "Why do you put in the extra effort?" he asked quickly, hoping to find a more comfortable subject. "You're here almost every night."

Eir shrugged, her shoulder rubbing against his. "I told you, I don't sleep much."

"But you don't have to come here and train. Why do you?"

Eir was silent for a while and Iro glanced at her to

find her eyes closed, a frown on her face. Then she sighed. "My mother is Eclipse Eyildr."

The name sounded familiar. Iro had definitely heard it before. Then like water draining away to reveal the plug, he realised it. "Your mother is the Silver Blade?" he asked, unable to keep the excitement from his voice.

Eir shot him a withering look and sighed again. "Yes."

Everyone in the fleet had heard of Eclipse Eyildr, the Silver Blade. She was even more famous than the Grand Hoppers. Neya used to tell Iro stories about her before bed. She'd tell him how she dreamt of one day getting to be in a squad with the Silver Blade. There were so many tales about her too. How she single-handedly stood against a swarm of two thousand rustlings, her arms never tiring and her blade never losing its edge. Or that she had one of the most powerful unique talents anyone knew of, the ability to store her current inside objects she touched, like a battery, and then retrieve that energy to give her a boost, or make the object explode, or a hundred other uses.

Iro's favourite story was how the Silver Blade had faced off against the Vhar warlord back on titan 01. Neya loved telling that tale, and it got more and more extravagant every time she told it. The Vhar warlord was the most powerful Vhar anyone had ever seen. Some said it was even the progenitor of all the Vhar. Where most of the Vhar were huge monsters, the warlord was no taller than a human. It had four arms and wielded a blade in each, and had a host of fist-sized flying creatures that crawled out of holes in its back whenever it fought. Each of those flying monsters had teeth that could sheer through normal steel and moved with a lurching speed no one could match. Yet the Silver Blade had challenged the Vhar warlord to single combat, and she had won. She was a legend.

"No wonder you're so good," Iro said. "I don't feel nearly so bad about you kicking my butt about for the past hour now."

Eir was silent. She even shifted away from him a little and he had the sudden thought he'd said something horribly wrong.

"Sorry," Iro said quietly, not really sure what he was apologising for.

Eir shook her head. "It's not your fault, Iro. Everybody always says the same thing when they realise it. *You must be so lucky*. Or. *What's it like having such a heroic mother*. And it's fine. She's fine. She's great. She's always been there for me when I needed her. She gave me extra training even before I manifested a talent." Eir went silent again for a few seconds. Then she shook her head and leaned against Iro's shoulder again.

"It's not her. It's everyone else. They all expect me to be her. Like I have to be a small version of the Silver Blade. I used to have long hair. People kept telling me I looked just like her, so I shaved it off." She ran a hand over her stubbly scalp.

"Oh, that's why," Iro said. "I just figured it was to make you more aerodynamic. It's clearly how you keep ducking under my strikes."

Eir snorted and shoved her shoulder against him. "Idiot." Then she sprang up onto her feet and strolled towards the door. "I'm off to bed. Don't stay up too late, Eclipse Iro, we're Hopping tomorrow." She pulled one leg up and hopped out the door.

Iro groaned at the joke, but she was already gone. He waited a few minutes, still leaning against the wall, his eyelids growing heavy. He wondered if Eir hated being compared to her mother because she thought she could never live up to the Silver Blade, or because she didn't even want to try.

Will I ever live up to Neya? Can I? She had been a Paladin, and tipped to be rising so meteorically she was bound to be a Grand, the first ever from the Courage. He was a Corsair, and so far not a very good one.

He shook away the maudlin thoughts, grabbed Neya's sword from where it rested against the wall, and made for bed.

Chapter Twenty

The wing of the titan filled the tiny window in the Hopper pod. As the pod thrusted closer, the indistinct peaks and troughs of the titan's skin grew more distinct, giving way to identifiable landmarks. There was a garden dome, there a solar farm, a towering structure that looked like an antenna but Iro guessed was actually large enough to fit half the fleet inside. He couldn't guess at the purpose of it.

The pod flew closer still to the titan and the scale of it really hit Iro. It took a full minute to pass over a single solar farm formed of hundreds of light collecting panels, each one as large as the Eclipse. Closer still and the terrain of the titan's hull became a blur passing by at such speed. Iro could just about make out individual docking ports where the pods could pass through some sort of membranous cross-hatch of lights that seemed to somehow keep the atmosphere of the titan locked inside.

Closer still and Iro could see nothing outside except the blurred ridges of the titan's hull. He was in amongst it all now, surrounded on all sides by its skin. A speck of dust, so small and insignificant in comparison. The thought scared him. It always did when he considered the size of the titans.

Green lights flashed around him as his pod passed through the atmospheric-locking cross-hatch. Then the landing thrusters fired, slowing the pod's speed and he touched down at their destination. His third time on titan 02 and he felt decidedly less nauseous this time. He hoped that meant he was getting used to the trip across.

Iro hit the button to open his pod's door and stepped out into a much smaller space than he had anticipated. Both

Hops before had been to cavernous areas. The engine feeder room had been huge, high ceilinged and stretching so far into the darkness he had never seen the end of it. The garden dome had been even larger, a massive space filled with a lush forest. But this area was much smaller, barely large enough to fit all their landing pods. The walls were dark metal and bowed outwards, and there were strange swirling designs etched onto them. The roof was cold, dark. Behind Iro, he could see the green mesh of light that kept the atmosphere in, and in the other direction, a large archway led into a well-lit corridor that ran deeper into the titan.

All the trainees were exiting their pods. Arne almost fell out of his, collapsed to his knees, and threw up his breakfast. Bjorn sauntered over to him, but Arne waved the bigger boy away and heaved again. Ashvild stepped out of her pod and immediately flicked her flashlight on. All the trainees had flashlights built into the left vambrace of their armor. It was standard design for Hopper armor no matter if it was heavy or light. A flashlight on the left vambrace, and a comms tablet on the right. Except none of the trainees had comms tablets.

Master Rollo stood near the archway at the far end of the dock, talking to a Hopper Iro had never seen before. The newcomer was a large woman and wore a bulky, rigid backpack that had a single mechanical arm poking out the top, a claw resting dormant at the end, a host of tools sheathed along its prehensile length. That was a Surveyor's autodage.

Iro drifted closer, staring at the mechanical arm. The autodage twisted about on its own as he drew near. Its gears whirred and pistons slid as it lowered itself until the claw was of a height with Iro's head. The thing looked like it was staring at him. Except, of course, that it didn't have eyes. A bright light behind the claw flicked on, blinding Iro for a moment. He raised a hand to shield his eyes.

The Surveyor laughed. She was just a few inches taller than Iro and plump. Her burnt orange armor barely looked like it fit her, but then Iro wasn't one to talk. She had an easy smile that looked like she used it a lot. "Careful," she said in a husky voice. "Snappy is curious enough at a distance, but get too close and he might go for your nose." The claw snapped shut with a clack, then drew back and went dormant hanging over the Surveyor's shoulder once more.

Master Rollo raised a hand to shield himself from the claw's flashlight. "Turn it off."

The Surveyor craned her neck to look up at the claw. "Don't argue. He's in charge of this one. Do as he says." A moment later the flashlight went dark.

Iro found himself grinning as he stared at the autodage. "I didn't think they were actually autonomous."

The Surveyor snorted and shook her head. "They're not. They have rudimentary intelligence at best." The claw clacked in response. "I didn't call you stupid at all. Shut up. Rudimentary intelligence, but more than enough personality to fool most people.

"I'm Burning Ember Franka," the Surveyor said with another smile and slight bow of her head.

Iro returned the bow. "Eclipse Iro."

"Is this your first exploratory Hop?" Franka asked.

Master Rollo yawned, his half lidded eyes sweeping over the disembarking trainees, his hands in his pockets. He wore the same suit of lightweight, navy blue armor as the last Hop, though judging by some of the smudges and dirt stains, he hadn't bothered to clean it.

"It is," Iro said when it became clear Master Rollo wasn't going to answer. "Any hints on what we might expect?"

Snappy clacked its claw and Franka nodded. "Traps and monsters most likely. We're not going too deep so it's nothing our Rollo here can't handle." She nudged Master Rollo in the side with an elbow. He sighed.

"Late again," Master Rollo said as he stepped past both Franka and Iro. Four more pods were passing through the green lights. Three of them came to a relatively graceful stop. One of them all but dropped the last few feet to the deck. Iro smiled as he recognised the flightless bird symbol on the pods. It appeared Roret still hadn't got them all working properly.

Franka leaned in closer to Iro and lowered her voice. "Are you aware you're wearing a woman's armor?"

Iro considered explaining again, but decided there was little point. "Yes."

"Hmm," Franka said and sounded almost pleased. "Good on you. Own the choice."

Before Iro could consider what she meant by it, the malfunctioning pod's door slammed open and Mia launched out of it with something like a battlecry. She hit the deck, turned, aimed a kick at the pod. "I hate you. I scrapping hate you!"

Iro saw Ingrid scowl and lean in to whisper to Ylfa. The slighter girl raised a hand and chuckled behind it.

"Master, why do I always get the scrapping malfunctioning pod?" Mia shouted.

Master Tannow climbed out of his own pod. He looked tired, weighty bags under his eyes. He was gaunt too, as though he had lost a lot of weight very quickly. "Because it's your pod."

Mia pulled her great hammer from over her shoulder and raised it high to slam down on the pod.

"Don't!" Master Tannow said, his voice hard and sharp. Mia slowly lowered her hammer. "I'll get the tech to look at it when we get back." He clasped arms with Master Rollo and the two of them moved off a short way to share some whispered words.

"Ooooh," Franka said. "That looks like Hopper stuff." She strolled off to join the two masters. Snappy turned its claw about to face Iro, flashed the light at him once in what felt like a warning somehow, then turned back around again.

Iro spotted Emil standing alone by his pod, arms crossed, frown beaming out at anyone who moved too close. Mia was busy introducing Cali to everyone as though they were all best friends. Eir was next to them. She said something. Mia laughed. Cali glanced over at Iro and shook her head. Iro felt his cheeks warming and had the sudden urge to both run over and demand to know what they were talking about, and also to leap through the hatch of green lights into the cold void of nothing beyond.

"You ready?" Bjorn asked as he sauntered over to Iro and draped a heavy arm across his shoulders. Bjorn was solid enough on his own, but his armor was so bulky it felt like someone had dumped a titan on Iro's shoulders. He slumped under the weight.

"For what?"

"To witness my thrilling heroics!" The bigger boy grinned and pulled Iro uncomfortably close.

"He hasn't shut up about how he's going to save the Hop this time," Torben said as he closed in on them. "A wounded pride burns hotter than any fire."

Bjorn let go of Iro and cracked his knuckles, his gauntlets groaning. "I can admit I did wrong last time. I foolishly tried to steal all the glory myself."

Torben chuckled and Bjorn pointed at him. "You helped. Complicit in my failure and humiliation."

Torben shrugged. "A dull blade should never blame

the whetstone."

Bjorn shook his head, turned, and gestured to the waiting archway. "Not this time. I'll be the point of the spear and lead you all to victory as one unified squad, working together." He raised a fist in triumph.

"Very rousing," Torben said flatly.

Iro grinned at him. "I wonder if Ashvild still has some spots left on her squad?"

"Trainees, line up," Master Rollo called out. He, Master Tannow, and Franka were marching toward them. Iro and the others scrambled to get into a line before the archway.

Master Rollo waved a lazy hand at Master Tannow. "You want to run this one?"

Master Tannow shook his head. "You're the highest ranked Hopper."

Rollo shrugged. "You have seniority."

Franka rolled her eyes at them both and stepped forward, raising her voice to address all the fidgeting trainees. "This is an exploratory Hop." Snappy's torch flicked on and the claw swept the beam over all the gathered trainees. "Thank you, Snappy. They're all paying attention." She shook her head. "Sorry about him, he gets carried away in positions of authority.

"As I was saying. This is an exploratory Hop. That means there's no mission critical resource to bring back. Of course, we may well find something worth bringing back anyway. The wonderful thing about exploring is that titans are full of loot and no one will have nabbed all the best stuff. Half of Snappy's parts, including his processing unit, come from exploratory Hops." Snappy clacked his claw. "Yes. You never know what you'll find. The downside of this is that no other Hoppers have cleared the way. We have no idea what we might run into. That makes things a bit dangerous.

Nobody has disarmed any traps or swept the monster nests, or marked out blocked routes. That's my job, of course, keeping the map updated and spotting… hopefully spotting any traps before we come across them.

"There was one time, during my own training, when my squad stepped on a pressure plate. It wasn't me, but someone missed it." Snappy clacked his claw. "No, it wasn't me. Anyway. The doors slammed shut and the chamber started filling with water. I'm going to assume none of you can swim?"

Iro didn't even know where to start with swimming. Judging by the looks on the other trainees' faces, neither did they.

"I didn't think so," Franka continued. "We should probably hope we don't run into a trap like that then. I can see it now. A dozen drowned trainees all because no one thought to teach you all how to swim."

Master Tannow stepped forward, putting a hand on Franka's shoulder. "I'll think I'll take over."

Snappy lurched at Master Tannow's hand, claw clacking, but Franka smacked the claw off course. "That's probably for the best," she said. "I'll go get started on the first room." She turned and strode through the archway into the waiting room beyond.

Master Tannow blew out his cheeks and nodded to them all. "Stories about drowning aside, she's not wrong. Untriggered traps and monsters nests will be the biggest concern. Keep your eyes open and watch your squad mates. Franka will lead the exploration. Give her room to work. Master Rollo will follow her, and then you all, and I'll guard the rear. If you see or hear anything you think is suspicious, do not hesitate to call a stop and query it."

Master Rollo cleared his throat. "And do not engage any enemies unless I give you permission."

Iro watched as everyone formed into small groups and started out. Bjorn, Torben, and Arne were the first to follow after Master Rollo. Then Ingrid and Ylfa. After them, Eir and Ashvild appeared to have adopted Mia and Cali. Mia was grinning and Eir laughing. Emil trailed after them at a distance, arms crossed and a scowl darkening his face and warning all the others away.

Iro had an odd feeling crawling through his body. An ache in his gut, bony fingers clutching at his heart, his throat tight enough that swallowing was painful. He was scared. Fear locked him in place just like it had on that first Hop. Just like it had when facing the bhur beast.

"You OK, lad?" Master Tannow asked. The old Hopper was standing beside Iro, watching him.

"Mhm." Iro forced a short-lived smile onto his face. He tried to move, to follow after the others, but it was like his legs just refused to budge. He stood there, rooted to the spot.

"I'm right behind you," Master Tannow said. Iro felt a hand on his back and then was pitching forward. His legs lurched beneath him and he stumbled, found his footing, kept walking.

He passed beneath the arch and into the looming corridor beyond, but he couldn't shake the fear. He couldn't dash the feeling that something was about to happen.

Emil tensed. His shoulders bunched, his arms strained, his hands clenched inside his gauntlets. He had to force himself to relax a little. Bunching up wasn't good. If anything leapt out at them, or a trap sprung, he would be too tense to react.

The corridor stretched on so far into the distance it looked endless. Somewhere in front of them, a light was flickering, occasionally casting the entire section into darkness. They'd passed through a similar blinking light just thirty seconds ago, it was disorientating being suddenly and completely thrown into darkness.

It was strange to find such human-sized hallways. Wide enough for three people to walk abreast comfortably, and high enough even the tallest of them would have to jump to touch the ceiling. That didn't make sense to Emil. He had no idea who had built the titans, if anyone had built them, but they were populated by monsters which came in all shapes and sizes, many of them so big they wouldn't fit in the corridor. Yet here it was, almost perfectly sized for a group of Hoppers and leading on from a landing bay.

They stopped as the Surveyor called a halt, she and that contraption on her back were searching the corridor for something.

"Surveyor's talents aren't combat orientated," Iro said as he stopped beside Emil. "They mostly function as trap disarmers, path finders, and combat support." He stared straight ahead as he spoke.

"You think I don't know that?" Emil snapped. "Suddenly you're living on a fancy ship and you think our education is scrap?"

"No. I didn't mean…"

"I've been training to be a Hopper all my life. You've been one for five minutes. So don't go assuming I don't know anything."

Iro's jaw tightened. "Alright then. So you tell me, what's our Surveyor doing?"

Emil shrugged. "Looking for traps."

"How?" Iro asked. "What talent is she using?"

Emil considered stalking ahead, leaving Iro behind, but the group still wasn't moving. And besides, he couldn't let Iro win. Up ahead, he saw the light flickering in the distance. "If you don't know, then maybe it's your fancy ship education that's lacking."

"So you don't know," Iro said. He turned to face Emil, face screwed up in frustration.

Emil rounded on Iro, squaring up to him, their armored breastplates clanging together. "I know. It's you who doesn't know, and I'm not telling you." Iro glared at Emil and Emil returned it as furiously as he could.

Master Tannow cleared his throat behind them. Iro didn't look away, so Emil refused to either. "Surveyors are skilled in a variety of trap detection methods. There are, of course, often visual cues for spotting traps, or sometimes auditory cues. Many Surveyors also have talents allowing them to boost their natural senses. And they affix tools to their autodage that can help in detection. Some Surveyors can even learn talents that allow them to focus the current through their eyes to provide extra-sensory data."

Iro finally lowered his gaze. Having won the staring competition, Emil turned away with a victorious snort, and set to blinking furiously to get rid of the tired dryness. He saw a light flickering behind them. One of the malfunctioning fittings they'd passed under a while ago.

"How long have we been walking for?" Emil asked.

"Not long," Master Tannow said. "Ten minutes. Long corridor, this one."

"Tired already?" Iro asked.

Emil rounded on him. "You'll tire long before I do."

Iro shrugged. "I doubt it. I run every day."

Emil ground his teeth in frustration. It was too much. He'd been training his entire life for this. And Iro had been at it for a few weeks and thought himself better just because he had been transferred to one of the fancy ships. Because everyone looked down on the Courage and he had forgotten where he had come from. Emil clenched his hands into tight fists inside his gauntlets and stared a burning hole through the other boy. "I can run further and faster than you, or anyone on your lazy ship."

Iro's face went red and furious. "Lazy? We're anything but lazy. You think your training was hard? You never did anywhere near as much as we have to."

"OK, enough," Master Tannow said. He stepped forward between them, put a hand on each of their shoulders and turned them both away from each other. "Look, we're moving again."

Up ahead, the Surveyor was striding forwards down the uniform corridor. Slowly the entire group got moving. Master Tannow dropped back a few paces and Emil found himself walking next to Iro. At first he thought he was imagining it, but Iro was increasing his pace, slowly moving ahead of him. Emil lowered his head, snarled, and increased his own pace to move ahead of Iro. Soon, they were shoulder to shoulder, surging past Mia and Cali and the two Eclipse girls, the bossy one and the bald one. Emil heard some of them laugh, but didn't care. He wasn't going to be beaten by Iro.

They were almost running by the time they passed the other two girls from the Eclipse, the fat one and the vicious-looking one. The boys from the Eclipse all turned to stare. The biggest of them, a chubby Corsair whose armor looked ill-fitting, grinned as he stepped aside. "Go on, Iro. Show him Eclipse pride." He laughed and the others joined in.

"Run, Emil," Mia shouted from behind. "Don't let Useless win."

Iro lurched forward another step, increasing his pace. Emil matched him, increased his stride, pulled out ahead. They passed the Eclipse boys at a jog. Then the Eclipse master was there, standing before them, one hand in his pocket and the other raised. He didn't look annoyed so much as bored.

"Stop," the Corsair master said.

Iro staggered to an immediate stop. Emil made sure to finish a pace ahead of him. He felt his heart racing, pulse pounding in his neck, breath fast and shallow. Iro was all but panting too, despite the fact that neither of them had even broken out into a run. Just ahead of them, beyond the Surveyor, one of the lights flickered.

"What are you two idiots doing?" the Corsair master asked.

Emil didn't have an answer for the master. At least, not one that didn't seem petty, so he kept his mouth shut.

"We were walking fast?" Iro said. "Well, we started slow, but then Emil pulled ahead so I matched him."

The Corsair shook his head and sighed.

The Surveyor was crouched down ahead of them, staring at something on the floor. Her autodage clacked its claw a couple of times. The Surveyor nodded. She stood and turned to face them. "You two seem to have a lot of energy. Do me a favour, run back to the dock."

"Sure," Iro said.

"Why?" Emil asked.

The Surveyor glanced up at her autodage's claw as it hung above her. It clacked. "I, uh, dropped something. A battery pack? Yeah, that'll do. Run back and get it for me. Make it a race."

Emil sighed, about to tell her to go back and get her own damned battery, but Iro took off, jogging back past the Eclipse boys. Well, Emil wasn't about to let him win. He launched into a sprint, trying to ignore the jeering of the others.

Iro had a head start, but he was shorter than Emil and his longer stride allowed him to catch up before they raced past Master Tannow who had his head in his hands.

They ran along the gloomy corridor side by side. Emil glanced at Iro, found the other boy staring back. The corridor passed in a blur of dark metal, pale yellow light, featureless walls. Up ahead, the light flickered, momentarily casting the corridor in complete darkness. Emil didn't like running into or through darkness, but he didn't have time to stop.

The light flickered again and for a moment he could see nothing. Not the floor beneath his pounding steps, nor Iro running beside him. Then the light flicked back on and the Corsair master was right in front of them. The Surveyor had stepped to the side, leaning against the wall, but the Corsair master was still watching down the corridor. Emil lurched to the side to avoid the master, Iro threw himself to the other side. They both stumbled. Emil managed to slide to a stop, panting and sweating, heart racing. Iro tripped, tumbled, crashed to the ground and rolled to a stop, moaning. The Corsair master let out a surprised cry, his eyes wide with confusion.

"What the scrap just happened?" the Corsair master asked.

Emil leaned against the nearby wall, still struggling to catch his breath. Still struggling to understand. They had been running away from the group, back towards the docks. And then… suddenly the group was in front of them. He coughed, sank down to sit on the floor, his back to the metal wall.

"I thought as much," the Surveyor said, one hand on her chin. "We're caught in a trap."

Chapter Twenty-One

Iro cradled his left hand to his chest. He'd skinned his palm when he fell and it stung like scrap. It was all fine and well his mother's old, dented armor covered his chest, arms and waist, but he decided he needed full gauntlets and some leg plates sooner rather than later.

"It's not uncommon for rooms just beyond docks to be trapped," the Surveyor said. "Some people think its to keep monsters away from the docks themselves, though I wonder if it's more to trap unwary Hoppers."

"I thought we brought a Surveyor along to stop us triggering traps?" Arne said. He had his arms crossed and was hunched on himself, glancing about fearfully.

"Don't be a smartass, Arne," Master Rollo said. "You're not nearly bright enough."

Franka chuckled. "Well, the problem is, you see, a lot of the traps we're encountering are entirely new to us. New titan, new problems to trip us up. We, the Surveyors that is, are keeping a compendium, but this is the heart of exploration. The fun part. The striking out into the unknown. I don't even know what triggered this trap, let alone how it works. All new traps and all new triggers.

"Just five days ago, Reinier came across a brand new trigger. It turns out it measured the ambient temperature of the room and sprung the trap when it raised. Very devious. It obviously wouldn't trigger if just one Hopper entered the room, but when the whole squad were in, the temperature increased and suddenly there were saw blades launching from every wall and angle. It got quite messy. Xavier, the Vanguard of the squad, lost his foot. Merelith, the Mage…"

"What about this trap?" Master Rollo asked.

"Well, I have no idea what the trigger is. Or was. Perhaps it detected motion or temperature or pressure."

"Isn't it your job to know?" Emil asked. "Why else have a Surveyor?"

The others were drawing closer now, listening in, everyone cramped together.

"Disarming, escaping, circumnavigating traps is my job," Franka said. "Not understanding them. But I would say it appears we are most likely trapped in some sort of loop. Perhaps there's a form of portal in the flickering sections of corridor. Or maybe we've been removed from time and space entirely and this corridor is all that exists now. At least for us."

A leaden silence settled over the group. Iro felt a shudder start at his toes and run all the way up him as he considered the possibility of being stuck in this dull section of corridor for the rest of his life.

"How long will it take us to starve to death?" Ingrid asked in a quiet voice.

"Weeks probably," Franka said cheerfully. "It's amazing how long a person can go without food. Much more likely we'll die of thirst first." She chuckled. "Probably more likely that Rollo here will go mad and kill you all long before that."

Master Rollo stared at the Surveyor. "It's a distinct possibility. How do we get out?"

"Now there's a good question," Franka said. She clapped her hands and Snappy clacked his claw in time. "I don't know. But I'll get working on it right away. Out of the way, kids." She started walking back the way they had come, wading through trainees trying to shift aside to let her pass.

"What should we do?" Ashvild asked.

Master Rollo shrugged as he leaned against the wall and sank down until he was sitting. "Try not to get in the way." He closed his eyes and in only moments looked like he was asleep.

The light in the corridor just ahead of them kept flickering. Iro stared down the dimly lit hall. It did seem to stretch on to forever. He was still peering into the gloom when the light flickered off and on again, and Franka was standing there where she hadn't been just a moment ago.

"Curious," the Surveyor said. "Which of you youngsters fancies going for a run next? Preferably someone who can keep a steady pace."

Iro stood up, ready to volunteer, but Bjorn put a hand on his shoulder. "You can't keep a steady pace to save your life, Iro. It's always faster and faster with you. Besides, I can run all day. I'll go. Where do you need me to run?"

"Just down the corridor," Franka said with a wave. "Clear a space for him. Keep running even when you loop back around. Don't stop until I say so."

Bjorn turned and set off at an even jog.

"You," Franka said, poking Snappy's claw. "Keep his time." She shuffled down the corridor, staring at the wall on one side, occasionally making marks on it with a pen.

Iro squeezed past Arne and Ylfa, apologising, their armor scraping, and stood next to Franka as she pressed her head against the wall. "Is there anything I can do?"

"Out of the way," Bjorn called as he reappeared in the flickering light and jogged past them, grinning like they weren't all caught in some devious trap. Snappy clacked after him.

"What I wouldn't give for a pair of Oversight Goggles," Franka said. "Alas, I never get to go on any spire climbs."

"Spire climbs?"

"On the outside of the titan there are towers, or spires. Very dangerous places filled with the worst traps and monsters you can imagine. But you can find some tasty loot at the pinnacle. Oversight Goggles give the wearer five different spectrums of vision. Don't tell anyone, but a pair of those do half the job of a Surveyor for them."

"You don't get to go on spire climbs?"

Franka shook her head as she shuffled sideways another step and ran her hand over a section of wall. "I'm too low ranked unfortunately. Most groups that go on spire climbs only accept Hoppers who have opened their third gates at the least." She glanced at Iro and rolled her eyes. "Most groups only accept applicants from the upper ships to be brutally honest."

"Still running," Bjorn shouted as he thundered past. Snappy clacked again and Franka stared up at the claw quizzically.

Eir laughed. She was standing around chatting with Mia and Cali. Mia was grinning too.

"Another pair of eyes might not hurt," Franka said. "Shift on over to the other wall and look along it, see if you can find anything that looks out of place."

"Like what?"

"Anything. A dent in the bulkhead, a smudge, a big ol' red button saying *press this to escape*. That would be nice. Make my life so much easier."

"How long am I doing this for?" Bjorn asked as he ran past again to another of Snappy's clacks.

"Thought you said you could run all day?" Franka shouted after Bjorn, not taking her eyes from the wall.

Iro rushed across to the opposite wall and started scanning it, despite having no idea what, if anything he was looking for. He looked up the wall, then down, then took a step to the side, repeated.

Bjorn jogged past again twice more, each time to a clack of Snappy's claw. On the third time, Franka grumbled. She glanced up at the claw hanging over her. "You're certain?" Snappy clacked. "Oh dear."

"What is it?" Master Tannow asked. He had taken to following Franka, lending his own eyes to the search.

"Well, I don't mean to alarm anyone," Franka said. "But our stretch of corridor appears to be getting smaller."

"How is that not meant to alarm us?" Ingrid asked, her voice rising.

"I said I don't mean to alarm you, girl, not that I wasn't going to."

"Does that mean I can stop running?" Bjorn asked.

"Nope. Keep it up." Franka looked up at the ceiling for a few seconds and Snappy clacked his claw. "Double check it." Snappy clacked again. "Right then. We have about ten minutes."

"Until what?" Master Tannow asked.

"Until our little stretch of corridor vanishes completely."

"What will scrapping happen to us?" Ylfa asked, her voice high and tight.

"A very good question," Franka said. "I imagine we'll all be crushed. Or ejected into the void. Or maybe just disintegrated."

"Enough!" Ylfa squeaked. "Stop telling us how we're going to scrapping die. What can we do?"

Bjorn jogged past again, silent this time. Iro continued searching along the wall as Franka directed Ylfa and all the other trainees to join him. Before long, they were all searching their shrinking stretch of corridor. All except Master Rollo who continued to sit back against the wall with his eyes closed as if their death wasn't steadily creeping in on them.

Iro worked methodically, up and down the wall then a step to the side. He ran his hands over the smooth metal bulkheads, stared at the edges of each plating in case he could see anything out of place. Time shrank to the regular thud of Bjorn racing past.

He stopped at a bulkhead, his hand pressed flat against it. It felt warmer maybe. He leaned in closer, pressed his ear against it, heard a faint electric hum. There was wiring behind the plating, a nexus of pathways. *How does that help?*

When he pulled away from the bulkhead, he found Eir standing next to him, her own face pressed against the plating next to him. "Am I doing it right?" she asked with a nervous smile. It faded instantly and Iro could see her trembling.

"I think so. I…"

The light flickered, casting them in darkness. When it came back on Iro found himself standing next to Master Rollo still sitting against the wall.

Bjorn appeared, charging past them. "We're getting cramped here," he called, already running towards the end of the corridor again.

"What do we do?" Ingrid shouted even though she really didn't need to given how little space they all had left. "What do we do?"

"Stay calm," Master Tannow said.

Franka ran a finger down the edge of a bulkhead plate, while Snappy tapped at the plate next to her. "Just keep looking for something."

"What?" Ingrid hollered. "Something what? We're all going to die here because you were supposed to detect traps, but instead led us right into one. You have killed us!"

Master Rollo sighed and pushed up and away from the wall. He closed in on Ingrid, took her aside and whispered something to her Iro couldn't hear over the sound of the other trainees and Bjorn's pounding feet, and the electric hum behind the bulkhead.

Something felt wrong and Iro couldn't quite put his finger on it. He pressed his palm against the bulkhead panel again. It was cool to the touch.

"Excuse me," he said as he edged around Eir. She stepped out of the way, watching him.

Iro was underneath the flickering light now. He pressed his hand against the bulkhead and found it warm. The electric hum was louder too.

The light flickered and Iro was standing a dozen feet down the corridor away from Eir. He saw her spin around, worry on her face, before she spotted him.

Bjorn ran past again. The light flickered and he was gone, running past Eir once more. Their stretch of corridor was small now, with fourteen bodies taking up their shrinking space.

Iro pressed his ear against the bulkhead, listened for the electric hum. It was fainter outside of the flickering light. He moved along the wall slowly, straining his ear, listening.

"Excuse me," he said, shooing Arne out of the way.

"You look stupid," Mia said as she backed away from the wall.

"I'd rather look stupid than dead," Iro said quietly, still listening to the wall.

He found a spot where the electric hum was louder, the bulkhead was warmer too. He looked up and found himself roughly halfway between the limits of the corridor.

"Here!" Iro shouted. "Franka. This panel is warmer and there's electrics behind it."

The Surveyor turned from the other side of the corridor. "You're sure?"

The lights flickered at both ends of the corridor and

the panel beneath Iro's hand cooled. "It moved." He pressed his ear against the panel again and followed the hum, stepped to the side once. "It's here now."

Franka hurried over, having to step around Ashvild and Cali. She shooed Iro aside and pressed her own hand against the wall. Snappy started tapping at the bulkhead.

"This is it," the Surveyor said. The lights flickered at both ends of the corridor. "Scrap it. Stop moving." She stepped to the side, found the spot again. "Behind this wall."

Mia stepped forward eagerly, great hammer already in hand. "Need me to smash it?" There was a slightly manic look in her eyes. Iro realised they were all on edge. Their entire world had shrunk down to the handful of steps it took them to cross the corridor.

"We'll call smashing it a last resort," Franka said.

Her crest flared to life behind her in sizzling yellow hues. It wasn't large, only as wide as the Surveyor herself, but Iro could see from it she had opened her first gate. Franka took a small pen from one of her pockets and started sketching lines and circles onto the wall. Iro quickly realised she was drawing a circuit on the wall, mapping out the wires and nodes behind the bulkhead. Her crest remained active behind her. It was all hard lines, and sharp turns and reminded Iro of an electrical diagram, very reminiscent of the circuit she was drawing on the wall. As he stared, he realised that one of the symbols on Franka's crest was glowing more brightly than the others. It was a circular design with small lines and lettering attached that looked a lot like annotations. It had to be a symbol representing a Surveyor talent, and Franka was using it. That was why the symbol was glowing brighter than the rest of her crest. He'd never realised it before, but now he wondered if all crests worked the same way?

The lights flickered again. "Scrap!" Franka snapped.

She stared at the diagram she had drawn on the wall, head twitching as she studied it. Then she started drawing crosses through circles.

"We're running out of room here," Master Tannow said. They were all pressed tightly together now. Fourteen bodies and only five feet of corridor between them. Iro found himself sandwiched between Bjorn and Ashvild, armor crushing him on every side.

The lights flickered again and they all squashed in even tighter. Franka crossed through another circle and stared at the three remaining.

"Well, this is one way to die you didn't mention." Ylfa said with a manic giggle. "Crushed into paste together."

"Quiet," Master Rollo snapped from somewhere.

Franka put a cross through another two of the circles and tapped the last remaining one. "Here. This is the one." Snappy clacked. "It better be."

The Surveyor shifted sideways, pushing Eir out of the way. "Move. Move."

The lights flickered again and Iro suddenly found himself squashed in on three sides as Torben appeared behind him. He really didn't understand how any of this was working. It looked like there was nothing behind Torben but empty space, yet he was squashed up against Iro as if pushed from behind.

"Give me some space," Franka growled.

Ingrid whined. "I can't."

Franka laid her palm against the bulkhead panel and nodded. She glanced over at her drawing on the panel next to her, traced the outline on the new panel, found the one circle she hadn't drawn a cross through. "Here!" She tapped the wall. Snappy clacked. "Just do it!"

Snappy shot forward, claw flattening against the wall where Franka had tapped. A spark of blue electricity arced out from the claw into the wall. Opposite the Surveyor, a door opened up in the wall with a whoosh of air. Arne tumbled out backwards through it with a cry.

"Go go go," Master Rollo said, pushing Eir after Arne. "One at a time. Go on. Through."

One by one they all bundled through the open door into a bright white room with a dark hole in the centre. Iro was one of the last through, only Master Rollo behind him.

They all stood around, breathing hard and staring at the doorway. The light flickered again and didn't come back on. Master Rollo pulled one of his knives out from its belt sheath and tapped it against what appeared to be solid black mass. It didn't ring like metal, but seemed to somehow absorb sound.

"Well," Master Rollo said, sheathing his knife again. "I don't think we're going back that way."

"What?" Arne asked. "How do we get back to the pods?"

All eyes turned to Franka. She was leaning back against the white panelled wall trying to catch her breath and wiping sweat from her forehead. Under the scrutiny of so many stares, Snappy drew back, shrinking to rest his claw on Franka's shoulder.

"I guess we'll have to find another way, won't we," the Surveyor said. "The joy of exploration. Annemie will be so jealous once she hears about this."

"She'll be jealous of us almost dying?" Ylfa asked. She was kneeling on the floor, hugging her arms to her chest as though she were cold, though her bulky blue armor made it look uncomfortable.

"Oh yes," Franka said. "Any Surveyor who discovers a new trap gets to name it. Annemie has been wanting to name a trap for years. It'll kill her that I get to name one first." She laughed and it sounded a bit manic to Iro.

"Perhaps I'll call it a Time Space Loop Crusher."

"It's a bit clunky," Iro said. "How about a Flicker Loop?"

Franka scowled at him and Snappy clacked his claw. "I quite like that. I'm still going to tell Annemie it was my name though." She pushed away from the wall and stretched out her arms, her elbows popping. "You have good instincts for a Corsair," she said with a nod at Iro. "Mostly they just sit about and wait for us Surveyors to do all the real work. Like Rollo there."

Master Rollo turned his head at the mention. His hands were buried in his pockets and eyes half lidded. "I'd have just got in the way like most of these idiots did. Speaking of doing your job." He removed one hand from his pocket and gestured at the room.

Franka sighed and Snappy sagged over her shoulder dramatically. "Surveyors do this. Surveyors do that." She smiled as she picked her way through the trainees to the front of the group. "I hope there's something to fight soon so you can do some work and I can take a break."

The new room they were in was cavernous with a high ceiling. It was cube-shaped, Iro realised, and they were actually standing on an elevated walkway about six feet wide that ran around the full length of the room. Everything was painted a dazzling white, from the panelled walls to the metal floor beneath their feet. He approached the edge of the walkway carefully, inching towards it until he could stare down at the floor below. Only there was no floor. The room extended down into a dark nothing.

Iro thought he could hear something, a whispering maybe. He strained his ears, tried to block out the sounds of the others chatting to each other. There was definitely a noise coming from down in the hole. A breath of wind tickled his face and it brought with it a single word whispered upon it.

"Slug."

Neya?

Iro had a sudden vision of Neya down in the hole, injured, leg broken, calling out for help. Calling out for him. He had to go to her, find a way down, help her, save her. This was his chance to have his sister back. His chance to prove to her that he could be a Hopper just like her. He'd bring her back and she'd come home and they could live together again, a happy family just like before. His mother wouldn't be so stricken with grief. Neya would smile at him, ruffle his hair, and call him…

"Slug."

Iro leaned forward over the edge and peered down into the darkness. He just had to find a way down. Steps or a ladder. Or maybe something just under the walkway. He leaned out further. And toppled forward over the precipice, the void rushing up to meet him.

He lurched to a halt, dangling over the edge. Someone was holding him back. A hand closed around the collar of his armor. Mia grunted in effort and dragged Iro back onto the walkway. He staggered away from the drop, fell to his knees. He was shaking, his breath quick and ragged, his pulse throbbing in his ears. He tried to remember what had just happened.

Neya! Neya is down in that hole.

"Scrapping idiot," Mia said. "What were you doing, Useless?"

"I thought I heard…" Iro trailed off. It was stupid. A trick. It had to be. Neya was dead.

"Heard what?" Mia asked. She turned to the drop, edged forward a little and pulled a face as she peered down into the darkness. "Ohhh…" Her voice went suddenly soft and beatific. "Mom?"

"What?" Cali asked. She strode to her sister's side and joined her staring down into the hole. "Mom!" Both girls leaned out further over the edge.

"No!" Iro shouted. He tried to get back to his feet, but his legs felt boneless and he couldn't move.

Emil rushed forward, grabbed both Mia and Cali by the arms and pulled them back away from the edge. "Idiots!" he snapped. "You were about to fall off the edge…" He trailed off, slowly turned his head to stare down at the hole. He wasn't the only one either. Iro realised that Bjorn and Ashvild were staring over the drop as well, leaning out. Ingrid, a step behind them, had a dazed look on her face, took a faltering step forward to peer into the void.

"OK, back against the wall," Master Rollo shouted. "All of you. Go on." He strode forward, pulling trainees back from the edge and pushing them to the back of the walkway. Bjorn was just about to pitch over into nothing when the Corsair pulled him back. The big boy shook his head and opened his mouth as if to say something, then closed it again. Iro had never seen him look so dazed, even after the bhur beast had smashed him against a tree.

"Go on, back against the wall," Master Rollo said again. He cajoled them into line. "Now, kids…" He grinned. "Hold hands." He waited expectantly.

Iro backed against the wall and looked at the people next to him. A hopeful part of him wishing he'd ended up with Eir, but she was up ahead, sandwiched between Torben and Ylfa. Iro found himself with Mia on one side, and Emil on the other.

Mia snatched his left hand into hers. "Urgh, why are you sweaty, Useless?"

Iro glared at her. "Why does your hand feel like cracked leather?"

"You cheeky ass!" Mia shifted, trying to bring her

other hand up to slap him, but Cali had hold of that hand. She settled on glaring back at Iro and stuck out her tongue at him.

On the other side of Iro, Emil had not taken his hand. The other boy stared straight ahead and didn't so much as twitch when Iro held out his own hand.

Master Rollo stalked down the line, stopped before them, stared down at their hands with an expression that was either boredom or a rage so extreme it had gone flat. "Did you not hear me?"

Iro held out his hand again. Emil hesitated, stared into Master Rollo's half-lidded eyes, then took Iro's hand. He was still wearing his oversized gauntlets and his grip was crushing.

"Good," Master Rollo said and took a step back. He scanned the line of trainees all clutching to each other's hands. "Stay close to the wall, and if you feel any of the others start to drift toward the hole, pull them back. Don't let go."

"What's down there, master?" Iro asked.

Master Rollo looked down into the drop, cocked his head to the side as if listening, then smiled wistfully. "Nothing. Follow the leader. Don't let go."

They skirted the yawning drop, staying as close to the wall as possible as they traversed towards the opposite side of the expansive room where an open door waited for them. Iro heard whispers drifting up from the drop. Some sounded like Neya, calling out to him, others were something else, promises of power waiting at the bottom of the hole. He felt Mia step out of line, angling towards the drop, and pulled her back into place. She shook her head as if to clear away the daze, but kept staring at the edge.

By the time the group had reached the far side of the room, they had all definitely heard the whispers. Only the full Hoppers seemed immune. Every one of the trainees had been pulled towards the drop.

"We call this one a Siren," Franka said as she ushered them all through the open door. "It's a fairly common trap, though it can come in many forms. First time I've seen one trying to get us to throw ourselves to death. The first one I ever encountered was in an exhaust room. I followed the voice of my brother and almost cooked to death in a plume of superheated air." She chuckled as if the memory of almost dying were somehow funny. "It rarely works on anyone who's opened their first gates though. Follow me, kids. Through we go." With that she strode through the doorway into the next room.

Emil shook his hand free of Iro and surged forward past them all, the third person to enter the room. Iro hesitated. He was still holding Mia's hand. She hadn't let go, seemingly hadn't even realised their fingers were still interlocked. She gave him a tug and they were moving forwards into the next room.

Iro glanced back at the white room and the walkway, the drop below it. One corridor and one room out from the dock and they had all almost died twice already. He found it somehow unbelievable that the traps were as terrifying as the monsters, and wondered all over again at how brave Neya had been to face it all with such enthusiasm.

Something squirmed in Iro's gut as he looked back at the traps they had just survived. It was that feeling that something bad was going to happen. It was still there. If anything, it was even stronger now.

Mia tugged on his hand again and Iro passed through the door out of the white room, and turned to see what dangers the next step would bring.

Chapter Twenty-Two

Rollo watched Iro back away from a large rustling. It reached up to the boy's waist and brandished a hand full of rusted shards of metal at him. Iro shifted stance, looked like he was about to strike, then shifted stance again and took another step back. The rustling gibbered something unintelligible and sprang at the boy.

Bjorn roared as he stepped in to save Iro. The bigger boy's sword cut through the air in a downward slash that would have split the rustling in two, but the monster heard the roar and rolled backwards away from the blade. The monsters weren't stupid. They were cowardly and primitive, but they didn't throw themselves onto swords. It gnashed its teeth as it spherical body stopped rolling. Then it gathered its legs beneath it, crouched ready to spring at Bjorn. It hadn't seen the trap. Eir darted in, thrust her sword through the monster's back and out between its eyes.

Eir backed up, wrenched her sword free of the dying rustling, grimaced as another of the monsters slashed at her. She couldn't get her sword up in time. Couldn't block and was wrong footed so unable to dodge. The rustling bounded into her, slashed at her with half a dozen rusty shards of metal. The metal scraped across her armor, carving dents into the surface, then hit her skin and skidded across her cheek with a spray of sparks. Eir looked as shocked as the rustling, and glanced sideways to find Mia grinning at her, hand outstretched, her apple-green crest shining in front of her and fading quickly as she pushed an enhancement of steel onto Eir.

The Paladins from the Courage were getting

involved in the fight too. Mia's sister, slightly the taller of the two but with less brawn, was carving up a rustling with her twin daggers, screaming at it. Rollo had seen Hoppers get like that before and guessed the cause. It was not the girl's first encounter with one of the little fiends, and it had apparently gone badly before.

Mia left off grinning at Eir, turned, ran to her sister, smashed her great hammer into the bleeding monster and sent it flying across the room to splat against the far wall. She was strong. Tannow appeared to be training them well.

They'd come across the small nest of the monsters and Rollo made the decision for the trainees to attack. Rustlings were weak enough that the eleven of them should have had no problem taking on eight monsters. He was right for the most part.

The room was small, metal walls, ceiling and roof, though instead of painted white or pristine and polished, rust spotted most surfaces. It always did when rustlings were nearby. Mounds of refuse were piled high all over the room, making it seem smaller than it was. Rustlings collected the stuff. Actually they collected just about anything and everything. They snatched scraps of cloth, discarded canisters, bones, exposed electrical wires. Anything the little monsters could get their hands on, they grabbed and took back to their nests, making these hills of scrap that they slept on.

Iro still hadn't moved. He held his sword up as if ready to thrust, pointing it at a rustling ten feet away engaged with Torben. Ashvild leapt in and stabbed a few holes into the monster. It cried out, tried to roll away, and Torben smashed his own huge blade down on it, crushing its bones. It twitched to a stop, bleeding out on the rusting floor. And then there were none left. Everyone, all the trainees had gotten involved, except Iro. Rollo hadn't missed that and he was sure the others wouldn't have either. He was starting to think maybe Alfvin had been right and he needed to push Iro. Then again, the mere thought of admitting Alfvin was right about anything made Rollo feel sick, so he decided it couldn't be the case.

"Let's rest up," Rollo said loudly as the trainees celebrated with each other. They all looked tired. Rustlings were weak, low grade fiends, certainly not dangerous enough to trouble a real squad of Hoppers. But the trainees were not real Hoppers yet, and they had been exploring for hours already."No one wander off alone. Have something to eat and a few sips from your canteens. Don't touch the scrap." Who knew what the rustlings kept in their nests. The last thing he wanted was to finally get his trainees home only to have them fall ill from rifling through monster leavings.

He made sure the trainees were sticking in groups. Most were clearly tired and welcomed the chance to sit down for a bit without the imminent threat of death hanging over them. Rollo chuckled. He did not miss being a trainee. He remembered it well enough, when just the sight of a monster made him want to wet himself, and every trap felt like the end of the world the moment it sprung. Years ago now. A titan ago. Scrap, but he was starting to feel old just thinking about it.

He remembered his own first Hop. He'd been late manifesting a talent and had only been a trainee for three years. But the Silver Blade was a better master than he'd ever be and she poked, prodded, and battered him into shape quickly enough. That first Hop had been to a garden dome. Alfvin had been so arrogant about it, striding off from the rest of the group. He claimed he needed to be challenged, and he'd never open his first gate while their master was around. He'd always claimed the threat of death was a requirement for encountering a gate.

Idiots! That's what they'd been. All three of them. Rollo, Alfvin, and Frigg. They'd wandered off on their own, and stopped by a lake. The first time any of them had seen any body of water larger than a puddle on the shower block floor. Then a marsh mite erupted out of the mud, tentacles flailing. It had caught Alfvin around the ankles right away. The mad man had actually laughed. He'd really expected that to be it, his path to power. His life was in danger and he was so certain his first gate would just appear for him.

Of course, it hadn't happened that way. Rollo had leapt at it with his knives, chopped a couple of tentacles up. But every time he sliced one, another reached up to take its place. They all took a beating. And then it had grabbed Frigg as well as Alfvin. Rollo just remembered the fear after that. The icy dread that Frigg was going to die. He'd pushed himself up. Despite the injuries and the exhaustion, he'd launched himself at the monster again. And then the world froze, and his gate appeared before him.

Alfvin had never forgiven him for it. Opening his gate first. They'd been fast friends up until that moment, but afterwards… Alfvin couldn't hide the resentment, didn't even try. The next Hop they went on, Alfvin had pulled Rollo aside and demanded he beat the other lad half to death. He'd wanted Rollo to force him to encounter his gate. Rollo refused, and they'd drifted apart after that. Rollo couldn't say he was too disappointed by it. Life was crazy enough with titans and monsters, that he felt no need to add madmen obsessed with power into the mix.

He tore his mind out of the past and found himself a nice spot where he could keep an eye on most of the kids. He turned an old metal crate upside down and sat on it. He fished out his canteen from his pack and sipped at the lukewarm water.

Tannow pulled over his own crate and sat down next to Rollo. For a frustrating moment, Rollo thought the old Paladin was about to strike up a conversation. He had no idea what to say to the man other than *Nice job training your kids, they're not all useless.* Luckily, Tannow just pulled a couple of dried bhur beast meat strips from his pack, offered one to Rollo, and started chewing on the other.

It was one of the best bits of being a Hopper. Even at times like this when food was still scarce, Hoppers were allocated the good stuff like dried meat to take on Hops. It was mostly because it was easier to transport than algae. Rollo was fairly certain half the fleet would riot if they knew what Hoppers got to eat while they were all still slurping down murky green paste.

He was still chewing on his strip of bhur beast when Tannow spoke. "You heard about the Stalling?"

Rollo stopped chewing, swallow a lump of the dried meat. He'd wondered how long it would be until people gave it a name. The Stalling wasn't exactly an imaginative one, but it fit.

Rollo lowered his voice to a whisper. "I wasn't aware it was common knowledge." Tannow might know, but the trainees couldn't be allowed to find out.

"It's not," Tannow said, still chewing. "I doubt anyone on the lower ships knows, but I have some contacts on the mid ships." He fell silent for a few seconds and Rollo hoped he'd let the matter drop.

"Must be hard on you," Tannow continued.

"Why's that?"

Tannow chuckled. "I've heard of you."

"I should hope so. This is our second Hop together." Rollo silently wished the old Paladin would take the hint and drop the topic. Of course, he rarely got what he wished, especially when it was for others to leave him alone.

"I mean from before. Back on 01. You were a legend in the making. Opened your first gate on your first ever Hop."

Rollo suppressed a sigh. He really hated praise, had no idea what to say to it. Mostly it just made him feel embarrassed. "Yeah."

"Everyone said you were close to opening your fifth gate. First Hopper ever to do it who wasn't from the upper ships. Then 01 exploded. And now this. Must be tough."

"Not really." Rollo tried not to look, but out of the corner of his eye he could see the man was frowning at him. "It's kind of welcome actually."

"Why?"

Rollo had that feeling he sometimes got when he knew, he just knew, someone wasn't going to let it go without an answer. He doubted Tannow would like the one he got.

"I was close," Rollo said. He smiled as he remembered it. It was like when the ship turned in just a way that the light from a sun shone in through a window on his face. He could feel the warmth of it so close, the power of it. Close, but also distant enough he wasn't ready to touch it. "I could feel it. I knew I was getting close to encountering it." He stopped smiling and tore off another chunk of dried meat, popping it in his mouth. "So I stopped training."

"What?" Tannow asked, incredulous. "Why? Didn't you want to open your fifth gate?"

"Urgh!" Rollo groaned and hung his head. "Have you any idea of the responsibility that would bring? I mean, they'd make me join the scrapping council of Grands for a start."

"Exactly! You'd have a say on the council. The first mid shipper ever."

"Riiiiiight," Rollo said, laughing bitterly. "A say. And

as long as I said whatever they wanted, it would be fine. Otherwise, they'd vote me out four against one. Pointless. And fifth gate means no more choosing my own Hops. I'd spend my entire time as a figurehead for the mid ships."

"And no more teaching either," Tannow added.

"Well, I didn't say it would be without benefits." Rollo shook his head. "I'm sure access to some of those fancy hidden talents would be nice, but… Nah. I'm better off, more useful as a fourth gate Hopper than I would have ever been a fifth gate. So I stopped."

Tannow was quiet a moment, then shook his head. "Sounds like laziness to me. You could have used your position to help people. To change things for the better."

Rollo did not enjoy having his motives or effort questioned, especially not when those questions hit a little too close to home. He knew he should just be quiet, let the conversation die. But a part of him wanted to hit back.

"What about you? Not many Hoppers quit." He caught Tannow's hurried glance. "Yeah, I heard of you too. I've been around long enough to know that those who quit usually have one of two reasons. Either they've lost everything and can't face it anymore, or they find something they can't bear to lose."

Tannow shifted aside a dented armor plate and scratched at his belly. "Never had a family. Never found someone willing to put up with me."

Rollo nodded. "That makes it lost everything then. Hop gone bad?"

"Have you ever been on a spire climb?" Tannow crushed the last of the strip of dried meat in his hand.

"A couple of times."

"They're something else, aren't they?"

"It's unusual for…" Rollo paused, tried to think of the right way to say, failed. "It's unusual for someone from the lower ships to get on a spire climb."

"I know. I used to think it was just haughty talk from the Legacy families. *Spire climbs are for the strong Hoppers from the upper ships. You low shippers can't handle them.* Now, I'm not so sure they were wrong."

Despite himself, Rollo found himself curious. This was why he preferred being alone, far less likely to get wrapped up in other people's dramas. "What happened?"

"The first few floors were easy. We were all low shippers. Vanguard from the Curse Hammer, Berserker from the Nighteyes, Surveyor from the Braided Fold, Mage from the Grave Chaser." He drew in a ragged breath, let it out slowly. "We dodged a few traps, killed a pack of kharapids. Tevita, our Mage, even found himself some loot. A purple pointy hat that boosted his current, made his crest as bright as a star. He'd only just opened his third gate, but the moment he put on that hat he said he could feel the fourth gate just beyond his reach. We celebrated that find. Loot the likes of which would normally be hoarded by the upper ships.

"Next level up it all went wrong. We encountered something new. A monster. It looked like a child, a naked babe suspended in a floating globe of water. It had glowing red eyes."

"A hydrid?"

Master Tannow sniffed loudly and started pulling the strip of meat in his hands apart into stringy threads. "We were the first squad to encounter one. When it spotted us… The room erupted. Standing pools of water shot into the air like geysers. Tentacles of water burst out of the monster, slammed into Terri, our Vanguard. She tried to block, but it was water. It flowed past her shield, wrapped around her head, ran into her mouth and up her nose, pushed into her eyes. I didn't know any enhancements that could stop that.

She drowned. And we all just watched it. Oskar, our Berserker burst into flames. Didn't know how or why at the time. I enhanced him with resistance to the fire. I couldn't put the flames out, but I tried to limit how much damage they would do. Then I heard Reinhold, our Surveyor scream. He collided with me. I lost concentration, then Oskar was screaming as he burned."

Tannow paused for a few seconds, face twitching as he stared through the floor, lost in his memory.

"It was Tevita, our Mage. Or it was the hat we had found. It had eyes, teeth biting into his skull. Tevita was gone, I think. Mouth hanging open, eyes vacant. He just raised his cannon and started shooting fire at us."

"A mimic," Rollo said. They were weak monsters as they were, but could camouflage themselves as items, clothing, weapons. It was true they made whoever held them more powerful, but once they had their teeth in a person, there was nothing left but a puppet for the mimic to control and drain of life.

Tannow nodded solemnly. "We ran, Reinhold and I. We probably should have tried to save the others. Save Tevita at least. Just before we reached the stairs, a tentacle of water snatched Reinhold around the foot, dragged him screaming all the way back into the room, flung him about." Tannow sagged. "I ran. Left him to die."

The old Paladin was quiet for a while then. When he spoke again, he seemed to have regained some of his composure. "I tried to get back out there a couple of times after that. But I just kept remembering Oskar bursting into flames, Tevita aiming his cannon at us, those teeth digging into his skull. You can't Hop with people you don't trust, and I couldn't bring myself to trust anyone. I just kept wondering what would happen if they turned on us. And the moment that starts, it's such an easy jump to stop asking *what if* and start asking *when*?

"After that, I swore I was done Hopping. Took up training instead. Not like I was any good as a tech, and the only other option was a drudge."

Tannow wasn't the first Hopper Rollo had known to quit after a tragedy. It was easy to make light of Hops as a trainer, to downplay the dangers so as not to scare the kids off. But the truth was Hopping was dangerous. Between the monsters, the traps, and the politics it was no wonder so few Hoppers made it to old age. What was rare though were people like Tannow. Hoppers who came out of retirement.

"You must have conquered your demons though," Rollo said, trying to sound supportive. "You're back out here now."

Tannow shot him a wry smile. "Not by choice. You really don't know how bad it is over on the Courage, do you?"

"Only that you're one of the poorest ships in the fleet."

A ship's worth in the fleet was dictated by the number and strength of the Hoppers it could marshal. Those with the Legacy families aboard were therefor considered worth most, and that made them the upper ships. They had prime access to requisitions, supplies, titan-forged items and gear. They also had a disproportionate voice when it came to fleet decision making. There were just five upper ships, but their collective voice was louder than all the mid and lower ships combined.

The lower ships, on the other hand, were the poorest, those who could field the fewest or weakest Hoppers. They rarely got a chance at anything above the most basic of requisitions. They were given the Hops no one else wanted. And when a manufactory was eventually discovered on titan 02, they would be right at the back of the line for vital parts to repair their ships.

"It's worse than you know," Tannow said. "Worse than we're letting on. The ship is failing fast. Systems are dying all over and we don't have even the most basic parts to replace them. We're having to cannibalise sections of the ship just to keep other sections running. At this point, almost half the ship is dead, sealed off from the rest and left to grow cold. Our people are stacked on top of each other in their cabins. Others are sleeping in the mess hall or observation lounge. The drudges are organising strikes as if the officers can do anything to change their lot."

"How is it that bad?" Rollo asked. He knew the lower ships got the raw end of the deal, but to think they were having to close down whole sections of their ships just to keep flying was obscene.

Tannow shook his head, lowered his voice to a whisper. "We haven't received any parts since 01 exploded. None of the lower ships have. It's been five years, Rollo. Everything is falling apart on board. The ships we lost since 01, those that stopped working and were left behind, their populations were shunted onto the lower ships. Everyone but the Hoppers. The Courage was over capacity even before the extra weight, and yet every time we requisition parts for repair, we're told there are none to spare."

Rollo nodded at that. *None to spare* actually meant *not for the likes of you*. "Can't you send out your own Hops? Maybe team up with some other lower ships. Salvage parts, pull them out of the walls if need be."

Tannow groaned. "There's the other problem. As of right now, I am one of two full Hoppers aboard the Courage. Phusone is the other, but he took a bad injury back on 01 and never properly recovered. We lost a lot of our Hoppers when 01 exploded. Most of them. Others have been injured since Hopping over to 02 began."

"Scrap! How many trainees do you have?" Rollo asked. Then he realised it didn't matter. If everyone really was Stalled, the trainees would never open their gates. They'd never be anything but useless.

"Exactly," Tannow said, apparently reading his mind. He was staring right at Rollo now, and must have seen the realisation dawn on his face. "Even if everyone wasn't Stalled. We have six trainees aboard."

"What? How so few? Out of a population of…"

"Almost seven thousand," Tannow answered the question even before Rollo could finish asking. "When you're as poor as the Courage, Hoppers look for any chance to get off the ship. If that means finding a partner aboard another vessel, raising kids there, better for you and your new family. Worse for everyone you're leaving behind."

He sighed. "The Courage is dying, Rollo. What do you think will happen when the ship fails completely?"

"You'll be taken as refugees aboard other ships."

"Will we? Which ships? Will the Eclipse take any?"

Rollo scoffed. "We've already taken one of you." He stopped himself, realised how it had sounded. "Sorry."

"It's fine," Tannow said. "Truth is, most of the lower ships are in the same boat." He laughed bitterly at the pun. "They can't afford to take any more refugees. The mid ships might take a few of us if forced, but they don't want us, especially as we can't provide Hoppers. And there's no chance the upper ships will take on a single one of us."

Tannow took a deep breath, popped the last of the dried meat into his mouth and swallowed without chewing. "Unless we find a manufactory soon, the Courage is dead, and I don't know what will happen to its people. Nothing good."

Rollo didn't know what to say to that. The Eclipse was a mid ship, it was safe. Non-urgent requisitions weren't quick, but they always arrived. He didn't know how to help the lower ships like the Courage, and nor was it his job to help them. It was his job to train the Eclipse trainees, and specifically his squad of trainees. Still, ignoring the matter now he knew about it seemed callous.

"Come on," Tannow said, patting his knee and standing with a groan. "Let's get moving again before our kids start falling asleep." He raised his voice. "Everybody up. Where are we going next Surveyor?"

Chapter Twenty-Three

"I froze," Iro said quietly as they walked along what appeared to be an empty promenade. There were small rooms to either side of them, empty windows staring out. Above, a walkway ran either side of the thoroughfare. Every dozen paces or so, a square planter filled with dirt stood in the centre of the promenade. Some had trees growing out of them, huge things that were spilling out of their designated space, roots erupting from the soil to quest along the metal ground in every direction. Others were empty, nothing but the decaying remains of the tree left to prove they were ever full.

"It happens to us all," Bjorn said, not bothering to lower his voice at all.

"It didn't happen to you."

Bjorn chuckled. "No. But I was making up for being swatted out of the air by a baby bhur beast last time. I can't be useless two Hops in a row!"

"Apparently I can," Iro said, feeling maudlin. The emptiness of the promenade wasn't helping. It had a strange feeling to it like it was meant to be populated. It was a huge open space and he could imagine it filled with people chatting, playing, offering goods or services. They used to do that, he'd read it in a history book. Once, before the fleet's ships had started to fail, people owned things, made things, sold things to others. "Every time there's a monster, I just freeze up. I can't move."

Bjorn shook his head, one eyebrow raised. Then he nudged Iro with his arm. "You're too hard on yourself, Iro. Besides, someone needs to hang back, protect the Paladins."

Iro was glad none of the Paladins heard that. They were all more useful than him against the rustlings. Every one of them getting involved, while he just stood there.

Franka held up a hand, calling for a halt. They all slowed to a stop around a particularly large and gnarly tree that looked like it was clawing its way out of the planter and up to the walkway above.

"Do you hear that?" the Surveyor asked. Snappy clacked. "Not you. Shut up. Anyone else? Hear the buzzing?" She pointed to her ear.

Most of the trainees shook their heads. Iro saw Ylfa lean across to Ingrid and whisper, "Looks like she's lost it."

Franka seemed insistent. "Well, luckily I hear it and you're all following me. So lets investigate."

Master Rollo looked like he was about to argue, but Franka turned and stormed off. Master Rollo sighed, shrugged, and followed without a word.

Franka led them off the promenade through an alley between two buildings Iro hadn't even realised was there until she pushed aside some old, dusty bones. Iro nudged one of the bones with his foot. Whatever they had once been, it wasn't human. It was easy to forget that monsters lived on the titan, breeding and hunting, and doing whatever it was monsters did when not attacking people. For some reason no one had ever explained, monsters banded together to hunt down humans who dared set foot on the titans, but the rest of the time they were more than happy killing each other.

They moved single file through the alley. Torben complained about the lack of space, his bulky armor scraping against the metal walls of the buildings to either side. Then they were through the alley, passing under a scar rent in the bulkhead. It looked almost like a giant claw had raked open the passageway in a riot of jagged and torn metal. Franka ordered them to be careful when passing through.

The space beyond was what lay between the rooms on the titan. Iro had never considered it before, but of course there had to be something in between. The titan was, in essence, a giant ship, just like the ships of the fleet. Wires, electrics, pipes all ran between the walls to deliver power and water and anything else that was needed to the various parts of the ship. The titan was just like their ships but on such a grander scale. The space between walls on the Eclipse might be a finger width at best, but the space between walls on the titan were huge labyrinths themselves.

Every suit of armor had a small flashlight built into the left vambrace and they all turned them on, sweeping the dark space with beams of colorless light.

Franka leapt over a small gap onto a cluster of pipes. The space below was dark but seemed to drop on forever. If anyone careened over the side they might fall for a long time, stopping only when hitting another pipe or something worse. The air was musty and close and too warm. Despite that, there was a breeze, the muted roar of gusting air somewhere far away, the distant whir of giant fans. *Could this be the ventilation system for the titan? Roret would love to see it.*

He felt a shiver on the back of his neck as he crossed through the dark space. It felt like eyes watching him, waiting, closing in.

"Don't look up," Master Tannow said quietly. "Keep moving. Quiet and sure. Crazy woman bringing us in here."

Iro walked across a grouping of wires each as big as his wrist. He overbalanced, reached out and grabbed another wire running vertical. It was sticky to the touch and when he pulled his hand away, some sort of viscous, ochre fluid stretched between his fingers and the wire. Despite Master Tannow's warning, and despite his own determination, he looked up.

The pale beam of his flashlight revealed glistening pods hanging above him. Sickly green in the darkness, each one as big as a person, bulging with whatever contents they held. Attached to each of the pods, a slimy monster pulsed, its pallid flesh rippling with every throb. Each of the torso-sized monsters stared down at the Hoppers through ten glossy, black eyes. As Iro watched, one of the monsters reared up away from the pod it was attached to, trailing sticky yellow fluid from its body. The fluid dripped from the underbelly, rushing past Iro into the darkness below. He realised the rear end of the monster had a dagger-like tail that was thrust into the pod, pulsing as if sucking something out from inside. As he swept his flashlight around, he saw dozens of them. More. Hundreds maybe.

"Just keep moving, Iro," Master Tannow said. "Don't look at them."

Now Iro knew the disgusting creatures were above them, he couldn't stop himself from staring at them. The group of Hoppers crossed onto a large pipe, walked along its length, their flashlights the only illumination in the space between walls. Then Franka found an exit, another gash clawed out of the wall, leading into a new room. They all hurried through. Iro wasn't sure how many of his fellow trainees had looked up and spotted the monsters, but no one wanted to wait around and see what the fat, grotesque creatures would do.

Iro rushed through the scar in the wall, almost shoving Arne out of the way in his attempt to flee. Master Tannow was the last one through and stared back into the darkness between the walls. "I would not recommend we backtrack through there," the old master said. "Those things were not happy with us passing through."

"What things?" Cali asked.

"You didn't see them?" Iro said.

"Obviously not!"

"Quiet," Master Rollo called from up front.

Iro scanned about their new location. It was a grand hall with a high ceiling. Eight great pillars, each one a good twenty feet in diameter stretched the length of the hall in four banks of two. Every now and then, surging electricity would race down one of the pillars in a crackling ring, starting at the roof and disappearing into the floor below.

Not pillars. Conduits. They were transferring massive amounts of power into something below them. Bones and refuse were scattered all over the floor. Scraps of clothing, piles of caked and stinking mud — or at least Iro hoped it was mud — decayed in the too warm air. Iro even spotted a weapon or two, rusting blades and an old hammer with a bent haft.

"Scrap," Master Rollo said, grinning. "You were right."

Franka held up her hand and Snappy slapped his claw against it. "I told you I heard something. Makes the trip through the walls worth it, no?"

"If it pans out."

Master Tannow walked past Iro and the other trainees, staring open-mouthed at the conduits. The furthest of them pulsed, electricity rippling down its metal length. "We have to find a way down."

Master Rollo glanced at the Paladin, then swept his gaze across the gathered trainees. "We call these rooms funnels. They're delivery systems." He thumbed over his shoulder just as another crackle of lightning raced down one of the pillars, circling its entire girth. "Electricity and materials are passed down those conduits, usually straight into a manufactory."

All the trainees started asking questions at once then.

Iro was the only one to keep quiet. They were right to be excited. With a manufactory under their control, they could produce replacement parts for damaged ships, new filters for air and algae maintenance, new tools to replace those falling apart. And for the trainees, they could produce titan-forged armor and weapons. If they really had found a manufactory, it was the most important discovery anyone had made yet on titan 02.

"So if we find it, we get to be the first with titan-forged blades?" Bjorn asked. He slammed a fist into a palm.

Master Rollo held up a hand. "Slow down, idiot. There's plenty of people who need things more than..."

A shrieking cry ripped through the air and silenced them all. Master Rollo spun about, uncharacteristically urgent. Iro squinted at the roof far above. He hadn't realised it before, but the walls and ceiling weren't smooth in this room. They were crenellated to provide extra support to the entire structure. And nestled inside one of the crenellations, almost invisible if not for its slow movement, was a green, scaly monster. It was almost humanoid, but with long, heavily muscled legs, each one ending with a claw strong enough to gouge furrows in the metal it clung to. The monster screeched again and unfurled its wings. Instead of arms, it possessed wings with a massive span, pale blue and membranous. It's face was elongated with gleaming red eyes, and fang-like teeth that protruded from its maw, extending outwards as if reaching for prey.

The monster dropped from the ceiling and spun about, its wings flapping once to right itself. It then tucked its wings behind it into a dive, heading straight for them. Iro reassessed the size of the monster in a moment. It was humanoid in shape, but easily three or four times the size of even Bjorn. It let out another keening howl as it soared toward them.

"Stay back," Master Rollo said as he strode into the room. "None of you get involved under any circumstances. This one is beyond you." The monster sighted on Master Rollo, tightened its dive toward him. Master Rollo stared up at it, reached into a pocket and pulled out a single little knife. "Now, Tannow."

Master Tannow's crest blinked into life before him, huge and bright as an electrical fire. He raised his hand. "Steel!"

The monster lurched in mid-air, flipping around to arrest its dive, its taloned claws aimed at Master Rollo. It hit the Corsair with crushing force, slamming him to the floor. Dust was blown into the air and Iro shielded his eyes as he tried to peer through the haze of particles.

The monster cried again, flapped its leathery wings and leapt, lurching back into the air. Two of the closest conduits, just a stone's throw away, pulsed with electricity, lighting the room briefly. Iro saw Master Rollo climbing back to his feet, entirely unharmed save for a few scratches on his already battered blue armor. The metal floor beneath him was dented from the force of the monster's strike, but Master Rollo cracked his neck to the left, spun the knife in his hand, then swiped up and to the right. His crest flared bright behind him, just for a second, a massive intricate whirl of emerald green radiance, then gone. He seemed to vanish as he was pulled through the air by his Blink Strike. Iro's own Blink Strikes were so slow by comparison.

Master Rollo completed his swipe at empty air thirty feet up, his feet against one of the conduits. The monster was already climbing higher, its head twitching about as it searched for its prey. Master Rollo swiped again and disappeared. He hit another of the conduits, again swiping at air. Above the Corsair, electricity rolled from the ceiling down the pillar. Master Rollo pushed off from the pillar, leaping into the air, swiped upwards with his little knife, vanished again. He reappeared above the monster as it struggled for height, wings flapping furiously. Master Rollo swung his knife down, disappeared again, reappeared just above the monster. His knife clashed against the scaly skin, sparks flying out, lighting the dusty air around them. The monster screamed and thrashed, a bloody gash torn out of its tough hide between shoulder and neck. It turned and flapped, soaring away.

Master Rollo was falling, tumbling through the air. Iro saw him reach into another pocket, pulling out a second knife. His crest lit up behind him and he threw the knife at a pillar in the direction the monster was fleeing, a golden thread of energy trailed behind the little blade. The knife sank into the conduit, the golden thread pulled taught, Master Rollo's fall lurched into a swing, quickly closing the distance on the monster once more. He threw another knife into a second conduit, leapt, letting go of the first golden thread, swinging forward on the new one. Then he was alongside the flying monster. Master Rollo pulled out another knife, launched it at the monster, golden thread trailing behind it once more. The knife sank into the monster's flank, just above its scaly tail. The Beast cried out, lurched one way, then the other, then turned sharply, banking in between two conduits. Master Rollo held on, dragged behind the fleeing creature, slowly pulling himself closer towards it hand over hand.

"We call them daeken," Master Tannow said as he strode to the head of the trainees, positioning himself between them and the monster should it return. "Grade five monsters. Beyond any of us save for Rollo. I've never actually seen one myself. Not a live one anyway." He sounded awed, either by the monster or by watching Master Rollo swinging through the room after it.

"Me either," Franka said. Iro noticed she was hiding back with the trainees, getting nowhere near the fight should it come back their way. "And I'm no happier now I have."

"You aren't itching to get in there and fight it too?" Bjorn said. The bigger boy was grinning, though Iro thought there was a manic edge to it. Smiling down the fear maybe.

Franka gave him a withering look. "Ah, no. I'm a Surveyor. The only way I like to see monsters is from a distance, thank you very much." Snappy clacked for emphasis.

The daeken flew back into sight, twisting, turning, flipping upside down. Master Rollo clung to its back between its thrashing wings, his crest now constantly lit, a glowing green spiral of arcane symbols and lettering floating behind him. He drove a luminescent white knife into the monster's shoulder. The daeken screamed, not rage anymore, but pain. It's injured wing wobbled, no longer catching the air properly.

The monster crashed into a nearby conduit, clearly trying to crush Master Rollo against the metal. But the Corsair leapt free at the last moment, launching another dagger up above him to sink into the metal pillar. He held on to the golden thread dangling from it and sprinted around the pillar even as the daeken clawed at the conduit, trying to find its own purchase. Master Rollo ran, completed his circuit of the pillar, coming face to face with the daeken. It roared, lurched forward, fangs snapping at the Corsair. Master Rollo leapt over the bite, still trailing golden thread. The thread fell against the daeken's chest as Master Rollo landed the other side of the monster. He pinned the thread to the conduit with another dagger, then leapt free, falling quickly the last thirty feet to the floor and landing with a roll.

The daeken thrashed, screamed, clawed at the

conduit, but couldn't break the golden thread holding it in place.

"I had no idea Thread Edge could be used like that," Ashvild said, her voice soft and wondrous. Iro realised then that Master Rollo had used just two talents so far in the battle. Blink Strike and Thread Edge.

The ceiling above the conduit the daeken was strapped to buzzed as electricity arced down its length. It hit the monster and the daeken's scream turned raw as the power sizzled its skin and cooked it inside and out. The electricity continued on, disappearing down into the floor, leaving a charred, smoking ruin of a monster behind.

Master Rollo dusted himself off, glanced up at the corpse of the daeken, then picked his way through the built up refuse and monster droppings back towards the group. He didn't even look out of breath, just thrust his hands back into his pockets and sauntered towards them. The only evidence he had just battled a monster at all, other than it's charred body, were the new scratches on his armor and a few spots of purple blood.

"Waste of three knives," Master Rollo said as he drew close. "But it's dead."

"That was amazing!" Ashvild said, her eyes wide and filled with awe.

"That's our master." Bjorn held up his hand for Master Rollo to slap only to be left hanging.

Torben rubbed his chin. "The silent sheathe hides the deadliest blade."

"Shut up!" Master Rollo snapped. "All of you. Idiots."

"We should turn back," Franka said once everyone had fallen silent.

Iro turned, stared into the hole in the wall. He imagined he could still hear the slimy drip of viscous fluids, see the pulsing larvae monsters attached to the pods. His skin crawled at the thought.

"Maybe not back through the hole, but there should be another way around," Franka continued. "We're heading deeper right now, and that's further away from the pods."

Master Rollo frowned and closed his eyes for a moment. Two of the conduits buzzed as crackling electricity raced down them. "You know as well as I that manufactories are often found just below these conduit rooms."

Snappy clacked and Franka patted his claw. "We just encountered a daeken. You are the only one who stood a chance against that thing."

"He scrapping killed it handily enough," Ylfa said enthusiastically.

"Shut up!" Master Rollo snapped at the girl.

Master Tannow took a step forward, joining the conversation. "It was a grade five monster. Out of my league."

Master Rollo flicked him a hard stare, frowned again, swept his gaze over the trainees. "If we can find a way down to the next level, we should be able to report back that we have located a manufactory."

"And what if there's something worse down there?" Franka said. "Something a single gate four Corsair can't handle alone? I've seen plenty of people die, Eclipse Rollo. I've seen traps that crush, chop, drop, slice, drown, burn, liquify…"

Master Rollo pulled a hand out of his pocket and held it up to stop her. "We still don't know how to get back to the dock or our pods. So we have to explore in order to get out."

"But we need to head up, not down."

Master Rollo sighed. "If we find the manufactory and report back its location, our ships will get first use of it." He gave Master Tannow a look. "If we report back that we might have found it, the Legacy families will send a squad and who knows how long it will be before anyone else gets the supplies they need?"

Neither Franka nor Master Tannow argued any further.

"OK," Master Rollo said, sounding far from certain. "We keep exploring. Head down as soon as we can, find the manufactory, then backtrack and find a way back up to our docks as quickly as possible. Easy."

He sighed. "Kids, from here on out things are likely to get dangerous. Touch nothing. Stay in line. Don't talk unless you see something suspicious. And do not under any circumstances try to fight any monsters."

Iro almost laughed. The way Master Rollo spoke, it was as though things hadn't been dangerous up until then. He took one last look into the deep darkness beyond the hole in the wall, thought he saw glistening eyes peering back at him out of the gloom. He turned and hurried to catch up with the others.

Fear coiled inside deep, clutching his chest tight, making him tremble. He almost drew Neya's sword, hoping the feel of it gripped tight would provide him comfort and courage. Neya had never been scared, she used to grin at the prospect of Hopping. He wanted to be brave like her.

Something touched Iro's shoulder and he jumped, spinning about and stumbling, almost tripping over his own feet. Master Tannow chuckled, his hand still extended. "Don't worry, Iro," the old Paladin said. "We'll protect you. Nothing to worry about."

Chapter Twenty-Four

Franka led them to an elevator and after a few minutes of checking it over declared it *probably safe*. They bundled in and found it surprisingly spacious. Certainly large enough for a stack of crates made from a manufactory. Iro thought that was maybe a good sign. Franka pressed a couple of buttons and the elevator lurched into a slow descent. It arrived at its destination a minute later with a jolt violent enough Ingrid stumbled. Master Tannow caught her before she hit the floor. A moment later the elevator door rumbled open, bathing them all in blinding light, deafening noise, and baking heat.

Franka stepped forward out of the elevator, squinting. "We found it. A working manufactory."

Iro stepped off the elevator, holding a hand above his eyes and blinking past the glare. He hadn't realised the rest of the titan had been so dark until assaulted by such light.

The manufactory was massive, easily as large as the conduit hall above. Iro saw the conduits coming through the roof, each one disappearing into a chunk of machinery he couldn't begin to understand. Conveyor belts whirred, sparks flew, massive construction machines clanged and span and poured molten metal into moulds. One of the machines belched out a metal crate, the contents unknown, deposited it on the floor next to three identical crates. A huge machine to the right had a mechanical arm methodically moving back and forth above it, printing something out of a silver resin. A dozen flying constructs buzzed about up high, occasionally darting forward with little torches, welding something Iro couldn't see. The hot, acrid stench of burning metal wafted down and made his nose itch.

They all moved further in. The first of the construction machines was just a hundred paces from the elevator. The ground between them was cold, hard, grated metal. Up above, there were criss-crossing walkways like a latticework. Iro thought he saw doorways on that level above them, leading out of the manufactory.

Each of the construction machines had a workstation with five flickering monitors laid out before it. Iro took a couple of steps forward, peering at the closest one. It was a menu system, like some of the more advanced systems on the Eclipse. It appeared to be an easy search selection of materials and components. On the monitor next to it, Iro saw a schematic builder awaiting input. It was all automated. You simply selected, or entered the design of whatever you wanted constructing or printing, and the manufactory would do it for you.

One of the conduits above pulsed with electricity, feeding power directly into the closest of the construction machines. The third screen blinked at Iro. He read the words *AWAITING INPUT*, but the rest of the screen was blank.

"Does this mean we can make ourselves some titan-forged swords?" Torben asked. Barely a day went by when he didn't complain how unfair it was that his sword had shattered against the bhur beast's skull, and his new one was just as flimsy.

"Probably," Master Rollo said. "But not yet. We'll report this discovery back to the fleet. The Eclipse and Courage will get first usage…"

Franka cleared her throat.

"And the Burning Ember," Master Rollo amended. "Though parts and supplies will get priority. But eventually you will all hopefully get titan-forged weapons and armor." He sighed and rubbed the back of his neck. "Me too. I could use a few new knives."

Iro stepped in front of the workstation to look more closely at the screens. The first appeared to be a basic selection of components along with a search function. He recognised many of the specifications you could select from. The menu responded to his touch and he scrolled through a recent list of items the machine had constructed. He saw a bulkhead listed with exact specifications on size and material. A plasma welding torch. Magnetic locking strips. All items to repair a damaged ship. He tapped the screen to select the bulkhead order. Five copies were ordered and the request was timestamped. Judging by the time and date at the top righthand of the screen, the request was put in just four hours earlier.

"Master Rollo," Iro said, pointing at the screen.

"Don't touch anything!" Master Rollo snapped, then went back to talking to Franka and Master Tannow. They appeared to be deciding on the best route back to the docking bay.

"How does it work?" Iro jumped at Mia's voice and spun to find her leaning down next to him, staring at the fifth screen.

"I… I don't really know. You select what you want, and it builds it, I guess."

"What's this one do?" she asked pointing at the fifth screen. "It says Awaiting Biometric?"

Iro looked at the screen. It was dark, the brief instructions written in glowing green text, a box outlined in electric green below it. "I think it wants someone to press their hand against it."

"Why?"

Iro shrugged. "Perhaps it wants to read your fingerprints? I don't know. Maybe it's a lock against people using the manufactory?"

Mia straightened up, stared at him quizzically. "I thought you were a tech, Useless. Shouldn't you know all this?"

Iro laughed. "I was a tech aboard the Courage. And a low grade tech at that. The most complex thing I had to deal with was *how do I make this square filter fit in that round hole*. The answer almost always involved tape."

Mia was still staring at him, her mouth turned up into a slight smile. Iro suddenly realised that despite how much he'd grown, he was still looking up at Mia. He'd always been looking up at her. She was taller and stronger than him. The prettiest girl on the Courage by far. She'd spent years mocking him for being useless, talentless, but now things were different and she wasn't nearly as obnoxious.

"Press it," Mia said, a mischievous glint in her eyes. She glanced at the fifth screen again.

"What? No. You press it!"

Mia moved her hand towards the screen, grinned, fingers just a breath from touching it. Then she bit her lip and pulled her hand back as if the screen had snapped at her. She shook her head. "No."

"Scared?" Iro asked.

"You're scrapping right I am, Useless. Look around. This place is scary."

Between the whirring, cranking, sizzling, and clashing the noise was a cacophony. He stared at the fifth screen awaiting its biometric input. He knew he should leave it alone, obey Master Rollo and not touch anything. But he was also sick of being scared of everything. He wanted to be brave for once. And he wanted to see what it did when someone pressed the screen.

Before he could reconsider, Iro thrust his palm against the screen. He stared at Mia, head high in something of a challenge, and saw her eyes go wide. The screen flashed, a green line flickering along it, then it was suddenly scorching hot.

"Ow!" Iro pulled his hand away, hugging it to his chest. The pain was intense and felt as though he'd tried to remove a heating element while it was still under power.

"What happened?" Mia whispered.

"Hot." Iro waved his hand in the air as if that might cool it.

The screen was changing. The box and text had disappeared, replaced by a small circle in the centre of the screen that seemed be very slowly filling. New text appeared above the circle. It read *Analysing Data*. The machine clunked to life, a behemoth of moving parts. Some of the flying automatons buzzed over. They were the size of a clenched fist, black, mostly spherical with a number of little silver rings on their chassis. The buzzing noise seemed to come from the rings and the air shimmered beneath them. Iro guessed it was those rings that were somehow keeping the little machines airborne. They surrounded him, buzzing all about, assaulting him with bright green lights. Mia squeaked and backed away. Iro tried to go with her, but the little flying machines moved with him, green lights still passing over his face and chest and arms.

"What did you do?" Master Rollo asked, striding over. He swatted at one of the machines and it buzzed away from him and let out a sound like an indignant fart.

The automatons then buzzed up and away from Iro all at once. They alighted atop the nearest of the production machinery and stayed there.

"What did you do?" Master Rollo repeated slowly.

"I touched the screen?" Iro said, cringing.

"After I specifically told you not to touch anything?"

Iro nodded. "Yeah."

"Why?"

Iro didn't have a good answer. He didn't think because he was showing off to Mia and trying to prove he wasn't a coward would be what Master Rollo was looking for.

"What's it doing?" Franka asked as she and Snappy hunched over the console, watching the circle slowly fill.

"I don't know," Master Rollo said. "Manufactories were different on 01. They only ever had four screens and worked with a keyboard. This is… more advanced."

"It says its analysing data," Franka said. "What data?" She glanced at Iro. "His data?"

Bjorn laughed and hung an arm over Iro's shoulders. "If it builds a second Iro, can we have the new one? This old one snores like a drill."

Iro fought free of Bjorn. "Master Rollo…"

"What?"

"The first screen." The Corsair glared at him and Iro lowered his gaze. "Before I touched the fifth one. The first screen said parts had been constructed just a few hours ago."

"Parts?"

Franka moved across to the first screen and tapped at it. "This is for repairing a ship," she said. "Did someone get here before us?"

Master Rollo sent one last glare at Iro, then turned to look at the screen. He frowned. "If they have, they didn't tell the rest of the fleet."

"Legacy family?" Master Tannow asked.

Master Rollo shook his head. "They wouldn't bother to hide it. Just claim it for their own and tell the rest of us to get at the back of a very long line."

"Master Tannow," Cali said. She was pointing at something further into the manufactory. "There's someone over there."

Master Tannow rushed to Cali's side, squinted in the direction she was pointing. "I don't recognise them."

"Everybody back into the elevator. Now!" Master Rollo's hands were out of his pockets. It seemed like a bad sign.

Iro left the workstation. The monitor still said it was analysing the data. His data. The circle was only filled a tenth of the way at best. He desperately wanted to know what it meant, but he stepped away, joined the others as they all started backtracking towards the elevator.

He could see the approaching figures now, picking their way between the machines and workstations and idle crates. One was a tall, pale woman with a long braid dangling from the top of her head, while the sides were shaved to stubble. She wore heavy crimson armor with a white fist painted in the centre of her chest. She also carried a metal staff in hand, each end sporting a large spherical head. Next to her walked a smaller, dark man with more hair on his chin than his head. He wore a grin that reminded Iro of a rustling, all malicious and hungry. His armor was lighter than the woman's, but the same shade of red, and had a grinning long-snouted animal painted on one of his spiky pauldrons.

"Leaving so soon?" a male voice called from above.

Iro spun about and looked up to see two more crimson armored figures above them on the criss-crossing walkways. One was a fat-cheeked man with messy hair and a sword dangling from one hand as he leaned over the railing. The other man was pale as bleached cloth and had an eyepatch covering his left eye. He sat on the railing and spun a single sai around his fingers.

"And here I thought we could use this opportunity to improve fleet relations," Chubby Cheeks said. He grinned and leapt over the railing, landing easily on the floor between Bjorn and the elevator. He was as broad as Torben, with a bulging belly, and his armor was heavy enough it made him look as bulky as the bhur beast. He had a few trinkets dangling from his belt, a small metal cup and a skull that had once belonged to a tiny animal.

"You mean start fleet relations, Kane," the tall woman with the white fist on her armor said. She leapt over a conveyor belt without breaking stride. Master Rollo faced White Fist and her companion down, not backing up as they closed in on him.

Master Tannow pushed past Iro and reached Bjorn, pulling the boy back and taking his place standing before Chubby Cheeks. Up above, still sitting on the walkway, Eyepatch let out a vicious chuckle.

"No need for the aggressive posturing, friend," Chubby Cheeks said, taking another step forward and twirling his curved sword. "We're just here to talk. After all, you did latch onto *our* titan. And without even a friendly hello."

Iro saw Master Tannow straighten. "You're from the other fleet." He reached over his shoulder and pulled free his ax, holding it before him.

"You seeing this, Eve?" Chubby Cheeks shouted. "This old junker just pulled a weapon on me."

"Very inhospitable," White Fist called back. She had reached Master Rollo now, was just a few steps from him. Her steel gauntlets creaked as she gripped her staff tight. Her companion was just a step behind her.

"Back off," Master Rollo said in a clipped voice. "The first meeting of our two fleets shouldn't come to violence.

"Bit late for that," White Fist said. "This is our titan. Very rude to kick down the door to someone's home and start taking things not yours."

"I couldn't have articulated it more eloquently

myself." A new voice.

Iro turned to see Eye Patch plummet to the ground and land bonelessly with a sickening crack. He didn't get up and Iro saw a trickle of blood leaking from his open mouth.

Looking up, Iro saw a tall man in a dark cloak, the hood up and obscuring their face. Beneath the cloak was pale grey armor.

Chubby Cheeks didn't bother to check on his fallen comrade. The man startled, then promptly ran around the gathered trainees to the safety of White Fist and the man with a rustling's evil smile. Though Iro had to admit, that smile was gone now, replaced by a worried frown.

"Now…" The new comer leapt off the walkway and landed on Eye Patch's body with a thump. He stepped off and walked straight forward past Master Tannow without so much as a glance. The trainees scurried out of the way, gawking at the cloaked man. "I seem to remember we've had this conversation before. Am I remembering that right, Shota?"

"Bah! Stop drawing it out, Goro," said another new voice. Iro saw a brute of a man standing near the elevator, but he was sure the man hadn't been there just a few moments ago. He wore the same dark, hooded cloak, but his armor was golden beneath it and large enough the cloak barely covered it. He leaned on a metal shield that was at least six feet tall and half that wide. Iro could see nothing of his face beneath the hood save for eyes that gleamed with the same dangerous light as the monsters between the walls.

Goro strode past Master Rollo. The three remaining Hoppers from the other fleet were backing off, and Goro paced after them. "I'm just adequately explaining the situation in a halcyon and informative manner. Now, did I, or did I not specifically admonish you? Yes, I remember it was you. Hard to forget those corpulent cheeks. Huh?"

Chubby Cheeks swallowed hard, nodded, backed up another step.

Goro stalked forward after the Hoppers, all mirth draining from his voice. "Stick to your wing. No lower than the fourth level. You were warned."

"We were," White Fist said, her voice quavering. "But this new fleet needed warning so we came here to..."

Goro vanished, the air buzzing in his wake. He reappeared an instant later in front of White Fist, his hand already swinging. His strike stopped a finger's width from her neck and Iro heard a sound like a bell ringing. White Fist's head snapped to the side and she crumpled to the floor.

Chubby Cheeks dropped his sword, turned, ran. The Hopper with the rustling smile screamed and charged Goro. He made it just two steps before Goro leapt to meet him, brushed aside his swinging sword blade, and delivered a punch to his gut so powerful the armor on his back exploded outwards. The Hopper with the rustling smile dropped beside White Fist. That left only Chubby Cheeks, sprinting away through the noisy machinery.

"Should I relinquish my pursuit, Shota?" Goro glanced over his shoulder. Shota said nothing. "You're equitable as infinity. We did relay them sufficient warning. It would be egregious to leave punishment only half rendered." He plucked a small metal disk from a pouch on his belt, extended his arm, and flicked. Iro heard the same ringing sound as before and the coin launched away in a spinning blur and struck Chubby Cheeks in the back of the head. The man toppled forward on top of a conveyor belt, unmoving as the machinery dragged him away.

"Time to go," Master Rollo said in a low voice. He held out a hand and waved at the trainees to move back towards the elevator.

Shota shifted to the side to stand right in the doorway of the elevator. He lifted his shield off the ground a couple of inches and slammed it down so hard dust erupted from the floor and the clang it made echoed throughout the manufactory.

"Now now now," Goro said as he turned and strode back towards them. "Let's not be overly hasty on evacuating the scene before sufficient discourse has been exchanged."

Iro shuffled back a step, felt his back bump against Emil who gave him a light shove away. All of the trainees were gathered close, Franka with them. Iro felt the same cold fear clutching at him, leadening his limbs. He felt his hand itch towards Neya's sword, desperate to hold it close as though his sister's spirit could comfort him somehow.

"We didn't know this was your territory," Master Rollo said. He faced Goro, refused to move as the man bore down on him. "We'll be leaving now. These Hoppers were nothing to do with us."

Goro stopped a few paces from Master Rollo and pulled down his hood to reveal his face. His skin was dark and latticed with pale scars that tugged up the left corner of his mouth into a sneer. His eyes were shining pits of oil. A scattering of stubble dusted his chin unevenly, and his wild, wiry hair was held back by a single metal circlet around his head. Iro saw small silver, metal rings on his gauntlets just like he had seen on the flying constructs.

"I see you are well on your way to comprehending the depth of your intrusion," Goro said, his hands waving about dramatically as he spoke. "But we cannot in good conscience allow you to exit before I have delivered the articles of our good faith."

Just in front of Iro, Arne leaned to the side and nudged Torben. "What's he saying? I only understand half the words."

"The rules," Torben said, his voice a low growl.

"Right you are, big lad," Goro said, pointing a gauntleted finger at Torben. "Rules." He turned his attention back to Master Rollo, the smile slipping from his face. "Article one: Stick to your wing. You have claimed this one. That's fine. It's a good wing. Probably my favourite. You try to leave it, explore any further and…" He winced and pointed to the body of White Fist on the floor just behind him. "An unfortunate fate awaits those who trespass."

Master Rollo didn't move, didn't even glance at White Fist's body. "Fair enough."

"Wonderful," Goro said happily. "I do love it when the proletariat are agreeable and communicative.

"Article two: anything level five or below is out of bounds. Do not descend past level four anywhere in your wing. The results and consequences expatiate for themselves." He paused then pointed at White Fist again.

Master Rollo didn't answer straight away. He glanced over his shoulder at the rest of them. "Our fleet needs a manufactory or…"

"Don't care," Goro said. "That is your predicament and none of our distress. Stick to your wing. Stay above level five." He looked past them all towards his companion. "That's it right, Shota? Just the two articles?"

The huge Hopper leaned on his shield in front of the elevator and grunted. "Assurances."

"No cause for such drastic measures," Goro said. "They comprehend the extent and futility of their station." He looked at Master Rollo again. "Right? You do comprehend, junker?"

Master Rollo nodded slowly. "We get it."

"See!" Goro grinned again and spread his arms wide. "An accord has been reached with all parties mutually agreeing upon the articles to ensure good faith is maintained."

"Assurances," Shota growled again.

Goro sighed. "Rules must be followed. I understand. Even we are not above the law. Mores the pity." He smiled again, his scars stretching to make him look ghastly. "We're going to take custody of one of your…" He gestured at the gathered trainees and for a brief moment his gaze passed over Iro. Iro felt his heart hammer in his chest. There was something about meeting the man's gaze that was terrifying. He had no idea how Master Rollo could stand there before it. "One of your whelps. As an assurance that you and the rest of your fleet will abide by the accords. If…"

"Not happening," Master Rollo said sharply. Iro had never heard that steel in the lethargic Corsair's voice before. "We understand your scrapping rules. We'll leave now and not return. You have my word."

Goro winced. "And if I had my way, that would be sufficient enough, compatriot. But it's not. We'll be taking one of your brats now."

Chapter Twenty-Five

Iro couldn't tell who struck first. Both Master Rollo and Goro moved so fast. One moment they were standing still, facing each other down, the next they were half a dozen paces away, dancing around each other as Master Rollo stabbed a flurry of blows at the black cloaked man.

Master Rollo darted in close, knife in hand, stabbing low into the chest. Goro turned away from the blade, arms still hanging by his side, dodging with footwork alone. Master Rollo chased after his opponent, slashed low again, brought a second dagger up in his other hand and stabbed high. Goro leapt, spun in mid-air, somehow occupying the space between the two strikes. His cloak flapped out like a whip, snapping against Master Rollo's face and the Corsair staggered back a step, bringing both knives up and ready in a strange stance, one hand held before him and the other hidden behind his back. Neither of them had activated their crest yet. That meant they were fighting without talents.

"Get ready to run for the elevator," Franka whispered low enough Iro was sure the black cloaked men wouldn't hear over the sound of the machinery. The Surveyor squeezed through the crowded trainees and repeated the order to the others. Bjorn and Ashvild had their swords out, held loose in hand. He slowly reached up and drew Neya's blade over his shoulder. He felt better holding it, knowing if he had to fight, he could. Or if he had to flee, he could Blink Strike over to the elevator faster than he could run.

Goro appeared before Iro, towering over him, grinning. His eyes seemed to drink in the light and reflected nothing. The pale latticework of scars made his face a terrifying motley of blacks. Iro squeaked in alarm, tripped, fell backwards onto his ass.

"Now now, kid. Drawing a weapon is an act of aggression." Goro's grin widened. Iro glanced past the man to see Master Rollo was striking at another Goro. There were somehow two of them. "You wouldn't want me to consider you aggressive, would you?" The Goro in front of Iro laughed. Then his image seemed to buzz, the air around it growing hazy, and it drifted apart like scraps of cloth ripped to the wind.

"What the scrap?" Mia asked. She was stood just behind Iro and held out a hand. He took it and she pulled him easily to his feet.

Goro, the only Goro left now, fighting with Master Rollo, glanced Iro's way, raised a hand to his face and tapped his cheek just below his eye then flicked the finger at him.

Master Rollo stabbed low and angled up, Goro was already stepping back. Master Rollo's emerald crest lit up behind him, he flicked the knife behind his back to the side and vanished, reappearing a half dozen steps away. He flicked the knife again, still hidden from Goro, and vanished again, reappearing behind the other man. His knife plunged into Goro's back with the sound of a bell being struck. Master Rollo leapt away.

Goro turned lazily, yawned. "I suppose it's time I took this seriously. Come on." He motioned for Master Rollo to attack him again. "I'll give you one more."

Master Rollo glanced over towards them for just a moment. Then Master Tannow raised a hand and whispered, "Speed." His lilac crest lit up behind him.

Master Rollo vanished, dust billowing in the space behind him. It wasn't a Blink Strike this time, but the power of a third gate Paladin backing the Corsair up. Master Rollo reappeared in front of Goro, knives flashing out at him.

Goro cried out in alarm, still smiling. He blocked both blows with his hands, each one ringing like a struck bell. Master Rollo didn't let up, dancing around Goro, darting in, stabbing high, slicing low, each attack so fast Iro could barely follow. Goro blocked each attack with the same ringing sound, stepping back and giving ground before the onslaught. Master Rollo's crest was a constant searing emerald light hovering behind him now, but Goro still hadn't even activated his own crest. He was still fighting without talents.

Something shifted, something beyond Iro's comprehension, and the battle turned. Suddenly Goro was on the attack, swinging gauntleted fists at Master Rollo. The Corsair gave ground, on the defensive, he dodged and spun and leapt back. Goro darted after him and Master Rollo flicked a knife to the side, vanishing and reappearing a few feet away with a Blink Strike. Goro didn't even break stride, but was on him again, fist thundering out even as Master Rollo reappeared.

Master Rollo brought a knife up to block. That same ringing sound echoed out along with a circular shockwave of force exploding outwards from the punch. Master Rollo's knife shattered in his hand, steel shards flying. Goro shifted, punched with his other fist.

"Steel!" Master Tannow said, pointing.

The bell sound rung out again and Master Rollo staggered back. The punch had hit him in the chest and his armor cracked from the force. Iro gawked.

That's impossible. He just cracked titan-forged armor with a single punch!

Master Rollo gagged, spat blood onto the manufactory floor, but didn't go down.

Goro took a single step back, frowned at Master Rollo, slowly swung his gaze to the gathered trainees. The black-cloaked man chuckled. "What is it you people like to say? *Always protect your Paladin*." He turned away from Master Rollo then and started walking towards them.

"No you don't," Master Rollo growled and tried to leap after Goro. He pulled up short, his left leg trailing. Iro didn't know when Goro had done it, but there was a little circle like those all over his own grey armor attached to Master Rollo's leg, another one on the floor below him. A thin line of hazy air connected the two and no matter how much Master Rollo struggled, he couldn't break free. "Get back here!"

Goro continued his lethargic pace towards them all. Bjorn was the first to stand in his way, sword raised and trembling only slightly. Goro glanced up at the big boy, and Bjorn paled, his sword dropping from his hands. Goro simply walked past him. Straight towards Iro.

Iro held up Neya's sword before him, hating how much it trembled in his grip. He locked his knees, tried to push down the fear threatening to bubble up and pull him down into a quivering heap. Goro bore down on him, stopped, looked Iro up and down, then reached out a single hand and flicked Neya's sword with a sound like soft chyme. The blade vibrated in Iro's grasp, wriggling free of his sweat-slick fingers and clanging to the ground. It continued to bounce there as if somehow alive and struggling. Goro brushed past Iro and continued on.

Master Rollo stabbed a knife at the little circle attached to his leg plate, trying to remove it. Then he gave up and dug the knife in beneath the plate, cutting it free, getting his fingers beneath it to tear the armor away.

"And you must be the Paladin," Goro said.

Master Tannow swing his ax at the black-cloaked

man. Goro grabbed the haft in one hand, punched it with the other. The bell rang again and the ax's haft shattered, spraying titan-forged steel across the manufactory floor. Goro plucked the falling ax head from the air, spun it about, drove it into Master Tannow's chest. His armor cracked and shattered from the force, and the ax bit deep into his flesh.

Master Tannow wavered for a moment, staggering as if punch drunk. He frowned, glanced down, then his crest blinked out and he collapsed backwards, hitting the floor with a damning thud.

"No!" Master Rollo ripped the leg plate free and swung his knife, vanishing. He reappeared behind and above Goro, stabbing his blade down at the black-cloaked man's exposed neck.

Goro's hand shot up to block the strike, his cloak billowing. Iro saw then that his entire suit of armor, not just his gauntlets, was covered in the little silver rings. The sound of a bell rang again and another shockwave of energy pulsed outward, throwing the nearby Arne to the floor. Iro saw Master Rollo's knife frozen in mid air, blocked by a shimmering shield of air just a finger's width from Goro's hand.

"Is he a Mage?" Ashvild said, her voice a breathy whisper. Iro knew little about the talents of Mages other than they were somehow able to use their current to manifest things like fire or ice. They were usually backline artillery, but Goro was going toe to toe with a fourth gate Corsair and appeared to be winning. Besides, Mages had to focus their talents through a cannon just like Corsairs did a sword.

Goro lurched into motion, reaching past his shimmering shield and grabbing Master Rollo's wrist. He pulled the Corsair closer with one hand, then delivered a thunderous punch with the other. It sounded like a gong had been struck and Master Rollo's titan-forged breastplate exploded. The Corsair was launched backwards, smashing into a stack of metal crates fifty feet away.

"Ooops," Goro said and giggled. "That might have been a bit more than he was ready for." He turned to the trainees and spread his hands. "Look, I'm really not trying to expire any of you here." He stopped, looked down at Master Tannow's body. Franka was knelt over him, checking for a pulse. "OK, I'm not trying to expire *all* of you."

The stack of crates erupted and Master Rollo, battered and bloody appeared a few steps away from Goro. He held one of his knives in each hand, but the blades were glowing blue and had extended to two feet long. His crest was huge, glowing like an emerald star behind him.

"Well, that's problematic," Goro said. Both he and Master Rollo vanished, reappearing a few feet away. The bell rang out and Iro saw Master Rollo stabbing with both glowing blades, Goro blocking with crossed arms. Then they vanished again, reappeared next to a distant stack of crates, another bell ringing out, Master Rollo's strike blocked again. They vanished and Iro lost track of them.

"Now!" Franka shouted. "Move."

It took only a second of milling about before all the trainees, Iro included, started running towards the elevator. Iro snatched Neya's sword from the ground as he ran, noticing the crack in the blade had snaked further along, reaching the centre now. Shota was still standing in front of the elevator. He watched them all running at him for a couple of seconds then raised his shield and slammed it to the floor again. The metal beneath him buckled and waves of force rushed out, hitting Torben and Ylfa first, then the rest of them. Everyone was knocked off their feet, falling backwards in a mess of tangled limbs. Iro fell backwards onto Franka and a moment later felt Snappy clacking next to his ear. He rolled off the Surveyor and rushed to his feet, finding himself the first one standing again.

Shota made no other move. Master Rollo was back in view, still chasing Goro, but the black-cloaked man was dancing away easily, even laughing. Then Master Rollo used a Blink Strike backwards, putting a dozen feet between the two of them. He crossed his glowing blades in front of himself, then slashed them apart to the sides. A shimmering wave of cutting, golden energy released from the blades and shot towards Goro.

Just as the energy wave reached him, Goro brought both hands together in front of him and caught the wave between his palms, the air ringing like a chorus of struck bells. His feet slid back on the metal as the wave pushed him, and Iro saw the black-cloaked figure grimace.

Master Rollo switched attention and swiped his dagger. He vanished and reappeared in front of Shota, already moving to stab around the giant's shield. Shota shifted his door-like shield a little to block the dagger. Master Rollo leapt, spun over the top of the shield, brought his other dagger around and down at Shota's face. The blade thrust into the giant's cheek. Shota's crest exploded into light around him. It was golden, the same hue as his armor, and was the largest and most complex crest Iro had ever seen, with not just one circle, but three, connected by searing bright lines, almost as if he had three separate crests.

Iro stood on his toes to see what was happening over Shota's shield. Master Rollo clung to the slab of metal with one hand, squatting on his haunches on top of it. His blade sizzled with energy, the air around it hissing and popping. But Shota's skin was unbroken. The blade rested against his cheek. Where the two's crests collided, the air crackled and sputtered like a plasma torch.

Master Rollo leapt backwards, flipping in the air and landing on his feet before the shield bearer. Shota's crest blinked out and the huge man jerked his head, nodding towards Goro.

"He's your opponent," Shota said, his voice grinding like a rusty servo.

Goro jerked his hands and the wave of energy he had gripped between them shattered into sparkling shards that quickly faded to nothing. He wiped his hands together as if trying to shed some foul residue. "A ranged encounter, are we switching to? I think you'll find that's far more to my liking." He reached into a pouch at his belt and pulled out a small metal coin.

Master Rollo backed away from Shota and slipped into a ready stance, both glowing daggers held before him.

Goro flicked his fingers and the bell rung. Master Rollo's left leg snapped out from beneath him and he went down with a cry, crashing to the ground. The energy surrounding his blades dissipated and he was left holding a couple of normal knives again.

Master Rollo struggled back to his feet, dragging his left leg. The bell rung again and he crashed back to the ground, crying out again. His right shoulder twisted unnaturally and one of his daggers dropped from his limp grasp.

"Stay down," Shota rumbled.

Master Rollo groaned from the ground, shuffled about. He was panting and bloody, his left leg and right arm broken. But he slowly struggled back to standing again.

The bell rung again. This time the coin struck Master Rollo in his chest, where his armor was already shattered. It flung him back to the ground a few feet away and he didn't move.

"Well," Goro said as he leapt over the conveyor belt and approached. "That was almost a workout." He swept his cold gaze over them all. "I assume our point has been made and the accords will be acquiesced to." He still hadn't even activated his crest once.

"Assurances," Shota said.

Goro turned to his companion, opened his mouth, then shut it again and nodded. "Fine. You, come here." He pointed at Iro.

Iro felt his heart freeze. His legs went numb. He suddenly felt as though all the other trainees were pulling away from him, leaving him to his fate. The room seemed distant, spinning. He couldn't breathe. He couldn't remember how to breathe. The floor crashed into his knees and he realised he'd collapsed.

"Not him," Shota said.

"Why not?"

"Too weak."

Goro laughed. He paced forward and grabbed Mia by the arm. She swung a punch at his face, but he didn't even flinch. Mia, however, cried out and pulled her hand back as if burned. "How about this one then? She has some fire."

Shota let out an affirmative grunt.

"I won't… let you," Master Rollo growled as he shifted again. White arcs of energy shot off him like a sparking wire. The metal plates beneath him rattled as he got back to one knee. The air around the injured Corsair visibly darkened as his crest flared brighter and brighter still. "You won't take anyone."

"Well, Shota, will you observe that," Goro said. "He's almost of a height to play with the adults."

Master Rollo reached his feet, favouring his right leg, his right arm hanging limp by his side. His armor was cracked and shattered. Blood ran down his face, dripping from his chin. His skin almost glowed and his crest was so bright Iro couldn't look at it.

Iro didn't even see Shota move. One moment he was standing in front of the elevator, and the next he was before Master Rollo. He swung his shield and smashed the huge metal slab into the Corsair, sending him flying across the manufactory into a wall twenty feet away. The metal dented from the impact, Master Rollo wedged into the indentation. The power that had been collecting around him was gone, his crest vanished.

"Done," Shota said and crouched. He leapt up onto the walkway fifteen feet above and started walking towards one of the doorways leading from the manufactory.

"Such impatience," Goro said. "I was actually about to engage in some jocularity. Ah well." He turned and started walking, dragging Mia away from the group.

"Let go of her." Cali ran at Goro, one of her daggers in hand and struck. The bell rang out again and the dagger shattered in Cali's hand. Goro just kept walking. Cali locked her hands around Mia's trailing arm and tugged, but Goro pulled her along too with seemingly no extra effort.

"Abide by the accords and hopefully we shall never make acquaintance again," Goro said. He stopped walking, turned back to them all and glared at Cali. She met his gaze and staggered back, dropping to her knees, still clutching at her sister's arm. "Fail to abide and the consequences will be dire. Especially for this one." He tugged Mia's arm, wrenched her from Cali's grip, then scooped her up in both arms and threw her up and across the manufactory as easily as he might a toy. Mia screamed and tumbled through the air. Then Shota caught her in one outstretched arm, and ducked through the doorway and out of the manufactory.

Goro leapt up the fifteen feet onto the walkway and started following his companion. "Inform your people about the accords. And good luck to your fleet. I truly hope you survive." He vanished through the same doorway as Shota.

Chapter Twenty-Six

Emil had never seen death before. He knew it happened, of course. People had died aboard the Courage. Sometimes of old age, sometimes of illness. One of his father's friends had been crushed by a collapsing bulkhead last year. A sad accident that could have been avoided if the ship had been properly repaired. His father raged about it, cursed, swore vengeance on the officers lounging about in the *fancy part of the ship*. He'd soon forgotten all about his friend though. Emil hadn't seen the body, there'd been no need to. He'd never seen any lifeless body before. But now Master Tannow was here and dead, and it all just felt so unreal.

He'd known Master Tannow his whole life. He'd been training with the man his whole life. It had been Tannow, not his father, who taught him how to throw a punch, to tuck his elbow in rather than sticking it out. The old Paladin had taught him how to use his first talent, to activate his crest and let the current flow. He couldn't be gone. And yet, Emil was staring down at his body. Glassy, unfocused eyes stared above at nothing. His mouth was slack, a trickle of blood leaking from the corners. His own ax lodged in his chest.

For a crazy moment, Emil felt like dropping to his knees, pulling free the ax, beating on Tannow's chest until he stopped playing around and stood up.

"Help me get Rollo down," the Surveyor said as she ran past. Two of the Corsair trainees, the bald girl and the fat boy rushed to help her. They slowly extracted the Corsair trainer from the metal bulkhead and carried him back to the group. As soon as they laid him on the floor, the Surveyor bent over him, her hands moving to check his vitals. Her little autodage clacked and poked at the body.

It still didn't seem real. Emil had been studying the gates all his life. He knew more than any other trainee. They were physical representations of locks in place to stop Hoppers from accessing too much of their power before they were ready. The titans gave the gates form, allowed Hoppers to open them. The only way to encounter a gate was to be ready, to train your body and your current to the point where it could handle the extra strain. Everyone said the Corsair trainer was a fourth gate, bordering on opening the fifth. But he had been beaten so easily. That rangy, scar-faced black cloak had said it was barely a warmup. He hadn't even activated his crest.

"Can you fix him?" the huge Corsair boy said.

"Fix him?" the Surveyor said. "He's not a leaking pipe."

"Just do it!" The big Corsair stood and swept his gaze over the rest of the trainees. Emil knew the type. Whether he was suited to it or not, this boy was assuming control. "We're on our own now and a long way from home. We need to backtrack and hope the shrinking corridor is open again."

"That's madness," said the fat girl with her hair in braids. "Even if we make it back, and even if its open, and even if the Surveyor can disarm it a second time, we have no way of knowing it will spit us out on the docks."

"We can't go back that way," the Surveyor said, still not looking up from ministering over the Corsair's body. "We disturbed the monsters between the walls. It will take them time to settle down again and without any Hoppers, it would be suicide."

"You're a Hopper," the big boy said.

"I'm not suited for combat."

"That why you just let Master Rollo get beaten up?"

The Surveyor stood at that, staring up at the boy. "Those black cloaks were…" She paused as if searching for the right word. "Beyond any of us. I could barely see them move. What should I have done?"

The big boy took a step forward, towering over the Surveyor. "Something."

"Enough, Bjorn." This came from the severe girl who liked to boss people around. She was the one who had come up with the plan to beat the bhur beast. The big lad stared at her for a moment, clenched his fists, then stepped away and shut his mouth.

"You're the Surveyor," the girl said as she knelt down next to her trainer. "Lead us out of here. We're the Corsairs, so we'll protect you from any monsters."

The Surveyor laughed, a note of panic in it. "You're trainees. Not a one of you has even seen a gate. I'm stronger than all of you."

"But we've been trained for combat," the severe girl said slowly and calmly. "Just tell us what to do and how to get out of here. We'll deal with any monsters."

"No," Cali said. She was still on her knees, eyes red and puffy, but the tears had stopped now. "We have to go after them. They have my sister."

"We can't," the severe girl said. "They're too powerful for us. Maybe too powerful for anyone. We need to head back to the fleet and tell them what happened. They'll send a squad to rescue her."

Cali shook her head. "We can't leave her."

Emil couldn't look away from Master Tannow's body. He would never have left Mia behind. He would have fought to protect her no matter the odds. He died to protect her. To protect them all.

"I'll go," Emil said before he could decide otherwise. He stepped over Master Tannow's body and started looking for a ladder up to the walkway. He suddenly remembered both the black cloaks easily leaping the fifteen feet up as if it was nothing. But of course he couldn't do anything like that.

"I'll go with you," Iro said.

"I don't need your help."

"You can't go alone."

"No one is going," the severe Corsair girl said as she stood from her trainer's body. "We have no idea where they've gone or how to follow them. And even if we did, look at what they did to our trainers." She shook her head, braid whipping about. "We are all sticking together, and we are all getting off this titan." She turned to Cali then. "The fleet will send Hoppers after your sister. The only thing we can do for her now is survive and get back to the fleet to tell them what happened."

Emil hated to admit it, but she was right. It just felt wrong not to be doing something to help. He paced about as the others made ready to leave. The Surveyor declared she had done all she could for the Corsair trainer and he needed a medical bay aboard one of the ships. She then set about scavenging some materials and constructing a makeshift stretcher to carry him, her autodage's plasma torch fusing together materials to build it. Once that was done, they all started towards the elevator.

"What about Master Tannow?" Iro asked. He had stopped by the body and was staring down at it.

"Leave him," the Surveyor said. "He's dead and we need to move quickly."

Iro hesitated and for once Emil understood him. It wasn't right to leave his body behind for the monsters. He knew it was often the fate of Hoppers who died on the titans, but it wasn't right for Master Tannow.

Emil knelt by the body, reached down and grabbed Master Tannow's arms. With a wrench and a grunt, he hauled the body up onto his shoulders. His legs wobbled as he pushed back to his feet, his back ached from the strain, and he felt sweat beading on his forehead, but he made it to his feet. Then he staggered the first step. It felt like Tannow was trying to resist, as if his body was somehow connected to the spot he died and some force was trying to drag him back. The second step was even harder.

"Let me help," Iro said, rushing forward.

Emil pushed the other boy away with a grunt. He almost overbalanced and toppled, but managed to plant his feet. "I… don't… need… your… help." He punctuated each word with a step toward the elevator.

Master Tannow was so heavy and the elevator seemed so far away. Iro hung around like an annoying smell, but Emil did his best to ignore the other boy. He could do this alone. He had to do it. He reached inside for his current, as if it could somehow strengthen him. It was so unfair that Paladins could only use it to buff others. It was his power, he should able to use it when he needed. He tried to force the current to flow into his limbs, without any target or talent. He almost felt like it worked, could imagine that warmth spreading through his veins making him stronger. The next step felt a little easier. But it was a lie.

By the time he made it to the elevator, sweat was pouring down his face. And the worst part was the journey home had only just begun.

⚙⚙⚙

Iro huddled in the back of the elevator feeling small. He pressed himself into the corner and wished he could fall back into the cold metal at his back, disappear entirely. Guilt and shame assailed him like rustlings stabbing at his heels.

He had been terrified when Goro had pointed at him,

chosen him. So scared his blood felt cold, pumped like paralysing poison in his veins, and his legs turned to stone, dragging him down. And then Goro had picked Mia instead and… Iro hated to admit, hated himself for the truth of it.

I was relieved. That wasn't right. It wasn't brave.

He clutched the hilt of Neya's sword to his chest, squeezed it tight enough his knuckles popped and ached. She had told him to be brave for their mom. But he couldn't. He couldn't even be brave for himself.

The elevator rumbled to a stop. They had gone further up, the level above the conduit room, as far as the elevator went. Ashvild pulled open the door to see what lay before them. She had taken charge of them all, slipping into the role easily.

Ashvild had her slender sword drawn, held mostly steady in her hands. She and Franka edged out of the elevator slowly, staring about a cramped corridor they would struggle to walk down two abreast. It bowed out at the sides like a tube being squeezed. The floor and ceiling were grated, bundles of wires and pipes running along above and below them. The lighting was soft and yellow, beamed out from a series of frosted globes set into the walls.

After a brief consultation, Franka declared she knew the direction that might hopefully lead them back to the docks. Iro didn't hold out much hope. The titan was massive, its passageways and rooms labyrinthine. The chance of them finding their way back home seemed impossible.

The others stumbled out of the elevator in near silence. Bjorn and Ingrid carried Master Rollo on the stretcher. Emil staggered forward every step under the weight of Master Tannow's body across his shoulders. Iro held back, waiting in the elevator, pressed into the corner. For a mad moment, he thought about pressing the button for the manufactory. The doors would close, no one would be able to stop him, and he could go after Mia. But then what? He'd never find her, never make it past whatever traps and monsters lay between them. And even if he did, he wasn't strong enough to rescue her from the black cloaks.

Iro left the confines of the elevator and ambled after the others, still lost in his maudlin thoughts. What would happen to Mia now? What would the black cloaks do to her? Would the fleet try to rescue her? Or would they not care about one missing girl?

Iro heard a tapping, scraping sound behind him. He stopped, turned, stared down the winding tunnel. The frosted globes set into the walls gave everything a hazy light, almost like staring through hanging smoke. Dreamlike. There was nothing behind him and the sound had stopped. He clutched Neya's sword tight, peered through the twilight.

Something heavy slapped his shoulder and Iro turned, yelling, bringing up Neya's sword to defend himself.

Torben took a step back, holding up both hands in surrender. "Don't skewer me," the bigger boy said. "I was just keeping you coming. We're pulling ahead up front."

Iro's heart was pounding, he heard a sound like water rushing through pipes in his ears. He took a few deep breaths and looked past Torben. The rest of the group was getting further away. Even Emil, burdened by Master Tannow's body, was slogging along at a good pace. Iro lowered his sword, closed his eyes for a moment, then nodded.

"Come on." Torben put a hand on his shoulder again, steered him on. "Good on you, being the rearguard though. You know what they say, history is as important as the future."

Iro shook his head as they plodded on. "Who says it?"

Torben chuckled and rubbed at the back of his neck, flicked some sweat from his gauntleted fingers. "Books mostly, I guess."

"You read a lot." Iro had so rarely read anything other than technical manuals, not after finishing mandatory classes as a child, but he wanted Torben to keep talking. He wanted the company, the noise. The distraction.

"What I can, sure," Torben said. "It's problematic. Our history is broken. There's bits missing. Not just specific books, but whole sections from the books we do have. Ingrid says the files have probably just become corrupted, but it seems too convenient to me. None of our history books go back any further than finding titan 01. What happened before that? None of our books say. There's anecdotes but no facts, no descriptions of what life was like. If it was just one book; sure that's odd. Two; a coincidence maybe. But all of them?" He shrugged and had to re-position his giant sword across his back.

"Maybe we came from the titans?" Iro said. "Monsters live on it. Maybe we used to." He heard a tapping of something hard against metal again, glanced over his shoulder. The corridor was still empty behind.

"Except we can't," Torben said. "Monsters are drawn to humans. We can't live here. And if we came from the titans, then where did the fleet come from?"

"I don't know."

"Exactly. No one does, and the books are corrupted. I hope to find the answer one day." Torben grinned, staring ahead at nothing. "I figure there has to be a library or something aboard this titan. Maybe it tells us where humans came from. Or maybe the other fleet still has all their history."

"But what does it matter?" Iro glanced over his shoulder again. He could still hear the distant tapping, but there really was nothing behind them. The corridor had curved so the elevator was long out of sight.

"Didn't I just say, history is as important as the future. You have to know the mistakes you've made in the past, so you don't repeat them in the future. Scrap, that's half of a Surveyor's job. Knowing the traps they've encountered in the past, so they can disarm or circumvent them. History informs the present, the present resolves the future, the future defines history. Without history, we're lost."

Iro groaned. He only understood about half of what Torben said. "We are lost though." He couldn't decide if the tapping was getting louder or fainter. Perhaps it was echoing from far away. He imagined the elevator working, Goro and Shota deciding they were going to slaughter everyone after all.

"For now, sure," Torben said. "But we've been lost before. I said we still have anecdotes. Did you know, ancient ships, before they figured out how to use sensors, used to use something called North to guide them."

"What's North?" Iro asked.

"I'm not really sure. It's one of those maddening things. We have a few mentions of it in books, but the context has all been gutted. I know that captains used to look out at the stars and follow the North to get them home. It told them where they were and where they were going. A guide no matter how dark things got."

"I wish we had a North with us now," Iro said. The tapping was definitely louder now. "Do you hear that?"

"I was ignoring it." Torben's voice trembled a little. "Hoping it was all in my head."

They both stopped, turned, stared down the snaking corridor behind them. It was empty. Frosted light seemed to hang in the air, gently smudging the details so the corridor faded into a mingling blur. Still that same, incessant tapping noise. It was louder now, more frequent.

"What is it?" Torben asked.

Iro sighed, lowered Neya's sword so the point tapped against the metal grate below his feet. Something niggled in his mind, a thought he couldn't quite form. He raised the sword an inch, tapped it against the grate again. The noise sounded worryingly familiar. Torben realised it too, the bigger boy's eyes were wide as a moon.

The space between the grates was thin, small enough that as Iro looked down the corridor it almost looked like solid metal below and above him. But there was space below their feet. He could see pipes and wiring in large, bound clusters running along the length of the place. But there was enough space around the clusters for a child to squeeze. Or something the size of a child.

The tapping grew more incessant and Iro realised it wasn't a single source, but lots of them. Lots of little things tapping on the metal grates. "You don't think the grates come up, do you?"

Torben shrugged, bent, wrapped his fingers around one and hauled up a small, square section of the floor. Down below it was dark and oily, and Iro could see the wires were coloured, the pipes glistening with condensed moisture.

"Have a look," Torben said, gesturing to the open square of flooring.

"I'm not looking!"

"I pulled up the floor. It's only fair you look."

"That's a terrible deal." Iro sank down to his knees, then lowered himself further to peer along the amassed cables. He didn't see anything. "It's too dark."

"Here."

Torben fumbled his torch out of its vambrace housing and passed it over. Iro spent a moment positioning it. Then he flicked on the switch. The beam of light seared away the darkness revealing dozens of long, sinewy bodies slithering along the cables, clawed hands clutching at the grating, black eyes shining back at him.

Iro cried out and rolled back just as the first of the monsters erupted from the floor in front of him.

Chapter Twenty-Seven

Torben hauled Iro out of the way as the little monster flew at him. The slimy creature lashed out with a bladed tale, the edge scraping along Iro's breastplate. It landed on the floor and quickly scurried up onto the wall.

The monster was like a sword given terrible, disgusting life. It was long as Iro's leg, thin like a flattened length of tube. All along its sides was serrated armored plating and its tale ended in a shovel-like blade. Its head was small, childlike but elongated with two gleaming black eyes and a mouthful of dark daggers for teeth. On its underside, just before its head, were two claws each with a trio of taloned fingers. It was oily-looking, a green so dark it was almost black, and it clung to the wall, slithering along and up to the ceiling. And it wasn't alone.

"Run!" he screamed, already pushing Torben ahead of him. The bigger boy was slower to get moving, but he had all the motivation he needed. Within moments, they were both sprinting down the corridor. The monster leapt from above, screeching, flailing with its bladed tail. Iro and Torben split, each dodging around the monster, slamming into the walls and barrelling on. Torben cried out, clutched a hand to his hip, but kept on running.

Some of the others didn't hesitate, were already running. Arne and Ylfa had stopped to stare. Ashvild pushed past the others to the back to see what was happening, squeezing around Bjorn and Ingrid as they hustled along with Master Rollo's stretcher bouncing between them. Emil was the furthest back, struggling along under the extra weight he was carrying.

Behind them, Iro heard more of the flooring launched free as the swarm of monsters erupted from beneath the grates. Arne's eyes went wide, Ylfa staggered back a step and almost fell. Ashvild grabbed them both and dragged them back, pushed them into a run.

Emil laboured on under the strain of carrying Master Tannow's body. Iro and Torben caught up to him quickly. Iro slowed.

"Drop him, Emil. We have to run." He turned to stare back into the corridor. He couldn't count how many of the monsters there were, they slithered over and across each other, confusing the eye. They filled the tunnel, surging onwards in a clawing, undulating mass.

"I'm not leaving him," Emil snarled. He grit his teeth and struggled on a little faster.

The monsters kept coming, gaining on them too quickly. "Then let me help."

"I don't need your scrapping help!"

One of the monsters clinging to the ceiling leapt at them. Iro swung Neya's sword at the creature. As the blade connected, the monster contorted, wrapping its serpent-like body around the blade, claws clutching at the hilt, little face darting forward, teeth snapping at Iro. He cried out, staggered back, swung Neya's sword against the wall. The blade sheared through the monster's body about half way up it's length, spraying foul, nauseating ichor all over Iro's legs. The monster screeched, leapt free of the sword, leaving its tail behind, and ripped up a section of floor then disappeared back into the dark.

Iro didn't have time to think. He grabbed Emil's arm and pulled him on.

"Get off!" Emil snarled. He was panting, shaking, sweat dripping from his chin. The others were ahead. Slowed by Emil's pace, not willing to leave him behind. Iro saw Ashvild grimacing at them, Cali with her hand over her mouth.

Another of the monsters scrabbled along the floor, leapt at Emil. It landed on Master Tannow's body, dug its little talons into his cold flesh, finding the gaps in his armor, then swung its tail up and wrapped it through the grating above. Emil staggered, his momentum brought up short, and Master Tannow's body slipped from his shoulders. The monster swung the corpse away to land with a thud on the floor behind them and a mass of the swarming creatures fell upon it.

"No!" Emil shouted, starting forward as if to wade into the tangle and pull Master Tannow's body free.

A monster leapt out of the swarm at him. Emil swung a gauntleted fist at it. The monster slipped around the punch, wrapping its oily body along Emil's arm, digging talons into his bicep, finding gaps in the armor plating. "Cali, Steel me," Emil shouted as the monster gnashed at him with its teeth. He brought his free hand up, shoved his gauntlet in its mouth, growling in pain.

Cali stood, staring, not moving, not enhancing. Her eyes were wide, her face a picture of horror.

"Scrap!" Emil staggered. The monster had somehow managed to constrict his other arm, pulling both together, then manoeuvred around to strike at his face with its tail.

Iro launched forward and grabbed the tail before it could find Emil's face. He struggled with it, the sinuous strength almost too great to hold back. "Don't move." He stabbed with Neya's sword, the point biting into the monster's body just below its claws. Stinking Ichor washed over Emil's arms. The tail and lower body of the monster went slack and Iro pulled it free. The upper body and head were thrashing about, screaming in Emil's grip. He stared at it for a moment, then threw it into the mass of swarming monsters as they devoured Master Tannow.

"Come on!" Iro urged, grabbing one of Emil's hands and pulling him. The other boy resisted for a moment, staring into the swarm. Then he shrugged Iro's hand away, turned and started running.

They fled, the others running ahead of them. Ashvild had tugged Cali into a run as well, though the other girl only seemed to move when someone made her.

He heard the monsters start swarming after them again, the tapping of their claws, the chittering of their armored bodies scraping against each other. He saw flashes beneath them, darkness against darkness below the grates as more of the monsters raced forward.

Ahead, one of the monsters reached a claw out of the grating, caught Franka's foot. The Surveyor screamed as she fell, hitting the floor hard. Eir was running just behind her, leapt into the air, flipped upside down, stabbed her thin blade down between the grates to a monstrous shriek, landed on the other side of Franka and grabbed hold of the Hopper, hauling her to her feet. She did it all without breaking stride and both women were running again in moments.

More of the monsters were launching up out of the floor ahead of them now. Ylfa had to dodge to the side as one leapt straight up, tail slicing for her. She spun around it, slashed out with her sword, but the blade did nothing but knock the monster aside. She ran on and the creature hissed and darted back under the flooring.

Ahead of Torben, a square section of grating fell from the ceiling and one of the monsters crawled out and stabbed its tail down at him. He slowed for a moment, grabbed the tail, hauled on it with all his weight and strength and ripped the monster free from the ceiling. He swung it against the wall with a slick crack, then dropped it, leaving it dazed, and ran on.

The corridor snaked around to the left. Iro saw figures ahead, hazy in the frosted light. There were four of them, but Iro couldn't tell if they were a Hopper squad from the Home Fleet, or more enemies. If they were from the other fleet, would they help? If they were black cloaks, had they come to finish the job?

"Burning Ember Franka," Franka shouted at them. "Help us."

The new Hoppers consulted briefly. The Vanguard of the group, a tall, broad woman with dark skin and a round shield strapped to one arm gestured to another. The other Hopper grinned and stepped forward, his long brown coat billowing around him and Iro saw a small Mage cannon strapped to each side of his hip.

Franka was the first to reach the new Hoppers, Eir just a step behind. Both slipped through their ranks and slowed to a stop behind them. Bjorn and Ingrid were next, Master Rollo's stretcher carried between them. Then the Mage drew both his cannons in a single, slick movement, activated his rusty red crest and opened fire.

Flames belched from his cannons as the Mage chanted his litany. Mages needed a cannon to focus their power and the chants were somehow necessary to give it form. Iro heard the monsters screech behind him as bolts of searing plasma tore past him, scorching the air. He felt the heat on his skin and ran on, trusting the man's aim.

A square of grating dropped from in front of Iro, a monster crawling out a few paces ahead of him. The Mage fired again, a flaming bolt arcing up to strike the monster. It burst into flames, dropped from the ceiling and thrashed about. Iro leapt over it and ran on. He and Emil sprinted past the line of Hoppers at the same time, and for the first time since the manufactory he actually felt safe.

"Finally, I can cut loose," said the Mage.

He started chanting faster, firing more and more bolts from his hand cannons. A storm of fiery blasts raced down the corridor, each one striking a monster, incinerating them. It was over in seconds. A swarm of monsters that had almost killed a full squad of trainees, and all it had taken was a single Mage to burn them all.

Iro found himself staring at the man in awe. He was short, wiry, pale and completely bald on the head but with a bushy black beard. His armor was painted brown, an emblem on the breast of his two Mage cannons crossed against a flame. His coat stretched almost down to the floor and was a darker brown than his armor, it smelled of bhur beast leather. His chanting, his litany to power his cannons was a song about a girl with emerald eyes, though he sang it tunelessly.

"That's enough, Willer," the Vanguard said. "You got them all."

"And I'm already sick of your song," said another woman, this one wearing yellow armor. Her voice was blunt, her skin brown, and she had a large, prominent scar across her nose. "Can't you learn to carry a tune?"

The Mage, Willer, stopped chanting, his cannons falling silent with him. He laughed and twirled his cannons in the air. Smoke trailed from the barrels. He whipped his arms down, billowing out his coat once again, then slotted the cannons back into their holsters. "You may consider yourself saved, Burning Ember Franka." He bowed low at the hip, looked up at Franka and winked.

The Vanguard stared down the corridor a moment longer, then turned on her heel to face them all. Her back was straight and she was powerfully muscled. Void-black hair tied into a bun on top of her head, the sides shaved to stubble. She wore silver armor with an emblem on the breast of a snarling monster head.

"Vermillion Gadise Samir," the Vanguard said with a nod to Franka.

Ylfa gasped. Ashvild's eyes went wide as she stared at the woman. Torben nudged Ingrid in the side so she almost dropped the stretcher, and whispered *Legacy family* to his sister. Ingrid just nodded in return.

Everyone knew of the Legacy families. They always produced the strongest Hoppers. They were also the only people in the fleet who had two names to go along with their ship.

"Thank you," Franka said. She clasped her hands together. Even Snappy lowered his claw in something like respect.

Gadise Samir narrowed her eyes, gaze lingering on Master Rollo unconscious in his stretcher. "What happened?"

"We were on an exploratory training Hop," Franka said, keeping her eyes down. "A training group from the Eclipse and the Courage."

Gadise Samir swept her cold and inscrutable gaze across them all.

"We found a manufactory," Franka said.

That got all their attention. Even the fourth member of their group, a squat man Iro guessed was a Surveyor by the brace of autodages strapped to his right arm. Franka had just one autodage, Snappy, but this new Surveyor had at least five and all seemed to be moving independently and ceaselessly. He pushed his goggles up on his forehead and stared hungrily at Franka.

"Did you claim it?" asked Gadise Samir.

"Yes!" Emil said quickly, taking a step forward, squaring up to the Vanguard. "The Courage laid claim to it first."

Franka laughed nervously, gripped hold of Emil's arm and pulled him away. He tried to shrug her off, but her grip was like iron and she was clearly stronger than him. She had already opened her first gate and there was simply no denying the strength that gave a person. Emil struggled a moment, but Snappy clacked at him and he quieted.

"No," Franka said once Emil was behind her. "It's unclaimed and unsecured. We encountered other Hoppers, not from our fleet. Our Corsair was injured." Snappy pointed at Master Rollo on the stretcher. "And our Paladin was killed."

"Other Hoppers?" Willer asked, sounding excited. "From the fleet on the other side of the titan?"

"Yes and no," Franka said.

Gadise Samir crossed her arms, somehow seeming even more imposing. "Explain."

Franka launched into the telling of their story. The Hoppers all remained standing throughout, but Iro leaned against the wall of the corridor and soon found himself sliding down to sit with his back against it. He wasn't the only one, most of the trainees took the chance to rest. Bjorn and Ingrid slowly lowered Master Rollo's stretcher and then slumped. Eir and Ylfa leaned against the wall and whispered to each other. Arne lay down and closed his eyes. Cali sunk to her knees and stared blankly at the floor. Only Emil and Ashvild remained standing.

"Weaklings," Willer said when Franka finished her telling. "I say we march down there, secure the manufactory for ourselves. I'll burn any of those black cloaks who come calling." He tugged on his beard and grinned.

Gadise Samir stared at Master Rollo's unconscious form. He was still in bad shape and had yet to wake. They needed to get him back to a ship soon so the medics could help him.

"You would take them all on yourself?" Gadise Samir said. "Unlikely. You have only opened your second gate, Willer. That is Eclipse Rollo. He was not weak. They took him down with ease, you say?"

Franka nodded.

"Not they," Iro said. "It was just one of them. Just Goro." He suddenly realised who he was talking to and shut his mouth.

"Who are you?" Gadise Samir asked.

Iro struggled back to his feet and brushed himself off. "Eclipse Iro."

"He's just one of the trainees," Franka said.

Gadise Samir gaze was so intense Iro couldn't meet it. There was something imposing about her, like staring into the void of space and knowing you meant nothing to it.

"Why is he wearing women's armor?" Willer asked.

"You know what those low shippers are like, Willer," said the Surveyor. "They'll wear scrap and call it armor."

Willer tugged on his beard again, frowning. "I thought the Eclipse was a mid ship?"

"Didn't they say they were from that drudge ship?" asked the Surveyor. "The Courage or some other junker?"

"Enough," Gadise Samir said. She uncrossed her arms, tightened the straps holding her shield to her arm. "We'll escort these trainees back to the docks and have their pods brought across. Then we report the location of the manufactory to the council and await new orders."

Willer groaned but didn't argue. Franka quickly bowed and offered her thanks. And with that, Gadise Samir strode onwards, leading the way. Everyone else hurried to catch up, eager not to be left alone.

Iro waited, his feet leaden and unresponsive. The cool, frosted light made the charred monsters seemed nothing more than lumps of smoking flesh. It had all gone so wrong. Master Rollo injured, Master Tannow dead, Mia kidnapped. And they had all almost died to the monsters. There wasn't a one of the trainees who didn't have an injury of some type. Iro couldn't help but wonder if this was what all Hops were like? How had Neya faced it every time with a grin? How had she been so brave?

After everyone else had gone, he turned. Cali was still knelt on the cold, metal grating. She was staring down the corridor as if waiting for Mia to come running down it, perhaps shouting that the black cloaks had let her go after all. Did she blame him for having been chosen first and being too weak to make it a sport for Goro?

She should. I'd blame me.

Iro stooped and took Cali under the arm, lifting her to her feet. She didn't resist. He led her away after the others. She said nothing, but turned her head to stare down the corridor. It was useless. No one followed them.

Chapter Twenty-Eight

Alfvin paced down the perfect halls of the Eclipse, his footfalls a well-timed staccato rhythm against the metal flooring. Someone ahead waved to him. It was Finn, a foolish old Hopper so far past his prime he was more hinderance than help to any Hop that was foolish enough to have him. Alfvin lowered his head and paced on, ignoring Finn's greetings. He had no time for it. Not the small talk, or the humbly worded request to be sent on more Hops, nor the eventual refusal he would have to give. Easier, quicker, and ultimately more satisfying just to ignore the old fool entirely.

He rounded a corner. There were other people in the corridor. They saw him coming and moved out of his way. It was as it should be. He was the Lead Hopper aboard the Eclipse. He had worked hard to get to that position, far harder than any of his peers. Even those who had managed to open their fourth gates. He had earned the respect.

Alfvin stopped outside the infirmary door, pulled out his tablet, and opened up the file on current injuries. It showed only one of his active Hoppers was severely injured, Gyda, suffering from a nasty infection caused by deep laceration by a rustling blade. Alfvin considered that a moment, then added a new entry for Rollo. He left the status blank.

He pushed open the infirmary door and almost recoiled from the sharp antiseptic tang that wafted out at him. It reminded him far too much of his childhood, of a mother who couldn't stand even a single mote of dust to mar her perfect quarters. Of being stripped down and scoured clean after every training session lest he *track muck* into the place.

Scrap, but Alfvin hated the way certain smells could trigger a memory and send his mind careening down useless paths. His mother was dead, he hadn't been a child for many years. That part of him was gone, given to the black along with his mother's corpse. He pushed the memories away and strode into the infirmary.

It was exactly as he remembered it. A large open room with a single bench next to the door, three beds against the wall to his left, then a series of cabinets once filled with supplies and drugs, now almost bare. Beyond the cabinets sat a desk where the doctor could work while not seeing patients, and behind that a single cot where the doctor could sleep. That was his mother's addition to the infirmary. Towards the end of her life, she had not liked to leave the place, preferring to eat and sleep close to her *supplies*.

To the right were four doorways, each leading to a private room. Alfvin's Hoppers would be in those rooms. His Hoppers were always provided the private rooms rather than being treated out in the open where anyone could walk in and see them at their weakest. It was important to keep that distance. The techs and drudges, and even the officers needed to believe the Hoppers were strong. They weren't allowed to see their heroes weak and injured.

Alfvin approached the first door on his right and peered in the window. He saw the old medic, Knud fussing about at Gyda's bedside. He pulled the door open and stepped inside. Both medic and patient looked up at him. Gyda gave him a smile tight with pain, Knud just frowned a little harder then went back to peering at the wound in Gyda's side.

"I'll be back in Hopping condition in no time, boss," Gyda said. Knud poked at her wound and she hissed in pain.

Alfvin drew in a deep breath. He knew that rich, sickly sweet scent on the air. Infection. Either the drugs weren't working, or they simply didn't have any left. He made a note in his tablet to requisition some. Though, in truth, he wasn't sure the upper ships would respond. They were closing ranks, cutting off the mid ships as well as the lowers. Alfvin could already see where things were headed, and the fleet-wide Stalling only seemed to be accelerating the incoming divide.

Alfvin nodded. "I'm counting on you, Gyda," he lied. "We'll beat this thing together. Anything you need to get back on your feet, it's yours." It was sometimes easier to tell people what they wanted to hear. It saved a lot of wasted air and tears.

Alfvin pushed the door open again and waved for Knud to follow him out. Once outside, he asked the real question. "Will she survive?"

Knud paced over to the empty bench and sank down into it with a hefty groan. "I don't know. She's strong, but I've not seen this type of infection before. New titan, new problems. Would help if I had a full larder." He waved vaguely towards the near empty cabinets.

Alfvin ignored the gesture and pulled up his tablet again. He marked Gyda as out of action permanently and pulled up the roster. They were now two Hoppers down and that was two too many. It would hurt their standings within the fleet and that could lower their priority for supplies. He made another note to put Finn back on active Hops. The old Corsair was next to useless, but as long as he could hold a sword, he counted as a Hopper. It was a thin line.

"Rollo?" Alfvin asked.

"Room four," Knud said. "He's unconscious. Has been since they brought him in."

"Will he survive?"

Knud shrugged. "Honestly, I'm scrapping surprised he made it this long. I give him fifty-fifty."

Alfvin opened the door to room four and stepped in. Rollo was in the bed, hooked up to a machine that displayed a number of vital signs, most of which looked low to Alfvin's eye. He was swathed in bandages, his mouth hanging open, breath barely moving his chest. Frigg sat at his bedside, staring up at Alfvin through puffy eyes. He shouldn't have been surprised by that. Frigg and Rollo had always been close. Even as children, they had been near inseparable. Alfvin had hated that. He'd always felt excluded by the two.

It was oddly satisfying to see Rollo brought so low. He'd always been stronger than Alfvin. Always one step ahead in training, in opening the gates, in everything. Alfvin pushed the thought down, smothered it in cold regard.

"The council is panicking," Alfvin said, not taking his eyes from the gentle rise and fall of Rollo's chest.

Frigg wiped her eyes, sniffed. "They're right to. The other fleet appears hostile, and there's something even worse. If the black cloaks don't allow us access to a manufactory, ships will start failing soon."

"Allow us access…" Alfvin pinched the bridge of his nose against the headache that pulsed along his brow. "The council are too afraid of the Stalling. They're unwilling to take action that might reduce our number of Hoppers."

Frigg sniffed again, pulled out her own tablet. "I'm not convinced about the Stalling yet, Alfvin. We don't have enough data. I've been going over…"

He waved a hand at Frigg to get her to stop. She'd talk for hours about the data if he let her, and as usual her only conclusions would be that it was too early to draw conclusions. That was why he was made Lead Hopper instead of her. Frigg was terrible at taking decisive action, preferring instead to continue to gather more data. She was just like the council, too paralysed to take action. They didn't understand that sometimes decisions needed to be made, action needed to be taken. And if it was the wrong action, well, that didn't matter. You just made it right afterwards. Data could always be altered, history rewritten.

"His trainees will need a new master until Rollo is awake again," Frigg said eventually.

Alfvin grimaced. Most of the trainees were stalled at that level, useless trash who would never be anything but a drain on the Eclipse. But the Courage boy was different. If he could open even his first gate, it might be enough to convince the council that not all hope was lost. Then they might actually take the risk of securing the manufactory. The fate of the entire fleet rested on that low shipper's ability to progress. He needed to be pushed harder. He needed to be given a reason to struggle. Shown what was at stake and what he had to lose.

Alfvin raised his terminal, tapped at the screen. He put in a request to dock with the Courage. They had some supplies they could spare, enough to keep that scrapping hunk of junk flying for a while longer. It would provide ample opportunity for the Courage boy to visit his family.

"Should I take over the training?" Frigg asked.

Alfvin shook his head as he turned for the door. "No. You have your own duties to attend." He couldn't let her anywhere near the Courage boy. Frigg was far too soft, just like Rollo. The time for coddling was past. The boy needing guiding with an iron hand now. And if that failed, he needed beating into shape.

It had been a long time since Iro had been able to sleep in. So long he couldn't actually remember. Maybe back when they were attached to titan 01, before he had been given duties as a tech. Six or seven years ago maybe? Eight?

Childhoods were short aboard ship.

He really wanted to enjoy the sleep in by actually sleeping, but he couldn't. He was awake and there was no denying it. He'd barely stripped out of his dirty clothes before collapsing into bed the previous night, and had dropped off to sleep instantly, but now he was staring up at the bunk above bowing beneath Bjorn's weight. The events of the previous day's Hop kept repeating in his mind. Things he could have done differently. If only he'd been stronger, strong enough to stand up to the black cloaks. Strong enough to be the one taken instead of Mia.

In an attempt to distract himself, Iro activated his crest and stared up at it. It had grown again, more sweeping lines connecting it, sectioning bits of it. More symbols he didn't understand. There was one which looked a lot like a rectangle with a single solid line stabbing out of it. When Iro tilted his head slightly, it almost looked like a hammer. Like Mia's hammer. The crest was still no brighter. A cool, dim blue like ice.

He pulled up the crest index on his tablet and scrolled through the mountains of symbols, checking each of them against his crest. The crossed tusks was definitely the symbol for the bhur beast. His first monster kill. A momentous point in his life, forever etched onto his crest. He trailed a hand through the symbol, the soft, icy blue light fuzzing around his fingers.

Near the centre of the crest, he found the symbol for the Blink Strike talent. All the talents had corresponding symbols and they were well-documented. For the Blink Strike, it was a single slash like the cut of a sword, but sheared in two, starting in one place and finishing somewhere else.

The arcane lettering that flowed along the lines was still a mystery to him. Hoppers had been studying it for generations and still no one understood the language. Some people insisted it was just gibberish, but Iro didn't believe that. It had to mean something.

Then there was the symbol at the very centre of his crest. Three sword slashes overlapping each other in the shape of a triangle. There was nothing in the index about that symbol and Master Rollo had seemed surprised by it. Iro wanted to know what it meant. Was it something to do with his manifesting a talent? Was it different because he had manifested aboard titan 02 instead of 01? The index provided no answers.

Eventually Bjorn rolled out of bed and pulled Iro up a few moments later. They headed out to the showers, not bothering with the usual morning run. Iro spent longer than he normally would under the running water, staring up into the stream and letting the drops pelt him in the face.

Dressed in clean training uniforms, they made their way to their hall. Eir and Ashvild were already there and Iro gave them a brief smile. Eir smiled back, but it seemed a shallow thing. They gathered together to move through the stretches and said nothing past polite greetings. The others arrived slowly. Arne and Torben first, then Ylfa and Ingrid.

Iro stared at the doorway and waited, hoping to see Master Rollo saunter through like normal. Maybe a little bruised and grumpier than usual, but otherwise unhurt. He'd leap up onto his usual perch, hands in pockets, eyes half lidded. Then he'd tell them all to line up, and explain in excruciating detail what they'd all done wrong. It was a vain hope.

Eventually a woman strolled through, a tablet clutched in one hand. She was tall with braided brown hair and a gentle face. She gave them all a friendly smile then waved at them to stand easy.

"Some of you know me, some not. My name is

Eclipse Frigg," the woman said as she paced into the training hall. "I'm here because Rollo can't be."

"Is he alright?" Iro asked quickly.

Frigg frowned. "You must be Iro. Rollo mentioned you were short." She smiled. "Rollo is… He's hurt. Badly. He hasn't regained consciousness yet, but the medics think he will eventually. For now, that obviously means he won't be training you."

"What about the manufactory?" Arne asked.

Bjorn nodded eagerly. "And those black cloaks. What's being done?"

Frigg held up a slender hand for silence. "All of that is above my clearance. I'm sure the Grands will make a decision and statement on it soon enough."

Ashvild stepped forward, clasped her hands behind her back and waited.

"Go ahead, Ashvild," Frigg said.

"Will you be training us from now on?"

Frigg shook her head. "I have my own duties. Alfvin, the lead Hopper here on the Eclipse, will be assigning you a new trainer in a few days."

Iro felt his limbs grow heavy. He liked Master Rollo and he didn't want to change trainers.

I just want things to go back to how they were. He clenched his fists against the frustration. "Will it be temporary?" he asked. "Will Master Rollo be coming back when he's better?"

Frigg frowned at him again, almost as though she were sizing him up. "I don't know. *If* he wakes up, he may have a long recovery ahead of him."

Iro didn't like the way she said that. He was sure Master Rollo would wake up. He just knew it.

"In the mean time," Frigg continued. "You all have three days downtime to rest up. What you went through was an ordeal. Take the time you're being given to recuperate."

Iro looked down the line at the others. They were all milling about, unsure of what to do. Three days off was probably more than any of them had since they were children. Like Iro, they probably didn't know what to do with so much free time.

Frigg smiled. "That's it. Be back here on time in three days to meet your new trainer. You're dismissed. Oh, and Iro, we'll be docking with the Courage for two hours tomorrow. You're welcome to visit your old ship during that time, but be sure to be back aboard the Eclipse before separation."

Emil walked into the empty training room, unsurprised by how bare it felt. It was two days since the Hop and no one had been to see him, not here or at his quarters. Master Tannow was gone and Emil guessed no other trainers wanted him. Mia was gone and her father had stepped down from captaining the ship. That had made Emil's father happy, seeing one of the officers brought low, and the captain of all people. It was like the man didn't even consider the reason behind it, too caught up in what he thought was some sort of vicious karma. Emil hated that. He'd slept here in the training room the previous night just to get away from the old man.

All but one of the training dummies had been completely removed, cannibalised for any working parts it might contain and given over to the last remaining full trainee squad on the Courage. Emil guessed he and Cali would be squeezed in to their ranks soon enough. For now, though, he had the training room all to himself. It was quiet and dark, all but one of the lights removed to be used elsewhere, and even that one flickered occasionally. Where paint still clung to the walls, it was peeling, and where it wasn't the rust was busy consuming the metal. The padded floor was ripped in places, patched over with silver tape in others. Crates and boxes were stacked haphazardly against the far wall, some locked up tight, others cracked open and stinking of moldering contents. Still, there was plenty of room for one person.

Emil dropped his gauntlets by the door and walked over to the training dummy. He pressed the button with his foot to set it spinning on its medium difficulty. Then he stepped into its range, ducked a swipe, blocked another with his arm, delivered a couple of lightning jabs to the dummy's face, stepped back out of range. The dummy accepted the beating with bland stoicism and kept on swinging its arms, its pink and purple smiling face unmoved.

It felt like it was attacking in slow motion. Emil could track the movements with ease, knew how to slip around them or block them without injury. He danced inside its reach again, weaved around a combo of strikes, ducked a swing, pounded out a one-two punch against its chest, blocked a retort, then rose into an uppercut that rocked the dummy's leering head back. Emil jumped back out of reach again and the dummy kept swinging. It wasn't too long ago the scrapping thing on this difficulty setting would have battered him about and left him bleeding on the floor. Now, beating it was all too easy. And he didn't even feel like he was moving quickly. He felt sluggish, unmotivated.

Emil pressed the button on the floor to deactivate the dummy. He wasn't feeling the fight today. Maybe a run around the ship would raise his spirits and put him in the mood. Or some strength exercises. He felt like training his talent, drawing on the current inside and using it to enhance, but without a partner to work with there was simply nothing he could do. He turned for the door and found Cali there.

"Hey," she said quietly. She was talking again,

moving on her own. Emil thought that was a good sign. He'd been worried after seeing her catatonic when they got back from the Hop. Still, she seemed different. More distant and reserved. She was wearing a fraying officer's uniform instead of her training gear, and carrying a tablet instead of her knives.

"Hey," Emil shot back. "Ready to get started? I need a partner for talent training."

Cali winced and looked away, pulled her worn jacket tighter across her chest. "I, uh… I'm not here to train, Emil. I'm dropping out. There's a spot opened up for a junior officer and I'm going to start the training for it."

"What? Why?"

She stared at the floor. "Hopping just isn't for me. I thought it would be but…" She shook her head.

It felt like a betrayal somehow. But that wasn't right. "That's a load of scrap, Cali." She looked up, shocked. "You're strong. A gifted Paladin. You're just scared."

Cali's face crumpled, then hardened into a glare. "Of course I am! Every time I set foot on that titan something bad happens. The first time I was hurt. The second time Mia was taken. What will happen if I go again? I can't. I just can't."

No it wasn't betrayal. It was abandonment. Cali was leaving him just like everyone else. First Tannow, then Mia, and now Cali. Now there was no one left and he would be alone. Well that was fine. He didn't need anyone else. He'd been training alone for half his life. Living alone for the other half because it was more comfortable than staying in his own quarters with his father. Empty store rooms or training halls or pod bays had always made much more comfortable beds. He'd never really had many friends either, just never had the time for them. But he'd counted Mia and Cali as friends. Until now. He knew it wasn't fair to blame them. But he was also too scrapping angry to care.

"Fine. Go. I don't really need you anyway. You were just holding me back."

Cali looked confused, but that soon gave way to anger. Emil preferred that. He was more comfortable with anger. Knew what to do with it, how to handle it. "Scrap you, Emil! Just…" She let out a wordless growl and turned away, stopping a few paces out the door.

"Here." She tapped on her pad a couple of times and Emil heard an alert from over near his gauntlets where he'd dropped his own tablet. The one Cali had given him. "Mia liked to draw in her off time." Emil watched her wipe an arm across her face. "That one is of you." And then she was gone, storming off down the halls of the ship and out of Emil's life.

He waited for her to go, to be certain she wasn't standing down the hall, then he approached his tablet. There was a message from her, a picture attached to it. He opened it up to see a black and white sketch of himself. It was terrible really, all smudged lines and incorrect proportions, a rough sketch at best. But it was clearly him. He was smiling in it, holding up one fist as if in challenge. He looked… happy.

Emil scoffed and moved his finger over to delete the image, paused, finger hovering over the button. Like it or not, Mia had been his friend and this was the only thing he had left of her. She had cared enough to draw him.

He shook his head. He didn't need friends. He didn't need allies. He didn't need anyone. No matter what the universe threw at him, Emil would face it alone. He mashed his finger down on the delete button far harder than he needed to as if to prove a point, and when the image vanished from the little screen he squashed the feeling of loss that tried to rise within him.

Emil threw the tablet to the floor and turned back to

the training dummy. He tapped the button on the floor to get it spinning and then upped it to the maximum difficulty. Its whipping limbs became a blur of movement he couldn't track, the whirring of its gears a mocking, hateful rhythm.

He stepped inside the dummy's reach and immediately took two hearty blows to the ribs. Brought his arms up to block, took another smack to the face. He staggered back, wiped a sleeve across his face. No blood, but his cheeks were wet. Had to be sweat. If only he had a partner to enhance him, he could stand inside the dummy's reach and take anything and everything it threw at him. But there were no more partners. He had to do it all himself.

Emil activated his fiery red crest and let the current inside of him flow. "Steel," he said, and stepped back into the dummy's flailing limbs. A crack across the face sent him staggering. A jab to the gut doubled him over. An uppercut knocked him back to crash down on the floor.

Of course it hadn't worked. Paladins couldn't buff themselves. Without a target, the current had simply flowed through him and dissipated.

Emil lifted his legs, flipped up onto his feet. Activated his crest again. "Steel," he growled and darted back at the dummy once more. It hit him in the arm, the chest, the head. Drew blood and sent him crashing down again.

Emil climbed back to his feet, activated his crest. "Steel!" He screamed the word as he launched himself at the dummy.

Chapter Twenty-Nine

It was the smell that hit Iro first. After so long aboard the Eclipse and its pristine floors and walls, and the pervasive stink of disinfectant, the smell of the Courage was stale. Like air left too long without being passed through a filter. There was mildewy scent to it. A fuzzy heat like dust cooking on a heater unit. He smiled, had to wipe a sleeve across his eyes. It smelled like home.

A couple of drudges from the Eclipse hustled Iro out of the way, struggling with the crates they were carrying. They were delivering supplies to the Courage, much needed things like new clothing, unstripped screws, and fresh filters. Things the Eclipse had to spare, but the Courage had been needing for years. Iro didn't know why it was happening, but he was glad. Anything to keep his old ship flying.

"Smell that?" one of the Eclipse drudges, a man with no chin, whispered to his colleague.

"Lower ships," said the old woman with grey hair laboring with the same crate. "They don't wash."

Iro's mood soured and he turned away before he overheard anything else. He walked through the halls of the Courage and looked at it with new eyes. He'd always seen the rusting bulkheads, flickering lights, and exposed sparking wires, of course. He had been a tech aboard the Courage and was trained to see and fix them where he could. But having spent so much time on the Eclipse he saw it slightly differently. It didn't have to be this way. If the lower ships were given the same supplies the others were given, the Courage wouldn't be falling apart. They weren't lazy. They worked just as hard as the Eclipse crew, maybe harder. But they didn't have the means to fix everything that was going wrong.

The passing crew of the Courage nodded to him as he went. He wasn't even sure they recognised him. He was a little taller now, cleaner for certain, his hair neatly trimmed. He was also wearing an Eclipse Hopper uniform, freshly printed and crisper than anything he'd ever worn while living on the Courage. Probably that was all they saw. Not the young tech who used to get underfoot trying to fix servos that were long past dead, but a foreign Hopper striding purposefully through their ship. Certainly no one addressed him by name. Those who did speak to him just lowered their heads and deferred, quickly moving on. He felt oddly out of place, an outsider on his own ship, just as he was back on the Eclipse.

His feet knew the way even without thinking about it and Iro soon found himself outside his quarters. *Mom's quarters,* he corrected himself. He didn't live there anymore. That thought brought an odd tightness to his chest and he struggled to breathe past it, took a moment to collect himself. He reached for the door handle, paused, then drew back his hand and knocked instead.

After a few seconds the door opened, grinding against its frame as it always did. His mother stood on the other side, her hair half brushed, her eyes wide. "Who is this mighty Hopper standing at my door?" she asked, grinning.

Iro felt tears springing to his eyes. He tried to say something, found his throat too tight, coughed. "Hi mom."

His mother stepped forward and wrapped her arms around him. Iro sniffed loudly and hugged her back. It really felt like coming home, like a weight he hadn't realised he'd been carrying was just lifted from his shoulders. And yet, something was different somehow. His mother seemed smaller. She had always been taller than him, a giant almost, to his eyes. Now they were the same height.

Iro heard footsteps in the hall, people passing, having to squeeze around him as he stood in his mom's embrace. He cleared his throat.

"Huh?" his mom said. "Oh, we're in the way. Sorry, Isis." She waved to the woman squeezing past behind them. "My son the Hopper has come home for a visit."

Isis laughed and waved as she continued on down the hall. "Nice to see you again, Iro." He waved back, but Isis was already moving on.

"Come on," his mom said. "Let's get inside. I just need to finish getting dressed. I'll be two minutes." She rushed away past the kitchen and disappeared into her room.

Iro stepped inside, pulled the door shut behind him and took a moment to bask in the feel of home. The smell of it. Nothing had changed despite how long he'd been away. That felt strange somehow. Strange and also right.

He opened the door to his room and looked in. His bed had been made and he certainly never did that himself, but otherwise it was just how he had left it. The same box full of parts and wires, his old radio hidden at the bottom. His drawer of clothes that never quite closed properly because the roller had fallen off and he'd never found time to replace it. The dusty smudge against the window where he'd spent so long leaning his forehead, staring out into the black.

His old titan bestiary was out, lying on his bed. He walked over, sat down, flipped open the cover and stared at the childish drawings. He'd had limited colours to choose from and no real idea what the monsters looked like past Neya's excited descriptions. He'd drawn a rustling as a wobbly red circle with two black dots for eyes. His old depiction of a kharapid looked like a wavy green wire with little legs and flailing arms.

"Iro?" his mom called.

Iro shut the bestiary and smiled. Things were different now. He'd seen some of the monsters in his little book first hand. He'd even fought a few of them. "Coming."

His mom was waiting for him in the kitchen. She had her bridge uniform on, the jacket slung over one of the chairs, and her hair was no longer a wild tangle, but a tamed frizz. She smiled at him, rounded the table, and squeezed his arms. "Look at you. So big. What do they feed you over there?"

"It's this wonderful new substance," Iro said. "You won't have heard of it. They call it algae."

"Mmmm. Sounds tasty."

Iro nodded. "Sometimes they do flavour it to give it a… taste." They both laughed. "The portions are larger over there though. And I can shower every day."

His mother pulled out one of the chairs and sat. "Sounds wonderful."

Iro just nodded. It was easier than correcting her. He sat down opposite her, tried to meet her gaze but found the frank appraisal oddly awkward. He felt like he wasn't worth the pride she was beaming his way.

"Tell me about it, Iro," she said excitedly. "Tell me everything."

He wanted to. He wanted to tell her about how hard the training had been at first, but how fun it had become. About everything he was learning. About the new friends he had made and working with them to bring down a bhur beast. He wanted to tell her about Master Rollo and how he pretended to be hard on them all, but they all knew how much he cared. And how strangely comfortable it was spending time with Eir. There was so much to say. So many happy times so she wouldn't worry. Instead, though, he found himself telling her about the last Hop. How something had felt wrong from the start, and the encounter with the black cloaks and everything it had cost them. And worst of all, he told his mom about how Goro had wanted to take him, but his cowardice had made the black cloak take Mia instead. His words came faster and faster as he told the story, tumbling out over each other in a frantic bid for freedom.

His mom just listened throughout. She didn't interrupt or try to offer condolences or encouragement. She didn't condemn him for his actions. She just listened.

"I'm a coward," Iro admitted eventually. Finally putting his most damning thought into words. "I locked up. I keep freezing. All I ever wanted was to be a Hopper. To be like Neya. To be brave like her. But I'm not. And because I'm a coward, Mia was taken. And the worst part is..." He paused, sniffed, wiped his eyes, swallowed hard and had to force the words past his constricting throat. "The worst part is I felt... I felt relieved. That someone else was taken instead of me." Hot, shameful tears streamed down his face and he buried his head in his hands to hide them.

His mother was silent. Damning him. Hating him. Seeing her own son for the first time as the coward he was.

"I'm relieved too," she said quietly. "I know Galen and Cali and Mia, but I'm still relieved these black cloaks took her instead of you. I wouldn't wish it on them or on anyone. But I'm still relieved they didn't take you. Does that make me a bad person?"

Iro looked up at his mother. Her face was lined, seemed greyer than before, and her eyes were shining. "No, but..."

"Does it make me a coward?"

"Of course not! But I froze. And that's why they took Mia instead. I froze against the rustlings as well. And the bhur beast. And the kharapid. I keep freezing."

"So give up."

"What?" Iro looked up to find his mother staring at him, her eyes hard.

"Give up. Come home. The Eclipse won't stop you from returning if you give up being a Hopper. Your room is still here. Engineering will welcome you back as a tech. Your little friend with the big nose is rushed off his feet."

Would it really be that simple?

He could just give up and go back to being a tech. The Courage did still feel more like home than the Eclipse. He had friends here. It seemed simple. A life of fixing things, of pulling systems apart and putting them back together. But it was the life he'd already had.

The life I wanted to escape from.

"But I want to be a Hopper. I've always wanted to be a Hopper."

"Why?"

Iro had spent a long time considering just that question, though he'd never said the truth out loud. "I used to want to go on Hops with Neya. To share in her adventures. To see her at her best instead of just listening in to her comms. But she's dead. And I didn't have a talent, so… I almost gave up."

He shook his head. "But now I have a talent and… I want to be like her. I want to be someone Neya would be proud of. To be strong and brave like she was."

"Would you like to hear the truth about your sister, Iro? Neya was scared. Every single Hop, she was afraid. The titan scared her, the monsters terrified her. But worst of all, she was always so worried she wouldn't make it back. That she would leave you and me alone." His mother drew in a ragged breath and nodded to herself. "She was always scared. That's why she grinned like that before every Hop.

Because she didn't want you to see the fear. She was so desperate for you to see her as brave and indomitable. You always looked up to her and she wanted to be someone worth looking up to, so she hid her fear behind smiles and she went out there anyway. Every time."

"But that just proves I'm a coward. She faced her fear, overcame it. I don't. I just freeze, let other people get hurt in my place."

"No you don't, Iro. You've never hidden from it. That kharapid, the one that attacked your friend Emil. It would have killed him if you hadn't stepped in front of it."

Iro opened his mouth to argue, but his mother barrelled on.

"It was your sword that killed the bhur beast. You didn't give it to someone else. You stepped into harm's way to help strike that killing blow."

"It's Neya's sword," Iro said weakly.

"From what you've said, you didn't lock up against the rustlings. You were doing exactly what your trainer has told you to do. You were protecting your Paladins."

"But what about the black cloaks? What about Mia? I froze then. I dropped to my knees and couldn't move and they took her."

His mom nodded to his words, condemning him. "Maybe. But the truth is, Iro, you can't win every fight. You are going to lose some. What you can do is survive the losses. Learn from them. Get stronger and don't lose again."

Get stronger and don't lose again. The words spun about in his head like algae being stirred in the vat. It was an impossible task. The black cloaks were too strong. Even Master Rollo couldn't hope to beat them. He stared down at his hands. *Get stronger and don't lose again.*

"So are you going to quit?" his mother asked. He looked up and found a kind smile on her face. "I won't lie,

Iro. It would make me happy. I would love to have you back here and safe. But would you be happy?"

Get stronger and don't lose again. He shook his head. "I'm a Hopper," he said, his voice quiet and weaker than he liked. "I'm a Hopper." More firmly this time. "Or I will be one day. After training. I'll become someone Neya would be proud of."

His mom sniffed, wiped at her eyes, and smiled at him again. "And I have just the thing to help." She stood and rounded the table, moving down the rusting halls to the bedroom doors. She paused there, placed a hand against Neya's door.

She pulled the door open and disappeared inside, reappearing a few seconds later with a red scarf clutched in one hand. Iro recognised it. Neya had always worn it tied around her left arm whenever she went on a Hop. But thinking back, he couldn't remember seeing it on her arm the day titan 01 exploded.

"Here." His mother held out the scarf to him. It was old and faded, covered in little stitchings where rips and tears had been hastily repaired. He took it carefully and stared down at it. He'd never noticed it before when Neya was wearing it, but there were some old dark markings on it. A symbol so faded he couldn't make out what it had once been.

"It was your father's. The only thing he left behind." Iro looked up to find his mother staring at the table. She never spoke of his father. Never answered any questions. Almost like it was too painful for her to even think about. "Neya always wore it whenever she Hopped. But that last time she… I suppose she forgot it. And now it's yours." She rounded the table, took the scarf from his hands and tied it loosely around his left arm. Just like Neya had worn it.

When she was done, his mom stepped back and

looked at him, smiling, hands clasped before her. "She would be proud of you, Iro. Never doubt that."

Iro spent the entire stay with his mother. She asked about his training and he finally got to tell her about it all. His new friends, Master Rollo, how much fun sparring was despite losing every single bout. He couldn't quite bring himself to tell her about Eir. He found he was oddly embarrassed at what his mother might say.

Eventually the alarm sounded, a five minute warning that the two ships were about to separate, and Iro said a hasty goodbye, disentangled himself from his mom's crushing hug, and ran for the docking umbilical. He'd meant to find time to visit Roret, but that would have to wait until next time. He hoped his friend would understand.

Faces passed by a in a blur. Some nodded to him and he nodded back, unsure if it was recognition or just a sign of respect to a Hopper. Some of them moved out of his way, others he had to dodge around.

He almost missed Cali. She wasn't wearing her Hopper uniform, but a patchy officer's suit. She stared at him through shadowed eyes and didn't move out of his way. He slowed to a stop and faced her. They were blocking the hallway, but no one else was close enough for that to matter. Iro searched for something to say, the right thing to say. Cali just stared at him, her face flat and unreadable.

"I'm sorry." The words fell from his lips quietly. They were inadequate, but he didn't know what else to say.

Cali stared at him, face blank and dark eyes boring into him.

"It should have been me," Iro continued quickly. "Not Mia. They should have taken me."

Cali's silence assaulted him far worse than any insult she could have spat.

Iro searched for the right thing to say, for anything to say. His mother's words bubbled to the surface in his mind. *Get stronger and don't lose again.*

"I'll bring her back," Iro said before he could think better of it.

Cali's face contorted. First pain, then anger. "You? You're useless. I wish they had taken you." She turned away from him, stalked down the corridor.

"I promise," Iro called after her. "I'll get stronger. I'll find Mia and bring her back."

Cali ignored him, turned a corner and was gone.

"I promise," Iro repeated quietly, knowing it was all to himself now. "I will get stronger. No matter what it takes. Even if I have to break open my own gates. No matter how many times I have to lose, I will survive and learn. I'll get strong enough to beat the black cloaks and bring Mia back."

Chapter Thirty

Iro came awake with that vague sense that something was wrong. He couldn't quite put his finger on it, but it was almost like the ship's gravity had been altered slightly, just enough things felt off. Then the beds shook as Bjorn unleashed a rumbling snore that almost convinced Iro the bigger boy was choking on something.

He checked the time and felt a grin spread across his face. Bjorn had overslept. Usually they'd all be out the door and jogging around the ship by now, struggling to keep up as Bjorn steadily increased the pace. As if to confirm the mini victory, the big Corsair snored again, the sound like a grinding ventilation fan.

Iro rolled out of bed and stood. Bjorn was sprawled out, the sheet wrapped around his legs, one hand splayed out, his mouth hanging open. Another brutally loud snore split the peace of the little room in two.

Creeping so he wouldn't accidentally wake the bigger boy, Iro opened the door to their room and crossed over to Torben and Arne's door. It was closed and no sound issued from within. He pulled it open slowly and saw the other two boys also asleep in their bunks. Something was definitely wrong, Iro never awoke first. Most days he was wrenched out of bed by Bjorn and pushed out the door while he was still pulling on his clothes. But today… today was different. Today was a day of vengeance.

All the quarters aboard a ship had a comms device to communicate with the bridge. Normally they were only used in emergencies or to report accidents. However, they also functioned as alarms in case of proximity warnings or general alerts. His old quarters on the Courage had the same comm system and long ago Iro had taken it apart to figure out how to tap into it with his own little makeshift radio. While playing around with it, he had also learned how to trip its various functions on a local level.

He made sure the doors to both his own room and the other boys' room were fully open, then opened up the panel on the comm device and twisted one of the wires into a new position. A blaring alarm like a hundred screaming Vhar casters tore through their little quarters. It was loud enough that even expecting it, Iro winced and jumped. He heard a muffled cry and then a thud that he guessed was Bjorn falling out of bed. Some shouted curses were probably Torben. Arne was the first out of his room, careening into the doorframe, eyes wide and face wet with drool. Bjorn was next, staggering forward with his hands clasped over his ears.

Iro untwisted the wires and the alarm cut off immediately. He couldn't keep the smile from his face.

"What the scrap?" Arne yelled, then looked shocked at the loudness of his own voice.

Bjorn groaned and grabbed Iro's arm, physically pulling him away from the comm device. "You trying to deafen us?"

Iro just grinned wider and assumed the worst Bjorn impression he could muster. "Lazy scrap, what time do you call this?"

"Huh?" Bjorn checked the clock. "Oh scrap."

Iro switched to a terrible Torben impression. "Oversleeping is the mark of a lazy mind."

"I hate you, Iro," Arne said, already turning and staggering back to his room.

"Love you too, Arne," Iro said loudly. Arne flicked him a rude gesture over his shoulder.

Bjorn was still staring at him bleary eyed. Iro just stared back. Then the bigger boy laughed and nodded. "Alright. Up, lazy scraps. Let's get this day started right. We're got to meet our new master later and we're gonna give a good impression."

Arne poked his head back out of the room. "I'm tired."

"Exactly why we're gonna do the morning run at double speed today."

Arne groaned.

"You can thank Iro."

Arne glared. "I hate you, Iro." He smiled and ducked back into his room. "Torben's gone back to sleep."

Iro raised his voice. "Tell him to get up or I'll trip the alarm again."

"Scrap you!" Torben shouted. "I'm up. I'm up."

Bjorn wasn't lying about pushing them hard to make up for the accidental late morning. He thundered through the ship's corridors at a pace that none of the others could match. Iro gave it his best shot though, pushing himself harder than he ever had before. Even so, Bjorn was waiting by the showers, leaning casually against the wall when Iro collapsed before him. He struggled to catch his breath, wiped sweat from his forehead, then again as more sprang up instantly. Arne was next to arrive, also gasping and red-faced. He collapsed next to Iro.

"I don't hate you… anymore, Iro," Arne said between great, panting breaths. "I hate him instead." He pointed a shaking finger at Bjorn.

Torben was the last to arrive. He was panting, his eyes wide, a hand pressed to his gut. "I got a stitch," he said as he slowed to a stop. Then he bent over double, unleashing a series of "Ow ow ows."

They rushed through the shower so quick Iro almost

thought they were back on water rations again. Then they jogged to the mess hall and Bjorn rushed them through breakfast too. He shovelled the algae into his mouth in five seconds flat, then berated them all for eating too slowly. As soon as they were done, Bjorn marched them to the training hall. Iro was already regretting waking up the bigger boy.

When they rounded the corner, they saw the girls had beaten them to it as usual. They were already moving through their stretches, and they were also already lined up which was a little unusual.

"Don't you four ever sleep?" Arne asked as he shuffled through the door. He punctuated the statement with a loud yawn.

Iro caught Eir's gaze and raised his hand to wave, but her eyes were wide and she gave a short shake of her head.

"You're late," said a man Iro hadn't seen before. He was tall and rangy, his hair close cropped and his face all hard angles. He stood at the far end of the room, close to the perch Master Rollo usually lounged on, but unlike Rollo this newcomer stood rigid, his arms crossed against his chest, a disapproving look on his face like he had stepped in something foul.

"No we're not," Arne said. He pointed at the clock. "Right on time."

The newcomer did not look impressed. "Rollo may have run things with such a lax discipline, but I will not. You are expected to be here, warmed up and ready, by the time training starts. From now on, anyone arriving after myself will receive punishment."

"What type of punishment?" Arne asked.

Bjorn grabbed the smaller boy and pulled him into line. "Shut up, Arne."

The newcomer glared at Arne for a moment longer. He didn't elaborate on the promised punishment and somehow that made it worse.

They all lined up quickly, Iro and the other boys joining in the girls' warmup stretches. The newcomer watched them in silence for a minute, his gaze somewhere between hostile and judging. It seemed to linger on Iro and he found himself staring at the floor rather than suffer beneath the man's venomous eyes.

"I am Eclipse Alfvin," the newcomer said eventually. "Master Alfvin to you. I will be taking over from Rollo in your training. Do not for a moment believe I will be as lenient as him."

Master Alfvin stepped forward, approaching them all, then walked down the line of trainees as he spoke. "You have been coddled. Made weak by your trainer's weakness. No more. I will mold you into Corsairs. Hoppers worthy of the name. You will become the pride of the Eclipse and the shining beacon for progress in the entire fleet." He reached the end of the line, staring hard at Ashvild. Even she, normally so confident seemed to wither under his disapproving stare. Master Alfvin turned on his heel and started back the other way.

"I will make you strong. Burn away all the impurities and leave pure titan steel behind." He stopped in front of Iro, turned to face him fully. Iro met the man's goggling eyes, then looked away. "I will push you through your first gate even if I have to break you in the process."

Iro stared hard at the floor. *He will push us through our first gates.* He made it sound like a threat. But it couldn't be that because it was exactly what Iro wanted. He needed to get stronger. If he was going to chase after the black cloaks and bring back Mia, he needed more power. His first gate was the first step. He had to open it no matter the cost. If Master Alfvin was promising him that, then good. Perhaps he could succeed where Master Rollo had failed.

Iro looked up, met Master Alfvin's burning gaze, and nodded.

Master Alfvin half smiled, the corner of his mouth turning up just a little, then it was gone. He turned and strode away to the other side of the room, stood facing them all with his hands clasped behind his back. "First, I need to assess your abilities. Rollo's notes on you all are maddeningly vague beyond a simple ranking."

"Ranking?" Arne asked, grinning. "He ranked us?"

Master Alfvin pulled a tablet out of his pocket and tapped at it. "Speak out of turn again and you will be punished. If you wish to talk, raise your hand and wait for permission."

Arne laughed bitterly. "We're not kids. You can't…"

Master Alfvin removed a small metal stylus from the top of his tablet, held it loosely between thumb and finger, then stabbed it casually at Arne. Arne doubled over with a loud *oof,* clutching at his stomach. He dropped to his knees, mouth gaping as if struggling for air in a vacuum. None of the others moved.

Iro knelt beside Arne, unsure of how to help. "Just try to stay calm," he said. "Breathe. Don't panic." Arne stared at him, eyes wide and full of fear. He sucked a high, whistling breath through his lips, then another a little deeper.

Iro stood and stepped forward, facing Master Alfvin. "Arne didn't deserve…"

There was a brief flash of silver light behind Master Alfvin and he stabbed his little stylus. Something hit Iro so hard in the chest he flew backwards, crashing down on the mats a good five feet away. He rolled with the fall, coming up onto his knees. His chest throbbed from the impact. He clutched at the pain, expecting to find a wound, but there was nothing but the agony.

"It figures the two lowest ranked would be the most troublesome." Master Alfvin sighed pointedly and looked back to his tablet.

Iro struggled back to his feet, but the pain was so intense he quickly fell back to his knees and decided to take a moment. Most of the others were staring straight ahead and he had never seen them all look so rigid. Eir glanced back at him, eyes wide. He nodded to her, hoping to reassure her he was alright. She just rolled her eyes and nodded back toward the line. Iro caught her meaning and staggered upright and back into line. Arne was still kneeling, gasping down lungfuls of air. Iro held out a hand and helped the other boy back to his feet in silence.

"Now then," Master Alfvin said without looking up from his tablet. "As I have said, Rollo's notes on you all are lacking past a basic ranking. I need to assess your abilities personally. We'll start with pure combat, no talents. Single matches to the first down, not hit." He tapped at his tablet a couple of times. "Bjorn and Iro, step forward. Collect your training blades."

Bjorn was first out of line, striding over to the wall to pick his usual weighty sword. It was a long blade so he'd have the reach over Iro and it was also heavy so combined with his greater strength and size, he'd have a significant advantage in every way except for speed. Though, Iro had to admit, Bjorn was faster than was fair for someone his size. There was a reason he was top of the class when it came to combat and no one had ever managed to beat him. Only Eir and Torben had even managed to land hits before.

Iro was still rubbing at his chest between his armor plates as he selected his own training sword. It was the same shape as Neya's sword, with a wide blade and a double edge, but a finger shorter. It also wasn't titan-steel so it was significantly lighter.

Bjorn grinned down at Iro as they moved into the centre of the hall. "I'm gonna make you regret waking me up this morning."

The other trainees backed away, giving them space to fight. Iro rolled his left shoulder in its socket, then his right, and bent over, quickly stretching. "I already regret it. But don't go easy on me. I'll beat you at your best or not at all." He returned Bjorn's grin and settled into a ready stance, light on the balls of his feet with his training blade held before him in a loose defence.

Bjorn chuckled. "Not at all then."

"Begin," Master Alfvin said flatly.

Bjorn launched forward into a wide sweeping slash, using his extra reach. Iro ducked underneath the arc, rising and lunging forwards, his blade stabbing. Bjorn somehow pivoted his sword around to block with the flat of the blade, braced against his shoulder and shoved. Iro couldn't hope to match strength with Bjorn so jumped back with the force of the push, his feet sliding on the mats. Bjorn gave him no time to recover and dashed forward, swinging his blade around again with lightning speed. Iro had no time to duck the strike. He brought his blade up in an attempt to block but Bjorn was too powerful. Iro's defence crumpled and his sword was knocked aside. Bjorn's blade smashed into his chest with such force it knocked Iro off his feet and slammed him down onto his back hard enough he felt the wind blasted from his lungs. Armor was great for blocking damage, but being hit still hurt like scrap.

A few sharp intakes of breath from the others let him know it looked as bad as it felt. Iro gasped air back into his lungs and rolled onto his hands and knees, coughing.

"Sorry about that," Bjorn said, holding out a hand to help Iro up.

"Again," Master Alfvin said coldly.

Iro accepted the hand and Bjorn heaved him to his feet as easily as he might a child. "I'll go a bit slower," he said with a nod. It was disrespectful any way Iro looked at it. Bjorn no doubt thought he was doing Iro a favour, but all he was really saying was *you're not good enough and I'll prove it*.

"Don't you dare," Iro snapped. He rubbed at his chest again, wriggled to get his mother's old armor to settle back into place, then stepped back into position.

Bjorn stared at him, all smiles gone. "Look, Iro…"

Iro wasn't about to let him finish condescending. He launched himself at Bjorn with a wild cross slash, then manoeuvred into a jab. Bjorn stepped back, wrong-footed, barely getting out of the way of the slash, only just bringing up his sword to parry the jab. He growled as he swung his heavy sword upwards in a strike that would have cut Iro in two had it connected. Iro spun to the side only to find Bjorn had rushed inside his guard. Bjorn's hilt cracked into Iro's chest plate, lifting him up off the ground, then slammed him back down onto the mat hard. Iro's head bounced off the foam, dark spots dancing before him, sparkling lights flaring. He blinked them away and found the tip of Bjorn's sword hanging an inch above his nose.

"Again," Master Alfvin said.

Bjorn turned his head to look at the master, frowning. Iro knocked the bigger boy's sword aside with his own blade and rushed back to his feet, taking his position again. Bjorn was slower, looked like he was chewing over something he wanted to say as he shuffled back into a ready stance.

Iro waited, got a hang on his breathing, watched the bigger boy.

His reach and strength are the biggest problems. He's fast, but so am I. I can't hope to match his skill. There has to be something else. Something I can use.

Bjorn stepped forward, hefting his sword from across

his shoulder and swinging. Iro sprang into motion, darting forward into the strike, his sword catching Bjorn's blade halfway down its length, robbing the attack of most of its strength. He pushed the blade away, slashed down with his own in a strike that should have cut across the bigger boy's torso. Bjorn twisted his sword somehow, bringing the cross hilt up to catch Iro's attack. Then he pushed further and the pommel of the sword cracked Iro across the face, sending him reeling, white lights flaring. The pain hit a moment later and he tasted blood in his mouth. He barely had time to register it before Bjorn's sword cut his legs out from under him and put right back down on the mat again.

Crawling away, not knowing whether to clutch at his face or his leg, Iro groaned and spat a gobbet of blood onto the mat. He was glad a tooth didn't go with it, but one of them did feel loose.

"Again."

Iro heard Bjorn grumble. "Master Alfvin," the bigger boy said in a respectful tone. "I think he's had enough."

"I'm fine," Iro slurred. His mouth felt swollen and stiff. He used his sword as a crutch and pushed back to his feet, turning to face his opponent again. Bjorn gave him a pained look.

"Again," Master Alfvin repeated.

Iro was starting to understand something. It went beyond the other boy's skill. Iro was starting to realise the way Bjorn fought. The understanding of it flickered on in his mind like a control board lighting up.

He uses his reach to distract. It's ruse. He should have less control up close, and he knows it. He knows I know it. That's why he switches it up whenever I get close, using the cross guard and pommel to defend and attack. Great. Now how the scrap do I counter it?

Iro's arms ached already, his legs were limp straws,

and his chest had given up telling him which bit hurt and had gone for wholesale pain. Despite that, he refused to give up. Not until he scored a hit. That was his goal, his first small step. He knew knocking Bjorn down was impossible at this point, but that didn't mean he couldn't aim for small, achievable goals. A hit. A single hit on the bigger boy and he could be happy.

Iro feinted left and Bjorn fell for it, his blade already moving to intercept. He spun right, slashing out at Bjorn's legs. Bjorn shifted, wrenched his sword back to block with the cross guard again. Iro leapt into the air, spinning. Bjorn's blade caught his trailing leg, spun him about and he lost all sense of up and down right up to the point where the floor hit him. Iro sprawled on the mat, groaning.

"Is this your way of giving up?" Bjorn asked with a friendly smile. "Sure is easier when you jump into my sword."

"Again."

Bjorn winced at the word. Opened his mouth to say something. Iro cut him off by lurching back to his feet and tapping his blade against Bjorn's chest plate. There was no power behind it and he was sure it didn't count as a true hit, but it was better than nothing. Bjorn turned a dangerous stare his way.

Iro fell back a couple of steps and took up his stance once more. "Again," he said, smiling bloody teeth through the pain.

They clashed twice more. Both times were brief, painful exchanges and both ended with Iro down on the ground with Bjorn's sword hovering above him. After that sixth clash, Iro gave himself a couple of seconds to get his breath back. He was panting and shaking, and it felt like something was on fire someone inside his chest, burning and out of control, making his heart race.

"Again."

"He's had enough," Bjorn said, then added, "Master Alfvin."

"I'm good," Iro said as he struggled back to his knees then leaned back and gasped at the pain. "Just taking a breather. But I can go again." He planted his sword tip on the mat and leaned heavily on it as he pushed back to his feet and staggered from the effort. He had to squint at Bjorn who appeared to be wiggling in front of him. The whole room was waving, spinning, blurred whites and greys exploding together in a riot of washed out sparkles.

Bjorn frowned and shook his head. "You may be, but I'm not." He hefted his sword and rested it against his shoulder. "I'm tired. So Iro wins this round."

Iro let out a manic laugh. "Victory at any cost." He staggered and used his sword as a crutch to steady himself again, then limped back to the line of trainees. It was hard to tell for sure given the room was still wiggling a bit, but he thought some of them were shooting him concerned stares.

Master Alfvin stared at Iro a few seconds longer, then tapped at his tablet again. "Eir and Arne, step forward and choose your swords."

Iro watched as closely as he could. He still hurt like he'd been set on fire by a fuel spitter, but his eyesight was clearing by the second and he found himself able to stand a little straighter.

Eir was clearly the superior fighter, but the bouts lasted longer than they should have. She drifted around as though gliding rather than walking, her feet sliding so artfully across the mats. She spun around slashes, leapt over cuts, turned aside stabs with the barest flick of her slender blade. And when she struck back it was with precision jabs and slices that would have cut flesh and pierced vital points had the blades been real. But she didn't knock Arne down.

At first Iro thought she was toying with him, certainly she was smiling the whole time. But the longer it went on, the more he could see the truth of it. Eir was strong, yes, probably stronger than him, but she was not built for powerful attacks. Both her weapon and her style were suited to pinpoint strikes.

Eventually Arne just collapsed backwards onto his arse, his long blade spilling from his battered fingers. If the fight had been real, Eir would have severed those digits long ago. Arne groaned, panted and held up his hands. "I give up. Scrap it, Eir, I give up. Just stop hitting me." He all but crawled back into line while Eir gave a flourish with her sword then skipped back into place.

Iro was still considering it when the next match was called out, Ashvild and Ylfa stepped forward to do battle. They seemed evenly matched at first. Both were of a height and a similar build, and even wielded swords of an equal reach. They traded a few blows, seeming to take it in turns to attack and parry. Then Ylfa appeared to gain the upper hand, beating Ashvild back. Ashvild gave ground again and again. Both girl's blades moved with such mesmerising speed, the clash of their contacts filling the air with a constant percussion. Then Ashvild shifted just slightly, firming her stance and pushing forward. Ylfa, caught off guard, took a hasty step back, her trailing foot catching on a torn corner of the mat. She stumbled. Ashvild rushed in and drove the edge of her blade into Ylfa's stomach, between two armor plates, doubling her over. As Ylfa cried out, eyes goggling from the pain, Ashvild swept her legs from under her and sent her crashing onto the mat, her sword point hovering a breath from her throat.

The two girls smiled at each other and Ashvild helped Ylfa up. They moved back into line, exchanging a few quiet words. Iro kept analysing the fight in his head.

Ashvild switched stance at just the right moment to make Ylfa trip on the edge of the mat. She manoeuvred Ylfa into the exact position she wanted.

Torben and Ingrid stepped forward as the final bout. The brother and sister were closely matched though Torben was a little bigger. They beat the scrap out of each other, both focusing mostly on offence and willing to take crushing blows on their armor in order to strike back. Torben won in the end, landing a thunderous slash with his great sword that knocked Ingrid's sword from her hand. He then barrelled into her, throwing her to the ground. They laughed as they moved back into line, despite the beating they had just heaped upon each other.

It did not escape Iro's notice that only he and Bjorn were made to fight more than once. After the sparring, they ran through some drills, Master Alfvin working them all to the point of exhaustion. It was the most gruelling day of training Iro could remember since his first, but he suffered through it, pushing his body on past the point where he wanted to collapse into the corner. He was determined to get stronger, no matter what. If Master Alfvin said this was the way, then so be it. Iro would excel. He would get stronger.

"I am unimpressed," Master Alfvin said when the training session came to an end.

Iro was only standing by pure willpower and could feel every muscle in his body trembling. He wasn't the only one either. With just a brief glance down the line, he could see the others struggling to stay upright. Arne was clutching his side and wincing, his hair a curly mess around his forehead rather than its usual slickness.

"I'm sure Rollo never shared his rankings with you all, but I feel it is important to know who among you is your superior." Again his gaze found Iro and seemed to lock on him. "It is a system for the weak to pull themselves up to a higher level."

He tapped on his tablet with his little stylus, took a deep breath then nodded to himself. "First: Bjorn. Second: Eir. Third: Torben. Fourth: Ashvild. Fifth: Ylfa. Sixth: Ingrid. Seventh: Arne. And right at the very bottom: Iro."

Iro had been expecting it. More than that, he'd been sure of it. He'd only been training for a few months whereas all the others had been at it for years. Some of them, like Eir, were born to fight, trained for it before they could even stand. It still hurt to hear his name last and said with such disappointment.

"Tomorrow I will assess your talents," Master Alfvin said. "Do not be late."

Chapter Thirty-One

Emil liked to think he was used to the cold. The Courage had never been the warmest of ships. His father blamed it on the bridge officers, of course. The old man claimed they funnelled all the heating into their own quarters and let the drudges freeze. Emil doubted it, he'd seen the way the officers wrapped up in multiple layers these days as they marched to duty. He thought it was far more likely the ship was failing, and with almost half of it sealed up and left to the void of space, heat was being leeched away from them all.

He liked to think he was used to the cold, but he still hated it. He sat in the training hall, nestled between a couple of old crates that didn't smell too bad, wrapped up in a threadbare yellow blanket. And he shivered. He'd been awake for a good thirty minutes, shivering, stewing in resentment, trying to work up the effort needed to get up and start the day of… of what?

Master Tannow was gone. The rest of his squad was gone. No one had come to give Emil new orders. He felt forgotten. His routine was trashed. He didn't want to go home while his father might be there, couldn't face the disappointment because apparently it was somehow Emil's fault the Hop had gone bad. His father… his cowardly, hateful old man blamed Emil for not being able to stand up to the black cloaks. He had no trainer anymore. He was alone. Not even sure if anyone would tell him when he was supposed to go on a Hop.

That thought twisted him up inside. Hopping was his existence, his reason for being. He wanted to change the system, to make all the ships equal, but there was no way he could do that as a nobody aboard the poorest of ships. If he wanted to make any difference at all he needed to progress, to Hop, to bring wealth to his ship and the fleet. And once more the universe had proven to him he couldn't rely on anyone else. He had to do it alone.

Breath misting on his lips, hands blue and trembling, Emil picked up the tablet Cali had given him. She'd gifted it to him with a bunch of books she liked to read. Fiction, fanciful tales of heroes and people living on giant rocks instead of ships. It was all useless scrap, but that didn't mean the tablet was useless. It was connected to the ship's library and that library contained a whole host of texts. Emil accessed the Hopper services, scrolled through the available texts until he found what he was looking for. *Basics of Pod Control*. He couldn't rely on anyone else to organise his Hops, certain now that he had been forgotten, so he would do it all himself. First, that meant learning how to fly one of the pods. Once he could get himself over to the titan, he could start making small, exploratory excursions.

He was reading the technical manual, his mind aching from the effort to go along with his body aching from the cold, when someone walked into the training hall. It was the little tech with the big nose and he was humming to himself as he sauntered over to the last remaining training dummy.

Emil realised he had been overlooked. Nestled away amongst the crates, wrapped up against the cold, the tech hadn't even seen him. It seemed fitting. Even the lowly techs now ignored Emil. His chest suddenly felt tight as though the ship's gravity had shifted to crush him down into dust.

The little tech dropped his toolbag by the dummy and pulled out a wrench. He knelt down to get at the base, still humming to himself, and started working on the bolts that connected the dummy to the floor.

"Don't you dare!" Emil snarled.

The little tech jumped, banged his head on the dummy's skirt, and skittered away on his ass. "Ow!" he said, rubbing at the back of his head with one hand while brandishing his wrench before him like a weapon with the other. "And also, scrap! You scared me."

"Good," Emil growled the word with as much menace as he could, though his chattering teeth made him sound weak. He slowly began to uncurl, fighting the chilly ache that had crept into his bones. Everything hurt to move.

"What are you doing here?" the tech asked. He lowered his wrench and glanced about, his eyes passing over the blanket, the empty bowl of green gruel, and Emil's gauntlets. "Are you living in here?"

Emil stretched, had to suppress a whimper of pain as his joints cramped. He limped over to the dummy and gave it a thump. It wasn't on, but it felt good to give the thing a beating. It leered back at him in mocking silence. "So what if I am?"

The little tech climbed back to his feet, straightened his stained, patched together trousers. "You can't. They're closing it off. Next week this whole section is being shut off and sealed."

Left to join the rest of the decaying ship, swallowed up by the void. "They've given up on the manufactory then?"

The tech frowned as he advanced on the dummy with his wrench again. "What manufactory?"

Of course the rest of the fleet hadn't been told. It made sense. With the black cloaks defending it, the fleet might not be able to claim it. And even if they did mount a significant Hop and claim it, no doubt the Legacy families would monopolise it for themselves, shutting out the

Courage altogether. Emil sighed. He'd tried. He'd staked the Courage's claim on first usage, but they all just ignored him. He thumped the dummy again in frustration.

"Whoa," the tech said. "I have to take the dummy down now. I'm moving it to training hall A."

Emil stepped in front of the dummy, towering over the little tech, glaring at him. "No, you're not."

The tech backed up, waving his wrench in the air. "Okay. I'm not going to try and fight you for it. But they are going to shut this section of the ship off. You think it's cold now? Wait until this room is swallowed up by the black."

Emil continued glaring at the little tech. He knew it wasn't the boy's fault, that the decision had come from higher up; the bridge crew most likely. He knew that, but he didn't care because right now the tech was here and he was the avatar of the decision. He was the only one Emil could stand up to and say *no*.

"I'll come back in two days. How does that work?" the tech said. "I can put off this job until then. But they are going to shut this section down and you can't be here when they do."

Emil nodded grudgingly, still not moving from between the tech and the training dummy. It was odd how protective he felt of the scrapping thing. It beat him bloody on a regular basis, and besides that it was just an object. But it was also the only partner Emil had left. The only one he could rely on. And even that was being taken from him.

The big-nosed tech skirted around Emil like he was a rustling about to bite, threw his wrench into his toolbag, snatched the bag from the floor, then made for the exit.

"Hey wait," Emil said quickly.

The tech stopped, turned his body sideways as if readying himself to flee if Emil made an aggressive move. Emil hated to admit it, but he needed someone. The dummy could help him train his combat skills, but he couldn't enhance the dummy. He could only enhance another person and that meant he needed someone else if he wanted to train his talent.

"Come here." Emil waved for the over boy.

The tech edged back towards him, eyes narrowed in obvious suspicion. "Why?"

"Have you ever been enhanced?" Emil said, already knowing he wouldn't have. Hoppers didn't go around enhancing random techs just for fun.

The tech shook his head, dumped his toolbag on the floor again, and approached. "I always wondered what it was like."

"Okay, stand here," Emil pointed to just in front of the dummy. He pressed the button on the floor to start it and the dummy's arms started whirling, spinning, whipping forward in blurred attacks. The tech took a step away and Emil shoved him roughly back into position.

"Just stand there. When I say *steel*, your skin will get tighter and you'll feel like you've doubled in weight. When that happens, step forward into the reach of the dummy."

"Uhhh…"

"You'll be fine." The dummy was on its second to highest setting, its arms flying about with a dizzying speed, the force easily enough to send an unenhanced person flying. Emil took a step back and calmed his breathing just like Master Tannow had first taught him so many years ago.

"Is that it?" the tech asked. "Do I move?"

"Not yet," Emil said impatiently. "Wait for me to say *steel*."

The big nosed lad nodded nervously. "I have more work to do."

Emil raised his hand to point at the boy. He activated his crest in front of him, a glowing complex of lines and arcane symbols. It looked like fire and lightning clashing. "Steel."

"Oh my," the tech said as the enhancement took hold, buffing him up and making him tough as steel. "This feels very strange. Um. Now?"

Emil nodded, teeth gritted past the strain. Holding an enhancement on someone for more than a couple of seconds was so difficult. His crest was already flickering.

The boy stepped into reach of the dummy, wincing as though he expected a beating. The dummy flailed at him, arms bouncing off his armored skin. He was shoved this way and that by the force of each attack, but with a steel buff on him, the boy barely felt the blows. He grinned wide and laughed. "This is amazing."

Emil's crest wavered, the fiery glow dying down, then vanished. He lost control of the enhancement at the same time. The tech's laughs turned to a strangled cry of pain and terror as his skin softened and the dummy smashed him in the leg, the chest, the arm, and finally a slap to the face that sent him tumbling across the room into a mewling pile.

Emil doubled over, a wave of exhaustion almost knocking him from his feet. It was the longest he had ever held an enhancement for, but it was still nothing compared to the time even a first gate Paladin could achieve. And it left him feeling raw and weak-limbed.

A strangled sob brought his attention back to the tech. The boy was crying, his face bloody. Emil ran to him, but the boy squeaked in terror and crawled away. He reached his feet just before the doorway and barrelled out, disappearing around the corner without a word.

Emil cursed himself. He should have put the dummy on the lowest setting. He was trying to train for length of enhancement, not potency. He should have pulled the boy back before the buff became too much for him to hold. He should have… He pressed the off button on the dummy, then thumped it in the face as it slowed to a stop. He hadn't meant for the tech to get hurt, he just needed someone to train with so he could work on his talent.

He shoved the boy's toolbag towards the door with his foot. No doubt he'd return for it soon and this way he could retrieve it without having to speak to Emil again. That would probably be for the best. The little tech was clearly a weakling, a few hits from a dummy sending him crying and running. One more person Emil couldn't rely on.

The dummy stood still and silent, laughing at him, mocking. That had been Mia's doing, drawing a leering face on the scrapping thing. She had said it helped her focus, having someone instead of something to hit. It was probably Mia who wrote Emil's name on the thing as well.

Emil pressed the button to start it up again and the arms flailed into life, reaching for him like a monster held just barely at bay. He had no one left. No one to turn to. No one to rely on. Entirely on his own, and that was for the best. He'd just have to learn to do everything on his own. He'd learn to fight, learn to fly a pod, learn to enhance on his own.

"I don't need anyone," Emil said it out loud and stepped into the dummy. It smacked him twice before he could get his guard up. He blocked two swinging arms, but a third knocked him sideways out of range.

"I don't need anyone." He activated his crest. The lines of it were fire again, the current inside him recharging quickly. "Steel." He stepped into the dummy again, lowered his arms and let it batter him, staggered back with a bloody lip and a bruised hip.

Again. He activated his crest. "Steel." He stepped into the dummy and it beat him about the head, brought flashing stars to his eyes and threw him back with a gut shot.

"Again." He had to wait a few seconds for his crest to glow to fiery life once more. "Steel." He approached the dummy. It's flailing arms battered him around the chest, the shoulders, the face. He weathered every strike, barely feeling the blows. Then another arm cracked him around the face and he felt that one, staggered back from it. But those first few attacks. It had been like… like he was enhanced. They had felt like distant taps, dull and forceless against his skin.

Emil smiled a little. Maybe it was his imagination. Maybe he was just tricking himself into thinking he had achieved something. In the utter lack of having anyone to enhance, he had somehow turned his current on himself. And if that was the case then he really didn't need anyone else.

Emil pressed the switch on the dummy to up it to the highest level, squared his shoulders and activated his crest. He stepped into reach of the spinning limbs. "Steel."

Chapter Thirty-Two

The Power Acceleration Chamber was a fancy name for sure. It was also a section of the ship Iro had never seen before. Master Alfvin led them all there in silence, mostly because all the trainees were afraid to talk around him without permission. Even Arne and Ylfa kept quiet and they were usually the most outspoken people Iro knew.

He goggled at the chamber as they entered. It was large enough to fit the training hall inside of it twice over. All over the walls and floor and ceiling at evenly spaced intervals were bulbous protrusions like spongy spheres had been embedded into the bulkheads. He had never seen anything like it before and was certain the Courage didn't have such a room. He forgot himself and quickly ran over to one of the half spheres, extending a finger towards it. It almost seemed to hum with a ferocious energy of its own. Not the background fuzzy crackle of electricity running through a ship's systems, but more like the feeling when he drew on his own current inside, flooding his body with the energy.

Something hard hit Iro's leg and he tumbled to the ground, crying out from the pain of the impact.

"Do not touch the spheres," Master Alfvin said, stylus in hand once more.

Iro rubbed animatedly at his leg, trying to work some feeling back into it. He soon regretted that as the feeling that flooded in was pain. Ashvild walked over to him quickly, held out her hand. He took it and let her help him up. She pulled him in close enough that their shoulders were almost touching, her hand still locked around his.

"Do as you're told," she said. He almost took it as an admonishment, but there was something about the way she said it, the urgency and the worried look on her face. "Keep your head down and don't give him a reason."

"A reason?" Iro said.

Ashvild opened her mouth, but Master Alfvin started speaking and instead she turned and pulled Iro into line, then shook her hand free of his.

"This is the Power Acceleration Chamber. Some of you may have heard of it, but I doubt any of you have used it before. Yes, Eir?"

Eir had her hand raised. She stepped forward when named, grinning. "I've used it."

Master Alfvin narrowed his eyes at her. "I suppose being the daughter of a hero comes with certain benefits."

Iro watched the smile slip from Eir's face.

"The chamber is mostly used for Hoppers to train their talents between Hops," Master Alfvin continued. Eir, realising she was dismissed, stepped back into line. "It is designed to absorb the current that escapes a Hopper when they use their talents, then throw the energy back at them. In this way, it is the most accurate form of simulating the atmosphere of the titans we can create aboard ship."

Iro raised his hand. Master Alfvin's eyes snapped to him. "Yes, Iro?"

Iro stepped forward, caught Ashvild shaking her head at him, but couldn't stop. "I don't understand, Master Alfvin," Iro said as respectfully as he could. "What do you mean by simulating the atmosphere of the titans?"

Master Alfvin pinched the bridge of his nose. "Did Rollo teach you children nothing?" He held up a hand. "No, do not answer that." He flicked his hand, clearly indicating Iro should rejoin the line.

"You have all been on multiple Hops by now.

Perhaps you realised that your current was stronger aboard the titan. Your crests glowed a little more brightly. You could use your talents more times without waiting for your power to recharge. Or you may even have noticed your talent seemed more potent. That is because of the ambient energy within the titan. It is invisible, intangible, and ever present. It seeps into you and permeates you and strengthens you. Your current is stronger aboard the titan, it replenishes quicker. The energy you can push into a talent is also higher as talents absorb some of the ambient energy when you use them."

Iro considered it. He had been able to use Blink Strike more often aboard the titan. He'd thought he was simply getting stronger, but maybe it was more than that. He raised his hand again.

"Yes, Iro?" Master Alfvin said impatiently.

"Is that why I only manifested my talent when I accidentally went aboard the titan?" He paused, glanced around at the other students, certain most of them already knew. "I was talentless until we encountered titan 02."

Master Alfvin smiled briefly. "I believe so. Perhaps your innate current was simply too weak to manifest before stepping aboard the titan, and it was only the ambient energy in the atmosphere that allowed you to reveal your attunement to the blade.

"This chamber is an imperfect approximation of the atmosphere aboard the titan. The spheres you see on the walls are designed to rebound expended energy, allowing Hoppers within the chamber to reabsorb some of the current they expel. In this way, a Hopper can train aboard ship for longer and with greater efficacy." He held up a single, slender finger. "However. It is reused energy and we have discovered that it has diminishing returns.

"Think of the current you expend as a basket full of

apples. Each time you use it, you take out an apple. Each time you use it, the power becomes less. In fact, it is worse than that. Each time you use the same portion of energy, you take a fresh apple out of the basket and replace it with a rotten apple. When the ratio of apples to rotten apples swings in favour of the rotten, you can become sick. Current sickness is a plague that, once started, consumes a Hopper. Therefor, it is important to be mindful of using the acceleration chamber. No more than fifteen minutes at a stretch, and then waiting another fifteen minutes for the toxic ambient energy to dissipate. Understand?"

Iro nodded along with all the other trainees. He'd never heard of current sickness before, but it didn't sound pleasant. He imagined it came with boils or rotting teeth or something nasty.

"Excellent," Master Alfvin said. He brought out his tablet again and tapped at it with his hateful stylus. "The goal today is to evaluate your progress with your talents and your available current. I do hope your status will be less disappointing than yesterday." He took a few steps back to make some room between himself and them all. "Iro. Your manifested talent is the Blink Strike. Demonstrate."

He stepped forward and drew Neya's sword from over his shoulder. At least he still had that. The blade bolstered him, made him stronger as though Neya were watching him through it. He knew it was stupid, but he liked the idea. His eyes locked on the snaking crack halfway up the blade. It was now a full finger's length through the titan steel. He needed the sword reforged before it broke, but that required a manufactory.

"Any time, trainee," Master Alfvin said.

Iro activated his crest. It had grown again. New arcane letters had appeared, skirting the edge of a faint line that appeared to be an unbroken outer circle. At the top side of that larger circle was a smaller, empty circle. He recognised it. It was his first glimpse of the lock. Did that mean he was ready to encounter his first gate?

Master Alfvin cleared his throat.

Iro shook his head to clear his thoughts and drew on his current, letting it flow into the blade. He swung Neya's sword. The world felt like it lurched around him, like gravity shifted and pulled him to the side. He slid to a stop a moment later and fifteen paces away, completing the arc of his swing and cutting through the air with a shimmer.

"Again," Master Alfvin said.

Iro hesitated. "What?"

Master Alfvin glanced up at him from his tablet, stylus poised.

Iro decided not to tempt fate. He activated his crest again. It was dimmer than before, but still glowing icy blue. Iro swung, Blink Striking back across the room to the other side, completing his slice. He took a moment to steady himself, still not use to the disorientation.

"Again."

His crest was flickering now, barely brighter than a distant star, but Iro let his current flow a third time. He swung Neya's sword and felt the force take hold again, exerting on him and dragging him across the room a third time, more slowly than before. He completed his swing and staggered, feeling exhausted and dizzy.

"Again."

"I… can't," Iro said. He dropped to one knee, leaning on Neya's blade as the room spun around him. He couldn't tell if it was the disorientation from being dragged around by a force that wasn't quite gravity so many times, or if it was a side effect from having used up his power supply so utterly and so quickly. He could feel it seeping back in though, the current a trickle but still willing to flow.

"Again."

Iro staggered back to his feet, swaying. He activated his crest and it flickered once, then vanished. He swung Neya's sword and… nothing happened. He looked up to find Master Alfvin watching him, waiting.

Iro waited five seconds, ten, fifteen. He activated his crest again with a brief flare of icy blue light. Then he swung, Blink Striking across the room again. He all but fell over after completing his swing and felt so nauseous he was amazed he didn't retch all over the floor.

"Hmmm," Master Alfvin said. He did not sound impressed. "Back in line. Eir step forward. Your talent is Riposte. Do you need a partner?"

"Sure do," Eir said eagerly. She danced forward, whipping her slender sword free from its sheath.

Master Alfvin stepped forward to meet her. He flicked out his wrist and his little stylus grew in length to half the size of his arm. It had no edge, but then Master Alfvin had opened his third gate, he didn't really need an edge on his weapon to do damage. He swung lazily at Eir with his telescopic stylus and she blocked, floating through the air along with the strike. They did it again and again. Ten times until Eir was panting, sweating, her violet crest fizzing in and out of existence. On the eleventh strike, she blocked and rather than gliding with the blow, it simply clanged to a halt against her blade. Master Alfvin made a shooing gesture with his hand and then tapped some notes onto his tablet.

He called Ylfa next and tested her ability with her Shadow Blade talent. It was something to do with light folding around the sword and making it invisible in Ylfa's hands. It was tough to follow given that Iro couldn't really see what was happening. But from what he could tell, Ylfa could keep her sword invisible for a long time as long as she didn't move it, but when she moved the sword, she could only keep it from being seen for a few seconds at most. Master Alfvin did not seem impressed.

He called each of them up in turn and had them demonstrate their talents, sometimes making them use the talents in different ways in order to test multiple factors. As he watched, Iro realised he still knew so little about being a Corsair past the basics. If he managed to open his first gate, he'd manifest a new talent, and be able to learn a third talent. Which ones he learned would dictate how he would fight, which monsters he was most capable against. It was a lot to consider. It might even influence his career moving forward as a Hopper, who would want him in their squad, and which sections of the titan he'd get to visit. It needed consideration, but until he opened his first gate, there seemed little point.

Master Alfvin read out his list of rankings. He seemed to like ranking them all. Of course, Iro found himself sitting squarely at the bottom. He wanted to not care, to be happy for everyone else being further along in their training than him, but he couldn't deny it hurt. He wanted to not be last. He wanted to improve. He needed to be stronger.

Sleep seemed to be coming harder and harder to Iro these days. He'd spent all day with Master Alfvin and the other trainees in the Power Acceleration Chamber and he knew he should be exhausted, yet he felt awake and energised. Or maybe it was just Bjorn and his bulkhead rattling snores that were keeping him awake.

He still missed his old room over on the Courage. He'd decided to stay on the Eclipse, to continue his training. He'd made that choice. But that didn't mean the homesick feeling went away. At least back on the Courage, his room had a window out into the dark. He could look through at the stars or the titan. Here the walls were bare except for a little paper picture Bjorn had stuck to one. It was old, the colours faded, the edges curling, and it looked like it had been ripped from a book. It depicted a scantily clad woman wielding a sword and wearing a crown that did nothing to constrain her flowing pink hair. Iro suspected her hair might have been red once, but the colours really were faded.

A soft ping sounded from Iro's bed and he turned to see his tablet screen flashing, indicating he had a message. He'd been reading from the bestiary before, trying to catch up on everything he needed to learn, but it was just so much. The bestiary of monsters, the compendium of traps, basics of pod control, understanding the titan ecosystem. That last one was mostly theoretical and sent Iro's head spinning. And nothing he had read in any of the books had even mentioned the black cloaks. Surely they were a greater threat to Hoppers than most of the monsters or traps?

He tapped the tablet screen to read the message. It was from Eir. Just two words. *You coming?*

Iro grinned and all but threw his tablet back onto the bed. He was out the door in a flash.

Eir was already moving through her final routine of stretches when Iro rushed in through the training hall door. She raised an eyebrow at him. "And here I thought you were going to make me train all alone."

Iro immediately sank down into the stretch next to her. "I just thought you'd be too tired to train after today. It's fine to admit you don't have my stamina." He grinned at her and she shot him a look of mock outrage.

Eir rolled out of her stretch and immediately flowed into her free-standing handstand. Iro sighed, tried to copy her, collapsed as usual. Eir chuckled, which had the effect of unbalancing her and she too collapsed onto the mat. They lay there laughing, staring up at the panelled roof. He'd never had a friend like Eir before. She was just so easy to talk to. So comfortable to be around. Even when she was challenging him or knocking him senseless in sparring. Perhaps especially then.

"Whatever you do, don't quit," Eir said eventually. "Don't let him make you quit, Iro." She was being serious. There was usually a lightness to Eir's voice, an energetic humour. But not now. It was like when she had talked about her mother, the humour giving way to an earnestness she normally hid.

"It's not just me then." Iro sighed. "He really is picking on me."

"He is. We've noticed. We've talked about it."

"We?"

Eir rolled her head to the side and gave him a withering look. "Me, Ashvild, Ylfa. Even Ingrid, though she doesn't really care."

"Oh. You've talked about it. About me?"

Eir snorted. "Don't let it go to your head. Most of the time if we talk about you it's just discussing how useless you are."

Iro smiled at that. He was used to being called useless. It was oddly more comfortable to think of people talking about him that way than any other.

"I spoke to my mother about it, too," Eir continued. "About Master Alfvin. She trained him, you know? Him and Rollo. She... uh..." Eir sat up, crossed her legs beneath her. "She said, my mother, that is. She said Alfvin was always a bit of an elitist. Believed himself better than everyone else, and said the low shippers were trash. That sort of thing."

"Oh." It all started to make sense. Iro was a low shipper. A poor kid from a poor ship who had been given a spot he didn't deserve aboard a midship.

"Apparently Alfvin and Rollo were rivals of a sort, always competing against each other." Eir grinned and shook her head. "Feels weird thinking about them both at our age, squaring off and knocking each other about. Maybe in this hall." She glanced around as if she could see through to the past where Masters Alfvin and Rollo were fighting.

"My mother said Alfvin had some odd views about the gates. Something about needing pain and danger to encounter them. He really wasn't happy when Rollo opened his gate first. She said he kept chasing after Rollo, but could never catch him.

"But the point is, don't give up, Iro. Because I'm pretty sure that's what Alfvin wants. He wants to prove that low shippers like you can't compete with those of us born on mid ships. It's scrap! So don't give up." She frowned at him then, fell silent and expectant.

"I won't," Iro said, holding up his hands placatingly. "I never intended to give up. I promise."

"Good. I'll hold you to it."

Iro realised that was the second promise he had made recently. First to get stronger and bring Mia back, and now to never give up. They both seemed like worthwhile promises to make.

Eir rolled forward onto her feet and into a back-cracking stretch. "Come on then, up you get."

"Now?" Iro asked. "I thought we were having a moment."

"Sure we were. Do you know how long moments last for?" Eir grinned at him. "A moment. So get up and lets spar because I feel like hitting something and you're the closest thing we have to a training dummy here."

Iro climbed to his feet. "That's wonderful. You tell me not to give up then compare me to a training dummy."

Eir grabbed her training sword from the wall, then picked out Iro's and tossed it to him. "You know the thing about training dummies?"

Iro caught his sword and rolled his shoulders,

settling into a stance. "You're gonna say they don't give up, aren't you?"

"They don't give up," Eir said. She winked at him once, then darted in at him.

A jab, followed by a wide shimmering slash. Iro parried the first, stepped back out of range, then back into range with his own cross-strike. Eir twirled away from the tip of Iro's blade with such obvious ease. Iro felt a jab in his side and looked down to see Eir's sword poking him in the ribs. He stepped back, rubbing at the spot.

"How did you beat Bjorn?"

Eir rubbed a hand over her bristly scalp and tossed her sword to her left hand, settling into her usual stance but mirrored. "I've never *beaten* Bjorn. I've landed hits on him plenty of times, but he's built like a bulkhead and refuses to go down."

Eir rushed forward with a furious combo of jabs, slashes, and twists. Iro stepped back, parrying, looking for an opening. Eir paused for a brief second, righting her footing, and Iro rushed in. A moment later the floor hit him in the face and he really wasn't sure how. He felt something tapping the back of his head and knew it was Eir's sword.

Iro rolled onto his back and sat up. Eir was grinning at him. She gestured for him to stand up.

"Okay, how do you land hits on Bjorn? He wiped the floor with me the other day. Literally, I think. He could have sprayed me with water and called me a mop."

Eir snorted out a laugh, then held a hand over her mouth. "Sorry. I land hits on Bjorn by not fighting like an idiot."

Iro sighed. "Helpful."

"Isn't it!" They traded a couple of blows again and once more Iro found himself stabbed with a training sword and rubbing at a soon to form bruise.

"Look, do you want to know why everyone in the squad can beat you, Iro?"

"Because I'm a terrible Corsair?"

"Exactly! But also no." Eir grinned, switched her sword back to her right hand. "It's not because you're the weakest of us. You are." A wink. "But I'm weaker than most of the squad yet I can still beat them."

"So I just need to learn to…" Iro gyrated his body in a terrible impression of Eir slipping away from his strikes. "Wriggle like you do?"

Eir raised an eyebrow at him and laughed. "Please never do that again." She shook her head and took a moment to collect herself. "You don't lose because you're the slowest either. You're actually not the slowest. Torben moves like grease down a pipe, but when you're that big and sturdy, you can afford to be slow.

"It's not even because your form is the worst of the group, Iro. You lose to everyone because you fight like you're in a rush to lose. Or win, I suppose, but given your track record lose is more appropriate."

Eir gestured at him and Iro sprang into motion. He jabbed to her left, spun with her parry and brought his sword up in a punishing vertical strike. Eir yawned as she stepped aside and poked him with her sword.

"Thank you for demonstrating my point," she said.

Iro retreated again, stretching out the pain.

"I'm no trainer, but I'll try my best." Eir grasped her chin in one hand and stared at him in such a thoughtful expression Iro almost laughed. "Okay, everyone fights differently, Iro. You understand that much? Pleeeeease tell me you get that."

He nodded. "You glide away from strikes as easily as a breeze. Bjorn is a titan in human form."

"Right, right. But there's also how we fight."

Iro considered. He'd been thinking about that before, during his matches with Bjorn. He'd almost managed to grasp something back then. "Bjorn uses that big sword. He has the reach on us."

"Sure… and?"

"But it's a distraction. It makes you think you can get in close for the advantage, but then he switches it up, uses the blade like a staff and hits you with the hilt and cross guard."

Eir grinned at him. "That's a good start!"

"Ashvild analysed the training hall and manoeuvred Ylfa into a position where she tripped."

"Yes!" Eir said. "So you can think. It's progress. You, on the other hand, Iro, always fight in one way."

"I do?"

"You do. You fight like you're in a hurry. Like it has to be all or nothing. You commit to every strike like it has to be the final one. Win or lose on a single move. Either you attack first and all I have to do is parry or dodge then you're wide open for a counter. Or I strike first and you block and then you commit to a final attack."

Iro closed his eyes, shutting out the light of the training hall and tried to think about every fight he'd lost. Eir was right, of course. Every one of his fights was lost within moments of beginning. Whereas some of the others fought for minutes, trading blows, moving across the mats.

"Let's try this," Eir said. He opened his eyes to find her approaching. She stopped just within striking distance. "I know Master Rollo likes to tell us that half of any fight is moving your feet as well as your arms, but right now I don't want you to move your feet at all. Just stay there and defend."

She started slowly, swinging her sword at him in lazy strikes a child could have seen coming. He blocked each one with the edge of his own sword. Every now and then he met her gaze, found her eyes dark and intense. Slowly, she began to get faster, her strikes less lethargic. There was still no power behind them, only an ever increasing speed. Still, neither of them moved from their spot. After a couple of minutes, she was all but whipping slices and jabs at him and he struggled to keep up. Sweat prickled his skin and his arms ached like fire in his veins.

"That's good," Eir said, not letting up her attacks. "Now start retreating as I advance." She stepped forward and Iro took a hasty step back, almost tripping over his own feet. His defence wavered and one of her jabs just touched his chest, not even hard enough to bruise. "Ignore it. Keep moving. Keep defending."

She chased him all across the training hall, instructed him to start moving to the sides as well, and then chased him back across it. Iro could feel his biceps trembling with the effort. His legs were unsteady beneath him, and every other step felt like a lurch. And to top it off, his head hurt from concentrating so hard on following Eir's strikes.

Suddenly Eir stopped attacking. She smiled at him and nodded. "Well done. Now attack. Not like you usually do, all charge in and try to end it. Attack me like I was attacking you just then. Remember all the strikes that Master Rollo drilled into us. Use them."

Iro took a couple of seconds to breathe, catching his breath, letting his muscles recover just a little. Then he launched into an attack.

Eir brushed the stab aside with ease. "Slow down. Start slow."

Iro did as he was told. Eir had seemed almost lazy at first so he emulated her, moving through attacks just as Master Rollo had taught them. Eir blocked and parried, and for a minute or two neither of them moved as he swung his sword at her over and over again.

"Faster now," Eir said, smiling at him over their crossed blades.

Iro had to concentrate, but he managed to move through the same series of strikes faster than before. It was difficult. A part of him demanded he push forward, commit to the attack and force an opening, but he managed to keep his feet planted as he moved through the blows.

"Good. Now push forward," Eir said. "Don't try to win the fight by rushing in, just push me back."

He stepped forward, swinging his sword in a cross-strike, then flowing into a stab. Eir moved with him, blocking the first, then parrying the second. Just like before, they moved across the training hall. Iro felt sweat dripping down his face, into his eyes, fought the urge to pause and wipe it away.

"Okay, stop," Eir said eventually.

Iro all but collapsed. He was so tired. His limbs felt like a weird cross between jellied algae and lead. He was breathing hard and his uniform felt soaked from sweat. Training had never been so hard before. He'd never realised Eir was such a savage task master. He glanced up to find her breathing deeply too, catching her breath. It was a minor consolation, but one he was happy to take.

"You did well," she said. She stretched one arm across her body, then the other. "But that was the easy part."

Iro groaned, doubled over, still struggling to catch his breathe.

"You want to give up?" Eir asked, suddenly serious. "If this is too hard for you, just say. We can give up now and you can go back to being useless and bottom of the class."

He looked up at her, glaring with as much force as he could muster. It was not much. He couldn't give up. He'd made a promise. To Cali and to himself. He promised he would get stronger, no matter what it took. He couldn't give up.

Iro stood up straight again. "What's next?"

Eir smiled, nodded at him encouragingly. "Next, we fight back. Just like before, don't over commit. I'll start by attacking, but when you feel like you see an opening, go on the offensive."

Iro nodded slowly. This was going to be tough. He had to not just concentrate on Eir's attacks, but also had to look for an opportunity to switch things up.

Eir swung for him, not quite as slow as when they started, but not fast. Iro blocked, then again as she followed up. He stepped back, accepting her attacks and brushing them aside, blocking, parrying. Then he saw the opening, a moment where Eir drew back as if resetting for another attack. Iro stepped forward into the space, swinging his blade for her neck. Eir grinned at him over their swords as they clashed and she stepped back. Iro advanced, swinging, stabbing.

The momentum shifted again, Eir taking the opportunity to go back on the attack, moving faster than before. Her sword whipped at him, gaining speed and Iro retreated, struggling to defend. She chased him all the way across the training hall. Then he saw the moment he was waiting for, brushed her sword up and aside and flowed into his own downward slash. She stepped back out of range and he followed up into a stab.

They flowed faster, dancing together back and forth across the training hall. At some point Iro realised Eir was no longer grinning. She was concentrating as hard as he was. Their exchange evolved from chasing each other back and forth into brief flurries of blows, wearing the same small section of mats down with their passing. Iro's arms ached, but he ignored it, pressed the attack, fell back into defence.

Faster they moved until Iro couldn't even see their swords past the blur and the instinctive feeling, knowing where to block, parry, stab, slash.

For a moment, Eir's defence faltered in a way Iro couldn't even understand, but he stepped in and struck. His blade slid along hers, past it and struck home. A light slicing across her ribs on the left side. Or at least, it would have been if the blades were real. They both paused in shock, staring down at Iro's sword against Eir's chest.

"I did it," Iro said, not quite believing it. "I scored a hit."

Eir hadn't taken her eyes from the sword. "You did," she said quietly, shocked.

"You don't have to sound so surprised."

"Oh, this isn't surprise. I'm just deeply disappointed in myself for allowing you to win."

"Allowing me?"

"Yep. No other way to explain it." Eir looked up at him, a grin spread across her face and she laughed. Iro couldn't help but laugh with her. Then they both collapsed onto the floor, exhausted.

"That was actually a good work out," Eir said, watching him out of the corner of her eyes. "For once."

Iro sighed, leaned back and let himself sprawl on the mats. "That was exhausting. I almost preferred getting crushed by Bjorn."

"Oh sure. I was watching that and it looked a lot of fun. But what have you learned? How did you do it?"

"I, uh…" Iro squeezed his eyes shut, tried to think past the aching of his body and his racing mind. "I saw the way you were fighting. Matched it. Then there was a moment where…" He opened his eyes and looked at her. "You faltered. An opening and I took it."

She grinned at him and tapped the side of her head.

"You analysed the fight and found your moment instead of throwing yourself into it. Now, if you can do that against Bjorn…"

"I'll win?"

"No. He's far too good. But you might make him think for a moment before he swats you."

Iro drew in a deep breath and let it out slowly, staring up at the metal panels above. "It's a start."

Chapter Thirty-Three

It was rare for the Power Acceleration Chamber to be empty. There was only one on the Eclipse and every Hopper had to book a slot to use it. For the trainees, they also had to organise those slots around their normal training. And as all the trainees kept the same training hours, the available slots were in high demand. On top of that, the chamber could only be used for fifteen minutes, and then the built up ambient current needed to dissipate for another fifteen minutes. So it was booked out in thirty minute slots. So, Iro realised as he stepped into the chamber, he had precisely fifteen minutes to train his talent. And he wasn't likely to get another chance for days.

Iro looked around the chamber to make sure no one else had snuck in to watch him. It was empty. Then he hurried over to one of the dark spheres half embedded in the bulkhead floor, and prodded it with a finger. It was oddly spongy. Just pressing his finger against it left a buzzing, prickly feeling tingling his hand. He wondered how the chamber worked, whether the techs aboard the Eclipse knew, and if they'd be willing to teach him. Perhaps, one day, he could take that knowledge back to the Courage and they could build their own.

He was running out of time and every moment he spent poking and prodding the spheres was a moment wasted. He was there to train his talent and that was what he meant to do.

Iro drew Neya's sword from over his back and activated his crest in front of him. It glowed with a fierce, icy blue light. So much brighter and stronger than normal. That was the effect of the Power Acceleration Chamber, he was sure. He could see the unbroken outer circle clearly now. The lock. It meant he would get no stronger unless he encountered his first gate and opened it. Unfortunately he had no idea how to do that.

Taking a deep breath, Iro shook away all the thoughts of his gate and activated his crest behind him instead. He swung Neya's sword and felt the strange force of his talent take control of his body, pulling him through the chamber as if gravity had shifted. He finished the Blink Strike ten paces away, slashing at thin air. Just a few months ago it had been so difficult. He'd needed to slash the sword through his crest as a crutch to use the talent. And just one strike left him exhausted and trembling as though he'd run around the ship a dozen times. Now, a single strike was easy. Too easy. Too basic.

It wasn't just about how many times he could use the Blink Strike, or how far away he could attack with it. He needed to figure out a better way to utilise it. Just like when he had used it to dodge the bhur beast. Or how Master Rollo had used the talent to fight against the daeken. It wasn't about the strike itself, the final delivery of the attack. Instead it was about the mobility the talent offered.

He activated his crest and launched into a run, sprinting from one side of the chamber to the other, avoiding the spongy, dark spheres. Then he swiped Neya's sword and used a Blink Strike to drag him sharply to his left. He completed his swipe, his feet slipping on the ground. He overbalanced and careened forwards, throwing the sword to the side so he didn't accidentally impale himself on it. He crashed down and rolled to a painful stop.

It was the change in speed. The sudden acceleration as he was pulled forward, then the deceleration as he completed the strike. He needed to learn to compensate for the shift in velocity.

Iro picked himself up and plucked Neya's sword from the ground. He checked the time. He'd been at it for a few minutes already. Had barely ten minutes left to practice. So little time to learn something so complex.

He started into a sprint again and swiped to the side. The force gripped hold of him, dragged him. His legs felt wrong, like he was trying to run on nothing. Then he was ten paces from where he had been, sword slicing through the air. He tried to keep his balance, slid, tripped, stumbled to a halt, but didn't fall.

It was progress. Slight though it may be, he'd take any progress he could. Iro breathed deep, released it slowly, nodding to himself. It was time to try again.

Iro thrust himself into the practice. Running, Blink Striking to the side, keeping his footing, running on. It was all about mobility. If he could just learn to keep his balance, he could Blink Strike around a battlefield, hitting monsters where they were weakest and then darting away.

I'll never be as big as Bjorn or Torben. I can't take a beating like they can, nor hit as hard. I need to fight more like Eir, maybe. Strike at weak points, dodge away before a reply can land. Or perhaps I can learn to analyse a battlefield like Ashvild. Figure out how to herd opponents into unfavourable footing, use the perils of the environment to help out.

He kept at it. Running, Blink Striking, running. He kept going until his crest flickered out and his limbs felt like lead. Then he let himself rest for a few seconds and tried again. He wouldn't let himself give up until he had mastered it. Until he could use his talent to cross the entire chamber in a series of consecutive strikes, faster than anyone could hope to run.

Iro felt sweat running down his cheeks, dropping from his chin. He pushed down the weariness and launched himself forwards again, sprinting on wobbly, leaden legs. He activated his crest, felt an ache deep inside, ignored it, swiped to the side and let the Blink Strike carry him. Pain seared through his chest and he gasped from it, his vision exploding into white stars. The force of the Blink Strike spat him out and he flailed, couldn't see where he was. He bounced off one of the spongy spheres, careened away to sprawl on the floor. His body felt like it was on fire, bolts of lightning racing through him. His pulse thundered in his ears. His heart was trying to force its way out of his chest. He tried to sit up, spasmed, fell back down to the floor, his legs kicking without command.

He lay for a while, whimpering in pain and fear, until the spasms stopped and the sharp agony faded to a dull ache. Eventually he managed to sit, pried his fingers open to release Neya's sword. He looked at the time, already terrified of what he might see. He'd been in the chamber for twenty five minutes. He'd gone over the fifteen minutes he was allowed to use it. The pain, the seizures. It was what Master Alfvin had warned about. Current sickness.

The Eclipse infirmary took the pristine appearance of the mid ship and polished it to a painfully sterile shine. Iro felt out of place and dirty just being there. He sat in a metal chair, clutching his trembling hands in his lap, terror sitting just below the surface. He felt sick, like he was about to throw up. His throat was tight, made it hard to breathe. He didn't know if it was the current sickness or the fear, but he wanted to scream from the tension.

The medic, an old man with grey hair and more wrinkles than a pile of dirty washing, pulled open a cupboard and rummaged around inside for a few moments. He looked over at Iro and smiled in a way that was probably meant to be comforting. Then he sauntered over and shoved something in Iro's ear. Iro trembled, unsure how he was supposed to act, but unable to stop the shaking. After a few moments, the thing in Iro's ear beeped angrily. The medic pulled it out, looked at it, grunted. Then he took one of Iro's hands and held it, fingers pressed against Iro's wrist. He grunted again.

"You were in the acceleration chamber too long, weren't you?"

Iro pulled his hand back, clutched them both together hard enough his fingers creaked and cracked. "Am I going to die?"

The medic burst into laughter, which wasn't helpful in the slightest. "No, lad. What have they been teaching you?"

Iro breathed out a sigh of relief and crumpled, burying his head in trembling hands. He felt tears of relief stinging his eyes and squeezed them shut. "Master Alfvin said current sickness consumes a Hopper."

The old medic backed up a couple of steps and sat down on the edge of his desk. "It can. If you let it get to the point you're at too many times, it probably will. But it'll take more than overdoing it the once. Take it as a lesson though. Current sickness hurts, so make sure you don't overdo it in the chamber. Or on the titan."

Iro nodded, stared down at his hands. No matter how tightly he clutched them together, they wouldn't stop trembling. "What do I do?"

"Do?" the medic said. "Rest. You're young. By tomorrow, you'll be bouncing off the walls again and barely remember how awful it felt." The old man stood and walked around his desk, sinking down into the chair with a sigh. "Now go on. Get out. Find a bed and sleep it off."

Iro stood unsteadily, holding onto the chair to make sure he didn't fall. He paused before the door and looked back. "Is Master Rollo here?"

"Huh? Rollo? Sure. Room four."

"Can I see him?"

The old medic nodded, his steely hair flopping in front of his face. He quickly ran a hand through it to push it back. "He won't see you though. Still unconscious, I'm afraid."

Iro pulled open the door to room four and stared in. It was sparse. A chair, a couple of cabinets, some machinery Iro didn't recognise. And a bed. Master Rollo was in the bed, unmoving save for the gentle rise and fall of his chest. He had some wires attached to his arm. They led to a machine that had a few numbers flickering in a pale, washed out green. Every now and then, it beeped. Iro moved around to the chair and collapsed into it. Master Rollo still didn't stir.

"We're doing alright, master." Iro clutched his trembling hands together and stared down at them, unable to look at Master Rollo while he lied to him. "You just take your time to get better. Don't worry about us. We're doing fine."

The machine attached to Master Rollo's arm beeped again, but the Corsair didn't awake.

Chapter Thirty-Four

Alfvin waited outside the captain's lounge. It was a small room just a few steps from the bridge. A place where the captain of the Eclipse could rest or draw up plans or take communications away from the rest of the officers.

Alfvin heard tinny voices within, some were raised, others soft and commanding. The words were too muted by the closed door though and he couldn't hear what was being said.

"You, too, huh?" Frigg said as she stopped by the door and leaned her back against the bulkhead wall. "Well, if she wants to see both of us, I guess I'm not in trouble."

A stab of pain rushed through Alfvin's head and he pinched the bridge of his nose. It wasn't right. Wasn't the way things should have been done. He was the Lead Hopper. Any communication or order that needed to reach Frigg should go through him. The captain had no business calling Frigg as well.

"What do you think it's about?" Frigg asked. She was eyeing Alfvin with the wary composure of a beast deciding whether to bolt or stand its ground.

"I heard Grand Mandla Samir's voice," Alfvin said quietly. He was one of the four Hoppers in the fleet who had opened his fifth gate and that put Mandla Samir on the Council of Grands. It also meant he was the most powerful Vanguard in the fleet, and a member of the Legacy family Samir.

"New orders then?" Frigg said. She brought up her tablet and tapped at the screen. Alfvin fought the urge to do the same. "Nothing via messages."

Something strange was happening and Alfvin didn't know what. He didn't like the mystery.

The door opened and Captain Ragnhldr stood on the other side. She was tall and pale, her face covered in freckles, and set in hard lines of age and worry. Her uniform was pressed, immaculate, and her posture was rigid enough even Alfvin was impressed.

"Inside," the captain said. "Both of you. Close the door."

Frigg slipped inside and Alfvin followed her, closing the door behind him. It's was a sparsely furnished office. A small cot, a smaller desk, a table with a coffee machine that had recently been on and was filling the space with a smell suspiciously more like coffee than algae. Alfvin immediately wondered if it was possible the captain had squirrelled away some of the last coffee the fleet owned. He glanced at the machine, half tempted to throw caution to the wind and make himself a cup. In the centre of the room was an integrated display table. It had screens for displaying information, and a well-preserved comms device that was for captain's use only. That meant it was connected directly to the council.

"New orders," Captain Ragnhldr said as she rounded the table. She picked up her steaming cup and Alfvin saw the contents were brown instead of green. Definitely real coffee. The captain tapped on one of the screens on the table and it brought up a representation of the Home Fleet. "See what you make of it."

Alfvin stared at the screen. A number of dots with names attached written in white. All the ships in the fleet and their positioning flying alongside the titan. They were moving slowly, the formation shifting.

"Oh scrap!" Frigg said. She had a hand over her mouth, her eyes wide.

Alfvin stared at the screen again, watching the dots move about. He didn't see it. Whatever it was the others saw, he didn't. He simply didn't have a head for ship movements and fleet positions. What did any of it matter to a Hopper anyway?

"When?" Frigg asked.

Captain Ragnhldr sipped at her coffee. "Two days."

Alfvin pinched at the bridge of his nose. It didn't help. "I don't know what I'm seeing here."

Frigg pointed at the first screen. "Ship manoeuvres." Then at the second screen displaying a list of names and numbers. "Transfer orders."

"Transfers?" Alfvin said. A sour feeling curdled his stomach and suddenly the smell of coffee, even real coffee, made him nauseous.

Captain Ragnhldr nodded slowly. "In two days, the five poorest ships in the fleet; the Courage, the Nighteyes, the Braided Fold, the Grave Chaser, and the Curse Hammer are to dock with a series of mid ships. All active Hoppers of rank two and higher are transferring across, along with essential food and printing supplies. The transfers will happen by force, if necessary."

"They're stripping them?" Alfvin asked.

Captain Ragnhldr downed the last of her coffee and with a trembling hand placed the mug on the table. "Yes. The rest of the fleet will then move to the fore wing. We're leaving the five poorest ships behind to fend for themselves."

"After taking their food and fuel and all their Hoppers," Frigg said. "It's a death sentence."

Captain Ragnhldr placed both hands on the table and lowered her head, nodding. "Without a manufactory, those five ships are a drain on resources we can't afford."

"There are over ten thousand people on those ships."

Frigg's voice rose higher.

"The council are too afraid to risk the ire of the black cloaks, or the other fleet. Not while our own Hoppers are stalled. We have no way to replace those who are injured or killed. We are also stopping all training of new Hoppers."

Alfvin looked up sharply. "What?"

"It's too much of a drain on resources. The trainees are as stalled as the rest of you. A better use of your time is to gather as many resources as we can. We are to start stockpiling."

"When?" Alfvin asked.

"Effective immediately. The official order will come tomorrow." Captain Ragnhldr seemed to deflate, as if she had been holding herself together only until the orders were given.

Alfvin stalked away from the meeting with the captain, Frigg rushing to keep up with him. "You look like you have a mission, and I doubt it's on the captain's orders," she said.

Alfvin pinched his nose and shook his head. "I'm the Lead Hopper on the Eclipse," he said. "I don't take orders from Captain Ragnhldr. I take orders from the council, and they have not given me any orders."

"Yet?"

"Yet," Alfvin agreed. He pulled out his tablet and tapped at it, sending a flight plan to Frigg. "Have the pods fuelled for the trainees."

Frigg stared down at her own tablet as she followed along behind him. "You're taking them on one last Hop?"

"I haven't given up hope," Alfvin snapped. "Just because the council are cowards and fools who would rather scuttle half the fleet than accept the possibility that a new generation of Hoppers can come from the lower ships, does not mean I have to accept that judgement. Not yet. I will push Courage Iro through his gate, no matter what it takes."

Frigg slowed to a stop behind him. "What if it doesn't work."

Alfvin stormed on. It had to work. He would make it work.

Three days since they shut down his training hall, sealed it up, and let the void take it like so much of the ship. Three days Emil had been living, sleeping, training in the secondary pod bay. At least they hadn't shut this part of the ship down yet. It gave him somewhere to call home. He wondered if his father missed him, if the old man had even realised he was gone. Probably not. No one seemed to care where he was or what he did these days. He was just glad they hadn't revoked his food and shower privileges.

He no longer had a dummy to punch and dodge, so he couldn't do much in the way of combat training. But he had learned to do the impossible. Everyone said a Paladin couldn't buff themselves, only others. Well, Emil had proven them wrong. He had turned his talent in on himself, proving once and for all he really didn't need anyone else. He trained his talent and his current daily, hourly, every few minutes. He steeled his skin and held it for as long as possible. His maximum was ten seconds. It didn't seem like much, but it was already a world longer than the two seconds it had been.

At least living in the pod bay gave him sufficient time and opportunity to familiarise himself with the pod controls. Of course, most of the pods had been taken apart to repair counterparts in the primary bay. Only Master Tannow's old pod was still functioning. It was strange sitting in it, almost like he could feel Tannow still there, watching him through the window. Emil chastised himself whenever he considered that. Tannow was dead. Dead and eaten by monsters. He deserved better than that.

Emil stared at the tablet screen, at the diagram on display, and then at the controls in front of him. He understood acceleration control, breaking thrusts, flight management. But the diagram also mentioned *sub-velocity atmospheric boosters, main core cooling vents, guidance interboard assistance,* and *focused wave wings*. He didn't have a clue what any of those things were. All he needed to know was how to fly the scrapping thing from here onto the titan. Master Tannow had always made it look easy, and Emil and the others had just engaged the automated guidance to follow the leader. Now he had to do it all on his own and he had horrible visions of crashing down onto the skin of the titan and exploding long before he made it on his first solo Hop.

He stared out the pod window at the titan. The Courage had drifted far enough away from it that he had a good view for once. It looked a monster itself. Some great leviathan swimming through space. Four massive wings, each one the size of a moon. Emil couldn't see them, but he knew that over on the other side, clinging to one of the other wings was the second fleet. He'd heard nothing about them since the previous Hop, neither them making contact again, nor the Home Fleet making any gestures towards them. But they were hostile, that was for certain.

That made four things Emil had to be careful of when he finally figured out how to pilot the pod and fly over to the titan. Monsters, traps, black cloaks, and Hoppers from the other fleet. He wasn't stupid enough to think that he, a solo trainee who hadn't even opened his first gate could hope to defend himself against them all, so he had to play it smart. He'd need to start out small, find low grade monsters close to the surface. He'd also need to dodge squads from his own fleet. If they found him out there on his own, they'd probably drag him back.

"One thing at a time," he told himself. There was no point dreaming up all the possible ways he might fail before he'd even tried. And right now he would never get to try if he didn't figure out the pod controls.

He tore his gaze away from the window and went back to staring at the tablet and the control board. He flicked over to the next page of the instruction manual. It claimed that coordinates could be used to automate much of the flying, but docking with a titan would need manual control or follow the leader guidance. None of which helped because he had no idea what coordinates he could enter and he doubted typing *take me to the scrapping titan* would work.

Emil growled in frustration and stalked out of the pod. He had too much energy to study, that was the problem. He'd never been good at reading when he was bursting with the need to move. Maybe if he went for a quick run to tire himself out a little. Then his mind would be able to settle down and focus. It was getting tougher with so much of the ship closed off, but he knew of one route that would take him about five minutes per lap. If he ran that ten times, then maybe spent a little time training his talent, surely he'd be tired enough to study properly.

He was halfway out the door and halfway convinced of his own lie when he heard his tablet chime. He paused and considered. It chimed again and he knew that meant he had a message waiting. Emil groaned and gave up on the idea of a run. It was only a distraction anyway, throwing himself into something he could do to delay failing at something he knew he couldn't.

He squeezed back into the pod and tapped on his tablet to wake it up. He had one waiting message from an unknown sender. He opened it up and read it.

"Oh scrap!"

Chapter Thirty-Five

Master Alfvin hadn't told them where they were going. He'd sprung the Hop on them and rushed them all into their pods. Iro stared at the titan out of the window, watching the contours of its skin, the pocked impressions and looming ridges. The occasional spire reaching out like a finger pointing into the void. According to Torben, who seemed to know a lot about those sorts of things, the spires occasionally lit up like filaments with a current passing through them, glowing against the dark skin of the titan. When that happened, the door to the spire opened up and a Hopper team could enter to brave the trials within and hopefully loot the place. But the Home Fleet had been limping alongside titan 02 for months now and no spires had lit up yet, at least, not any close enough for them to reach.

The pods took a sharp turn and Iro felt himself pressed hard into his seat. Then they were passing through the crosshatch of green lights into the titan, the pod thrusters breaking hard.

The door hissed as it opened and Iro stepped out to find a place he recognised. It was the thruster feed, the same one the fleet had boarded on their first encounter with titan 02. The same one where Iro had manifested his Corsair talent. It was dark now, lit only by the occasional yellow glow of an embedded light wire running along the walls. Silent, too, where before it had been a maelstrom of noise. Iro remembered the deafening roar of the fuel feed as it churned up pellets to feed the titan's now dormant thruster. The shouts and screams of Hoppers as they fought against the native monsters. The terrifying sight of the metal clad fiend towering over everyone, breathing fire and tearing down Hoppers as if they were tiny children at play.

But that monster was dead now. The Legacy families had sent one of the Grand Hoppers over to deal with it. And besides, hadn't there been an explosion? Iro thought the whole section had been vented into the black and that was why the feed was silent, the thrust it supplied dead. Had the breach been repaired? And if so, by who? Surely no one aboard the Home Fleet could have done it.

"Gather," Master Alfvin snapped.

They all rushed to obey. Master Alfvin had, as far as Iro could tell, not brought his hateful little stylus with him. However, he did carry a long baton hanging from his hip that could no doubt serve the same job just as well, if not better. Though, just like the trainer's stylus, it had no edge to it. Iro started wondering if the edge was needed at all. Corsairs had to focus their power through a sword, but what if it didn't need to be a sword?

Ylfa staggered away from the group and retched, spilling bile all over the floor. She still didn't deal with pod travel well. Master Alfvin pinched his nose and shook his head.

"This is what I call a foundational Hop," Master Alfvin said. His voice echoed around the silent, cavernous chamber. In the wake of it, Iro thought he heard the noise of skittering claws across metal flooring. "Nothing we encounter will be new to you, but it is important to familiarise yourselves with being aboard a titan. The way has been cleared of traps, but it is impossible to keep monsters from moving back in so you will encounter some of the more low grade atrocities."

Ylfa rejoined them all, wiping her mouth and looking a little green and very unhappy. Ashvild put her arm around the other girl and hugged her awkwardly past their armor.

"You will do as you are told," Master Alfvin continued. "Follow my orders to the letter. I will likely order some of you to combat some of the things we encounter alone. It is to assess your abilities." His gaze locked on to Iro. "And to push you to your limits. Now follow." He turned away and strode into the yawning chamber.

The roar of thruster fire sounded behind Iro and he turned to see a battered, old pod slam down against the floor, bounce, spin sideways through the crosshatched green lights, and careen past them all as a dizzying gray blur. It crashed into the closest feed belt, scattering loose fuel pellets and reducing a section of metal plating to dented scrap. One of the rear thrusters on the pod sparked again as if trying to fire up despite the pod being wedged inside the belt mechanism it had smashed into.

A muted, percussive thump resounded from the pod, followed by another and another. Finally the door popped open with a vacuum hiss. Emil spilled out of the old pod, gasping for air, his face an unhealthy shade of blue. Frost laced the edges of his bone-white armor. He crawled a couple of paces away from the pod and collapsed.

Iro was the first to rush over to check on the other boy. The rest of the trainees just stood around looking confused. Master Alfvin appeared more angry than anything else. Emil was still sucking down wheezing gasps of air. His skin was cold and his eyes were bloodshot. Iro sank down to his knees beside the boy, but honestly had no idea what to do.

"I think…" Emil's teeth chattered. "The pod… is compromised."

"Who are you and what are you doing here?" Master Alfvin asked as he approached. He spared Emil only a glance and then set about investigating the pod.

"His name is Courage Emil," Iro said.

"Shut up," Emil snarled. He was breathing more deeply now, colour starting to return to his cheeks. "I can talk for myself." He crawled onto his knees, then pushed up to stand on his feet and swayed a moment, hugged his arms around his breastplate and shivered. "Courage Emil. I'm on the Paladin squad assigned to you."

Master Alfvin frowned. "Your master is dead, your squad disbanded. What are you doing here?"

"Not letting you go without me," Emil growled.

"Who told you we were on a Hop?"

Emil shut his mouth and trembled belligerently.

"Trainee, you will tell me who." Master Alfvin glared. Emil only clenched his teeth, his jaw writhing.

"Your pod is scrap, how do you plan to get back?"

Still Emil was silent.

Master Alfvin pinched the bridge of his nose and took a deep breath. "One more useless, stalled out fool to cart around."

"Stalled out?" Iro asked.

Master Alfvin coughed loudly and turned towards the dormant thruster feeds. "Follow me and do exactly as I say." He strode off, picking his way around the busted feed belt and the carnage of torn metal and scattered crates the pod had left.

As they all started following, Iro ran to catch up with Emil, leaping over a toppled crate. He fell in beside the Paladin. "Where's Cali?"

"Gone."

"What?"

Emil stepped around a pool of something that looked like dried blood. It dawned on Iro then that there were no bodies. Monsters had died here in the hundreds. Hoppers had died here too. It had been months ago, true, but there were no bodies. Not even bones of the creatures that had been slain. If they had been picked off by scavengers, devoured, either they were eaten entirely or were dragged off somewhere else first. There was still just so much he didn't understand about the titans.

"Cali quit," Emil said eventually.

"But why? She was..."

Emil glared at him then. "Because they took Mia. Now she thinks she's bad luck or something." He stopped, advanced on Iro and pushed him up against blocky machine housing with multiple feed belts leading into it. So close their chest plates were touching. "So now, instead of three Paladins, there's just me." He gave Iro a final push, then stepped away. "But at least all of you from the Eclipse are still alright. Lucky you."

"That's not..."

Emil waved a dismissive hand at Iro. "Just leave me alone."

Iro watched the Paladin go for a few seconds, then slammed a fist against the machine housing he was still leaning against. The noise boomed, echoing around the gaping vastness of the chamber. Iro looked up as if following the noise and could swear he saw glittering eyes peering back from the darkness high above, nestled in between the mammoth piping that curled around the ceiling.

"He seems nice."

Iro jumped at the whispered voice. Eir was stood beside him, grinning. How she could move so silently even in her armor was astounding. "You look nervous, Eclipse Iro."

"It's not nice to sneak up on people," Iro said.

"It's not wise to get left behind." She gave him a light shove and he took the hint, started walking again, skirting the dormant machinery. "So what's up with your friend? He's very angry."

"He's not my friend," Iro said, hating how sulky he sounded. "I barely know him. I don't think he even registered me as a person before I manifested my talent."

"Ooooh. One of those." Eir nodded sagely, leapt onto a discarded crate, twirled, and landed on the other side. "Elitests. I know a few. If you're not a Hopper, you're not a person, just an object to be used or ordered around."

"No. He's not like that," Iro said. "I don't think." He didn't really know. Certainly didn't know why he felt the need to defend Emil. Perhaps because they both came from the Courage. Even if Iro had moved to the Eclipse, that gave them a kinship of sort. They had grown up around each other if not together. They experienced the same poverty and hardship. And yet, Iro couldn't help but feel like Emil resented him for having gotten out. Or maybe it was for having left everyone else behind.

"Hey, could you help me with something?" he asked.

Eir pouted at him. "Haven't I helped you enough?"

Iro smiled and shook his head. He reached into one of the little pouches on his belt and pulled out Neya's red scarf. His father's red scarf. "Could you tie this around my arm? I tried, but I couldn't do it with my armor on."

Eir plucked it from his gauntleted fingers and quickly wrapped it around his right arm. "It's a bold choice, Eclipse Iro," she said, grinning as she tied a little knot in it. "I do enjoy your flair for the dramatic."

Master Alfvin reached the far end of the chamber, turned and even from a distance Iro could see he was frowning. He and Eir picked up the pace, all but sprinting across the remaining ground to catch up with the others.

"From here on out it will get dangerous," Master Alfvin said.

"Why are there no monsters, master?" Iro asked. "I know the fleet sent a Grand Hopper to clear the chamber out, but I thought monsters always moved back in to sections that we've cleared."

"They do," Master Alfvin said. "And they have." His crest glowed to life softly behind him and he raised his baton. It started to glow, projecting a beam of bright alabaster light straight forward to the ceiling.

"Scrap!" Ylfa said in a small voice.

Above them all, monsters writhed. Iro had thought them pipes before, lacing the ceiling, but they were long, segmented beasts scuttling about the bulkheads above on chitinous legs. Each of the monsters had a squat head with a multitude of black eyes gleaming in the projected light. Their bodies were grease black, sinuous and undulating.

"Corpse crawlers," Torben said, his voice soft.

Master Alfvin snuffed out his light and hung his baton from his hip once again. "Correct. Big ones." He turned and strode through the door out of the chamber.

Iro felt like he could still hear the corpse crawlers moving, writhing against each other. He imagined them dangling down from the bulkheads, scooping up unwary passersby and devouring them. He turned and fled the room, unwilling to be left alone with the monsters.

Master Alfvin led them through a short corridor that went from slate grey walls, slowly lightening and gaining colour until they were surrounded by a cerulean glow. It didn't seem to bother the Corsair at all and he lectured as he walked.

"You will find that most monsters you encounter can be classified into one of two types regardless of how powerful they might be. On the one hand we have the mindless beasts like rustlings and corpse crawlers. They have no real intelligence beyond the drive to kill and feed and reproduce. On the other hand, you have those who possess real sentience like the various forms of Vhar. They are generally far more dangerous, but are still monsters and should be treated as such, just with greater respect for the danger they possess.

"The corpse crawlers, as we have just seen, can be relied upon to act as their nature decrees. They are not predators but scavengers. They congregate where there has been bloodshed and feed on the dead, scooping them up and digesting them. You will rarely see them moving about as they are one of the monster species who use the space between the titan's walls to travel from section to section, always seeking more carrion to feed on. Here."

He stopped before the corridor ended. Iro was glad of that. It seemed to get brighter and brighter the longer they walked down it and if he peered down the remaining length he could see nothing but a burning pearl-coloured glow.

Master Alfvin walked down another short stretch of corridor, then pressed a button on the wall. Ahead, a large door opened, the two halves splitting diagonally and retracting into the floor and ceiling. Master Alfvin stepped through into what appeared to be a council chamber of some sort. On one side there was a huge raised stage made of smoky metal. It was large enough all ten of them could have stood on it, stretched out their arms, and still not touched each other. On the other side of the chamber were a series of concentric steps rising almost all the way to the ceiling, each one half as tall as Iro. It was almost like the classrooms he used to sit in as a child while the teacher lectured them all on basic ship maintenance from the front, except on a much grander scale. And it was all lit in a pervasive sepia light that blared out of eight glowing strips above them.

Iro stared around the room, wondering what sort of purpose it might have once served. He couldn't imagine monsters gathering here for a meeting, so surely it had been designed and built with humans in mind. But humans couldn't stay on titans for long periods of time without monsters hunting them. And the longer they tried to stay, the more powerful the monsters that lumbered up from the depths of the titan. A peril that was only made worse by stronger Hoppers. The higher gate the Hopper had opened, the more dangerous the monsters that hunted them. And Master Rollo had said that opening a gate reverberated around the titan like an alarm, stirring all those nearby into a killing frenzy. So who, if not humans, had this hall been built for?

Master Alfvin was still walking, past the platform and the tiered seating, not even glancing at them. His tablet was attached to the right vambrace of his armor and he tapped once at the screen, then changed direction slightly. There were three doors side by side at the far end of the chamber and he strode towards the left one, largest by far. He pressed a button on the wall and the door slid open so quietly Iro marvelled at it. Unless the servos were being regularly maintained, they had to be made of something far superior to those used aboard the fleet.

The hallway was wide, tapering out until all the trainees could have walked side by side if they wanted. It stretched off at an angle to the previous chamber and Master Alfvin walked it with confidence, as though he feared no traps or monsters.

"Have you been here before?" Emil asked. "You seem to know where we're going."

Master Alfvin glanced impatiently at the boy. "It has already been mapped out by Surveyors. Once you've reached Hopper status and had your own suit of titan-forged armor made, it will be fitted with a navigation and communications tablet like mine." He sighed. "Well, you won't."

"What does that mean?" Emil asked.

"Quiet!" Master Alfvin snapped as the corridor ended at a huge archway of a door. He pressed a button to the side and the door split crossways, one half lowering into the floor and the other up into the ceiling. An ethereal cobalt glow assaulted them all from within the vast chamber beyond.

Ingrid was the first through the doorway, mouth gaping and eyes wide. "It's beautiful."

It was even larger than the manufactory, maybe even as big as the garden dome. Everywhere Iro looked he saw colossal glass tanks full of water stretching from the floor all the way to the ceiling high above. Each of the tanks was maybe two hundred feet across and tubular and they seemed to be spaced at irregular intervals throughout the chamber, stretching so far back and to the side he had no idea how many there were in total. Some of the tanks were bubbling, air rushing up in great wobbling globules, while others seemed perfectly still. Most of the water was lit from somewhere above or below, the cobalt hue shining through the liquid to light the entire chamber with its mesmerising beauty. But at least one of the tanks had clearly malfunctioned somewhere along the way. The water was still and murky, looking almost like the contents of an algae vat but darker and somehow more septic.

The heat inside the chamber was oppressive and as soon as Iro stepped into it he felt his skin prickle as sweat sprung forth on his brow, trickling down his back. He would have scratched but the armor plating made that impossible. He heard the muted roar of rushing water somewhere, the steady, rhythmic splash of a leak in one of the pipes or tanks.

"What the scrap is this place?" Ylfa asked.

"Secondary thruster coolant and water heating," Iro said. Ylfa and Bjorn turned curious stares his way. "What? I used to be a tech aboard the Courage. This system is remarkably similar to the ones we use aboard the fleet." He saw Master Alfvin turn a narrow-eyed gaze his way and shut his mouth quickly.

"Go on," the Corsair said with a whip like gesture from one slender finger.

Iro wiped some sweat back into his hair and approached the closest of the water tanks. It dwarfed him so entirely. The amount of water it had to contain was mind boggling. "Well, I would assume it works on a similar system to our ships. The thrusters generate a tremendous amount of heat energy which bakes the metal to super temperatures. The ships systems are set up to recycle as much of that energy as possible. Water is run around the thruster housings constantly. It acts as both a secondary cooling system to the thrusters, much less efficient than the primary venting system. But it also super heats the water which we collect in storage tanks to be used when we need it.

"Every time you step foot in the shower and turn on the hot water, you're washing in water that has ridden the system around our thrusters. That's where the heat comes from. It's a much smaller scale than this." He hovered his hand before one of the glass tanks, but didn't feel any heat coming from it. He pressed his palm against it and found it cold to the touch even through the padding of his gauntlet. Water waiting to be passed through the thrusters. "A much smaller scale."

Now he thought about it, the scale was beyond behemothic. The sheer amount of water in a single one of the tanks was enough to supply the entire fleet for years even with the inherent loss present in any system no matter how closed. And there were dozens or even hundreds of tanks in the chamber.

"Does each thruster have its own secondary cooling chamber like this?" Iro asked.

Master Alfvin nodded, a shrewd look in his eyes.

"And each wing has thirty-two thrusters. With four wings that means there are one-hundred-and-twenty-eight chambers just like this one aboard the titan."

Bjorn whistled sharply. "That's a lot of water."

Eir stepped up beside Iro, pressed her own hand against the glass tank. "Oooh. It's cool." She pressed her cheek against it next and looked like she was trying to stare down into the glowing depths. With her face smushed against the glass, she looked so cute Iro found himself grinning.

Something was gnawing at Iro, a suspicion he couldn't quite name and also couldn't shake. "But if this system is so similar to our own, you have to wonder why? Did the titan's systems come first or did ours?"

"Not important," Master Alfvin said.

"I think I see something," Eir said quietly.

"Huh!" Torben grunted. "It's just like the fleet's origin. All our books are corrupted or missing so we don't know where we come from. But our ships are far too like the titans to be coincidence."

"Enough, trainee," Master Alfvin snapped so sharply everyone fell quiet.

"There's someone in the tank," Eir said, pulling her cheek away and looking back to the rest of the group.

They all flocked to the glass, pressing themselves against it, peering down into the azure depths. Even as clear and well-lit as it was, Iro couldn't see past the vast amount of water to the other side. But Eir was right. Below them, in the depths of the tank, there appeared to be a human floating in the liquid. They were naked, hairless, curled into a fetal ball. It was impossible to tell how old they were, or had been, Iro supposed. They couldn't still be alive.

"Step away," Master Alfvin said. His voice held such an iron jab of command, they all obeyed without question. "It may look human, but it's not."

Iro saw a few jostling bubbles start to rise from the water, the invisible currents dragging them too and fro and as they rose to the ceiling. The water was being sucked up into the heating system to begin its journey around the thruster, while hot water was flushed into the tank from the bottom. Yet the thing inside the tank didn't move.

"We call them hydrids," Master Alfvin said, waving at them all to move away from the tank. "Even a juvenile is considered a grade 5 monster." He didn't need to add that meant it would be beyond even his capabilities.

"Hydrids can control water like it's an extension of their limbs," Ashvild said. "It shields them, attacks for them. Some Hoppers also say they whisper into your mind as you fight them, convince you to lay down and accept defeat."

Master Alfvin nodded. "Correct. We believe they use the tanks to gestate."

"They can survive the super heated water then?" Iro asked.

Master Alfvin only nodded at that. They skirted the tank, moving away from it, and continued further into the vast chamber.

They passed the murky juniper tank and Iro peered into it. So much of the titan seemed in such good repair, he wondered if perhaps there were some automated maintenance systems. But this tank had clearly been inoperable for a long time. The water was thick and the glass festooned with strange fuchsia plants that clutched at the tank with wide suckers. Perhaps not everything could be repaired and even a mammoth construct like the titan could only continue for so long. Iro wished he could show Roret this chamber. He'd be fascinated by the systems and complexity on display.

There was another noise, past the roar of the water rushing through pipes, and the occasional sound of a bubble of air slamming against one of the tank's glass walls. It sounded like snorting, grunting, squealing echoing off and around the chamber.

They rounded another of the tanks and Iro froze, the rest of the trainees halting with him. Only Master Alfvin continued. Before them lay a shallow lake that spread out across the chamber floor. Water streamed down from a broken pipe above in a roaring waterfall that sent sparkling sprays in every direction.

At the far end of the lake, easily two hundred feet away, was a gigantic bhur beast. It had to be twice the size of the one they had faced back in the garden dome, and had ten spiralling tusks erupting from its bony skull. Its head was lowered to the lake, snout dipped into the water as it lapped at the surface.

Nestled at the bhur beast's feet was a swarm of rustlings. They gibbered in a constant chatter, dipped claw-like hands into the water and threw splashes into each other's toothy maws like children playing.

"Excellent," Master Alfvin said. "This will be a perfect chance to push you."

"You want us to fight that thing?" Arne asked, incredulous. "It's so much bigger than the last one."

Master Alfvin turned, glanced at Arne, then away. "Iro, you will fight it. Alone."

Chapter Thirty-Six

Master Alfvin raised his baton and it glowed again, flashing a glorious yellow like a flickering star, blinding and brief. The huge bhur beast looked up from the lake, its eyes two dark pin pricks amidst its armored skull and tangle of tusks. The monster stamped, snorted, sending pearlescent spray whipping up around its feet. The rustling swarm fled, chittering to each other as they scattered in between the tanks and vanished into holes in the chamber walls Iro hadn't even realised were there.

"Kill it, trainee Iro," Master Alfvin said. He hung his baton from his belt again and stepped back.

Iro glanced back at them all, a plea for help already forming on his lips. Bjorn looked raring to get involved, his sword already in hand, gauntlets creaking as he gripped the hilt. Emil seemed annoyed, as though *he* had wanted to fight the monster all alone.

Iro caught Eir's gaze and she winked at him, tapped the side of her head. She was right. He had to stop panicking. Stop thinking of ways to convince Master Alfvin to let the others help. Master Alfvin might not like him, might want him to quit, but he was a trainer, responsible for the lives of his charges. He wouldn't send Iro into a fight he couldn't handle. So Iro had to trust in himself and analyse the way the bhur beast fought. He had to find a weakness and exploit it.

He drew Neya's sword over his shoulder and stepped forward into the shimmering waters of the lake. The azure glow from the tanks reflected off the surface, caught on the waves and sent dancing hues in every direction. The bhur beast watched him advance, one giant hoof stamping the shallow lake, slamming against the metal floor beneath the waters. The closer Iro got, the more intimidating the monster looked. It had to be thirty feet tall. Its head, legs, torso were all armored with ivory bone. Its tusks seemed to promise painful death on their points.

"I can do this," Iro said to himself. He didn't sound very confident. He stopped before the halfway point in the lake, the water sloshing gently about his ankles, finding the gaps in the armor plating and soaking the fabric beneath. "Analyse the way it fights. Find a weakness. Preferably before it kills me."

The bhur beast snorted as if mocking at him, stamped the ground again, then lurched into a charge. It picked up speed so fast, water spraying around its every pounding step. In just moments it had crossed the distance between them, its head lowered and the thicket of tusks closing in around Iro.

He swiped with Neya's sword and the Blink Strike dragged at him, slower than he'd like as the water seemed to pull back, but the strike carried him out of the way of the charge. He stumbled to a halt, completing his swing. The water rippled about him as the bhur beast thundered around in a wide arc, focused on him once more, and sped into a stampeding charge.

It takes a few seconds to turn. Has to slow in order to shorten its turn. It wasn't much of a weakness, but it was a start.

Iro swept Neya's sword upwards as the beast closed on him. The Blink Strike pulled him out of the water, up and over the charge. The bhur beast raised its head as he passed and one of the tusks caught him, boosting him and throwing him out of alignment. Iro tumbled through the air, bounced off the beast's hairy back, fell to the water with a splash, knocking his knee against the metal flooring.

He struggled back to his feet, wincing at the sharp knives stabbing into his knocked knee. It was a pain he could deal with later. The monster had already completed its turn and was focusing up for another charge.

This is how it fights. Charge after charge. Always leading with its most armored and dangerous part. But its belly is soft flesh.

Iro activated his crest. Its cool blue light was dim, but strong and constant. He might have two more Blink Strikes before needing to let his current recharge. He needed to find a way to strike at the monster's soft underbelly. That was the only way to hurt it.

The monster leapt into its next charge and Iro steadied himself to meet it. A plan formed in his head. Two quick Blink Strikes and he had a chance. The beast closed terrifyingly fast, water spraying all around it. Iro slashed to the side and the Blink Strike wrenched him out of the charging path. Too slow. The bhur beast swung its head and one of the tusks caught him again, knocking him aside, sending him flying. Iro cried out as he careened away, hit the water, disappeared beneath the surface as it enveloped him. He'd never been submerged before. Panic gripped hold, racing through his heart, thundering in his ears. He tried to breath. Couldn't. Swallowed water. Choked. Then his knees were touching metal and he sat up, pulled his head out of the water and coughed. He sucked down air, gasping and choking at the same time.

The pain registered and he almost collapsed again. It felt like something was stabbing into his side, but he glanced down and couldn't see any blood.

He'd lost track of the bhur beast. Lost grip on his sister's sword. Desperately, he searched for Neya's blade, slapping his hands against the water. He caught a glimpse of the silver blade a few feet away and staggered towards it even as he heard the beast's thundering steps closing in on him from somewhere.

Iro felt a spray of water hit his back, heard the harsh snort of the beast's breath so close it sounded an intimate whisper. He threw himself down on top of Neya's sword, curling into a ball around the sword even as the beast's tusk plowed through the water for the final strike.

Emil almost turned away when the monster went in for the killing blow. He might not like Iro, or any of the Corsairs to be honest, but he didn't want to see the other boy die. To his surprise, Iro wasn't skewered by the beast's tusks. It missed him somehow. Its feet didn't though and Iro took a painful-looking kicking as the monster trampled him. To his credit, Iro stood up afterwards. He was swaying, his feet unsteady, his sword all but dangling from his grip. But he stood. Emil respected that.

The Corsair master stood ahead of the rest of the trainees, watching the monster pick Iro apart. Emil approached him quietly. He was talking to himself.

"Come on," the master whispered. "Open the damn gate, you little fool. You have to do it. You have to be better than the rest of these stalled trash."

That was the second time he'd called them stalled. It wasn't possible that they had all encountered their first gates and failed to open them. They wouldn't be here if that were the case. That meant that something else was going on. Some other reason the master was referring to them as stalled.

In the centre of the lake, the bhur beast charged again. Iro swung his sword, blurred, reappeared a dozen steps away, swung his sword back the other way, blurred again, and reappeared next to the back end of the monster. His sword clanged against a protruding section of bone armor, rebounding off it. The monster kicked out with its back leg, caught Iro in the chest, sent him tumbling away into the water.

"It's going to kill him," Emil said.

The Corsair master startled, half turned, glancing over his shoulder. Emil met his gaze and for a heart-stopping moment thought the man was going to lash out at him. His hands twitched for his gauntlets too late. If the man had attacked, he'd never had raised his fists in time to defend. The master stared hostility at him a moment longer, then turned back to watch Iro stumble to his feet and start wading to shore as the bhur beast finished its turn and focused on him once again.

"Then he will have to open his gate or die," the Corsair master snarled.

Iro spun about, water spraying from him, until he saw them all. He swung his sword, blurred, and then appeared in front of Emil, sword cutting harmlessly through the air next to him. Emil watched as Iro collapsed next to him, hitting the floor with a solid thunk. One of the others rushed to his side, the mammoth boy who looked like he'd been eating triple rations his entire life.

"Get back out there, trainee Iro," the Corsair master snarled.

"I… I can't…" Iro sat up with help of the huge boy. He was bleeding from a cut on his cheek, his eyes looked unfocused. He couldn't even lift his sword. "It's too strong."

"An adult bhur beast is a grade 2 monster." This came from the severe-looking girl who always seemed to be bossing people around. "None of us could hope to beat it alone until we've unlocked our first gates."

Emil saw the monster turn, legs pounding the water to white froth as it sighted them all and charged.

The Corsair master shook his head sadly, his face like

curdled algae. "And you never will." He stepped forward, his crest flaring to silver light behind him, feet sinking into the shallow water. He inhaled sharply. A bright amber light, no larger than a fist, ripped free of the charging bhur beast and flew towards the master, into his mouth. He swallowed it down and leapt into a charge, meeting the bhur beast head on. The Corsair master somehow grew to three times his normal size, bone plating blossoming out from his left shoulder.

One of the girls, the bald one, behind Emil made a cooing noise. "That's Master Alfvin's unique talent. He can temporarily steal attributes of his opponents."

The Corsair master slammed his bone-armored shoulder into the charging bhur beast's skull with a crash that sent waves of water flying and made the entire chamber reverberate so violently Emil was almost thrown from his feet. The monster was thrown backwards from the impact, rolling in the water, squealing, its legs thrashing.

The Corsair master shrank back down to his normal size, the bone plating that had erupted from his shoulder fell away into the water. He pulled his baton from his belt and it glowed crimson. Then the man swiped with the weapon and a wave of bloody light flared out from it, speeding across the water and slicing into the bhur beast's skull, chopping three of its tusks in two and driving into the monster's eye. It roared, squealed, thrashed. Water sprayed in every direction.

Holstering his baton, the Corsair master turned and started stalking slowly back towards the group of trainees. His face was thunderous. Murderous.

"Time to go," said the severe girl. "Everyone run back to the pods. Torben, carry Iro if he can't run."

None of the other trainees argued. They all fled back the way they had come. Emil spent a few moments staring at the rampaging bhur beast, at the master slowly walking away from it, his mouth moving in some sort of vicious litany. He had no idea what was happening, but he knew he didn't want to be left alone with the man. He turned and fled after the others.

Chapter Thirty-Seven

Iro hurt everywhere. He was pretty sure even his hair ached. He'd tried to beat the bhur beast. He'd done everything he could, analysed its attacks, come up with a strategy, struck at the monster's weakest point. None of it had mattered. It had simply been too strong for him. At last, when he realised he wasn't ever going to win, his mother's words had sounded in his head.

You can't win every fight. You are going to lose some. What you can do is survive the losses. Learn from them. Get stronger and don't lose again.

He knew then he had to run. Escape the monster and survive. He was still so weak. So far from being able to challenge the black cloaks and bring Mia home.

"You did good, Iro," Torben said as they charged along the corridor. It bounced all around them and Iro couldn't seem to make it stay still. Torben was half dragging him as they followed behind Ashvild and the others.

Iro wanted to sob and collapse. To scream and lash out. He wanted to win. "I lost."

Torben grunted. "We all would have. It took all of us to beat that baby bhur beast back in the dome."

"That was months ago."

"Yeah. You opened a gate since then?" Torben chuckled bitterly. "Ashvild says an adult bhur beast is a grade 2 monster. Master Alfvin had no sense sending you against it alone."

Ashvild reached the end of the corridor, slammed the button to open the great door. It slid slowly apart, each section disappearing into the floor and ceiling. Iro saw her glance back towards them, face tight with fear. He didn't want to know what she saw behind them all.

"Go." Ashvild shouted, waving the others through the open door.

"Stop!" Master Alfvin's voice rang through the corridor with the threat of punishment.

Torben slowed, dragging Iro with him, but Ashvild grabbed his pauldron and pushed him through the door. Emil was the last one through and Ashvild pushed the button to close the door, then ran on to join the others. They were all milling about before the raised platform, unsure, waiting for someone to take charge. Even Bjorn wasn't volunteering for that duty, but Ashvild strode into the centre of them all without hesitation.

"Why are we running?" Arne asked.

"You didn't see it?" Ingrid asked. "He's gone mad."

"What? The monster?"

Ylfa thumped Arne on the arm. "Master Alfvin, you scrapping dolt. It was in his eyes." She hugged herself.

"What do we do?" Eir asked. She was shifting from foot to foot, never stopping.

"Run back to the pods," Ashvild said. "The automated piloting has a return journey setting."

"Mine doesn't," Emil said quietly.

Ylfa shook her head. "Maybe because you scrapped it?"

Emil only shrugged in reply.

The door clanged and they all turned to stare at it. It was trying to close, but Master Alfvin's baton was blocking the two halves from coming together. Iro heard the grinding of servos for a second, then the door started opening again. Master Alfvin stood on the other side, a dark look on his face. As soon as the door had opened enough to admit him, he stepped through. The door shut slowly after him.

"Too late to run now," Arne said quietly. Iro noticed he had slunk to the back of the pack.

Master Alfvin stalked toward them. "I told you to stop."

Ashvild stepped forward to meet him. "Master, you…"

Master Alfvin backhanded her across the face and Ashvild careened sideways, crashing against the raised tiers of seating. She groaned and didn't get up. Master Alfvin didn't break stride and Iro realised his gaze was locked on him.

Iro pushed away from Torben just as the Corsair reached him. Master Alfvin grabbed him by the collar of his breastplate and tossed him up onto the platform. His vision spun as he crashed down on the metal flooring, rolling to a stop. He crawled onto his hands and knees, tried to stand, but he just hurt everywhere.

"What is it going to take?" Master Alfvin snarled. He leapt up onto the platform and kicked Iro in the chest hard enough to drive the air from his lungs and send him skidding across the floor.

"Master?"Bjorn's voice.

Master Alfvin spun about, waving a wild hand at the others. "Stay where you are. All of you."

Iro struggled back to his knees, clutching at his mid-section. He didn't understand what was happening. He had lost to the bhur beast, yes. He'd run away from a fight he'd known he couldn't win. But why was Master Alfvin so angry? Why was he attacking him?

"I'm sorry." Iro had to squeeze the words past the pain. He lurched to his feet, backed away from Master Alfvin as the Corsair advanced on him again. Iro raised his arm, a pitiful ward to the man's attacks.

"Sorry?" Master Alfvin stalked forwards, pushed

Iro's arm aside, grabbed him by the collar of his chest plate again. "Do you even understand what's at stake?"

"No!"

Master Alfvin pushed, throwing Iro backwards against the far wall. He hit it hard, bashed the back of his head against the bulkhead, rebounded, stumbled forward dizzy and wavering.

"You have to open your gate, Iro," Master Alfvin said as he closed on Iro again. "You are the only one who can. Everyone else is stalled." He drew his baton and swung. It smashed into Iro's chest, cracked his breastplate, sent him tumbling away.

"The council is panicking," Master Alfvin continued. "They're shutting down training of new Hoppers entirely." He waved a hand at the other trainees, gathered together near the base of the tiered seating. "There's no point to bringing weaklings like this aboard the titan. They'll never progress. Nothing but stalled out trash."

Iro lurched back to his feet, staggering towards the edge of the platform, towards the other trainees. He knew they couldn't help him, not against Master Alfvin, but he just wanted to get away. "What makes you think I'm different?"

"Because you manifested your talent here on this titan. The council don't believe it, so I have to prove it. I have to make you open your gate to prove to them all is not lost. Before they cancel the training and scrap half the fleet." He advanced on Iro again. "Now, open your gate, trainee."

"I don't know how!" Iro drew Neya's sword and held it in trembling hands. He staggered, trying to take stance in a loose guard, ready to defend, but he hurt everywhere and couldn't keep his arms from shaking. He didn't know what to do. Couldn't hope to beat Master Alfvin. Had no idea how to open a gate.

Master Alfvin swung his baton and Iro raised Neya's

sword, blocked the strike. He staggered from the impact, forced his screaming muscles into motion and backed up a step, raising the blade again. Another strike and Iro was knocked aside, barely keeping his feet below him.

Iro blocked another strike and was flung sideways from the force of it, feet skidding across the metal plating. Master Alfvin was relentless, following after him immediately, baton raised to hit him again. He smashed it down. The blow almost knocked Neya's sword from his grasp. Iro fell backwards onto his arse, scooted away, and twisted back to his feet.

"Do you think I won't kill you?" Master Alfvin snarled as another blow from his baton sent Iro reeling. "Unless you open you're gate, you. Are. Worthless."

Another strike. This time Iro wasn't quick enough and it knocked Neya's sword aside, smashed into his pauldron, shattering the metal and sending shards flying across the chamber. Iro sunk to his knees, arms trembling, barely able to raise the sword to block the next attack.

Master Alfvin raised his baton and it started to glow with the same crimson light as before. His crest flared to shining silver behind him.

"Leave him alone!" Torben's voice, roared from the other side of the chamber.

"Quiet!" Master Alfvin shouted back, swiping his baton to the side. A wave of ruby light shot across the chamber and hit Torben in the chest.

The bigger boy stumbled from the impact. His chest plate dropped away, sheared in half. Blood poured from his chest. He collapsed sideways without a word, hit the metal floor, and didn't move.

For a moment that seemed like forever, no one moved. Even Master Alfvin just stared at Torben's body, a look of shock twisting his face. Then Ingrid screamed, fell to her knees beside her brother, shaking him as if she could make him get up and admit it was all a joke.

Master Alfvin took a single step back, looked down at the baton in his hand. Iro saw his eye twitch, his teeth clench. He pinched the bridge of his nose.

There was no time. No time to think, to analyse, to plan. Iro roared, launched up to his feet and thrust Neya's sword at Master Alfvin's chest. The Corsair recovered from his shock in only a moment, swiped his baton sideways, knocking Iro's stab aside.

"You made me do it," Master Alfvin said. "I didn't want to, but I have to prove how far I'm willing to go. I have to show you what will happen if you don't OPEN YOUR GATE!" He roared the last and struck again and again and again. A flurry of blows whipped at Iro and he was battered in every direction. Neya's sword rang from the impacts time and again. Iro saw the crack in the blade spreading, creeping ever further across the metal.

"Open it or I will kill you too," Master Alfvin shouted, raising his baton again. Iro thrust Neya's sword up, blocked the strike. With a sound like a child's scream, the blade cracked in half.

Iro stared down at the half of Neya's sword in his hands, not comprehending it. The sword was now just a foot of cracked titan steel, ending in a jagged line of torn metal. The other half lay on the floor beside him.

"No more defences," Master Alfvin said, his baton glowing crimson again. "Open your gate or die, trainee."

Out of the corner of his eye, Iro saw Emil leap up onto the platform and launch himself towards them. "Enough!" His gauntlets on his hands, fist brought back and ready to punch.

Master Alfvin stepped back, calmly avoiding Emil's wild swing, slashed out with his glowing baton. Emil pulled back his hands just in time, raised them to block. The ruby light from the baton flared and Emil was flung backwards. He rolled with the momentum, sliding back onto his feet, fists raised and ready. Then his gauntlets fell apart, clattering to the ground in a dozen pieces. He stared down at them dumbly, flexing his hands as if not understanding.

A cruel smile tugged at the corner of Master Alfvin's lips. Then the Corsair dashed forward, raised his baton and brought it crashing down on Emil.

Emil's fiery crest roared to life behind him. "Steel." The Paladin raised his arm and the baton clashed against it with a metallic clang.

"That's not possible," Master Alfvin said, staring down at the Paladin.

Emil grunted, staggered back a step, then roared and pushed against the baton. He followed it up by launching himself at the Corsair, throwing punch after punch in a dizzying combo.

Master Alfvin gave ground, his brow pulled into a frown. He stepped out of the way of Emil's attacks, brushed aside others, kicked out with one foot, connecting with Emil's knee. The other boy fell away and Master Alfvin darted in, swinging his baton again.

"Steel." Again the baton clanged to a halt against Emil's steel-enhanced arm.

"How?" Master Alfvin growled. "Paladins can't buff themselves."

Emil grinned at the man. "I can." He pushed back to his feet and swung a wild haymaker. Master Alfvin swayed out of the way of it, then whipped his baton across the boy's face so fast he had no chance to enhance himself. Emil hit the ground hard, rolled to a stop, groaned as he struggled to get back up. It was clear that even though Emil had somehow managed to learn to enhance himself, without opening his first gate, he still had too weak a current to hold an enhancement for more than a few seconds.

Master Alfvin stalked towards Emil. The Paladin pushed himself back to kneeling. A large gash ran along his cheek, the flesh around it angry and dribbling blood. He blinked rapidly, staring up at the approaching Corsair.

"In the end, you achieved nothing." Master Alfvin's words seemed to hit Emil like a hammer blow and he reeled back, panting and staring up at his approaching end.

It was hopeless. Even if all the other trainees joined them, they stood no chance against Master Alfvin. He was a rank three Corsair. Too strong. Too quick. Too powerful. Before him, they really were nothing but children playing with toy swords.

Even Emil, who had always seemed so strong to Iro. Even with the ability to enhance himself, Emil was beaten so easily. He tried to protect Iro, and he would die for it. Just like Torben.

Master Alfvin stalked past Iro, not even sparing him a glance as he advanced on Emil.

His mother's words sounded in his head again.

You can't win every fight. You are going to lose some. What you can do is survive the losses. Learn from them. Get stronger and don't lose again.

Courage could come in many forms. One of those was running away. Surviving. He could do it now, while Master Alfvin was distracted. Iro could run, flee to the pods, fly back to the Eclipse. Survive. Survive long enough to get stronger. What else could he do? He was too weak. Too weak to stop Alfvin. Too weak to save Emil. Too weak to do anything.

Iro stared down at his sister's broken sword in his hands. At his mother's cracked armor on his chest. What else could he do but run?

Emil lurched back to his feet, swaying, swung a punch at Master Alfvin. The Corsair pushed the fist aside, kicked Emil in the chest putting him back on his knees. Then he drew his baton back, and swung it at the boy's head.

Chapter Thirty-Eight

Iro staggered to his feet, reaching for Master Alfvin, shouting at him to stop, knowing it was too late. He saw the baton swinging down, slower and slower. The crimson glow faded to flat gray. The whole chamber leeched of colour. The baton stopped moving, a hand's width from Emil's face. Master Alfvin's snarl was writ large on his frozen features. Emil's wince, seeing the fatal blow coming and knowing he could do nothing to stop it. All frozen. Colorless.

Iro turned around to see the other trainees frozen and gray too. Eir and Ylfa were busy helping Ashvild up, she was conscious again, but slick, gray ooze leaked down her face from the gash Master Alfvin had given her. Ingrid knelt over Torben's body, tears streaming down her cheeks, some frozen in mid air. Bjorn stood at the head of the group, sword drawn as if to defend them from something. Arne was frozen in mid run, barrelling towards the door that led back to the pod bay. Iro didn't understand it. Everything was locked in a frozen, colourless tableau. As though he was somehow trapped in the moment before Emil's death, knowing there was nothing he could do to stop it.

Am I dreaming?

But Master Rollo had said something about the world freezing. He'd said it happens when a Hopper manifested a gate. Iro spun about, searching. And there it was. Between Emil and Master Alfvin. It was in shades of gray just like everything else. Taller than Iro by a full head and twice as wide as him. It was not grand like he might have expected. The gate's frame was made from twisted, jagged metal that looked a lot like the broken end of Neya's sword. All along the arch were little scarfs tied around it. They looked just like his father's scarf. The one Neya had worn on every Hop. The same one now tied around his own right arm.

Iro approached the gate slowly, wondering what the door would look like. Master Rollo had said a Hopper needed to figure out how to open the gate once it manifested. That there was usually some sort of puzzle to solve or… But there was no door. The gate stood open. In its centre, where the door should have been, his crest hung in the air, detached from him, the only color in the whole world. Iro walked around to stand behind Emil's frozen form. The gate didn't look like it had ever held a door. It was an open archway. There was a word written on the crown of the arch.

COURAGE.

The word sounded oddly bitter to Iro. Courage. The one thing he had struggled with his whole life, it seemed. But what did it mean here? The Courage Gate. Already open with no door. Was the lack of door a trick? Was it the puzzle? Or was it trying to say he had been courageous all along? That couldn't be right. If it was, why hadn't he manifested the gate sooner? If he had, Torben would still be alive. Master Alfvin would have had no reason to kill him.

Iro growled and flung his head back, trying to reason out what it all meant. Above, creeping down from the ceiling, he saw color returning to the chamber. The ceiling was already white panels again. The walls were changing too, a line of color gobbling up the gray as it descended. Of course. Master Rollo had said that would happen too. Iro only had until color fully returned to the chamber to figure out what to do, or the gate would disappear and he would be forever stalled out. Unable to progress.

Approaching the gate, Iro tried to reason out the puzzle. Color was creeping back in quickly. He had only a minute at most before the gate disappeared. He had to focus.

The gate was between Emil and Master Alfvin. The Corsair was already swinging his baton for the killing blow. Even if the lack of door wasn't a puzzle, there was no way Iro could walk through the gate without getting in the way of that strike. That would probably be a record for the quickest death after opening a gate.

Iro walked behind Emil and grabbed him under the shoulders, tried to lift him. It was like he was made of solid steel. The boy didn't budge at all.

Iro glanced at the wall. The line of color was moving so quickly, maybe even faster than before. It drew level with the top of the gate and Iro saw that *COURAGE* was written in deep indigo lettering. The scarfs tied around the arch were indeed red, the exact same faded ruby of his father's scarf. But he didn't have time to stop and gawk.

He rushed around the gate to Master Alfvin's side and paused for a moment, waved a hand in front of the man's face. Iro couldn't quite shake the niggling fear that if he touched Master Alfvin, he would suddenly unfreeze and Iro would have to face him entirely alone in the gray expanse. Although, he had to admit, the chamber was more color than not now. The line had crept down far enough that Master Alfvin's hair was blonde again. Iro shook himself to chase away the thoughts, braced his shoulder against Master Alfvin's side and pushed as hard as he could. Nothing happened. The man didn't move at all.

Iro backed up a step, took Neya's broken sword in both hands, and thrust the jagged edge up into Master Alfvin's side. The broken blade bounced off the man as if he were a bulkhead.

The color had crept further now, was fully halfway down the arch of the gate. Emil's hair was black again, his face pale, no longer looking like a statue. He looked scared, watching his death come at him, unable to stop it.

And Iro didn't know how to stop it either.

Courage. The Courage Gate. His mother had said it was a form of courage to run away, to live and get stronger so you didn't fail again. But Iro had been doing that all along. He ran away from everything. The black cloaks, the bhur beast. He kept running away and he never got any stronger.

The creeping color had almost reached the bottom of the Gate now. He was out of time. Iro saw just two choices before him. Either he did nothing and the gate vanished, and Master Alfvin struck Emil down. Or Iro walked through the gate and took the blow instead. He was under no illusions. He wouldn't survive it.

Maybe that was the true essence of courage. Not being fearless, but being afraid and standing up to it just like Neya had done every time she Hopped over to titan 01. Of having a choice, the option to run away, but choosing not to. He couldn't win against Master Alfvin. He couldn't even survive the glowing red strike aimed at Emil's head. But he could choose to face down his fear and step into its path to protect the other boy.

The color had almost reached the bottom of the gate. Iro was out of time. He gripped Neya's broken sword in both hands, and walked through the gate to meet Master Alfvin head on.

Iro's crest exploded into icy light. The lock opened, a symbol of a flightless bird, the symbol of the Courage in the centre. His current surged through him like a reactor starved of fuel for too long and suddenly running at one hundred percent. It strengthened his limbs, seared his wounds closed. It crackled around him like a skin of frozen fire. That same energy rushed into Neya's broken sword and reforged it in pure cerulean light.

Master Alfvin's glowing baton clanged to a halt against the crackling energy of Neya's sword. The Corsair stared at Iro over their crossed weapons. The air sizzled between them, two opposing forces fighting to consume one another. Then the man grinned and pulled back.

Master Alfvin laughed, throwing out his arms. "I did it!" he shouted.

Iro glanced back over his shoulder at Emil. The other boy was alright. Still hurt, in shock probably, but alive. He stared up at Iro in disbelief. Iro grinned at him. "I guess you owe me one again."

He turned back to Master Alfvin, repositioned himself to make certain the Corsair couldn't launch another attack at Emil.

"Now they can't refute it," Master Alfvin said. The smile that cracked his face was somehow triumphant and menacing all at once.

Iro felt the new current inside like it had a will of its own, begging to be used. He felt stronger, so unbelievably strong. Like he could finally take on the bhur beast. Like he could take on an army of bhur beasts. He tried to control it, to force it back down, felt his limbs tremble. Not from exertion, but from the effort of restraint. He wondered if this was how all Hoppers felt when they opened their First Gates of Power. Invincible. All powerful. Dangerous.

"Come on," Master Alfvin said. "Back to the pods, Iro. We have to show you to the council, prove that you're not stalled."

Iro didn't budge from his protective position in front of Emil. He tightened his grip on Neya's sword. The hilt and half the blade was still warm titan steel, but the top half of the blade was made from the same fizzling icy energy as his crest.

"You killed Torben," Iro said darkly. He wondered if he could take Master Alfvin in a fight now. Probably not. The rush of energy inside seemed to promise him that he could. That he could do anything. It was a lie. Iro knew it was just the heady confidence of opening his gate for the first time. Master Alfvin was a rank three Corsair. Far beyond anything Iro could throw at him. Yet still. He was the only one out of all of them who stood any chance.

"So what?" Master Alfvin asked. "Stalled out trash like the rest of them. They don't matter, Iro. Only you matter. You are the proof that the fleet is not yet lost. That what we need is a new generation of Hoppers."

"Torben matters," Iro snarled at the man. "They all matter. The rest of the fleet won't let you get away with murdering one of their own."

The smile slipped from Master Alfvin's face. He looked over to the rest of the trainees, then back to Iro. "No. You're right. They won't." His knuckles tightened around his baton. "Unless they don't know about it."

"What?"

Alfvin pinched the bridge of his nose, clenched his teeth. Then his expression went flat and far too calm. "I understand. You'll tell them. If you get the chance. So I won't give it to you. You've already done the important part, Iro. You've proven me correct. An unfortunate accident then that neither you, nor any of the others survived. Your opening the first gate drew a swarm of monsters to us. Too many for even me to handle. A shame. But I'm the only survivor. Luckily, I bring back news of your encountering a gate here on titan 02."

Something loud rammed against the door leading to the chamber with the water tanks. It slammed against the metal again and again. Above him, Iro heard the sound of hundreds of claws scuttling against metal. Rustlings barrelling through the pipes.

Iro met Master Alfvin's hostile gaze again and the man lifted his baton, ready to charge. "A shame."

Master Alfvin dashed forward with a burst of speed. Iro barely brought Neya's sword up in time to block the first slash. He ducked away from a follow-up jab, swiped the blade sideways, Blink Striking a dozen paces away. Master Alfvin somehow beat him there, already swinging even as Iro slid to a stop. The baton smashed into Iro's chest, shattering what was left of his mother's breastplate so it fell away in chunks of jagged metal.

Iro used Blink Strike again, ripping himself back across the platform. He was ready for the pursuit this time, and as soon as he completed the strike, he swung Neya's sword back the other way. Master Alfvin dashed in front of Iro right into the path of his attack. He smashed his baton down on Neya's sword to knock it away, then punched Iro in the face with his free hand.

Iro crashed to the ground, blood filling his mouth, but didn't give himself a moment to worry about it. He activated his crest again, half expecting to see it had dimmed to a muted glow. Two quick successive Blink Strikes, along with maintaining the energy blade had to have drained it. Instead, his crest was bright as thruster fire. He swung his sword to the right, felt the Blink Strike carry him away on his back out of the crushing downward swing Master Alfvin levelled at him. Iro finished the strike at thin air, swung around and used the momentum to flip up onto his feet once again.

It was so good to feel strong, to feel fast. Like he could do anything. Every move he'd ever thought about in his head, but had never been powerful enough to pull off. He felt like now he could. He couldn't win. He knew he couldn't win. But if he could just keep Master Alfvin busy long enough for the others to escape, it would be enough. At the very least, it wouldn't be losing.

It was time to go on the offensive. He couldn't just keep running, so maybe it was time to see just what a Hopper could do after unlocking their first gate.

Iro shifted his grip on Neya's sword, thrust it forward. The Blink Strike carried him toward Master Alfvin. The Corsair grinned, stepped to the side, raised his baton to bring down on Iro's head as he passed. But Iro had aimed his strike short on purpose. He stopped short of Master Alfvin's blow, swung Neya's sword upward, and let a new Blink Strike carry him over the man's head, slashing out at him as he passed. Master Alfvin ducked out of the way. Iro hit the ground on the other side of the man, skidding to a halt, already swinging Neya's sword to attack again.

Chapter Thirty-Nine

Emil couldn't keep up. He'd trained so hard to match the speed of the training dummy back on the Courage. Setting it to its highest speed and getting used to its movements. But here, now, he could barely even see Iro and the insane Corsair. They zipped about the stage, Iro using that technique of his, in a mirage of shimmering strikes. Emil twitched left and right trying to follow them, but he just couldn't.

It wasn't fair. It wasn't right. He'd spent his entire life training to be a Hopper. It was his path, his way to claw himself out of the scrap and become something. And then drag the Courage up with him. They had all been third rate citizens for too long, living on the scraps the mid ships and Legacy families left for them. That needed to change. Emil had to change it. But how could he if he was stalled out? And what did that leave him? Even if they did somehow escape the madman, what awaited him back on the Courage? Without the ability to progress, to open his gates, to become the Hopper he had always wanted to be… He had no other skills. Just like his father hadn't had any other skills.

Emil tore his eyes from the fight and stared down at his own hands. He knew what it meant, what awaited for him back on the Courage. The life of a drudge. Cleaning the septic tanks, squeezing between bulkheads to chase out the vermin that infested the ship, The worst, most dangerous labor available aboard the fleet. And he'd live in his father's quarters with his old man. Listening to him gripe about his lot, never trying to change anything. A life of complaints and excuses and anger. And it would swallow Emil up, chew him into shape, then spit him out as a new version of his father. Bitter, impotent, alone.

The sounds of battle stopped. Emil stared down at his hands, at the gray metal floor below, and waited. He knew Iro couldn't win. That meant the Corsair had killed him. And that meant Emil was next. Good. He'd rather die than live his father's life. Emil waited for that death to come. And waited. Nothing happened. Everything was silent. The other trainees weren't speaking anymore. Even the sound of the monsters trying to bash their way through the door had quieted.

Emil raised his head to find the entire chamber painted in shades of gray. Before him stood a huge double door. The frame was forged of thick steel girders, decorated with the mocking face of the training dummy he had come to know so well. The doors themselves were sturdy-looking, whorly, slate gray and embossed with his crest glowing fiercely. They fit together perfectly apart from a slight seam running straight down the middle. Heavy chains wrapped around the entire doorway, securing it tight. And above, on the head of the door, was a single word written in a language Emil didn't know, but somehow understood all the same. It read *FAILURE*.

The *Failure* gate.

It seemed fitting. Perhaps it was meant to indicate that was what Emil was, or maybe it was prophesying his future. It didn't matter. Emil stood slowly, already determined he would beat this challenge just like all the others.

He glanced to the left, saw the rest of the trainees frozen, all color leeched out of them. They were stuck moving towards the door leading back to the dock. To his right, he saw Iro and the insane Corsair, their weapons crossed. Iro was grimacing, his back leg buckling as the man pressed down on him with greater strength. Above, Emil saw color starting to drain back into the chamber, a line of it slowly descending towards him, painting the walls white. He guessed that meant there was a time limit to opening his gate. And that meant there was no time to waste.

Emil ran to his door, pressed his hands against it and pushed. It didn't budge. He pressed his shoulder against it, braced his foot, shouted as he leaned every bit of himself into it. Still it didn't open. He tried to squeeze his fingers into the seam, cracked a fingernail, didn't care. He pushed, pulled, wrenched, tore another fingernail loose, red blood turning gray the moment it spattered against the floor. And still the door remained utterly, imposingly closed.

Breathing hard, a tight panic rising in his chest, Emil grabbed hold of one of the chains, wrenched on it as hard as he could. It rattled, the sound echoing strangely in the frozen space, but no matter how much he wrenched it, it wouldn't break.

The line of color continued to move down the wall. The white walls, the paint chipped and splotchy in places, seemed to mock him somehow. The very existence of the timed nature was an insult laid directly at Emil's feet. He stared at the word above the door again.

Failure.

He understood it now. It was an insult levelled at him. It was also a prophecy of his inability. It labelled him, defined him, encompassed him. His father had always said it. The gate was proving the hateful old man right.

Emil felt the panic in his chest now as the color reached the top of the Gate. He couldn't breathe deep enough, couldn't fill his lungs. His arms felt somehow tired, and aching with suppressed energy all at once. He wanted to move, to run, to hit something, to sit down and scream in frustration. It wasn't fair. Wasn't right. He would not...

could not allow himself to fail.

He ran at the door, roaring in anger and punched it as hard as he could. Pain erupted in his hand and the door still stood there impassive and locked. He punched it again, and again, and again. Split his knuckles, blood flying, didn't care. He screamed, kept punching. The color crept further down until Emil could see the doors themselves were brown like the trees he had seen back in the garden dome, his crest red like fire upon them. He threw himself against it, screamed, kicked the door. Still it didn't open.

Taking a step back, Emil reached inside for his current. It wasn't there. He couldn't feel it at all. Couldn't activate his crest.

"Steel." He willed his talent to work, to strengthen his body and make him steel. Nothing happened. He punched the door anyway, left a smear of crimson blood across the gnarly brown wood.

"Why?" he asked the door. "WHY? Why won't you open?"

He stared up at the word again.

Failure.

He was going to fail. The gate knew it. His father knew it. Everyone knew it. Emil knew it. He was going to fail.

The color was already half way down the gate and still creeping. Emil felt exhausted. It was all just too much. He glanced right to where Iro and the Corsair were frozen mid struggle. Their legs were gray, but colour had returned to their upper bodies. Emil could see the strain and fear on Iro's face, the azure light of his glowing blade almost making his eyes glow.

He staggered over to the locked combatants, screamed at them. No words only fury. They didn't respond, didn't hear him. Emil collapsed to his knees before them, the last of his strength fleeing him. It was all so scrapping unfair.

"Why?" His voice was a strangled, pitiful whisper. He hated that. "Why was it so easy for you?" He stared up at Iro. The other boy didn't respond, of course. The color had reached his knees now, his old, battered armor looking all the worse for the white paint that still clung to it.

The tightness in Emil's chest lightened and he sagged, felt tears prickling his eyes, blurring his vision. "Why did you open your gate so easily? Why do I have to struggle and fail? What do you have that I don't? I have trained my entire life and still I fail. And you…" He shook his head, felt like screaming again. "You've had a talent for five minutes and open your gate like it's nothing. Why? How?"

He had done everything on his own, pulled himself up from nothing, trained harder than anyone. When everyone else around him quit, Emil kept going alone. And Iro had been given everything. Gifted a position aboard a mid ship. A strong trainer, other trainees who didn't quit at the first hardship. He'd even been given a titan steel sword. And of course he had opened his gate first and easily. While Emil just failed all alone again.

The color was down to Iro's ankles now. Emil stared at that line of descending color, hated it. "How did you do it, Iro? How did you open your gate? Tell me. Please."

Emil heard the rattle of chains behind him, turned, saw the chains falling away from his gate, the door swinging open. The color had almost reached the bottom now, he had so little time. He twisted, lurched forward, scrambling on hands and knees, threw himself at the gate even as the chamber and everyone in it lurched back into colour and noise and motion.

Iro's back leg buckled and he dropped to one knee,

Master Alfvin pressing down on him, snarling at him past their locked weapons. He was too strong, too fast, too powerful.

A roar sounded off to the side like water rushing through pipes. Master Alfvin glanced at the sound, then backed up, releasing the pressure from Iro entirely.

"That's impossible," the Corsair said, staring.

Iro lurched back to his feet and followed Master Alfvin's gaze. Emil knelt on the metal stage, his fists clenched before him. Translucent orange flames danced across his arms, head, shoulders. His armor glowed in the burning light. And suddenly Iro understood. Emil had opened his first gate.

Somewhere far off, muted by closed doorways, something howled. The banging on the doors grew more frantic as monsters sought to batter their way in, drawn now by two Hoppers having opened their gates.

Emil unclenched his fists, staring at his hands, then clenched them again. He stood slowly, turned to face Iro, eyes wide and mouth open.

"You did it," Iro said, grinning.

Emil stared wide-eyed at him a moment longer, then closed his mouth and frowned. "Of course, I did. What? If you can do it, anyone can."

Master Alfvin shook his head. "Do you know what this means?"

Emil stalked over towards Iro, his gaze locked on Master Alfvin.

"Your talent manifested back when we were orbiting titan 01." Master Alfvin began pacing back and forth on the stage, tapping at the tablet on his vambrace. "If you can open your gate, then surely the rest of us can too. Something must have changed. Some way of encountering our gates." He stopped tapping, looked up, eyes wide and manic. "We're not stalled!" He took a couple of steps forward and Emil dropped into a ready stance, fists held up before him. "How did you do it? You must tell me."

The howl from somewhere deeper into the titan sounded again, closer this time.

"You can't fight him alone," Emil said quietly.

Iro nodded. He'd already figured that out. "And you can?"

Emil was quiet for a moment. "I'll defend. You attack."

"Can you enhance me?"

The Paladin shook his head slowly. *Does that mean he can only enhance himself?*

"Ready?" Emil asked.

"Wai…"

"Go!"

Chapter Forty

Iro was still deciding how best to attack when Emil rushed forward. He moved so much faster than he had before and Master Alfvin stepped back in shock, clearly not expecting the attack. Emil jabbed two quick punches at the man, both knocked aside as Master Alfvin recovered then struck back. Emil raised an arm, took the strike just below the elbow. His rusting armor cracked and fell away, but Emil was enhancing himself with steel and though the blow knocked him down onto one knee, it didn't fell him. Master Alfvin raised his baton for a second strike.

No time to think, Iro just attacked. He slipped in around Emil's side and thrust his glowing blade up at Master Alfvin's chest. The Corsair twisted away, then leapt back half a dozen paces, giving himself room.

"Saved you!" Iro said, grinning.

He didn't stop to see Emil's reaction. Iro had a feeling letting Master Alfvin collect his wits was a bad idea. He used a Blink Strike to close the distance, was dragged through the chamber with incredible speed, swiped his sword a foot short of Master Alfvin. The Corsair swung for where he expected Iro to be, missed.

Iro had no time to congratulate himself on fooling Master Alfvin. The Corsair followed his missed strike with astounding speed, stepping forwards and slicing with his glowing red baton. Iro heard Emil grunt, felt a hand on his back, pulling him out of the way of the strike. He stumbled, wrong footed, and Emil leapt over him.

"Saved *you*. Steel," Emil said as he landed and barrelled forward, leading with a barrage of fists. His crest glowed a fierce red behind him.

Master Alfvin swept his baton left and right in a dizzying crimson blur as he knocked aside every one of Emil's punches. Then the Corsair kicked out with one foot, pushing Emil's leading leg out from under him. Emil fell mid-punch, thrust his hands out and caught himself on the ground.

Iro stabbed his blade, Blink Striking in beside Emil and intercepting a blow that was meant to split his skull. Emil reared up, shouting, knocked into Iro and they both stumbled apart. Iro glared at Emil, saw Emil glaring right back.

"Stop trying to save me," Emil growled.

"Right back at you."

Master Alfvin surged in between them both. The first glowing baton strike smashed into Iro's arm and shattered his right vambrace, shards of printed metal flying everywhere. The second strike slipped past Emil's guard, hammered into his ribs and ripped a squeak of pain from the boy. Suddenly both Emil and Iro were on the back foot, retreating, shoulder to shoulder and desperately defending a flurry of attacks. Master Alfvin was relentless, tireless, beating them back.

Iro swung his azure blade to the side, Blink Striking away, then back in behind Master Alfvin as Emil steeled himself and took the full brunt of the man's assault for a few seconds. Over his shoulder, Iro saw his crest dimming, unable to sustain both the glowing blade and his frequent uses of Blink Strike. He completed his swing just behind Master Alfvin, turned, sweeping his sword across the man's back. Master Alfvin leapt straight upwards. Iro overbalanced, his momentum carrying him forwards just as Emil pulled his fist back for a punch. The two of them collided in the space Master Alfvin had been, toppling to the ground in a heap of tangled limbs.

"Get off me," Emil growled, pushing at Iro.

"You ran into me," Iro accused him, trying to roll free.

Iro saw a flash of red above them, looked up to see Master Alfvin twenty feet up, swinging his glowing baton. A wave of red light burst forth, arcing towards them.

Emil threw himself on top of Iro. "Steel." He screamed when the blast of crimson light hit him. The armor on his back was cleaved in two, and the entire chest piece fell away, crumbling into pieces. Iro threw Emil aside, raised his azure blade just as Master Alfvin fell towards them, swinging his glowing baton in for the kill. Blue and red met in a burst of violet energy that exploded outwards, knocking the other trainees off their feet even half the chamber away by the door that led to the docks.

Iro's legs collapsed beneath him and he fell onto his back, Master Alfvin pressing down. Sparks hissed from where their two blades met and Iro could feel his arms trembling.

Emil barrelled into Master Alfvin, carrying him away. The two of them hit the stage, rolled, both springing back to their feet. Master Alfvin was faster and cracked Emil across the jaw as he recovered. The other boy stumbled away, raised an arm and blocked the follow up strike. His crest was also dimming, the fiery red dulling to a belligerent orange.

This isn't working. We're not strong enough. All we're doing is throwing ourselves at him to save each other. There has to be something. Some way we can beat him.

Again Iro heard the howl, closer than before. It seemed to shake the very walls of the chamber. The scrabbling and banging against the door leading to the tank room became more frantic.

Stop trying to fight like Eir. Fight like Ashvild. Use the battlefield.

They couldn't win. Master Alfvin smashed his baton into Emil's arm and the blow flung the Paladin away. When he struggled back to his feet, his arm hung limp by his side.

Iro focused on the other trainees, saw Ashvild pulling Ylfa to her feet. He swung his blade, Blink Striking across the room to stand before them. Ashvild turned to him with a start, almost recoiling in surprise. If anyone would understand, it would be her.

Iro sucked in a breath. His chest felt like it was on fire. "Open the doors."

"But the monsters," Bjorn said. He still had his sword drawn, still hadn't used it.

Iro didn't have time to explain.

A smile flashed across Ashvild's face, gone a moment later. "Yes! Eir, get over there and open the other door."

"The one with all the banging?" Eir asked. "Sure. Why not." She set off at a sprint.

Iro didn't have any more time. He had to get back to the fight before Master Alfvin crushed Emil. He swung his sword, Blink Striking back on to the stage and let out a battle cry as he charged into the fray.

Master Alfvin turned, swatted Iro's wild strike away, then whipped his baton into Iro's side. He cried out at a sharp pain like a knife being driven into his flesh. Then Master Alfvin whisked his baton to the other side and smacked it into Emil's side. The Paladin barely seemed to feel the blow with his skin buffed with steel. Master Alfvin kicked Emil in the chest and sent him stumbling backwards. Iro was yanked along with the other boy and they teetered around each other for a moment, locked together by a glowing golden string of energy. Emil careened off the side of the stage and dragged Iro down with him.

Iro hit his head on something on the way down and found his vision far too bright and full of sparkling light. He tried to stand, staggered away a pace, and then was yanked back. He sprawled on the cold, metal floor next to Emil and the other boy frowned at him.

"Stop it," Emil said. Iro had to concentrate on him to hear the words. His ears were ringing. "Will you just cut the line?"

Iro shook his head, trying to clear the sparkling lights.

Master Alfvin leapt off the stage, kicked Iro in the chest and sent him flying backwards. He landed on his back on the floor and Emil landed on top of him a moment later. Emil growled something, pushed back to his feet and hauled Iro up.

"Cut the line," he snarled, holding up his one good arm as Master Alfvin stalked toward them.

Iro's head cleared and he remembered the golden line connecting the two of them. He swiped his azure blade at it, severing it in two and the gold faded away to nothing, disappearing entirely. Iro gripped his sword's hilt in both hands and settled into a stance, ready to attack. The azure light of his blade flickered and then vanished. He was left holding the battered, broken half of Neya's sword. His crest was all but gone, a fizzing icy light barely even visible. He'd burned through all his current, and they hadn't even put a scratch on Master Alfvin.

"I got nothing left," Iro said around panting breaths. "You?"

Emil sagged, leaning against him shoulder to shoulder. "Shut up."

Iro forced a tired smile onto his face. "At least I saved you more than you did me."

Emil reached across and gave Iro a shove with his

good arm. They stepped apart, both of them barely able to stand. "No chance. You still owe me at least..." He trailed off, staring across the chamber. "What's she doing?"

Eir had reached the door leading back to the water tank chamber. She slid to a stop and slammed the button.

"No!" Master Alfvin shouted, reached out a hand as if he could stop her.

The door opened quickly and the huge bhur beast charged through. Eir leapt into the air as a tusk collided with her. Her purple crest flared to life behind her and she slid along the length of the tusk. It flung her sliding off along the wall. She hit the ground running, a wild grin on her face as she sprinted for the other side of the hall. The bhur beast thrashed about madly, trumpeted, then charged Master Alfvin. A swarm of rustlings followed the monster in, chittering and thrusting rusty blades in the air as they swept forward like a crashing tide. On the other side of the room, Ashvild pressed the button to open the door leading towards the docks. More rustlings poured into the chamber. Some charged towards the centre, while others turned and started battling with the trainees. They really were on a timer now. They needed to fight their way free before too many monsters turned up, drawn by the opening of two gates.

Master Alfvin met the bhur beast head on, swinging his baton in two hands. The strike flared crimson, slicing into the bone armor of the monster. It's head snapped sideways, tusks digging into the metal bulkheads of the floor, and its momentum dragged its massive body up, flipped it over, and crashed it to the ground. Master Alfvin killed the beast with a single strike. The swarm of rustlings engulfed the Corsair a few seconds later and Iro heard them screaming as he chopped them down.

"Time to go," Iro said. He and Emil limped back towards the other trainees where they fought their own desperate battle.

Another of the wailing, echoing howls split the chamber. Iro saw many of the rustlings scamper, turning tail and running from the sound. He and Emil both turned together, staring back towards the water tank chamber.

A globe of swirling, bubbling water floated in through the door. Suspended in the centre of the globe was something that looked a lot like a naked man, his body smooth and hairless. But it wasn't human. It was the hydrid, broken free of the tank it had been suspended in, and drawn towards Iro and Emil's opening of their gates. The rustlings either side of it cowered away, bowing and scraping. The hydrid floated on, ignoring them, glowing black eyes fixed on Master Alfvin.

The Corsair swept his baton around in a red arc, clearing a space around himself by slaughtering a dozen rustlings with a single flare of red cutting energy. He spotted the hydrid and for just a moment, Iro thought he saw Master Alfvin's shoulders sag. Then the Corsair breathed in deep. A sparkling pearlescent light shot out of the hydrid and Master Alfvin sucked it in.

The hydrid howled again, its globe of water rippling with the force. Two huge tentacles of water shot out of the globe and thrust towards Master Alfvin. They hit him, water colliding around him into white rapids, and formed into a second globe around the Corsair.

"He's taken the hydrid's ability," Iro said quietly.

"Who will win?" Emil said. Then the other boy shook his head. "Scrap it! Who cares. Let's go."

Eir had already sprinted around the chamber, reached the others, and leapt into the fight. She was pressing back a rustling right into Bjorn's swinging blade. He cut the little monster down with a backswing, then ripped his sword free and stabbed at another. They were all holding the door, beating back a fresh wave of rustlings trying to swarm inside. It seemed an endless horde and the trainees needed help.

Behind Iro, he heard a crash of rushing water, felt warm spray splash the back of his neck, heard the hydrid howl again.

A thought occurred to Iro. "I have no idea if this will work."

"What will…" Emil squeaked in alarm as Iro grabbed him around the waist and pulled him close. "What are you doing?"

Iro didn't have time to explain. He swiped Neya's broken sword and used a Blink Strike to cross the room in a few heartbeats, holding onto Emil and dragging the other boy with him. They arrived stumbling, Iro's swipe overbalanced him and he let go of Emil's waist and would have gone sprawling if not for Arne catching him in open arms and keeping him upright. Emil staggered away a couple of paces and bent over, hands on knees.

"You definitely owe me one now," Iro said, grinning, wincing. He was aching everywhere again. His crest had vanished, and his current was a strangely aching void inside.

"Don't ever…" Emil paused, made a noise like he was about to throw up, struggled to keep it down. "Never again."

"Time to go," Ashvild shouted from the front lines. "Bjorn, push!"

With a bellowing roar, Bjorn surged forward, giant blade swiping, knocking rustlings back. Ashvild and Ylfa moved in behind him, covering his sides and stabbing out at the oncoming swarm. Eir danced behind them, restless as always, eager to get into the fight. Ingrid was stood at the back of them all, staring into the middle of the chamber.

Iro glanced back. Two massive, roiling globes of

water were crashing against each other, spray flying everywhere. He could just about make out the hydrid at the centre of one and Master Alfvin in the other. A watery tentacle erupted from Master Alfvin's globe, darted towards the other, was slapped aside by another tentacle from the hydrid. The rustling swarm from that side of the chamber was giving the battle a wide berth, and was closing in on the trainees.

"I hope you die," Ingrid said quietly, her voice full of venom. Then she stepped forward, drew in a deep breath and bellowed. "Die, you scrapper!"

"I got her," Arne said as he took Ingrid by the shoulders and pulled her away. There were tears running down her scarlet cheeks.

Iro extended a hand to Emil kneeling on the metal floor, still looking like he wanted to vomit. "Got a little bit of fight left in you?"

Emil glared up at him, slapped away his hand. "Shut up." He stood, took in the sight of the trainees slowly pushing forward against the rustling horde. Then ran forwards, leaping into the fight.

Iro moved into the corridor, pressed the button on the wall to close the door and watched behind as it slowly slid shut. The last thing he saw was the hydrid pulling water from Master Alfvin's globe, swelling its own. Then the door slammed shut.

Chapter Forty-One

Emil pushed through the other trainees, reached the front lines so he was standing shoulder to shoulder with the huge Corsair. The boy was swinging his sword wildly, beating back the rustlings trying to dart forward and stab him. Behind the immediate horde, Emil could see the corridor was clear. They were almost free.

He activated his crest, saw the fiery lines burning low. He didn't have long, but there was enough current left inside to use. And he wanted to use it. He loved how strong he felt. He may have lost his gauntlets, but that wouldn't stop him crushing the rustlings.

"Steel." Emil enhanced himself, felt his skin tightening as it grew heavy and hard as metal. Then he threw himself into the swarm.

Claws and rusty shards of metal stabbed at him from all sides, but none could hurt him. Some bounced off the remains of his cracked and shattered armor, others skittered off his hardened skin. He struck left, then right, jabbing and swinging punches at the little monsters. Pitted skin burst and bones cracked under his assault.

Emil was laughing as he battered his way through the other side of the horde. The rustlings he didn't break turned to stab at him, mindlessly intent on killing him. The Corsair trainees capitalised on the distraction and cut the last of the monsters down from behind. They were all spattered with pink blood, wading through twitching corpses. Emil looked down at his gore-soaked fists and felt strange. Exhaustion washed over him and he couldn't hold his enhancement any longer. His fire gutted out, his crest vanishing, and he staggered.

The big trainee steadied him with a hand on his shoulder and a broad laugh. "You are one crazy scrapper."

Emil shrugged his shoulder to remove the hand, drew in a deep breath and stood up straight again. He wouldn't show weakness to the mid-shippers. He had to prove the people from the Courage were strong.

"It was a compliment," the big lad called after him. "What? I meant it as a compliment."

Emil approached the t-junction up ahead. To the right led back to the docks. He angled towards it. Something large and green and segmented scuttled around the left corner. It took only a moment to close on him. A kharapid, long and sinuous with a half dozen bladed arms. It reared up in front of Emil and he raised his hands to block, tried to activate his crest but nothing happened.

Iro surged past Emil, knocking him aside. He thrust his sword up and into the kharapid, the broken, jagged blade sliding into the flesh between segments. The kharapid screeched. Then Iro ripped the sword free sideways, cutting the monster in two. Its front end fell one way and the rear end the other.

Iro turned to Emil, grinning. "Now you definitely…"

The kharapid moved, its upper half pulling itself upright and leaping off bladed appendages at Iro's back. Emil lurched in, caught it by one of the legs, felt the bladed limb slicing his palm. He span, swung the monster to the side and slammed it against the wall, held it in place with one hand, then punched it as hard as he could in the head with his other. The kharapid's head crumpled from the force, goo and blood exploding outwards all over the wall.

Emil stepped back, let the dead monster drop. He knew Iro was staring at him, probably waiting with some line about how he could have handled it. Emil didn't give him the chance. He rubbed his hands together. It did nothing but smear the monster blood all over them. Then he walked around the corner to the right, towards the docks.

By the time they reached the thruster feed chamber, the corridor was no longer clear of monsters. Master Rollo had said a Hopper opening a gate would draw monsters from nearby, but Iro guessed he and Emil were drawing them from everywhere. As they stepped through into the docks and pressed the button to close the door behind them, he saw a swarm of kharapids scuttling along the corridor behind them, closing fast. The door clanged shut, cutting them off, and he heard the monsters scrabbling at the metal.

"I hope there isn't another way in," he said, turning back to the others. He and Emil had killed one of the monsters, but he was exhausted and hurting and there were a lot of them out there.

"Get to your pods," Ashvild shouted, waisting no time.

They picked their way across the thruster feed chamber quickly. Iro glanced up at the monsters hanging from above, the corpse crawlers hadn't been summoned by the gates. They still writhed together, but didn't attack. He wondered if they were different somehow? If only certain monsters were drawn by the release of power?

The thruster feed chamber was dark and eerily quiet, the footsteps of the trainees echoing around them. Iro felt strange, like something else was coming and he couldn't figure out what. He hoped it was just in his head. He imagined Master Alfvin bursting through the door, vengeance in mind. Or the hydrid maybe, having won the battle and coming for them all. He tried to shake the images out of his head and doubled his pace, running past the empty crates and dead feed belts.

They reached the pods and immediately set about finding their individual ones. Iro supposed it didn't really matter which they jumped in, but there was something oddly personal about them. Emil checked on his own pod, still busted, sparking, and half embedded in one of the fuel feeders.

"Here," Ashvild called to him. "Get in Torben's pod. He…" She looked over at Ingrid and sighed. "He won't be using it."

Ingrid's jaw tightened. "What about that scrapper's pod." She aimed a savage kick at Master Alfvin's pod as though it were him. "I say we trash it. Make sure he won't be coming back."

"Waste of a pod," Emil said darkly. He pressed the button to open Torben's pod. "They have return settings. Just send it home empty."

Something rattled overhead. One of the pipes above. There was something moving through the ducts.

"Everyone in your pods. Now!" Ashvild shouted.

The rattling grew louder, closer. It hit the ventilation grate above Iro and he jumped, staring up. He gripped Neya's broken sword in two hands and waited for whatever it was to erupt.

There was a sound like drilling and a screw popped loose of the grate and fell to the floor, bouncing at Iro's feet. A moment later, another screw dropped down. Then the grate levered open a little and something small and metallic flew out.

It was about as large as a clenched fist, mostly spherical, and marbled copper and black in colour. It had a number of little raised, silver rings around it and Iro realised it looked just like the automatons they had seen in the manufactory. The little thing buzzed and turned in a circle. Then it spoke.

"Found you. Found you." It sounded just like Iro only tinny like his voice through an old radio transmitter. It buzzed again as it descended and hovered just in front of Iro. "Found you."

"Uhhh…" Iro looked around at the others, but they were all either stood around staring, or busy climbing into their pods. "Hello?"

"It has found you," the little automaton said in Iro's tinny voice.

"What has?" Iro started scanning the surrounding area, looking for monsters.

"It has found you," the floating automaton repeated.

"Do you mean you?" Iro asked. "Are you it?"

The automaton buzzed. "Agreed."

"What is it?" Eir asked. She had snuck up behind him again, but he didn't jump this time. It was comforting to hear her so close.

The automaton buzzed again. "It is your Autonomous Guide and Chronicler, created at your request."

Eir nudged him in the side. "What did you do?" She narrowed her eyes at him.

"I didn't… Oh." Iro remembered the manufactory, placing his hand against the screen on Mia's dare. He'd been scanned by the automatons and then the manufactory had said it was analysing his data. "Maybe I did. Back at the manufactory."

"Uh huh. So he requested your creation?" Eir asked the automaton.

It buzzed. "Agreed."

"Iro, Eir." Ashvild shouted. "Stop playing with whatever that is and get in your pods."

To emphasise her point, Ylfa's pod fired up its thrusters and rocketed away and out into the void, presumably on its return course.

Eir stepped forward to peer at the automaton, stretched out a finger to poke it. It buzzed, somehow seeming angry, and backed away, still floating though Iro couldn't see how. "Does it have a name?" She asked. "*Autonomous Guide and Chronicler* is a bit unwieldy."

It buzzed. "It has not yet received a designation."

Iro had the distinct feeling it was watching him, waiting.

"I'm going to call it Buzz," Eir said.

It buzzed. "Designation must be applied by Command."

"Command?"

It buzzed again. "It has found you."

"Ohhhh." Eir took a step back and grinned at Iro. "I think it means you."

"Eir, Iro. Now!" Ashvild shouted. More of the pods were taking off, filling the air with the acrid stench of burning fuel.

Eir waved a hand at Ashvild. "One second, Ash. Iro has to name his new toy." She turned back to him. "Go on. Call it Buzz."

"You're a guide?" Iro asked. "Uh. It is a guide?"

"It is an Autonomous Guide and Chronicler."

Iro remembered something Torben had told him earlier, during their Hop where they found the manufactory. He'd said that in the old days, back when all the records were still spotty, the fleet used a guide to keep them on course. "North," he said. "Uh. Command designates you North."

It buzzed. "Agreed. North has found you."

"Eir!" Ashvild grabbed hold of Eir by the arm and dragged her away. "Iro, get in your pod. I don't care what that thing is."

"I have to go, North." Iro pressed the button to open his pod door and climbed inside. North buzzed and floated over and inside before Iro closed the door. Four little metallic legs slid out of the chassis and it settled down on his shoulder. "Oh, you're coming with me?"

"North is your Autonomous Guide and Chronicler."

"Okay." He really wasn't sure how to react to that. "We're going to have to teach you to say something else."

North buzzed.

Iro spared one last look for the titan. It was dark in the thruster feed chamber, but he thought he heard something. A far off banging. A howl of rage. He pressed the button to close the pod door and set it to return home.

Chapter Forty-Two

There hadn't been any alcohol on the Eclipse for almost four years now. That wasn't strictly true. Rollo knew of a tech down in engineering by the name of Loke who had figured out how to make moonshine from algae. It tasted like unwashed socks and didn't so much get you drunk as knock you senseless after just a couple of sips. He'd tried it precisely once before swearing he'd never touch another drop of alcohol again. Or at least until they were making the real stuff again. Which was why it was such a surprise for Rollo to wake up feeling like he had the worst hangover in the history of his ship, the human race, and probably the whole universe.

He groaned, tried to sit up, failed. The medic ambled over and asked him a few inane questions like *where does it hurt?* Apparently Rollo's answer of *every-scrapping-where* wasn't good enough and the old, silver-haired medic set to poking and prodding him every-scrapping-where.

Rollo took the time, between gasps of pain, winces, hisses, and threats of violence to remember how he had ended up in the sick bay. It came back to him slowly, and when it did, he almost wished it hadn't.

He'd been beaten. Courage Tannow was dead. He had no idea how he got back to the Eclipse, but he assumed at least some of his trainees must have survived. Unfortunately, the grumpy medic wasn't very accommodating with answers and waved away Rollo's questions stating simply *The lead Hopper will talk to you about it.* Alfvin was pretty much the last person Rollo wanted to see, but the medic wandered off to summon him anyway, and Rollo leaned back and tried not to slip into unconsciousness. He failed.

Rollo awoke again to a slapping on the left side of his face.

"Hey!" The old medic said. "Wake up. Lead Hopper is here to see you."

"Ow!" Rollo groaned. He blinked away the fuzzy edges of his vision. "Surely it's not good practice to wake up an injured patient by slapping them?"

The medic barked a laugh. "I'm sorry. Did I hurt the big, strong Hopper. Want me to kiss it better?" He laughed again and walked for the door. "He's fine. Through the worst of it now."

Rollo took a moment to look around. He was in a private room of the sick bay, hooked up to a machine that displayed a bunch of numbers that made no sense to him. The walls were glaringly white and the whole thing had a sterile feel to it. Which was probably good, all things considered.

Frigg sauntered through the door, a tablet in one hand and something red, shiny, and spherical in the other.

"I was expecting Alfvin," Rollo croaked. "But you're much more welcome."

Frigg paused, glanced at the medic. He shook his head. "I didn't tell him anything."

"What?" Rollo managed to say, then coughed.

Frigg placed the red, shiny thing on the table next to Rollo's bed. She poured a cup of water and held it to his lips as he drank. All the while she said nothing. Only once he was finished with the cup, did she speak.

"The black cloaks really beat you up badly, huh?"

"Black cloaks?"

"That's what we're calling them. On account of the black cloaks they were wearing." She pulled a chair from against the wall and sat down at his bed side.

"That's a terrible name."

"Well… Maybe. It was your trainees who named them."

"Idiots. What happened?"

Frigg leaned back in her chair, frowned at Rollo. "You remember the manufactory?"

Rollo nodded. The room span a little, but it quickly settled back down. "I remember getting beating bloody. Did everyone get out?"

Frigg shook her head slowly. "Courage Tannow was killed. Courage Mia was taken by the black cloaks. Everyone else made it back from that Hop."

Rollo sighed, both happy and grief-stricken all at once. At least all of his trainees made it back, but Courage Tannow was a big loss. And the girl was taken. Hopefully the council would launch a rescue mission soon. Hopefully he'd recover quickly enough to be on it. She was his responsibility, after all, and he had failed her. That wasn't right. He needed to make amends.

"How long have I been out?"

"This is where it gets complicated," Frigg said as she tapped a single finger against her tablet. "You've been unconscious for twenty days, Rollo."

The room suddenly felt like it was spinning and Rollo had to close his eyes. That only led to an odd spinning in the dark sensation which was equally as unpleasant. "What…"

"The medics gave you a forty-sixty chance of waking up at all," Frigg continued. "I'm delighted to find you continue to beat the odds."

"It's a gift," Rollo groaned. When he opened his eyes and turned his head to the side, he saw the shiny, red thing Frigg had placed on his table. It was an apple. "Is that real?"

She nodded, plucked the apple from the table and dropped it in his lap. "We've started harvesting food from a couple of the garden domes. The fleet is no longer just subsisting on algae. No coffee yet, though. Apparently it's a non-critical resource. I tried to argue the point but the lead Hopper from a mid-ship isn't important enough to dictate that."

Rollo stared at the apple, lifted it in a bandaged hand and turned it about. "Lead Hopper? You?"

Frigg was quiet a moment, frowning at him. "A lot has happened, Rollo. I'll fill you in."

She spent the next hour telling him about Alfvin and the trainees. His taking over training them. The Hop and the reports that Alfvin had gone crazy and tried to kill them. Torben's death. Rollo felt like his chest was about to burst at that. One of his trainees was dead because Alfvin had finally snapped. Rollo had always known the man had violence in him, but he never thought that violence would be turned against his own. And a child at that. It was madness. And worst of all, it was all his fault. Frigg finished by telling Rollo about Iro and Courage Emil, their opening of the gates, and the escape from Alfvin and the hydrid.

"They did it," Rollo said. He was proud of Iro. Proud of Courage Emil too. "But Emil didn't manifest his talent on titan 02. That means… he's not stalled. We're not stalled?"

Frigg tapped at her tablet. "Well, we're not sure about that, yet. I have a theory. Want to hear it?"

"If I say no, are you going to tell me it anyway?"

"Of course. You'd only be lying to yourself, anyway. I know you, Rollo."

He bit into the apple while he waited for her to start. It tasted wonderful. So crisp and sweet and juicy. After years of algae, it was the most glorious thing he'd ever tasted.

"I have quite extensive records on both the boys,

transferred over from the Courage. They might be one of the poorest of the ships, but whoever they have in data collection over there is studious to a fault. Oh, what I could do with an assistant like that working for me.

"I also had a chance to interview the boys when they returned. A few chances actually."

Rollo narrowed his eyes at her and Frigg grinned at him.

"Yes, yes. I've interviewed our Iro six times already. And because they returned to the Eclipse after the Hop, I was also the first to interview them. Before the council sent over their own scribe."

"The council have been here?"

Frigg nodded, pulled a sour face, and tapped at the tablet again. "Twice so far. One of those times they came to look at you, too."

Rollo wasn't sure how he felt about being stared at while he was unconscious. But at least he didn't have to answer any stupid questions. "I'm glad I was out."

Frigg reached out, patted his leg. "Don't worry, I called them all idiots for you.

"Back to my theory though. And this is just a theory, so far." She paused, stared past Rollo for a moment as if collecting her thoughts. "The gates exist within all of us. Potential waiting to be unlocked. But there's something aboard the titans that brings them out, manifests them. Perhaps it's the ambient power that floats around the place or… Well, I don't have enough data yet. But one thing we know for certain is that aboard titan 01, physical strength and preparedness and need were the impetus for manifesting the gates. Train hard enough, fight enough monsters, Hop enough times, and really *need* the power of the next gate, and it was almost sure to appear. Whether or not you were strong enough or smart enough to open it."

She drew a little circle on the tablet, then another, and another as she spoke. Absentmindedly doodling on the screen. Rollo had always liked that about Frigg.

"I don't believe the Gates operate in the same manner here on titan 02. I don't think they respond to physical prowess. At least not in the same way. I have no doubt a person's body has to be prepared for the extra current opening a gate will provide, but I believe the causal event to manifesting a gate to be more emotional than physical."

She stood up, crossed to the door and closed it. "I interviewed both boys directly after the Hop and I asked them some questions which I think may have made them uncomfortable. I don't think they like me much."

"Finally, something I'll have in common with them."

Frigg rolled her eyes. "We both know you're completely infatuated with me, Rollo.

"Iro was the first to open his gate and he said it appeared to him when Emil was in danger. He said Alfvin was about to kill the boy and the gate appeared in between the two of them. He described it, his words, as a choice, to run away or to take a fight he knew he couldn't win for the sake of protecting another. He said the gate had the word *Courage* written on it and it was already open."

"I've never heard of a gate having words on it before," Rollo said.

Frigg sat back down in the chair by his bed and nodded thoughtfully. "When I spoke to Courage Emil… He was quite difficult. That boy does not like to share. But I dragged the story out of him. It took hours, much of it spent in silence. Odd boy.

"He said his gate only appeared when he gave up. When he admitted to himself that he couldn't win against Alfvin. His gate had the word *Failure* written on it and it was locked up tight. It wouldn't open no matter how much he tried. That is until he asked for help. Specifically, he asked Iro for help unlocking it."

"But if the gate was there then Iro was frozen."

"Correct. Iro didn't actually help Emil open the gate, but rather it was the act of asking for help that did it."

Rollo finished chomping on the apple and placed the core on the table beside him. "That's the oddest puzzle to opening a gate I've ever heard of."

"Because it's not a puzzle," Frigg said. She grinned at him, suddenly full of energy and he could tell she was excited to tell him her theory.

"I'm feeling tired," Rollo said, yawning. "I think I'll take a nap now."

Frigg punched him in the leg hard enough he didn't have to fake the exclamation of pain.

"The gates on titan 02 respond to emotional triggers rather than physical. That's my theory." She paused and stared at him expectantly. He stared back as blandly as possible. "Both boys experienced severe emotional responses.

"In Iro's case he realised he wasn't a coward and willingly met a fight he knew he couldn't win rather than run away.

"In Courage Emil's case, he had a traumatic realisation that he couldn't do everything alone. That he needed to go against his very nature and ask for help.

"Both are emotional triggers, Rollo. But I believe our two newest Hoppers are walking different paths."

Rollo laid his head back on the pillow and massaged his eyes. It was a lot to take in given he had only just woken up from a coma. "Different paths?"

"Yes!" He heard Frigg tap on her tablet screen with her finger. "Reconciliation and trauma. It's just a theory. I'm still figuring it all out."

"But we're not stalled?" Rollo asked.

"No. At least, I don't think so. The council doesn't either. They agree with me, with my theory. To a point. I haven't told them about the two paths bit yet. But they agree the gates operate differently on titan 02. We're not stalled. We just have to progress differently if we are to encounter our gates."

She couldn't hide the excitement, at least not from Rollo. He heard it in her voice, felt it in the tension of the room. Frigg had never been happy sitting at her third gate. When titan 01 had exploded, she'd been depressed for months. This was a lifeline for her, a chance to progress further, to reach for new power. Alfvin was the same, never happy with where he was, always wanting more. Rollo, on the other hand, had always been the foil to both their drives. He had the power. Opening the gates came easy to him back on 01. But he had never really wanted it. He was always happy where he was, rather than looking forward to where he wanted to be.

Rollo groaned and sat up, pushing himself upright. He hurt, felt like he still had a broken rib or two, and the world sparkled at the edges from the pain. "Help me up."

Frigg stood and rushed to his side, gently pushing him back down. "I don't think you should be moving, Rollo."

He flailed at her, struggling to push her away. "Stop it, Frigg. Help me up." She considered him for a moment, then pulled him up to sitting. He slipped from the bed, found his legs wobbly as loose wires beneath him. The room swayed and twisted, dizziness threatening to bring up the apple he had just eaten. He realised then he was wearing a loose gown, open at the back, his arse on display. When he caught Frigg's gaze, she grinned at him.

"You really shouldn't be up and moving about yet,

Rollo."

He shook his head, wished he hadn't as another wave of dizziness almost knocked him over. "I'm done lying around, Frigg."

Chapter Forty-Three

Emil stared up at the red docking light, waiting. He refused to look out the little window, to watch the umbilical of the two ships stretching to meet each other. He was too scared he might see his father's face peering through the window. And just as scared that he wouldn't.

The red light flickered over to green, indicating the umbilicals had connected and flooded the space with air. A moment later, the door hissed as it opened and Emil stared down the length towards the Courage.

There was no one to see him off, and he was taking nothing with him. His armor and gauntlets were nothing but shards of metal back aboard the titan now. All he had was his uniform, freshly printed from the Eclipse quartermaster. It was the newest, cleanest, and most comfortable clothing he'd ever owned. And it was also the least comfortable.

"Go on," an Eclipse tech said. "Don't have all day, Hopper."

Emil started down the umbilical, his head a whirl of conflicting emotions. Part of him didn't want to go back to the Courage. There was nothing waiting for him there. Master Tannow was dead. Mia was gone. Cali had quit. He didn't have a squad to train with, nor even space to train in. He had no doubt his father would somehow find fault with him, regardless of his achievement. There was nothing aboard the Courage for him anymore.

But there was nothing aboard the Eclipse either. It was better supplied, stocked with food and clothing and water. It smelled weird, but he could put up with that. Yet, even if he could stay, there was no one there to learn from.

He had opened his first gate. He was a Hopper now. But he hadn't manifested his next talent yet, and that annoyed him. Partly because Iro had. The moment the other boy opened his gate, his new talent had manifested. Everything came far too easy to Iro. But Emil needed to figure out his new talent, and he had to convince a Paladin to teach him another. He couldn't do that aboard the Eclipse. He needed help, and there was only one place he was going to get it. Back home. Back aboard the poorest ship in the fleet.

He passed the halfway mark down the umbilical and sensed a shift. It was in the air. A deep longing for the past welled up within him and he understood. Emil smelled the Courage now. He smelled his home. The slightly stale air, dust being cooked by the heaters. It was the noise too. The Eclipse was too quiet, too orderly. The Courage was a haphazard mess of noise. That was oddly comforting.

He was going home. After days of interviews, the same questions asked again and again, he was finally heading home. And even if he had the strange sense he no longer belonged, that didn't matter. Emil was going home, and the Courage needed him. He was a Hopper now. He could go on Hops, fetch supplies. Thanks to him, the Courage might pull itself up that little bit further out of poverty. They needed him. And he needed them. He needed to change things, even if they didn't want him too. Even if they hated him for it. He needed to break the system that held the low ships in poverty. And he'd start with the Courage. With his home.

Emil took his first real step onto the ship and breathed in deep, feeling a smile stretch his face. There was a woman waiting there. She was an officer, but she wasn't waiting for him. She peered around him, staring down the umbilical back towards the Eclipse.

"Is Iro coming?" she asked.

Emil shook his head. "They're still interviewing him about what happened."

"Oh," she let out a hefty sigh and pressed the button on the bulkhead. The docking light flashed from green to red, and the door ground shut. Then she turned to Emil and saluted him. "Welcome aboard, Hopper Emil. It's good to have you home." She left then, leaving Emil standing alone at the dock.

He didn't know what to think about that. Iro's mother had come to the docks with a thin hope of seeing her son. And even failing that, she had welcomed Emil home. His own father hadn't even bothered to come.

The crew greeted him as he passed. Word had apparently spread and everyone was quick with a kind word or congratulations. It was both surprising and not. The interviewers aboard the Eclipse had pointed out over and over again that he was some sort of hope for the future. That he was proof that Hoppers weren't stalled out, but just needed to figure out a new way to open their gates. They'd kept asking him how he'd done it, and never seemed pleased when he couldn't really answer them.

Emil stopped outside his father's quarters, his hand paused before the door handle. It dawned on him then that he'd always considered it his father's quarters. Never his own. He heard voices inside, muted by the metal door. Someone laughed, a harsh, braying sound. Emil briefly entertained the idea of going back to the pod bay. But no. He had to face his father at some point, and if not now, then when? He pulled open the door, hating the rusted squeal it made, and stepped through.

"There he is!" Emil's father said loudly. He was smiling. Smiling at Emil. It was unnerving.

His father wasn't alone. His friends were there. Four of them, all drudges, sitting around the kitchen table playing cards. They didn't have anything to play for, too poor to afford proper stakes, so they traded duties back and forth over it. Win enough hands and you might not have to smell the sanitation tanks for a week. Of course his father cheated, but the others didn't know that.

"Conquering hero," said Uncle Dimos. He wasn't Emil's real uncle, but had known him all his life all the same.

Dimos stood, his chair squealing on the kitchen floor, and wrapped his arms around Emil, pulling him into a hug, wrinkling his new uniform. The others congratulated him too, shaking his hand, clapping him on the shoulder. All except his father, who sat in his chair and stared, that odd smile on his face. Emil wondered if it was pride.

"Second Hopper in the fleet to open a gate on the new titan," his father said. "Such a grand achievement." His smile faded. "Or would have been if you'd managed it just a couple of minutes earlier. Had to let a mid shipper beat you to it though."

Emil clenched his jaw shut. He knew it. He knew it was too much for his father to be proud of him, even for a moment.

"Ahh, let him have a moment, Savvas," Uncle Dimos said. "The lad did well. Got further than you did."

"Shut up!" his father snapped. He glared Dimos down. In just a few a moments, a sullen silence settled over the group. Emil realised he was clenching his fist around the bottom of his new uniform jacket. He'd even managed to rip the printed fabric a little. All of one minute in a room with his father, and his new uniform was ruined.

The spare chair squealed across the floor as his father pushed it out with his foot. "Come on then, Second Place. Join us for a hand. Or are you too good to play with the drudges now?"

Emil stared at the chair. Part of him wanted it. To sit

down, join in the game of cards. To be welcomed. Finally on equal footing with his father. A peer, instead of a child. But he knew it would be a lie. His father didn't see anyone as peers. That's why he was so willing to cheat them all, even his friends. It was his way of showing his dominance over them, of claiming a petty power that was never his, and laughing at them all for being too stupid to suspect him.

"No thanks," Emil heard himself say as if from a distance. The room suddenly felt far away, even though he was standing in it. "You'd only cheat me, just like you do them."

His father surged to his feet, the chair bouncing off the cabinet behind him and clattering to the metal floor. The man rounded the table in a moment and squared off against Emil. He was smaller than Emil remembered; thin as a wire, but strong like a man used to daily manual labour. But not tall. Not anymore. Emil stared at him, jaw clenched and eyes hard.

"How dare you talk to me like that in my own quarters!" the old man snapped, getting close to Emil but not quite touching him. "I raised you, boy. Made you everything you are." He stabbed a finger at Emil's face. "Everything you are is because of me. Me! And you accuse me of cheating here, in my own home? You lie in front of my friends. I should knock you on arse where you belong."

"Do it," Emil said. He sounded so cold, detached. Felt like he was floating above his own shoulder, watching the conflict from afar. His father had opened his first gate, had the strength of a Hopper, but despite that he had never before been physical with Emil. Just tore him down with words instead.

His father sneered and turned away, shaking his head. Emil let out a trembling breath. Then his father spun around and lashed out, striking him across the face. Emil's crest flared to life behind him, lighting the kitchen a bloody crimson.

He staggered from the punch, his head snapped to the side, but he didn't go down. His father was flung backwards, across the kitchen table. He rolled, crashed into one of his friends, and they both sprawled in a heap on the metal floor.

Emil looked down at his hands. He hadn't moved. He hadn't hit his father back. He just… The kitchen was still lit in flickering red and Emil glanced over his shoulder at his crest. Suddenly he understood. His new talent had manifested.

His father was still on the floor, moaning and barely conscious. One of his friends was slapping him gently on the face, trying to bring him around. Emil ignored them, turned away and strode from the kitchen. Uncle Dimos scooted out of the way quickly, almost upending his own chair. Emil ignored him too.

He stopped outside his room, stared in, wondering if he should gather up some of his things. But then, he didn't have anything. Not really. His clothes were all scrap and now he was a Hopper, he could request new ones. His armor and gauntlets were gone. Most of the room was taken up by the junk his father collected. There was simply nothing for him there.

Emil pulled open the door to his father's quarters. It squealed in protest.

"Go then, you ungrateful scrap!" his father shouted. "And don't you dare come back. You ain't my son anymore."

Emil stepped out and pulled the door shut behind him with a smile. It was probably the only thing his father had ever said that he agreed with.

Chapter Forty-Four

Iro woke with a new energy even as Bjorn pulled him from his bed for their morning run. It was good to be back in the routine of things. It had been five days since the harrowing experience of the Hop. Five days since Master Alfvin killed Torben and almost murdered the rest of them too. Five days since Iro had opened his first gate. In that time, Iro had spent approximately ninety percent of his waking hours in interviews and medical studies. This was the first day since that he had no one trying to ask him how he did it, or poke him with things to see what made him different.

North buzzed as soon as it saw he was awake. It launched itself from the bottom of the bed into the air, floating around him. The little automaton didn't seem to know or understand much, but it was learning. The first night back from the titan, it had kept him awake by asking questions about sleep. It didn't seem to understand that humans needed to rest. But it had gone quiet once Bjorn threatened to scrap it.

Arne looked tired, haunted. He did every morning now. Torben's death was hard on him. The two of them had been living in the same room for years, in constant company. Now Torben was gone and Arne was struggling. Iro had heard him crying at night, but he didn't feel close enough to the other boy to offer a shoulder to cry on. He was also worried that Arne blamed him for Torben's death. Master Alfvin had been trying to force Iro to open his gate, and it was Iro's failure that had caused him to snap. If he had just managed it sooner, Torben would still be alive. He thought maybe Arne was right to blame him.

Bjorn dragged them out for the morning run and set a fast pace. Iro raced past him as if he had been born running. He had to wait for five minutes at the showers for the other boys to catch up and even Bjorn was panting hard by the time he did. Iro felt so much stronger and faster now. It went beyond having a deeper current flowing through him. He felt like he could run all day and not get tired. Bjorn grumbled something about it not being fair and Iro grinned, only assuring Bjorn the tables would surely turn once again when he opened his gate.

They showered and ate— mostly algae paste still, but every trainee got a piece of fruit with each meal now— then jogged to the training hall. Iro hadn't had a chance to go back there since returning from the titan, his days too full of interviews and the like, but Bjorn said the others had been gathering every day and had yet to be introduced to their new trainer. Instead, Ashvild had been pushing them all through training, pairing them up in sparring sessions and teaching them from the bestiary. Bjorn grumbled about that, but also admitted she was a better leader and teacher than he was.

North floated along behind Iro, the quiet buzz of the automaton's anti-gravity rings a worrying noise. Iro didn't like being monitored by the little thing constantly, but he'd tried to order it to go away and all it said was *Command Error* in Iro's own voice.

"Oh, look who it is," Ylfa said as Iro, Bjorn, and Arne walked through the door. "The mighty scrapping Hopper has deigned to grace us with his presence."

"You're just jealous," Eir said as she stretched down far enough she could have licked her own knee if she wanted.

"Am not."

"Of course you are. We all are. Don't worry, Iro. We're all just jealous of you. Hey, how strong are you now? Can you lift Bjorn?"

Iro glanced at Bjorn. The bigger boy glared back at him. "I don't know and I'm not going to try. I've learned when he starts looking like a rustling, it means he's angry."

"I do not look like a rustling," Bjorn snapped.

Ylfa laughed. "Oh scrap, Iro. You are so right. Look how red he's gone."

Ingrid was the only one of them who remained quiet. She stood apart from the others, stretching and staring off into the distance. It was the first time Iro had seen the girls since returning from the Hop and they were full of questions, asking him what it was like and what he could do. Eir spent even more time poking at North and asking it questions to which it clearly did not know the answer. Eventually the little automaton retreated to Iro and landed on his shoulder. It was so light he barely felt it.

"Line up, trainees." They all turned as one to find Master Rollo standing in the doorway. He had a metal crutch under one arm, was swathed in bandages around his hands and feet and neck, and looked gaunt. Iro spotted Frigg waiting just behind Master Rollo and wanted to slink away and find a corner to hide in. He never wanted to answer another one of her questions ever again.

"You're back!" Eir said loudly. "Tell me you're back. Please be back. Ash is so mean, she keeps making me fight Bjorn."

Ashvild shot Eir a look. "I've done my best to keep them motivated, master."

"What part of line up didn't you understand? Idiots." Master Rollo said. They all scrambled to get into position, but Iro glanced down the line and found them all grinning at the return of their old master. All except Ingrid.

Master Rollo limped down the line, staring at them all. His crutch tapped awkwardly against the padded floor and he winced with every step. Frigg followed him, her tablet in hand, finger poised above it like she did before every question she asked. She caught Iro looking at her and winked at him. He felt heat flush his cheeks and looked away, hoping she wasn't about to pull him out of class for another interview.

"Alright, let's do this," Master Rollo said. He looked unhappy and Iro had a feeling they were all about to get a dressing down. He handed his crutch to Frigg, then awkwardly lowered himself onto his knees and bowed his head.

For a few long seconds, Master Rollo knelt there in silence. Then he drew in a deep breath. "I'm sorry," his voice broke a little on the words. "Everything that has happened to you, it's all my fault. I wasn't strong enough to protect you. I failed you. Failed in my role as trainer. I couldn't keep you all safe."

Master Rollo sniffed, looked up, met Ingrid's blank stare. "Ingrid, I am so sorry. I know it's not enough. It can never be enough. But I am sorry. Torben was a good boy. I wish I could have protected him like he deserved."

Ingrid dropped her gaze to the floor, wiped at her eyes. Iro saw tears streaming down her cheeks, but she was silent. Ylfa edged closer to her, reached out and squeezed her hand.

"Command Query," North said, taking off from Iro's shoulder and floating towards Ingrid.

Iro reached out with both hands, pulled North back. "Not now," he hissed at the little automaton.

North buzzed, vibrating angrily enough Iro let it go. It quickly floated back into the air and hovered above his shoulder again. "Query delayed."

Master Rollo narrowed his eyes at Iro and again at North. Then he dragged his attention back to the rest of the trainees. "I promise you all, it will never happen again. As long as you are my trainees, I will not let anything happen to you. I will protect you. I swear it." He nodded to Frigg and she moved forward, took him under the shoulder and helped him stand again, handed him the crutch.

"I may need Ashvild to continue training you all for a few days though," Master Rollo said as he sagged against the crutch.

Ashvild stepped forward, back straight as a girder. "How long have you been awake, master?"

"About four hours," Frigg said disapprovingly. "I had to make him shower before coming to see you all. And I had to help him." She grinned.

Master Rollo limped towards Iro, pulling up short as North levitated forwards to meet him. "Command Designation Request."

"That's Master Rollo," Iro said. "North, get back here."

"Command Designation Confirmed. Hello Master Rollo, it is North."

Master Rollo narrowed his eyes at the automaton. Then leaned to the side slightly to look past it at Iro. "Why does it sound like you?"

"North is Command's Automated Guide and Chronicler," North said cheerily.

Iro stepped forward and waved a hand at North to get it to back away. It buzzed at him. "I, uh, accidentally ordered its creation back at the manufactory. I haven't figured out how to change it yet. The voice, I mean. It's weird."

Master Rollo nodded once. The rest of the trainees were already pairing off under Ashvild's supervision. Iro wanted to join in. He wanted to fight Bjorn and see if he could win now he had opened his First Gate.

"Well done, Eclipse Iro," Master Rollo said. "On opening your first gate, and on protecting Courage Emil and all of my trainees. I owe you a debt for that."

Iro shook his head, opened his mouth, but Master Rollo cut him off.

"You probably think this is it now, huh? You've graduated, opened your gate. You're a Hopper now?"

"Well… yes?"

Master Rollo snorted. "Idiot. Kid, your training has only just begun."

Snapshot
Willet

Willet checked the door to his quarters was closed. He couldn't have anybody walking in on him like last time. Not until he had it absolutely perfect. That took practice and he knew the others would only laugh if they found him practicing.

He checked the kitchen area and his sleeping room, just to make sure he was alone. Of course he was alone. He lived alone. Why would there be anyone else in his rooms? He double checked just to make sure, even pulling open his closet to glance inside. Empty. He was alone.

The underside of his kitchen table was reflective. He'd purposefully polished it to a mirror shine. He hefted the table onto its side and leaned it up against the far wall so he had enough space to move. Then he stood in front of the makeshift mirror and smiled at himself. He knew it was vain to think it, but scrap he was handsome. He popped the collar on his brown duster and danced a couple of steps on the spot, then pointed at his reflection and grinned.

"Down to serious business," he said. "No smiles. Just do it sparky."

Willet settled down, flexed his shoulders a couple of times, then went still. He stared at his reflection and it stared back.

"Draw." He whisked his duster back, grabbed his cannons and drew. His right cannon got caught in the tail of his coat and he struggled to pull it free, raised it and pointed. It looked stupid.

"Scrap that looked terrible." He spun the cannons on

his fingers and slotted them both back into their hip holsters. "Gotta get this right, Willet. Can't look a fool."

He settled back into position, staring at his reflection. Gave it a wink.

"Draw."

Again he whisked his duster back, grabbed his cannons, and drew on his reflection. This time they came free easily. His duster billowed out behind him looking sparky as a thruster under fire.

"That's right. That's it. You look good, Willet. You look sparky. You look like a titan-slaying beast." He grinned at himself, spun his cannons around on his fingers.

"Ahem," the voice came from his doorway and Willet startled, lost control and both his cannons flew from his fingers, clattering against cupboards and dropping to the floor.

Deiter leaned against the doorframe, arms crossed over his broad chest, one eye hidden by his hanging fringe.

"How long have you been there?" Willet asked as he knelt and grabbed his cannons, shoving them back into their holsters.

"Not long," Deiter said. "Captain wants to see you." He turned and disappeared out the doorway.

Willet sighed out his relief.

Deiter's head poked back around the doorway. "That's assuming you have the time, you titan-slaying beast."

Snapshot
Lara and Ben

"Block," Ben shouted at the humanoid monster as he drew his dual shields together. The monster's club smashed into the shields and rebounded. Ben dropped the shields, leaving them standing, darted in between them.

"Uppercut." He ducked a swiping claw, rose leading with his fist and delivered a punch that knocked the monster off its feet and into the air.

"Slam," he shouted as he grabbed the monster's thorny foot, twisted, brought the creature crashing down to the metal floor between his two shields. The monster bounced, its armored hide cracking from the force.

"Distraction," Ben said. He jumped back a step, put his hands on his hips and blew a kiss at the monster as it struggled back to its feet.

The monster roared stringy spittle flying, then hacked, coughed, spasmed, and finally drooled blood as the air shimmered behind it, revealing Lara dragging a knife down its back. She stepped back, kicking the monster aside and it sprawled on the floor, steaming insides leaking from the jagged hole in its back.

"Ahh, Lara, just in time as always." Ben sauntered forwards and leaned on one his shields, gazing at the short, gloomy woman. "What would I do without you?"

"Die a horrible, gruesome death."

Ben nodded. "You're probably right."

Lara flicked the gore from her knife. "It was a request, not a suggestion."

"Wounded," Ben said, placing a hand over his heart.

"Besides, you'd miss me. Who would you trade your barbs with if not me."

"Literally anyone else."

"And yet," Ben tapped on his wrist tablet to inform the squad leader they had dispatched the last of the monsters in the idyllic arboretum. "You do keep ending up on squads with me. A man can't help but feel it's not just coincidence." He winked at her. "I think you like my company really."

"Nope." Her searing white crest flared in front of her for a moment, the air shimmered, then she was gone. Ben couldn't even hear her moving she was so stealthy.

Ben felt a hard tap on his back, right between two armor plates and knew it was Lara showing off, saying she could have killed him. He let out a loud cry of fake pain, dropped to his knees and clawed at the air.

"Dramatic… death… scene…" He slumped forward onto the floor and lay there for a few moments. Lara did not reappear.

"How was it?" Ben asked. The only answer he got was the hiss of monster innards escaping their cracked shell. "Too much? Not enough?" He got back to his knees and looked around. "Lara? I need feedback, Lara."

He stood and picked up his shields again. There was no sight of Lara at all. "Yep. She definitely likes you, Ben."

"I'd rather kiss vacuum."

Books by Rob J. Hayes

The War Eternal
Along the Razor's Edge
The Lessons Never Learned
From Cold Ashes Risen
Sins of the Mother
Death's Beating Heart

The Mortal Techniques
Never Die
Pawn's Gambit
Spirits of Vengeance

First Earth Saga
The Heresy Within
The Colour of Vengeance
The Price of Faith
Best Laid Plans
The Fifth Empire of Man
City of Kings

It Takes a Thief...
It Takes a Thief to Catch a Sunrise
It Takes a Thief to Start a Fire

Science Fiction
Drones

Printed in Great Britain
by Amazon